Awakening

Jason Boa / *Woman's Day*

Natalie King has always had imaginary friends in her head. This proved a distraction during school and beyond, and she ultimately abandoned her various jobs as researcher, mystery shopper and recruitment specialist because she was forever imagining herself elsewhere. Fortunately she now locks herself in her little garden shed to spend her days scribbling the stories those imaginary characters entice her with.

Natalie also writes contemporary romance as Natalie Anderson. In this genre she's had more than twenty-five novels published, been translated into more than twenty languages and sold over two million books. A *USA Today* bestseller, she's also been a *Romantic Times* Award nominee and a finalist for the R★BY (Romantic Book of the Year). She lives in Christchurch, New Zealand.

Find out more at her website: nataliekingwrites.com

For Evelyn, Sylvie, Henry and Kathleen

PENGUIN BOOKS
Published by the Penguin Group
Penguin Group (NZ), 67 Apollo Drive, Rosedale,
Auckland 0632, New Zealand (a division of Penguin New Zealand Pty Ltd)
Penguin Group (USA) Inc., 375 Hudson Street, New York, New York 10014, USA
Penguin Group (Canada), 90 Eglinton Avenue East, Suite 700, Toronto,
Ontario, M4P 2Y3, Canada (a division of Penguin Canada Books Inc.)
Penguin Books Ltd, 80 Strand, London, WC2R 0RL, England
Penguin Ireland, 25 St Stephen's Green, Dublin 2, Ireland (a division of Penguin Books Ltd)
Penguin Group (Australia), 707 Collins Street, Melbourne,
Victoria 3008, Australia (a division of Penguin Australia Pty Ltd)
Penguin Books India Pvt Ltd, 11, Community Centre,
Panchsheel Park, New Delhi – 110 017, India
Penguin Books (South Africa) (Pty) Ltd, Block D, Rosebank Office Park,
181 Jan Smuts Avenue, Parktown North, Gauteng 2193, South Africa
Penguin (Beijing) Ltd, 7F, Tower B, Jiaming Center, 27 East Third Ring Road North,
Chaoyang District, Beijing 100020, China

Penguin Books Ltd, Registered Offices: 80 Strand, London, WC2R 0RL, England

First published by Penguin Group (NZ), 2014

Copyright © Natalie King, 2014

The right of Natalie King to be identified as the author of this work in terms of
section 96 of the Copyright Act 1994 is hereby asserted.

Designed and typeset by Jenny Haslimeier, © Penguin Group (NZ)
Additional cover imagery from iStockphoto.com
Printed and bound in Australia by Griffin Press

ISBN 978-0-143-57079-0

A catalogue record for this book is available from the National Library of New Zealand.

www.penguin.co.nz

MIX
Paper from
responsible sources
FSC® C009448

Awakening

NATALIE KING

PENGUIN BOOKS

CHAPTER ONE

OF ALL THE emotions, guilt leaves the greatest mark. While fear and happiness can fade, guilt remains as heavy and harsh as the day it arrived. Zelie Taylor's guilt weighed heavy, so when Kate Hearn asked, she couldn't say no.

Kate had that smell. Instantly recognisable, that weird combo of industrial cleaner and damp mustiness stung Zelie's guilt, rubbing at the scab on her heart.

Zelie had only met her once, after hours in the waiting room of her father's medical practice. Kate had blocked the doorway, her pixie-cropped hair too thin and wispy to be cute, her skinny jeans swamping her. She'd been flanked by her two oversized uncles – a good thing given she looked like she could hardly stand unsupported.

Talk about awkward. The three Hearns had stared at Zelie with the eerie, unblinking kind of gaze usually employed by sociopaths, and stayed silent. With their identical, gas-flame-blue eyes wide, they'd waited for who-knows-what to happen, until finally Kate had sort of smiled, stepped forwards from that trance-like minute, and introduced herself with her laryngitis-rusted voice.

The grim uncles had said nada. Either too wealthy-station-owner snobby to say hi or just too concerned about their dreadfully ill niece to bother.

Zelie had nodded at Kate and grabbed the chance to slip out, because it was hideously apparent Kate Hearn didn't have long left on the planet. Aside from all else, that death smell gave it away.

So what was she doing now, hanging out all alone at Lake Tekapo on such a cold morning?

'Are you sure you should be out here?' Zelie crossed her arms tightly, a useless attempt to brace against the freezing wind as she hesitated, then walked to the bony girl who'd called her name.

The rest of Zelie's class had already disappeared through the trees to the waiting bus, so now the lakefront was bare, no people or plants, just snow and stones. Bagging trouble for being last on the bus wasn't on today's to-do list. Her first school field trip in this place sucked enough already.

'I need to get it out. Can you reach it for me?' Kate was staring into the water, her thin canvas shoes half a millimetre from the sinking wet.

Reach what? Zelie walked closer. Her teeth ached and her eyes watered as the icy wind stabbed. Its effect on Kate must be a million times worse. Yeah, it wasn't nail polish painting her nails purple and it wasn't make-up deepening the hollows of her cheeks. If Kate – 'twiglet' – Hearn stuck her hand into the ice-cold water it'd be suicide.

'It's my necklace. It's precious,' Kate said softly.

'What, like magic-ring *precioussssss*?' Zelie joked lamely.

Kate didn't laugh.

Zelie suppressed a shiver and walked closer. She'd overheard her father talking about Kate – his new pet project – so she knew she was home-schooled on the ginormous merino sheep station further round the lake. She was too vulnerable to mix with other students for fear of picking up some virus that would take her down. Death chased her hard and right now it looked moments from victory.

'I really don't think you should be here.' Zelie coughed away the rasp clogging her throat. She'd hardly spoken all morning – hadn't met Mr Webb's eyes at all so he wouldn't ask her any questions. Being the new kid gave her partial exemption, but she also knew how to avoid attention. She hated talking one-to-one, let alone in front of all of them. But now she stretched her lips into a smile – not easy given the way she was clenching all her other muscles to stop the shivers skittering down her spine.

Sickness creeped her out. Getting involved wasn't her thing either, but Kate's soft request forced her close to both.

'Think you can reach it?' Kate asked again.

Zelie sighed, her breath forming a cloud between them. 'I'll try.' Really she had no choice. That creepy smell was suffocating, making memories return and pressing salty guilt deeper into her wounds. She had to at least try, because last time she'd been too late to help.

She peered into the famously weird-coloured water. The ancient glacier upstream had pulverised the rocks in its path into powder. That 'rock flour' came down the river to hang suspended in the lake, turning the water milky-blue and making the stones at the bottom hard to see. Mr Webb had warbled on about it for the first fifteen minutes they'd been there, even though almost every kid in the class lived locally and knew it all anyway.

'How'd it get in there?' Zelie asked.

'I lost it ages ago.' Kate shrugged, her sharp bones jutting despite her bulky jersey. 'I just spotted it.'

How had she done that? Zelie squinted down; only a fragment of the chain was visible. 'Just now?'

Kate kept staring as if she thought the chain would disappear if she blinked. Which it probably would. Zelie was amazed Kate had ever seen it again. But this request was something she could manage. She pushed up her polar-fleece sleeve, squatted down and plunged her hand into the water. The sooner she got it, the sooner she could go. But the lake was deceptive; the chain sat deeper than she'd realised. The water rose past her elbow. She gritted her teeth. The fleece soaked up litres in seconds.

She jerked her arm out and shook it, flinging drops onto her face. She sucked in a breath to stave off the stinging sensation. *Way* worse than she'd expected. She took off her fleece, tossed it onto the stones and rolled her T-shirt sleeve into her bra-strap.

She sank her arm back into the cold, turning her head, trying to find the chain by feel rather than sight. She gripped the large rock beside her to keep from falling in. She'd be hypothermic in less than a minute if she did.

Every cell in her arm shrieked. Her jaw ached from clamping her teeth together. She was about to give up when she saw Kate's hand spread wide on the rock beside her. The skin was mottled white and purple and ended with those blue-tipped bony fingers. If Kate Hearn tried to fish out the chain, she'd get a chill. She was sniffing every other second already. She shouldn't be out in this hellish winter, but here she hovered, staring – fixated, desperate, sick.

Zelie's legs hurt as she leaned over as far as she could without toppling in. Her muscles both stretched and cramped. As useless as raw sausages her floppy fingers scraped on the stones, too slow to follow the instructions her brain was issuing. She closed her eyes to concentrate but all that did was make the wind blow louder in her ears.

Then she felt it. Colder, harder than the rocks, the tiny links of the chain. Cautiously she bent her thumb, hooking the thin metal with her nail, pressing her index finger over the top to secure it. Precarious, but almost in place. She twisted her wrist so the chain fell against the palm of her hand.

'I've got it.' Triumphant, she fisted her fingers around it.

'You have?' Kate's voice scooted up thirty octaves. 'Are you okay?'

Brilliant. She was brilliant. Now she could get out of here and nurse her practically frostbitten arm. But she pulled it out slowly, not wanting to lose her grip on the chain or her balance. She wasn't about to dive in. Not even for death-cheating Kate Hearn.

Once again she inhaled deeply to block the prickling as the warmer air needled through her numb, wet skin. Carefully she lifted her hand high enough to see what was so precious about this necklace. It was silver, a circular chain with another straight piece of chain hanging from one link in the centre. On the end of that swung a pendant. A misshapen silver rectangle with a worn engraving on one side. Heavy, untarnished, unusual. And for just a moment, envy hit.

She instantly shook the bad vibe off and held the chain out to Kate. 'Here you go.' Her smile came more easily this time.

But rather than reach for it, Kate shrank back, her focus now wholly on the metal – wide-eyed, almost hypnotised. Was she scared?

'It's yours, right?' Zelie held it out further, despite the ache in her arm.

Kate sniffed.

Zelie's patience evaporated as the pain in her arm intensified. 'Come on, take it.'

But Kate's already pale skin now turned all but see-through. She took a step backwards.

Zelie hurriedly stood, catching the silver pendant with her other hand as it swung on the chain. Her fingers curled round the silver lump, convulsing tighter at its shocking coldness.

The sigh was deep, long and loud. A strained sound. Relief tinged with pain? Startled, Zelie looked at Kate. That had been too big a noise to come from someone who looked like she'd been chewing on a million appetite suppressants. But Kate was five feet away – and moving further, faster.

'You got it out. You keep it,' she called as she turned, tucking her chin into the neck of her jersey.

What on earth was going on? 'But –'

'I'm not strong enough.'

'For what?' Zelie couldn't make her fingers unclench and drop the frozen thing, even though it burned worse than dry ice.

She didn't hear Kate's low-voiced answer because this time the sigh was louder. It echoed the water slipping over the stones, the wind stirring the trees. She could have sworn she heard a word in the inhumanly long gust of air. A hissing fragment she couldn't quite catch. She whirled towards the sound, towards the eerie milk-blue water. A large ripple was spreading across the beautiful lake as if a passing boat had roused waves to lap against the stony shore. But there was no boat. There was nothing out there, no one on the beach but Kate and her. Not even a bird.

Shocked at the rawness of the sound reverberating in her head, she turned back to Kate. Now the walking skeleton was statue-still, staring at Zelie with her wide eyes, her pupils pinpricks in a scary gas-blue sea.

'What was that?' Goosebumps slithered over Zelie's skin.

'Put your jacket on,' said Kate. 'You'll need to keep warm.'

Zelie swallowed the irony and picked up her fleece with her free hand. While Kate permanently looked like she was about to keel over, now Zelie felt weakness invading her muscles. A weird rushing noise filled her head, like howling gales were coming from all directions right at her. The sun held as much heat as a toy torch against the ice-edged wind.

'But –' Zelie broke off as her teeth began to chatter.

Kate backed up another couple of paces, then turned away. Only she staggered as she went.

'Kate?' Zelie panicked.

'You should run,' Kate said breathlessly, half bent over. 'You don't want to miss the bus.'

'But I've still got your –'

'Run!' Kate straightened and shouted, only her cry cracked in the middle.

Zelie recoiled.

Kate's scary wide eyes had changed. The whites had turned luminescent *yellow*. Worse still, something was hanging from her nose. Zelie swallowed back the sourness in her mouth. Who knew jaundice could hit that quick? And now she realised what was on Kate's face. Blood. A thick glob of dark blood. And as Kate repeated the command, Zelie saw that blood also trickled from her ear, the scarlet a shocking slash against her sick-white skin.

The coldness of the water and the metal necklace sank into Zelie. Her stomach twisted. Bile burned its way up then down her throat as she swallowed again.

The deep red ran faster from Kate's nose but she just wiped it with the back of her hand. The stench rose. Zelie's tears rose too. She couldn't move. Couldn't help. Couldn't hide.

'My uncles . . .' Kate lifted a hand to wave but dropped it to her thigh as she struggled to stay upright.

Zelie looked behind her – two tall men were running out from the stand of trees further along the lakefront.

Thank God. They might be the ultimate in taciturn, but they were big and strong and responsible.

'Kate!' The nearest man shouted as he moved closer, his heavy boots loud on the stones.

Relieved tears stung Zelie's eyes. She didn't have to deal with this alone.

But suddenly Kate turned that psycho-killer stare back on her and started spitting, hurling words in a crazy language Zelie hadn't heard before and sure as hell didn't understand. All she knew was that, whatever Kate was saying, it sounded wretched, scary shit.

Zelie moved. Fast. Faster. From stagger, to run, to sprint. She had to get away from her. From *them*. Images flickered in her head. Brutal, ugly images that she tried so hard to forget yet never could. She knew it was being near someone sick that did this to her, but now wasn't the time to remember.

She ran faster. Her legs hurt, her heart thundered. Hell, she was unfit.

Only once did she turn to check on Kate. One of the uncles had his arm around her, lifting her. His furious words carried on the malevolent wind.

'What have you done?'

Scrambling over the uneven stones, Zelie pushed on, a stitch sawing into her side. But she kept going. Her lungs burned and jerked. She stumbled along the beach and up the icy path, her fingers curled tight.

That strange sigh sounded again and the world seemed to tilt. Giddy, she had to stop. She bent over to let blood come back to her head. She was *not* going to faint.

'Zelie?' Someone strode heavy-footed down the path. 'Are you okay?'

She squeezed her eyelids shut, trying to stay conscious and not drown in the blackness encroaching on the edges.

'Zelie?'

He rhymed her name with Celie not belly. She gasped for breath, amazed he even knew it, let alone how to say it properly. Mortified he was the one who'd come down.

Otis Hayes.

She straightened and looked up. His cocoa eyes were both warm and wide in an expression that mixed curiosity with concern. And she was impersonating a failure at fat camp. Brilliant.

Otis had never looked at her before. Well, not when she was sneaking peeks at him. Which, okay, might be a little often. But then every girl looked at Otis.

'Why are you running so fast?' he asked.

'I – I . . .' She couldn't tell him. 'I thought I was going to miss the bus.'

'Another few minutes.' He smiled. That smile had caught her attention on her first day at school here, two weeks ago. Slow, slightly lopsided and gorgeous. She'd never expected him to turn that smile on her. She blinked but it was too late, her brain was beginning to melt. His eyes were the kind any girl would drown in.

'You should try for the cross-country this season,' he said. 'You powered up those stones. You're really talented.'

Thus spoke the school's number one all-round athlete. But he didn't look like he was joking, he looked surprised.

'Um, no,' she muttered, struggling harder for breath as her embarrassment seemed to thin the air. She had no talent. Just cowardice.

His gaze skimmed down and his eyebrows flickered, reminding her she was sweating and puffing and no doubt redder than a traffic light. So not the time to have snagged his attention.

'You sure you're okay?' Otis stepped closer. 'You're bleeding.'

She lifted her hand and almost puked. There was a smear of blood on the back of her fist. Kate's blood. She frantically wiped it off on her jeans. Dad would kill her. Worse, his endless OTT attempts at hygiene indoctrination must be working because she really wanted some sanitiser gel. 'It's nothing. Just a scratch.'

'Are you sure?'

'Yeah –'

'Yo, O!' One of his crew called him back to the fold. They were up on the path near where the bus was parked.

Otis waved and whoever it was fell silent. Conscious of them watching, Zelie struggled to meet Otis's eyes. Like the sun it hurt to look at them. And, like the sun, Otis was the centre of this school's solar system. The popular girls referred to him as the Big O. She'd heard the giggles as they dissected his merits – and those of every other male in school. They had names for everyone. Otis was *the* man. And yeah, Zelie totally agreed. But high school hotties didn't ordinarily look at the quiet, in-the-corner girls like her. Humiliation central, to be caught staggering up the path so out of breath she could hardly talk, with blood on her hand and her T-shirt all wet and heavy and not in a hot, beach-competition kind of way.

Now they were all looking at the mess she was. Oh to be able to shrivel behind a rock.

As she studied the ground she sensed Otis was still looking at her, but she couldn't think of a thing to say. It would be impossible anyway because her puffing only worsened the more she tried to control it. Almost as bad as one of her little brother's asthma attacks. And despite her goosebumps, she knew her face was flaming. She wished she could slink across the park and go straight home, rather than have to go all the way back to school for the rest of the afternoon.

But she turned and walked up the last stretch of the path to where everyone waited, conscious of Otis keeping pace just behind her.

'See ya, Zelie.'

She heard his grin as he joined his mates.

Well yeah, she would be seeing him. They all had to go back on that too-loud bus together. And she was mortified.

Not only that, she was freezing. She looked down at her hands. In one was her fleece, and in the other?

The necklace. The pendant she'd pulled out for Kate was locked in her fist, the chain dangling in the air. In the panic of seeing Kate sicken so quickly she'd forgotten it. Shit. Now she had to get it back to her.

Maybe she'd get her dad to drop it off when he did his daily house call – though hopefully Kate was on her way to see him already.

She dropped the fleece and uncurled her frozen fingers. The faint engraving on the metal caught her eye, but it was so worn she couldn't make out the picture. She gnawed the inside of her lip, feeling guilty that she still had it, that she'd run from Kate like such a chicken.

But the safest place for the pendant to be was on, right? She'd put it on for now and get it back to Kate later. She quickly fastened the clasp behind her neck, dropped the pendant beneath her tee, then put her fleece back on.

A crashing sound of stone on stone made her turn. The clattering grew louder as someone ran up the last of the rocks. Adrenalin whooshed through her system as she recognised one of the men who'd run to Kate – one of her uncles. It was the taller one with the perma-stubble and a nose that looked like it had once been broken and healed wonky – giving him a retired pro-rugby-player look. That day in the waiting room he'd looked like the ultimate wealthy landowner in his clean jeans, leather boots and pressed shirt, his expression giving nothing away. Now he was red-faced and puffing, his jeans splattered with snow, mud and blood. Emotion blew ahead of him in a violent, invisible cloud, but she didn't know if it was fury or fear.

Zelie's chills returned, obliterating the remnants of warmth from her embarrassed moment with Otis. Kate wasn't with him. Was Kate okay?

He was searching. His head turned quickly as he looked at every person he passed. Suddenly she knew who he was looking for and just as suddenly she knew she didn't want to be found. She didn't want to be involved. They should just take Kate to the doctor. Better still, take her all the way to the hospital. While he was a good doctor, Zelie couldn't be sure her father was working at full capacity yet and she didn't want to find out he wasn't in the worst possible way.

She pulled the elastic tie down the length of her ponytail and off. She never normally wore her hair out, but as she walked into the midst of the others she kept her chin down to let her hair curtain her face.

Mr Webb whistled loudly. 'Come on, everyone.'

She hid among the bodies that formed the restless queue to board the bus. It was easy to be invisible when you were average height with average brown hair. Cold fear swirled in the space just below her ribs. She didn't want to know about Kate. She didn't want any more responsibility or any more guilt.

Yeah she was a coward, but at least she owned up to it.

Finally the bus doors opened to let them on. She got on as quickly as she could, said nothing to anyone. Mr Webb waited at the front, ticking them off his list as they boarded. She was aware his attention rested on her, but she kept her gaze fixed on the floor. She chose a row not too near the back or the front and slumped into the seat by the window. She stuck her bag on the empty spot next to her to stop someone from taking it, although it was unlikely anyone would. Already the others got that she liked her space.

Back in Manchester, when it had happened, her friends hadn't understood. Not even Sarah. She hadn't tried to help them. What was the point? She knew they were uncomfortable and didn't know what to say. So she made it easy for them and didn't talk about it. She also stopped saying yes to invitations. Said she was busy. Which was true. Soon enough there weren't any more invitations to have to answer. And that was good because she preferred to be alone. Alone she didn't have to pretend, didn't have to *try*. The effort was too exhausting.

She drew her feet up on the seat and hugged her knees, wishing she could sink deeper into her fleece. So damn cold.

Then she realised why. The pendant resting under her T-shirt was still ice-age temperature. It hadn't warmed at all, nor had the chain. Why not? Metal conducted heat, didn't it? Pots heated on the hob. That was the science of it. If she were braver she'd ask Mr Webb. Instead she pressed the heel of her hand to her chest, pushing the pendant through her clothing, shifting its position because her skin was sore. Was the pendant what the man was after?

With her hand still covering the lump, she looked out. Kate's uncle stood on the footpath, carefully studying each window of the bus until eventually he was looking at her. That's where he stopped. There was no point letting her hair fall forwards again. He knew.

She chewed on the inside of her cheek as she met his stare. His eyes were the same mass of colours as Kate's. A palette of striking blues with a touch of unhealthy yellow in the whites.

It *was* the necklace he wanted. But she didn't want to give it back yet. She had this weird urge to get both it and herself warm. Which was ridiculous. Like it was some magical piece of jewellery that once she'd put on, she couldn't give up? That she'd only hand over if forced to?

Yeah right. She'd take it back once she'd showered and was dry and dressed. And she wasn't going to give it to that man, but to freaky, barely-there Kate.

For now Kate's uncle kept staring at Zelie, stepped closer to the window, his eyes wide and weird. What did he think he could see by staring so hard? The inside of her head? Her heart thumped all the way into her throat as seconds seemed to take hours to tick by. Would he try to get on board?

The bus vibrated as the engine fired and rumbled. The doors hissed as they closed. She glanced up the front. Mr Webb was doing a double-check headcount – finishing with her. His eyes narrowed as he looked at her, then beyond her to the window.

Zelie's heart stopped. So did time. The only thing that moved was the frown line on her teacher's face as he saw who stood beside the bus. It scored deep into his brow. Then his mouth thinned.

Zelie was biting hard on her own teeth, instinct telling her to stay as silent as possible. Was he going to go out and ask Kate's uncle what he wanted? Or worse, ask Zelie what was going on?

Because it had to be obvious something was going on, right?

But after another agonising second, all Mr Webb did was blink. His frown smoothed in that instant. He swivelled to speak to the driver, his expression now bland.

Surprised, Zelie heard the mechanical groan of shifting gears. Way too slowly for her zigzagging pulse, they pulled out onto the road. A lurch forwards, a pause, then another lurch that eased into smooth progress.

As Mr Webb took his seat, his gaze grazed her. Not bland now, but serious. Concerned.

Unwilling to answer that wordless query, Zelie turned back to Kate's uncle. It was like the no-blinking contest had never been interrupted. Motionless, expressionless, all he did was watch – *her* – until the bus took her away.

She breathed out. She couldn't get home quickly enough. But first there was the drive back to school, then another hour or so of discussing today's field trip – the pros and cons of hydro power and the arguments against further construction around the lake. There was never enough power. People always used more than they had. Ya da ya. Right now Zelie didn't care. No way could she wait for school to be over. She'd make up an excuse and leave early. Crazy to have to do the thirty-minute trip to school and then drive back here to the small village again, but her car was there, and Zelie wanted to give Kate time to see her father and be gone again.

Her neck burned from the icy chain. She itched to pull the pendant out and study it, but she didn't want to draw attention by fidgeting. And she didn't want anyone else to see it.

'*Quelle heure est-il?*'

She glanced over her shoulder. Who was that? And why was he asking in French?

But there was no one in the seat behind her. Certainly no one near enough to whisper in her ear like that. Not so softly. The basketball boys were in the back row and it wasn't any of them. Otis, the brightest of that bunch, might do French, but from what she'd seen in class, he was as average at it as she was.

'*Quelle . . . Quelle heure?*' Whoever he was, he sounded confused.

She looked to the front even though she was sure the voice hadn't come from that direction. Ella and Clare were nearest, and while Tom was in the seat across the aisle he was busy playing a game on his phone. Although given the smile on his face, maybe he was looking at some dodgy picture.

A noise that could only be described as a growl startled her.

'*Quelle heure est-il?*'

Okay, this was strange. She did a 360-degree glance round the bus. How could nobody else be turning to see? Didn't they hear him too? Because he was getting louder. Angry.

'*Quelle heure?*'

More than angry. Every one of Zelie's muscles contracted, including her heart. Was there a psycho stranger on the bus?

No. She hugged her knees tight and told her heart to beat again. Of course there wasn't. Someone was having a laugh at her expense. She darted glances left to right, hunting for anyone acting weird, or giggling. But there was only chat – last week's game, next weekend's ball. The usual two topics. No strange guy grunting and asking the time in French.

Slowly she breathed in and out. *Relax.* Seeing Kate like that had done some damage to her cardiac muscle and she was tired, right? She looked out the window, trying to let the sight of the snow-tipped trees soothe her.

'*Répondez-moi!*'

She jumped, her pulse zipping back to frantic. There really was someone talking – shouting in fact. But she had no idea who he was, or where he was, or why he was talking. And why was no one else noticing?

'*Wo sind wir?*'

Was that German? She'd done a scrappy couple of months of that just before her dad had dragged her and Luke to this freezing speck of a town.

She lowered her feet to the floor and pressed her fists to her stomach.

'English. I try English.' The voice was stronger and not stopping. 'What time it is?'

Despite the thick accent she understood him. As much as she could understand a random voice that had appeared out of nowhere. This totally had to be a set-up, but she couldn't keep ignoring it.

'Just after midday,' she whispered, looking out the window and trying not to let her lips move much as a wave of hot humiliation swept over her. Whoever it was, they must be killing themselves laughing.

'You speak. English.' Another deep sigh – slightly pained, totally angry.

He'd heard her whisper? How was that possible? Had the sighing she'd heard at the lake been him? No way.

'Where are we?' he asked.

'Where are *you*?'

His short laugh held no amusement, only bitterness. 'Exactly where you left me.'

Where she'd left him? She'd never met this guy. She'd remember if she had. His accent – and anger – was that distinctive. The only foreigners she'd recently met were the punters at the winter play-park where she'd scored weekend work. They were either middle-aged wealthy types going for the spa treatments or shaggy-haired twenty-something travellers cutting up the ice rink. But no one she'd met recently had sounded like this.

'I don't understand.' She glanced across the aisle at Tom, who was still focused on his phone. In the rows ahead the others were relentlessly talking about the school ball. It seemed no one else could hear this guy. Which meant that maybe she wasn't hearing him either – not really. Maybe it was all in her head.

'I ask again, where are we?'

She was hearing a random voice and, stupidly, she was talking back. Was this the start of some psychosis? Had she flipped the switch and gone nuts? Had the chaos of the last few months finally sent her over?

Admittedly she hadn't been sleeping well, staying awake late to avoid the dreams, and she hadn't eaten breakfast this morning because she'd been running behind . . . but even so.

Fear solidified inside, a colder weight than the metal lump still searing her chest. The awful question circled like a vulture. Was she becoming as paranoid as her father? She understood the cause of his condition, but she didn't want to live with the rampant fears he had.

She pulled her iPod from her bag and stuffed the earbuds in. Now people would think she was singing along to music, not turning into the local Looney Tune. Then she whispered again.

'I didn't leave you anywhere. Where are you?'

There was a long sentence in a language she didn't understand. Neither French nor German; even weirder than the words Kate had spat. These sounded less polite than those too.

She scrunched down into the seat, rested her head back against the rough upholstery and tried to get a grip. This was some weird day-mare, or someone was playing a trick, or she was going crazy. She switched the music on. She'd ignore the voice completely.

'What noise is that?'

She didn't answer. He wasn't into dubstep?

The bass thumped but her pulse raced ahead of the rhythm. She listened close, focusing until finally her heart slowed to meet the beat. It was still too fast but better than before.

As the bus chugged past the white-blanketed fields, she slipped her hand under the neck of her shirt and ran a thumb over the cold chain, feeling for the clasp. She'd take it off and put it in her pocket; the cold pressure was too much. She thumbed round the length once, then again, but couldn't find the fastener. She frowned. She'd have to wait until she was alone and could look at it properly. Slow minutes passed, one song seamlessly flipped into another. No more strange voice.

There, see? Nothing. The pendant might burn cold, but it was inanimate. Merely a lump of metal. Nothing special. And the voice-hearing thing? Just an auditory hallucination caused by overtiredness.

'How long will it take?'

She snapped her eyes shut, wincing from the sudden shout in her ear. It didn't help that he sounded like one of the bad guys in an old-school Bond flick.

'How long will it take?' he demanded again.

'For what?' Her sanity to return?

'Do not pretend you know nothing. You did this.'

'I don't think so.' A bubble of nervousness gurgled out, a cross between half-drowned giggle and a snort. 'I have no idea what's going on.'

A couple of people in the rows ahead turned around and she tried to make the giggle-snort a cough.

He answered with another long sentence she didn't understand. Definitely not French. Definitely not pqlite.

How could her brain come up with a language she'd never heard before? Even if it was some kind of hallucination? Surely it would have to be based on things she'd experienced? Her ears had never experienced the sound of fast, low syllables like these.

Her fingers curled around the chain, just above the pendant. The colder-than-ice temperature was too much to bear any more. Despite that strange urge to keep it close, she pulled the chain so the pendant lifted away from her skin.

'Don't!'

She flinched. That violent shout hadn't just contained anger, there'd been fear there too.

'Keep it on skin. It *must* touch your skin.'

The pendant? She let go of the chain and the weight fell back onto skin that already felt blistered. 'Why?'

'Nothing warms a cold body like the heat of another.'

Her body hit pause for interminable seconds. A cold body? This wasn't a cold body, this was a piece of metal. She was turning into Queen Freak. Shaking her head she pushed herself off freeze-frame, curled her fingers around the pendant and gripped it in the centre of her fist. She could tolerate the temperature on her palm more than on her chest.

'Do not let it go.'

'I'm not who you think I am.'

'You are. You are the bitch.'

His accent made the B sound like a V. She figured he meant Kate. Her fingers tightened. Why would Kate have set her up for this kind of stunt? They'd barely spoken.

'I'm not her,' she whispered as vehemently as she could.

Silence for the first thirty seconds of the next song.

'Look in a mirror,' he finally answered, much quieter than before.

'Absolutely. As soon as I can. Then I can see where the damn clasp is on this chain and take it off.' Please let it be some incredibly sophisticated toy with a nano-sized speaker in it, like some gadget from *Doctor Who*. But it looked so genuinely old.

'You cannot take it off,' he said.

'As soon as I find a mirror that's what I'll do.'

'As soon as you find a mirror you will see I am right.'

'How do you figure that?'

'I will see you.'

The cold spread like anaesthetic in her veins. 'How will you see me?'

'The same way you see you. Looking in the mirror.'

The fear resurged, driving deeper into every cell. 'Why would my looking in a mirror help you see me?'

'Because I see through your eyes.'

CHAPTER TWO

'MR WEBB. I HAVE a really bad headache.' No lie. The speed and force of her heartbeats had brought on a killer headache.

He gave her one of those assessing you-can't-fool-me looks as she stood beside the bus in the school car park. He was a good teacher – smart, not easy to pull the wool over.

'You do look pale,' he frowned.

Well yeah, she'd just worked out she was going nuts.

'Migraine,' she muttered. 'I get them sometimes.' Again, no lie. Female hormones sucked. But this headache was way worse than those.

His mouth opened. But he paused before answering, his eyes sharpening with curiosity.

Zelie braced. She had no idea how to answer if he asked about Kate's uncle. But then he nodded, the questioning look vanishing. 'Can you get home okay, or should I call your father?'

'I'll be okay.' The last thing she wanted was Dad alerted. He'd be taking her temperature every five minutes and shining bright light into her eyes every ten. Even when her migraines were monthly-related he still panicked. Given what had happened to Mum she couldn't blame him. But it'd be easier if he didn't know yet. Not till she'd figured more out.

The others were already walking into the school building, but as she walked towards the student side of the car park she saw Otis turn and watch her. She quickly glanced away. Why was he looking? Why now when in the last two weeks he hadn't ever? Today he'd talked to her, now he was watching. Why?

Paranoia. Hearing strange voices. Doubting everything and everyone. She *was* going nuts. She got into her car, winding down the window a fraction. She needed fresh air despite the relentless chilling effect of the pendant. What she really needed was to curl into her bed and sleep the craziness away. She'd warm up with her electric blanket, maybe a hot-water bottle too, and try to relax.

'What are you doing?'

Her fingers clenched on the steering wheel. Damn. He was still there. In the silence in those few minutes since getting the escape nod from Mr Webb, she'd hoped the nightmare had ended.

'Driving home.' It was a relief to speak at normal volume. 'Or I will once I get the car in gear and take the handbrake off.' She did exactly that, deliberately avoiding the rear-view mirror. She didn't want to deal with the weirdness while driving and she wanted the private space of her bedroom to examine the chain.

'This is a car?'

'Obviously.' She rolled her eyes.

'Where is home?'

'The clinic.' The sole doctor's surgery in Tekapo, the tiny town on the edge of the massive lake they'd just visited on that wretched school trip.

Her father was on call twenty-four hours, seven days a week and happy about it. The locals had been thrilled when he'd taken the job because there wasn't a doctor for miles. The nearest hospital was almost a two-hour drive away, or a forty-minute 'copter ride if the weather permitted, which at this time of year it sometimes didn't. He'd dragged Zelie and Luke halfway across the world in his quest for an apparently *safe* spot where they could survive any pandemic in easily achieved isolation.

Luke hadn't cared. It had been sold as an adventure to him and he'd bought it, but Zelie hadn't been so sure. Then again, she hadn't been sure about anything for quite a while and that's what had enabled her father to convince her. There was nothing holding her back there, why not try here? And there'd been one reason Zelie didn't need to be told. She had to come for Luke. Her brother was too little to lose half his family in less than two years. And her father was too much of a workaholic to give Luke all he needed. Luke needed Zelie.

So she'd come. But here she stood out more than ever – the one with the strange accent. She couldn't be bothered trying to blend in. In reality she had no home anywhere any more.

But she didn't explain it all to the random voice. What was the point? If this was some high-tech tease then the perpetrators already knew where she lived, and if she was going nuts then she didn't want to overfeed the alter ego inside her. The less she said the better, then he might go away.

She drove slowly, carefully watching the road, conscious of the weight on her chest. She daren't risk looking at the pendant again yet. She turned the music up loud but could still hear the muttering of indistinct phrases in that weird language. She trod harder on the accelerator and tried to focus on the music again to block him out.

Twenty minutes later her headache was beyond horrific and that angry voice still echoed in her head. She pulled up outside the clinic. There wasn't room in the garage for her car so she parked it on the street, leaving the spaces in the sealed front yard for patients. She walked up to the path and glanced around. Dark clouds settled ominously low, closing the usually wide sky in on her. Her skin prickled – if she had hackles they'd be on end. Despite the lack of population, the lack of buildings, it felt like she was being watched.

Serious paranoia. But then, she had reason.

'Are you still there?' she asked quietly.

'You know I am.'

Yeah, she was being watched – by her own sweet crazy self.

She went in the back entrance so she wouldn't disturb any patients in the clinic at the front part of the house. Fingers crossed Kate had been and gone and hopefully Dad was too busy to notice she was home early. If he wasn't with a patient he'd be in his lab.

What would the locals say if they knew about the futile, unconventional research that consumed him? Would they shake their heads and put it down to eccentricity? The mad scientist? The bereaved doctor?

Zelie felt for him. Of course she did. But his obsession was increasingly intense and it left no room for her or Luke.

She ran upstairs to her bedroom, shut the door behind her and stripped off her fleece, tossing it onto the pile of clothes at the foot of her bed. The pile was so big eruption was imminent, but she turned her back on it.

Later.

She grabbed the neck of her T-shirt and pulled it down to a V so she could see the pendant resting a few inches below her collarbones. The skin there was mottled, pink and purple and white. The pendant looked dull, a couple of dents at one corner like it had been accidentally beaten. Across one edge a narrow loop was engraved. Like half a butterfly wing only smaller. Some other insect? Luke would probably know. She turned the metal over, another dent on that side. Maybe it had happened when Kate had lost it in the lake. It wasn't glowing. There was no precious or unusual gem set into it. Nothing otherworldly or anything. Just a lump of metal.

She dropped the pendant back on her sore skin and looked at the chain it hung from. She twisted it around her neck until she'd examined every single link. She couldn't find the clasp. She slid it around again and again. Still nothing. There must be some trick to it but the links all looked the same to her. None were any thicker or had any lever or anything. But there had been. She'd done it herself – pinched open the little hook to do it up . . .

She let the necklace go, dropping her fists to her sides. Her body boiled except for that one patch on her chest that remained icy. She had no more reason to delay.

With clammy hands she retied her hair into its usual loose ponytail and went to the mirror. It had been her mother's – antique, full-length and free-standing in a mahogany frame. She could hear roughened breathing. But she didn't think it was her own.

With her heart hammering, she finally looked up to her face.

She released the breath she'd been holding. It was still her. She was pale and a sheen of sweat gleamed on her skin, but it was still her. There was no scary yellow in her eyes.

'What do you see?' she prompted as she stared at herself, trying to spot a difference – any answer to the confusion her mind was suffering.

'You do not look like her,' he sounded surprised. Hoarse. Disappointed. 'You are not her.'

Raising an eyebrow, she stood taller. If this was some elaborate prank, whoever it was couldn't really see her.

'What do I look like?' She tested him, poking her tongue out at her reflection.

'Your tongue is quite long. You lift just one eyebrow. Strange.'

Zelie sucked her tongue back in so quickly she nearly swallowed it. He could see her right this minute? Just as he'd said he'd be able to? Sharply she glanced around the room. There had to be a webcam. But hers was switched off and she could see no other. How was she hearing this voice? How was he seeing her now? She checked behind the mirror to make sure there wasn't something planted on the back of it.

'What are you doing?' he asked.

'Looking for some kind of camera,' she said through a clenched jaw.

'Look in the mirror,' he snapped. 'You do not want me to tell you?'

She stood back and stared at her reflection. This couldn't be happening. She refused to believe it.

'Your hair is tied back. Brown. Your eyes are green with gold near the centre. You wear . . . men's trousers?'

He sounded puzzled, but he wasn't half as puzzled as she was. 'How can you see me?'

'I said. Through your eyes.'

She grabbed the pendant. There was no seam that she could see but even so she took it in both hands and tried to force it open. It wouldn't give. There couldn't be a computer chip in it. Nothing. It wasn't possible. It really was only a lump of metal that quite some time ago had been melted and moulded into an odd rectangle. There was no camera. No microphone. Yet she could still hear him and he could see her. She turned her back on the mirror, afraid to keep looking at herself. 'What can you see now?'

'You are in a room. A bed. A map on the wall. Colour. A plant by the window. Dead. A box on a desk. It is all . . .'

'What?' Why did he sound unsure? Maybe there was a camera somewhere and it didn't have good focus on objects at a slight distance. She strained her eyes as she tried to spot it. 'It's all what?'

'Strange. Everything is strange. I know some things, but most things are strange.'

He thought things were strange?

His voice was quiet. 'I have never seen anything like that.'

'Like what?'

'The box on your desk. The painting that moves.'

Her computer was on, her one total luxury. She'd insisted her dad get her a good one. How else was she to stay in touch with the outside world? Not that she'd emailed anyone back in the UK, not even Sarah, her former BFF. Which yes, she felt guilty about. But she'd deleted her social media accounts – she hadn't updated them in months anyway.

Now the screen saver was running with her favourite pictures on a slide show. 'That's my computer.'

'Your what?'

'Computer. You know. Com. Pu. Ter.' Zelie shook her head. Someone was playing one hell of a complicated prank – but why?

'Who is that?'

'Who?' Zelie spun, a full circle on the spot, but there was no one in the room.

'The woman on your . . . com . . . puter.'

Zelie looked at the picture on the screen but said nothing. In another moment it would fade and something else would pop up.

'She looks like you.'

Zelie was over this. Her vision blurred. 'Stop it.'

She didn't look like her. Her mum had been far more beautiful.

Zelie ran out of her room and down the stairs. She stormed out of the house, filled with a fiery energy that seemed fuelled by the cold, heavy chain. 'Go away and leave me alone.'

'I cannot.'

'Stop it.' She wanted it to stop. Not make her run through town talking to herself like the nutcase she'd turned into – starting to believe she was talking to someone *real*.

She headed towards the lake but then swerved, not wanting to struggle with the stony beach and the threat the slippery rocks posed to her ankles. Instead she raced between the trees a few yards back from the lakefront. She'd be safe under their cover, right? If someone was watching her from a distance, they wouldn't be able to see her in the thick green.

'We are outside now. You are running. I can hear you breathing. There are trees.' He knew she still doubted and he was giving her the evidence.

She didn't want to listen.

The necklace banged on her chest as she ran faster, striking her skin like a silver-tipped hammer. Words choked in her throat. 'What else? What else can you see?'

'Snow. A path up the hill.' His accent coloured every word he spoke, and then once more he was muttering strange words – sounds her brain couldn't possibly have invented.

'What are you saying?' she asked.

'I have been here before.' He sounded as surprised as she felt. 'I know this forest.'

Zelie froze, her muscles jarring at her quick halt. Suddenly the trees threatened. There could be someone watching – lots of people. The subtle noises of nature sounded as loud as cannon fire. The occasional drip of water, the snap of a twig, a rustling in the leaves. Birds, right? Or some small animal foraging. Even though she knew that's all it would be, it scared her. And she could hear another sound getting louder, a rhythmic thumping that grew more insistent until it was all she could hear – just thud-thud-thud-thud-thud-thud. For a blinded moment she couldn't work out what it was.

Dizzying relief rushed her system as she realised.

Her heart. It was her stupid heart racing as she panicked and her blood drumming in her ears. She took off again, running up the hill beyond the low forest, bypassing the ice rink at the side, out to the clear track that led to the barren peak of the hill from where she could see all around and across the lake. Halfway along the open track she stopped to look down at that unusual pale blue water.

Further up the hill was the observatory where scientists studied the night sky, watching meteors and stars, trying to find things beyond what the mind could imagine. Zelie looked in all directions but could see no one. Yet he was still here. She could sense him in her head, could almost feel him. Someone – some *thing* – inside her. Yet she was alone. More alone than at any time since the move, and since she'd lost her mum.

'Now you cry.'

She blinked as tears ran down her cheeks. 'How is this possible?'

'How do you think?'

'I can't think. It's impossible. This isn't real.' She was living a nightmare.

'It is real,' he said angrily. 'If you are not her, I need help. You to help.' He didn't sound pleased about that.

'Who are you?' She stared at the vast stretch of water, wrapping her arms around her middle in that old, useless defence against a vicious rising wind.

There was a moment when she thought she could actually feel his hesitation. Then his decision.

'Tamás.'

Both the name and the way he said it sounded strange. She turned her head away from the lake, blocking the crashing waves of wind in her ears. 'Where are you from?'

Another hesitation. 'I was born in France.'

'When?'

'1901.'

'*When*?' She half laughed, half choked. She'd heard him wrong. '1901.'

Nope, he really had said that. Twice now. 'But that's over a hundred years ago.'

'A hundred – what?'

'A hundred years. We're in the twenty-first century now, no wonder things look strange to you.'

'Over . . .' he sounded oddly uncertain. 'But she promised it would not be long. She promised I would stay –' He broke off, then launched into his own weird language. A mad scrabble of syllables, a full minute of gobbledegook before he suddenly stopped.

Even though she couldn't understand what he'd been saying, Zelie couldn't be immune to his tone – to the thread of fear running through it. Her eyes ached with a sudden sharp pain behind them.

'What's the last thing you remember?' she asked, listening to his laboured – panicked – breathing.

'The last birthday I remember was my seventeenth.'

Right, back in 1918?

'So you're seventeen. Give or take a hundred or so years.' Wow. Could he be an old man? No – he didn't sound old. Foreign yes, but not old.

'I must be,' he answered quietly.

Okay, this was definitely psychosis. She'd gone bonkers. But she couldn't pull out of it, couldn't stop herself asking more. 'Then where have you been all this time? Where are you now?'

'I have only just woken. I did not know how long it had been . . .' He trailed off.

Zelie waited but he said nothing for so long that she had to ask again. She couldn't resist. 'Where are you?'

She heard him draw in a deep breath before answering. 'I am not sure where she has hidden my shell. But it is just as she said it would be. I am cold. I cannot move my form, cannot feel it.' His words tumbled faster. 'But I can see and hear through you.'

His shell? What was he – a snail?

'Who's she?'

'The witch.'

'Witch?'

He'd said it more clearly this time and it seemed he really meant a W not a B.

'The one who did this to me.'

Zelie shut her eyes and shook her head, laughing. It was either that or cry some more. 'You're telling me you're under some kind of spell?'

Now she was sure it was a dream. She'd wake up any moment to find the day had yet to begin and that she hadn't been on the field trip yet.

'She was to release me when it was time.'

'Time for what?' Zelie wasn't getting to grips with any of it but she had to admit the hallucination was intriguing. 'Why am I involved? How come I can hear you?'

'The *amulette*.'

Amulet? 'You mean the pendant? The necklace?'

'Yes.'

'You're not telling me you're inside it?'

She didn't get an answer. She wasn't really getting any of the answers she needed. She chewed the inside of her cheek. 'Why did she give it to me?'

'Something must be wrong. You are not her.'

She sure wasn't. 'She said she wasn't strong enough.'

'Who did?'

'The girl who gave it to me. She's not well. She's really thin. She's my age but she can't come to school because she's so sick. Her name's Kate Hearn.'

Her words disappeared into the wind. There was no reply.

Zelie turned her head up sharply, sure she'd just seen something moving out of the corner of her eye. She blinked and checked again but there was nothing, only the pristine layer of snow over the barren high part of the hill. Her breathing quickened, her poor pulse was still chaotic.

No word from him. Had he gone? Was it over just like that?

'Tamás?'

'*Her* name was Hearn,' he said slowly. 'It must be her. She must have got the influenza. Perhaps she was not strong enough.'

Zelie frowned. 'It didn't look like flu.' You didn't bleed from orifices with flu. Ebola maybe, but not flu.

'You know influenza?'

'Of course,' she said. 'It's always around.'

'Always?' he asked, horrified.

'Sure. But I get a jab before the worst hits in winter.'

'A "jab"?'

'Yes,' she sighed impatiently. 'An injection to build immunity.'

Another lengthy silence.

'There is now immunity against the influenza?' he asked.

She rolled her eyes. How typical that her nightmare would morph into a dissection of this, her father's obsession.

'Influenza is beaten? It is gone?' His volume dial spun to loud again, but now he sounded amazed rather than angry.

'No. Viruses constantly mutate.' Was she really having a conversation with herself about this? 'They become resistant to the medicines, and the vaccinations don't protect from all strands. It's impossible to keep up with the changes but we try.'

But his questioning made her think. Had he really been born in 1901? Had they even had vaccines then? Jeez, she'd have to Google it.

She shook her head. She was definitely hallucinating. She probably had the flu right now and this was all because of a fever. No way could he have been born in 1901, and no way was she hearing him now.

'The flu kills too many.'

'You sound like my dad,' Zelie said tiredly. The doom doctor. The most paranoid GP on the planet. His sole aim was to find a vaccine or cure to protect the world's people from bird flu, bat flu, elephant flu – whatever strand it was that would threaten next. 'People do die from flu each year, but it's not as bad as it was. They keep predicting another killer strain but it hasn't happened yet.'

She shivered as the wind lifted higher. The clouds were a purplish colour that suggested snow. She should go back down the hill. It got dark early and she had no torch with her. A stupid risk. School would have finished. Luke would be home.

Luke.

Zelie wiped her face with her cold hands and started walking. She had to get back for her brother. She might be going crazy on the inside, but she'd stay normal on the outside – for him. Ditto for her dad. Life was tough enough already without her looping the loop on them.

'This Kate must be the witch,' Tamás spoke. 'I knew her as Catriona. It has to be her.'

'She can't be, she's not old enough,' Zelie said, impatient and sarcastic. 'She's a teenager. And there's no way she's a witch. There aren't any witches.'

'This would not be happening if they were gone.'

'They're not gone. They've never existed.'

There was a bitter laugh.

'No,' Zelie shook her head firmly. 'I don't believe in witches. Or vampires or zombies or any of that stuff.'

'Zombies?'

'The living dead. Very Hollywood.'

'Hollywood?'

He didn't know about Hollywood? 'You really were born in 1901?'

'If you do not believe in witches, do you not believe in me either?'

'Definitely not. I think I'm having some kind of hallucination.'

'No,' he said bluntly. 'You know this is real. That is why you are scared. You know what I have said is true.'

'No I don't.'

'You do. I can tell you things you see but do not notice. You know I am with you.'

Her confused mind certainly thought something was. But it had to be fever. 'And if I take the necklace off?'

'You cannot. It must not be taken off until it is done.'

'Until *what* is done?' She mightn't be able to find the clasp but she could lift the pendant away from her skin – what would happen then? She fingered the chain.

'Do not lift it.'

'You're not real. You're in my head. I'm sick.' She was sticking to that story.

'How do you know? What if you do lift it?' He paused. 'Could you kill someone?'

'That's not what would happen.'

'It would. Could you do it?'

Zelie glanced at the lake and chose to answer his question with one of her own. 'So what is it we have to wait for?' she asked. 'Tamás? Tell me what is going to happen.'

No reply.

Yeah, he couldn't answer that, could he? Because he wasn't real and her sick mind had yet to make it up.

She rubbed her fingers against her cold lips. 'I think I need to go and see Kate.' Maybe she'd picked up one of Kate's many viruses and this was a symptom of it. Zelie didn't want to go anywhere near that girl or her mad, staring uncles but she didn't have much choice.

'No,' Tamás said firmly. 'Do not go there.'

Zelie ignored the ninety per cent of her that wanted to agree with him. Just because he'd supposedly taken up temporary residence in her body, didn't mean she'd let him boss her around. 'Why not? They can't do anything to me.'

'They can and will. You cannot go there.'

To that big sheep station? Zelie might have only lived in Tekapo three weeks but she'd already heard about the huge property and the reclusive, loaded brothers who owned it. The fact they wouldn't allow the public access through to climb the mountain was a point of contention for the tourists who came, but not within the town. Everyone in Tekapo knew about Kate, even though she was rarely seen, so they closed ranks around the Hearn brothers and their right to restrict who came on their land. But maybe there was more to their fight for isolation?

'You think it'll be dangerous?' she asked.

'I know it will be.'

CHAPTER THREE

ZELIE RAN BACK down the path. Would going to Kate's be any crazier than continuing this conversation with a bodiless voice?

Snowfall started, light flakes easily floating to rest. It was a slow, steady dusting of icing sugar adding to the frozen layer that already hid the raw mud on the ground. It looked enchanting but would soon become deadly, blinding the way and freezing those exposed. If she got lost she'd end up hypothermic in less than an hour. Not an option. She ran faster – from the hill, from the cold that crunched her flesh. From him.

'You are not to go there.'

Of course she couldn't escape him, he was with her with every step she took. That was the problem with a newly split personality. But why should she listen to him? Follow his orders?

She might be crazy but she wasn't stupid.

'I don't have a choice,' she panted, amping up her pace to get through the trees on the lower part of the hill. 'I have to find out what's wrong with me.'

'You do not know what she can do.' His accent thickened the faster he spoke.

'No, I don't. But I'm not getting much info freezing up here. Why don't *you* tell me all about it?'

'I cannot.'

'Cannot or will not?'

There was nothing but the sound of her puffing and the scrunching as her shoes slammed down on the icy path.

'Both,' he answered eventually.

'So why should I listen to you about not going there?'

'You do not want to go there,' he growled.

Actually he was right, she didn't. But that wasn't the point. Zelie glanced up to the trees. Had the wind just picked up? Yes. Snow flurries blew into her face. The pretty-looking stuff stung.

'I need information first,' he said carefully. 'That way I can prepare you for what might happen.'

As if he was some kind of protector or teacher? She so didn't think so.

'Like what?' She had the stitch again so dropped to a walk as she got to the bottom of the hill and out to the road.

He didn't answer for a while. 'What is the worst thing?' he asked. 'Something worse than death.'

What was worse than death? Actually, Zelie knew one answer to that – being left behind. The endless agony of loss. During the day she tried to turn her back on it and pretend it wasn't there. For her the cliché hadn't worked; time hadn't healed that wound. And sometimes, in the darkness that stretched beyond midnight, she was jealous. The dead person had the easier run. At least for them it was finished. But then her guilt multiplied over that selfish thought – she was *lucky*. And she had responsibilities. She owed.

'They trapped me,' he said angrily. 'Imprisonment is worse than anything. To be unable to move. That could happen. You could be bound for years – helpless, hopeless, blind, mute . . .'

Wasn't she a prisoner now? To her own mistakes?

'Give me tonight,' he said. 'One night. I must trust you with the *amulette*, you must trust me on this.'

What did she have to lose? A little more sanity?

'Understand this,' he said quietly. 'I do not want you hurt, because if you are hurt I will die. Stay home tonight, nothing will happen.'

She rubbed the back of her neck. She didn't like it when he spoke all melodramatic life-and-death. Anyway, she didn't want to go to Kate's house in the dark. The brighter light of day might make her feel marginally safer. And the snow was falling thicker now and if it kept up the roads might close. The last thing she wanted was to be stuck out there.

'Okay. I'll stay home tonight and go there tomorrow.'

'I need information.'

What, she didn't even get a thank you? Nope, he was straight on to business. To what *he* needed.

'What kind of information?'

She quickened her pace as the snow flurries eased.

'I must know what has happened since 1918.'

She stifled a half-hysterical laugh. 'That's almost a hundred years.' And an action-packed time it had been.

'You can find out about it?'

'Of course.' She knew the basics and she had both the internet and the History Channel. But why did he want to know about it?

It was her conscience calling, that was it. She'd got slack with her schoolwork – so uninterested. Was this some weird latent guilt making her want to ace history? It was nuts.

But what choice did she have? It wasn't like she could run to her father and tell him. He'd helicopter her to hospital and make her have a million brain scans or something. She gulped in the cold air. Maybe *that* was her problem. She had a tumour. It wasn't a personality disorder or a lack-of-sleep psychosis, but a full-on cancer crushing her brain.

Oh my God, she was *dying*. Fear injected adrenalin into her muscles. She struck out, running again. If it was some weird virus, or cancer, shouldn't she start taking meds for it asap? Damn, she was going to have to tell her dad.

No, no and no again. Sweat dampened her skin. The clammy fear kind as well as the hot exercise kind. She pushed harder, trying to run from the nightmare. She couldn't die. She couldn't do that to Luke.

'Hey, Zelie.'

She looked up from her unblinking glare at the ground. That wasn't the voice of the foreigner.

The Big O stood sheltering just where the row of shops started. A plastic bag dangled from his hand and he wore jeans, an old rock-concert tee over a striped thermal and a smile on his face. He took a step sideways into her path but her legs had stopped already. So had her heart.

'Wow.' Otis cocked his head and cheekiness shone from his eyes. 'You're really into running. I thought you weren't feeling well?'

She stared blankly at him, taking ten seconds to believe he was really there, ten more to process what he'd said. Since when did Otis Hayes notice anything about her? Let alone twice in one day.

Faint colour clouded his cheekbones and he shifted the bag to his other hand. 'I heard you talking to Mr Webb.'

He'd been listening? He'd been *interested*? She felt her own colour deepen as she realised she hadn't blinked in minutes. Nor had she managed to say hello. She'd gone mute fangirl, like she was spellbound or something. She pulled herself together, forced a smile and tried to answer lightly, tried to be a little normal. 'I thought some fresh air might help.' Ugh. Squeaky-voice central.

'You really should train for the athletics squad. You're fast.'

Yeah. Even she hadn't known she had a sprint like that in her. But he'd been watching her for a while? Great. All wobble and bounce and certifiable craziness. 'It's a good day for a run,' she panted, dying inside – now from mortification, not the mind-maddening malignant tumour. Why did he have to cross her path every time she was sweaty and gross with stop-sign red cheeks?

She spoke to cover her awkwardness. 'It's not too hot.' She flushed harder as she realised the stupidity of that comment. It was winter. It was snowing. So definitely not too hot. And like she was an expert? And like people went for training runs in the jeans and grubby T-shirt they'd been wearing all day?

But he wasn't looking at her like she was a total loser. Okay, so he had that amused-by-you grin on, but it was also friendly.

She swallowed, dropped her gaze and rubbed the side of her head with her fingers. She wanted to walk away. Didn't want to. Couldn't seem to move anyway. Unsure of what he wanted and unwilling to even try to guess.

'And you like to sing when you run?'

She frowned. Nope, she hadn't been singing, she'd been talking to –

'Oh. Um. Yeah,' she babbled, her face now nuclear hot as she lied.

His smile widened – easily, lazily – totally fascinating. Heat burned through the rest of her. It was the first time she'd felt warm all over, inside and out, since she'd put the pendant on.

'I, um . . . better get back home,' she mumbled, embarrassed by her inability to speak a simple sentence.

'Sure.' That easy grin again.

Her insides somersaulted.

'Feel better soon, Zelie.'

She couldn't hold his warm brown gaze any more. How unfair

of him to be that good-looking and turn a mere mortal like her into a stammering idiot.

She moved past him, so self-conscious that walking took all her concentration. She didn't look back. The snowflakes hit her hot cheeks and instantly dissolved into drips of water. She brushed them from her jaw with the back of her fingers.

'Zelie?'

She groaned. Tamás was still there? For a moment she'd felt like something happy was only a breath away.

'That is your name?'

'Yeah,' she mumbled. He'd copied Otis and pronounced it right, but it sounded different with his accent. Exotic instead of strange.

'He talked to you this afternoon by the lake.'

Funnily enough she'd remembered that herself, though she didn't know why Tamás sounded disapproving. 'Otis.' The Gorgeous. Not that she highlighted that fact aloud. 'He goes to my school.'

'You do not need a chaperone?'

'A *what*?'

'You are a young woman. You should not talk to a man unaccompanied.'

Oh, he just had to be kidding. 'In New Zealand today,' she explained with slow sarcasm, 'a girl is free to talk to whoever she wants, whenever she wants, about whatever she wants. She can go anywhere and do anything and she doesn't need some guy's permission or protection. It's called liberation.'

'And you wear men's clothes.'

Seriously? More disapproval?

'You mean my jeans?'

'*Oui*.' He muttered another weird word.

Zelie rolled her eyes. She *so* wasn't going to start prancing round in ankle-length skirts.

Then Tamás spoke again. 'What was he wearing on his arms?'

Zelie laughed, light-hearted as the ridiculousness won over the fear. 'You know, Tamás, you've missed a hell of a lot in the last hundred years. But we can catch you up on the fashion styles of the last century at least.'

She walked in through the front door. Luke was parked on the sofa in the lounge, killing something on Xbox. A jar sat on the coffee table, a pile of twigs and green-brown leaves in the bottom of it. Somewhere under that debris there'd be another bug or slug to add to his collection. Gross. It'd be fine if he kept them in the jar, or let them go outside, but all too often he let them explore the carpet. And while he'd kill as many aliens as possible in a computer game, he'd freak if a bug got squashed. She stepped in front of the screen so he couldn't avoid her. 'Okay?'

He nodded and leaned his head to peer behind her at the action. She could hear the wheeze in his lungs. She picked up the inhaler from the low table and threw it at him.

'You finished your homework?'

'I will later.'

'No, you will now.' She turned around and flicked off the screen. Just because she was fast-tracking to failure at school, didn't mean she was going to let Luke do the same. All his teachers had said he was 'bright and quirky'. Zelie knew that was code for 'annoying and asks incessant questions', and she was going to make sure he reached all his special potential.

'Aw, Zelie!'

'You can put it back on once you've shown me your finished homework. Need a hand with it?'

He shook his head grouchily and stomped over to the school bag he'd let explode on the floor at the end of the sofa.

'Okay, well, call me if you do.' She walked towards the kitchen. An irregular banging sound greeted her and her heart sank – so not the day for her father to go all active-parent on her.

The week they'd moved in there'd been a stream of 'welcome to Tekapo' dinner invites, but her dad had declined them all. Once everyone had heard he was a widower with two kids, the locals had dropped off dinners instead – mostly home-made heat-and-eat casseroles. Zelie had been appreciative and was sorry the deliveries had dried up already.

Now her dad was at the bench, striking a knife through an onion with alarming inaccuracy. Damn. Preparing dinner was usually her job. Not because she fancied herself as the next Nigella, but because her father's cooking was awful.

'You're late home,' he glanced up.

Normally he wouldn't be out of his lab to notice.

'It's okay. I've got spag Bol underway,' he added.

Zelie stifled her shudder. It was his one dish. Even then he cheated by using store-bought sauce. She feared for his fingers as he went back to mutilating the onion.

'Great,' she lied as she backed out the doorway, hoping she was safe from interrogation. Then she heard the question.

'You were out with friends?'

She turned back to face him and bit the bullet. If she didn't tell him something now and minimise it, he'd make more of it later when he found out. 'No. Just for a walk. I had a headache and came home from school early.'

Her father immediately put the knife on the bench and walked to where she stood, his eyes professionally assessing, a huge frown on his face. 'Is the headache gone now?'

The one sure way to get her dad's attention was to tell him she was sick.

'Yes.' And it had. Maybe the rising wind had blown it out. Or the adrenalin was masking it.

Even so, he put his hand to her forehead. She looked down while he felt it, hiding the madness that must be obvious in her eyes. Then he felt her glands, made her open her mouth and say 'ahhhh'. Already all over the top.

'No temperature.' He stopped prodding. 'But you're soaked through. Go get changed, take some paracetamol and I'll keep an eye on you.'

The mini physical settled it. She didn't want him keeping his obsessive eye on her. If she was sick, she didn't want Luke suffering because of it. She didn't want long months of drugs and hospitals and more moves in the hunt for miracle treatments. Her father was already half-crazed. If she really was sick he'd make what was left of her life unbearable. And Luke's. Her baby brother had suffered enough. The later she left it, the better for everyone. She wasn't going to tell him. 'I'll have a quick shower then do some work upstairs before dinner,' she said, aiming to allay his concern. 'Catch up on what I missed this afternoon.'

'Sure.' Her dad hovered, his frown still super-sized. 'Dinner is only half an hour away. Don't do too much.'

That instruction was a first. According to her dad the move was supposed to help re-motivate her academically. She hadn't done much in the way of study for months now. Up until her mother had died she'd been a good student. But since then it hadn't been her first, second, third or even twentieth priority. Their house had been so empty, and there'd been so much to do. So much her father couldn't cope with.

Most especially caring for Luke.

Late most nights, when she'd finished organising things, she sat alone in her room. She should be studying but instead she listened to music. The beat sucked time the way Luke sucked a milkshake, so quick it was rude. Movies sucked even more time. But her addiction to trashy talent shows was the real time vacuum. Before she knew it, it was beyond late and she was too tired to concentrate on school stuff. But even then she didn't want to sleep. She hated the dream.

She walked back through the living room to check Luke was hard at work, then ran up the stairs to her room. Shivering again, she switched on the heater and turned the free-standing mirror to the wall. The guy might be a figment of her imagination but she still wasn't giving him a thrill. Besides, before she did anything about his supposed need for information, she needed to get warm and dry. She struggled to peel her jeans off. The saturated denim was glued to her thighs and the backs of her calves. Finally, in her undies, she dashed across the hall to the bathroom she shared with Luke and locked the door. She grabbed a towel then closed her eyes and stripped completely.

The steaming jet of water was a delicious torture as it pummelled her cold skin. It felt even more fantastic with her eyes closed; the needles of heat were a painful pleasure. Her other senses sharpened in the red-tinged darkness, especially sound and touch. Thankfully, the voice was silent and all she could hear was the streaming, splashing water. But the pendant was still as cold as a cube of ice. She held one side of it right up to the shower head and turned the water as hot as she could take it. But still it didn't get any warmer. It just didn't make sense. Then again, none of this made sense.

Back in her room she wiggled blindly into her underwear and then pulled on her navy trackies and a long-sleeved jersey. She pulled thick, hot-pink bed socks right up over her ankles and as an extra measure she stuffed her feet into her old fluffy slippers. Surely that would warm her up.

'You wear very strange clothes.'

Zelie bit back a laugh at that definite disapproval. Who was he, the new host of *What Not to Wear*?

'Zelie! Can you get the door?' her father yelled.

She hadn't heard the buzzer but she headed down the stairs. Swinging the front door open, she didn't recognise the woman standing outside with a large rectangular dish in her hands.

'You must be Zelie.' The woman smiled. 'I'm Megan Hayes. I live on the other side of the main road, in the new subdivision.'

Zelie made herself blink so she wasn't totally staring at the blue-eyed, brunette woman standing on the doorstep. Megan was beautiful. Her hair shone, so did her skin, but more than that her smile was real. She sparkled. Zelie's mum had been like that – so pretty.

'I wanted to welcome you to Tekapo. I thought I'd leave it a couple of weeks or so until the rush was over . . .' she winked.

Zelie giggled as she nodded, instantly warming to the older woman.

'Thanks, that's so kind of you.'

It was like her wish had been granted – she might have to suffer Dad's spaghetti tonight, but tomorrow there'd be this yum-smelling number.

'It's vegetarian, I hope that's okay. But my son doesn't eat meat so that's what I'm used to cooking.' Her shoulders lifted in an easy shrug.

Her son? Zelie paused. She'd said her name was Megan *Hayes*, surely she wasn't –

'Otis,' Megan nodded, like she'd followed Zelie's thoughts. 'He's in your year at school, I think?'

'Uh, yes,' Zelie cleared her throat awkwardly, suddenly conscious of heat flooding her face as she remembered what she was wearing. Hot-pink bed socks? Wow, great impression. Thank heavens Megan hadn't sent her son to do the delivery.

'We need to get working.'

Zelie looked down, trying to block Tamás's snarl.

'Um, thanks so much.' Eager now to get away, she took the amazing-smelling, heavy dish from Megan. But she couldn't be so snatch-and-run rude.

'Would you like to come in?'

'No, I won't hold you up, I know it's dinner-time.'

Zelie smiled gratefully. 'Dad would come and say hi but he's just . . . he's busy,' she said apologetically, embarrassed that her father would never come to the door and be polite. 'He gets preoccupied.'

'We all do,' Megan answered easily.

Yeah, no wonder Otis had that charm thing going. He'd inherited it from his mum.

'Who are you?' Luke suddenly pushed past Zelie and stepped outside.

'*Luke.*' Zelie winced.

'It's okay,' Megan laughed. 'I'm Megan, who are you?'

'Luke.'

'Hi, Luke. Nice to meet you.'

Luke nodded like Megan meeting him was the best thing ever.

'Are you one of Dad's patients?'

'No,' Megan shook her head. 'But I live in Tekapo. I work up at the observatory.'

'Really?' Luke's eyes widened, his interest snared. 'So you find black holes and meteorites and stuff?'

'Meteorites are my favourite thing,' Megan nodded. 'When they enter the atmosphere and burn up they're stunning.'

'Have you seen many?'

'Not enough.' Megan cocked her head, the way Zelie had seen Otis do. 'Have you been up there yet?'

Luke shook his head.

'Well, you're going to have to come. I'll give you the tour, if you like. Maybe Zelie could bring you later in the week? Though not a school night, right?' She looked up at Zelie with a conspiratorial smile.

'Really? *Epic*,' breathed Luke. 'Thanks.'

'Thanks.' Zelie echoed softly. 'He'd love that.'

Megan straightened and looked right into Zelie's eyes for a moment. 'Pleasure to meet you, Zelie.'

Zelie lowered her lashes, unable to hold that bright-eyed gaze. 'You too.' She lifted up the casserole in an appreciative gesture. 'Thanks again.'

The second she shut the door her father called them through for dinner.

'Coming!' she called back. 'Better go wash your hands, Luke.'

'What about information?' Tamás asked, machine-gun style. 'You have to help me.'

'I'm hungry, so we're eating first,' Zelie whispered tartly as she walked to put the casserole in the fridge and then wash her hands. 'I promise to eat fast and go straight upstairs to get on with it. That keep you happy?'

Silence. Not impressed, huh? Too bad, because she *was* hungry. She'd been too late for breakfast, hadn't had lunch and had spent most of the afternoon out in the cold. But not even hunger could make her mouth water over this dish. Some people thought spaghetti Bolognese was the ultimate in comfort food. But they'd never had the misfortune of eating her father's. He butchered it with large chunks of barely cooked onion and lumpy mince. She wished Megan had dropped off that awesome casserole an hour earlier.

But Luke was already into it when she sat at the dining table, seeing how fast he could suck up each spaghetti string. A piece went in whippet-fast and sauce splattered in all directions – on his nose, his shirt and across the table.

'Gross.' Zelie wiped her cheek. 'Stop it, Luke.'

He just grinned and did it again.

Ugh. She needed an umbrella at the dining table. Zelie sent her father a look, but he'd done his dad bit and was back to preoccupied mad doctor. She recognised his expression – he'd worn it almost constantly since their mother's death. His eyes were seeing something, but nothing that was actually in front of him. She knew that she could say something to him now and even though there was no other noise in the entire house, he still wouldn't hear her.

But she was used to his absence. So was Luke.

She shifted her seat further away from her cretinous brother and went back to eating.

'How long is this going to take?' Tamás asked.

Zelie swallowed. As if she could answer him when she was dining with her dad and brother. She just kept eating, for once beating Luke-the-gannet in the plate-clearing race. Not because she wanted to get back upstairs and obey the new Commander-in-Body, but because her father's pasta was only swallowable when still too hot to taste. She took her plate through to the kitchen bench and then opened the freezer. Before she bored her brains out with twentieth-century history, she needed a treat.

Ice cream was her absolute weakness. She'd been devastated to discover neither Ben & Jerry's nor Häagen-Dazs was available in New Zealand, but now she was working her way through the local options and some of them were pretty good. She opened the carton and sighed as she saw the pockmarks left by Luke. But she still spooned some into a bowl.

'Can I have some?' Luke banged his plate down on the bench.

She put the ice cream back in the freezer and slammed the door shut. 'You can get it yourself,' she said shortly.

Luke glared at her and fetched it from the freezer again. She didn't care; he'd picked out all the gummy lollies, so he could get his own leftovers – which he did, simply taking the container and a spoon out of the room with him.

'Go shower as soon as you've had it,' Zelie told him sharply. She leaned against the bench. Two minutes later she heard the video game starting up again. Her dad was already back in his den-like laboratory.

She sighed. She'd stack the dishes later, she had her ice cream to savour.

'What is this?' Tamás sounded appalled but she didn't care, too busy letting the flavour hit the spot.

'Ice cream. You've never had it?' Had ice cream been widely available a hundred years ago? She'd have to Google that sometime too. She grinned, her insane brain was surprisingly inventive. But right now she was having another spoonful.

'This is not iced cream. This is awful,' he said loudly. 'It is bright green.'

'Yeah. Lots of things that are good for you are green, didn't you know?' It wasn't neon but it was pretty lurid. 'It usually has lollies in it but Luke's eaten them all.' She raised her voice to holler at her brother. 'Go shower *now*, Luke.'

She took another mouthful of ice cream, heard the game go quiet, then the familiar thuds of her brother stomping up the stairs.

'It is too cold,' said Tamás.

What did he mean too cold?

'Can you taste it?' Okay, another step too close to the weird side. It was bad enough to think this persona could see and hear through her – but that he could taste what she ate as well? She had another mouthful and tried to get over the creepiness. After all, it was only some sick part of herself talking. This wasn't real.

'It is faint but I can taste it. It is sweet but too cold. Do not have any more.'

What did he mean 'do not have any more'? First demanding history lessons, now imposing diet restrictions? She wasn't putting up with that. With exaggerated deliberation, she loaded her spoon and slowly sucked the huge scoop from it, then smacked her lips with a doubled sense of satisfaction.

'I need to get warm. That will not help.'

Oh please, like her eating ice cream was going to make any difference?

'Feel the *amulette*.'

Could she hear his teeth grinding? She rolled her eyes but put her hand to her neck.

Okay, so the pendant *was* even colder.

'All right,' she sighed, feeling the tension headache returning. 'Let's try something else.' She rinsed the last of the ice cream from her bowl and watched it melt in the sink. 'Could you taste the spaghetti too?'

'Yes. That was good.'

He thought her father's rubbery pasta was good? That told her all she needed to know about his taste.

Sighing, she faced up to the mountain of dishes. How did her father manage to use every pot in the cupboard for something as simple as spaghetti? She rinsed and loaded plates into the dishwasher and did the pots by hand, ignoring the seething silence from Tamás. Once the mess was cleared, she was ready for something else.

'What is this . . . with all the food in it?'

'A fridge,' she said, full of faux patience. 'It keeps things cold. And beside it is the freezer that keeps things frozen. Like the ice cream.'

'We don't need more of that.'

'No, but we do need the milk.' She poured some into a small pan.

'Who are you talking to?' Luke walked into the kitchen, looking the ultimate in angelic boy, all pink and clean in his dinosaur-covered flannelette pyjamas. During the day he was grubtastic, but seeing him like this made her annoyance instantly evaporate. He was so young.

'Myself. First sign of madness.' She wasn't really joking but she smiled brightly to cover it. 'Want a hot drink?' That offer would distract him completely.

'Yeah.' Luke's eyes lit up at the purple packet she'd put on the bench.

She stirred the powder until it dissolved and then frothed the milk, pouring it on. 'You get the marshmallows.'

He didn't hesitate.

'Have you had a good day?' she asked him as she squirted a dollop of canned whipped cream in and then grated some chocolate on top.

'Yeah. I moved up a reading group.'

'Awesome,' she beamed at him and handed him his mug.

Luke lifted it, his eyes bigger than those of his plastic attack-of-the-mutant-bugs collection. 'Thanks, Zelie.'

Ahhhh yes, the drink was magnificent, even if she said so herself.

'Come on, you need to get to bed.' She walked with him up the stairs, went ahead into his room to pull back the covers from the bed she'd made this morning. 'Don't forget to go to the bathroom and brush your teeth before turning out your light.'

'I know.'

She flicked on the iPod speaker on the bedside table. 'You want to listen to a story?'

'Yeah.'

Audiobooks weren't the same as having your mum read to you, but they were pretty good. And Zelie had other things to do tonight. She touched the screen so the story started.

'Come see me if you need anything.' She tousled her kid brother's head.

''Night, Zelie.'

As Zelie walked along the hall to her own room she spooned up a marshmallow, its middle ringed with chocolate. *Yum.*

'What's this?'

'Hot chocolate.' She grinned as she swooshed the next marshmallow in the hot mixture so it half melted. 'Sweet and hot. Better than sweet and cold, right?'

'Much better.'

The warm liquid pooled just below her ribcage, heat spreading along her veins. So good. She swore she heard him sigh too. Even the pendant didn't seem quite as icy now. For the first time all day she relaxed.

Chocolate.

Was that all it was going to take to pacify her new alter ego? No biggie. She even managed a smile as she kicked her door shut behind her.

'All right then, Tamás, let's get the blanks filled in.'

CHAPTER FOUR

ZELIE JIGGLED THE mouse so her computer woke from snooze mode. 'You want an overview? There was another big world war, many smaller ones. All hideous. We've created the most destructive weapons you can imagine and killed millions of people. On the more positive side, a guy walked on the moon, women got the vote and a black man got elected as US president.'

'They sent someone up in space?'

'Sure. Several people and a chimpanzee.'

'A chimpanzee?'

'Yeah. And a dog too, I think.'

'Why?'

'I have no idea. Because they could?' She sat on the chair, wheeling it closer to the screen. 'Where do you want to start, past or present?'

'Tell me about now.'

'Okay. Let's see what's on the news.' She went to her favourites file and picked her number one news site. The video started playing and the newsreader was there with perfect hair, suit and diction.

'This is incredible.'

'Nice resolution, huh?' She split the screen so she could play the latest news video and have the newspaper headlines up as well.

'How does it work?'

'It's pretty simple. You move the mouse and get the arrow on what you want and then you click on it.' She wasn't going to even attempt some convoluted explanation of the internet and ethernet and all that technical stuff. 'We can get TV shows as well. We have the History Channel downstairs but we can get some stuff up here on You Tube. I can do a playlist.'

'TV? Playlist?' He inhaled sharply. 'Is it really the twenty-first century?'

'Sure is.' She pointed out the date on the banner of the online newspaper. 'And we can see whatever is going on from right here in my room,' she paused. 'Can you read?'

'Of course,' he said, frostier than the half-dead plant by her window.

She'd not inherited her mother's fabulous garden skills.

'I mean in English,' she clarified. 'I'm guessing it's not your first language.'

'Not my last either.'

She rolled her eyes. Maybe he could get a job as a translator in the European Union. But she couldn't resist asking. 'How many do you speak?'

'A few. Go to the next page.'

She wrinkled her nose. There was more than a little arrogance there. And didn't he want to chat?

'Would you like to go to a French newspaper?'

'Yes.' His answer was too quick.

New personality wasn't as clever as he thought then. She'd only had the main page of *Le Monde* up for a few minutes when he asked to see something else. Another obvious fail – she'd understood about one in a hundred words on that page. 'What about a history book, Tamás? One that covers from 1918 on or something?'

'Yes,' he answered abruptly. Still not managing any of the social niceties like please and thank you.

As Zelie typed, her brain tracked along other ways of researching. The dreaded annual library skills lesson might actually have come in useful. 'Many books are available digitally so you can read them on screen.'

No answer. Maybe he was getting his head round the whole computer thing.

She took a few moments to search, figured it'd be best to find a book that gave a broad-picture overview. She pulled her wallet from her backpack, glad she had money in her account – hooray for the part-time job.

The book downloaded in seconds. She pulled up the first page and settled in for a long, boring read.

'I am fast reader,' Tamás said. 'Quickly look at each page, I will have it.'

Speed reading, huh?

'Can you remember it all too?'

'Naturally.'

He had a photographic memory as well? Of course he did. Her alter ego was outsized.

'If I split the screen, you can listen to documentaries and read at the same time,' she said. 'Would that do, you think?'

'Yes.' Clipped as ever.

He didn't get sarcasm, did he?

'Okay then.' She stared at the first page of the book for a moment, then clicked onto the next. Then the next. She'd trip him up. 'That not too fast for you?'

'No.'

'Seriously?' How was it possible? How could he read it if she wasn't? He saw what she saw – by default, surely, he had to focus on what she did?

'You do not believe me,' he said aggressively.

'Nope.'

'Go back two pages. The third paragraph down begins, "In March 1939, Germany invaded Prague –"'

'Cool trick.' He'd so set that up. Maybe it was true that humans usually only used three per cent of their brains. Maybe she'd somehow tapped into another percentage point or two.

'You still do not believe me.'

'No.' But an uneasy feeling rippled beneath her ribs.

'You choose the page,' he said.

'Okay,' she'd get him. 'Go back four. What was the last line?'

'The causes of the military conflict –'

'Okay.' Zelie took a second to check. Her pulse picked up. 'Fifth line, two pages after that.'

'The Treaty of Versailles forbade such action.'

She clicked to it and stared at the words that he'd just uttered. Her hand shook so violently she dropped the mouse. She clenched her fingers into fists but they still jerked uncontrollably like a fish caught on a line. She pushed the chair back and spun away from the computer, her blood thumping so fast she couldn't think for the noise of it.

'Zelie?'

'This is true,' she muttered. 'This whole thing is true, isn't it?'

'You only believe *now*?'

There was no way her brain was playing tricks on her. She hadn't *read* those pages. She'd hardly glanced at them. She didn't have a split personality. She hadn't suddenly got some superpower from a massive brain tumour. There was no scientific explanation for any of this. This had to be magic.

Tamás had to be real.

Her body locked into fear mode, her brain screamed at her to run, run, run. But where? How could she get away?

'Open your eyes and look at the screen,' he said firmly. 'We have much to do.'

Learn the history of the modern world in an evening? Like that was possible.

'No.' Her hysteria rose. 'I want you to go. I want you to get out right now.'

'I cannot. You know I cannot.'

'I don't know anything. I want you out.'

She had an alien inside her. She rubbed the chain, fast enough and hard enough to leave red marks on her fingers and neck. She twisted her hand so the necklace looped around her fist. She'd pull it off. She'd throw the thing back in the lake.

'Zelie,' he said sharply. 'I will not hurt you.'

'No? You don't know that. You told me you didn't know what was going to happen.' Anything could happen. Her head was exploding with the possibilities and none of them were good.

'You cannot be hurt. Or I will be hurt too. I want you to be safe as much as you do.'

Only while he needed her for the heating-up treatment or whatever it was that was going on. What happened when he was warm enough?

'The best thing we can do tonight is find information,' he said firmly. 'Then I can help you face her tomorrow.'

She closed her eyes. Kate. What did she know of all this? Why had she done this?

'I don't want to see her.'

And she didn't trust Tamás. She didn't know him. Her fingers tightened on the cold chain.

'Try to break it.' His words were ultra-soft.

'What?' She moved, turning the mirror around so she could see her reflection.

'Try to break the chain. Try to pull it off.'

Her eyes looked wider than normal. The green was almost neon.

'Go on,' he commanded. 'See if you can.'

His arrogance was the trigger. She pulled. Pulled and pulled and pulled with all her strength. The chain slipped up her neck, back down again. Hurt like hell as it rasped over her skin and rubbed it raw. She used both hands, trying to pull the links apart. It only hurt more. And still it wouldn't give.

But she wouldn't give up. She leaned forwards and hooked the chain around the arm of the chair. She drew a quick breath and then pushed back from it, hard. She screwed up her face from the agony as the chain cut her skin. But she kept pushing, until with a pathetic yelp she dropped down again, letting it slacken. Defeated.

She turned her head away from the mirror and closed her eyes for good measure. She didn't want to hear his 'I told you so.' But that wasn't what he said.

'I am sorry, Zelie. But you have no choice.'

'I could ignore you.'

'For how long? I can talk and talk.'

'I could hold the pendant away from my skin.'

'You would listen to my screams as I die?' He sounded husky. 'You do not have that in you. You are not a murderess.'

Hot tears stung her eyes and slid down her cheeks. Angrily she swished them away. But she said nothing. Then she did the only thing she could.

She swivelled the chair back to the computer, pressed play on the next documentary and turned to the next page of the book. She had no choice but to do as he asked and hope that it would all be over soon. Otherwise she feared she really would go crazy.

After an hour she was cold from sitting still so long, doing nothing but staring at the screen, so she wrapped a blanket around herself. She flicked over each page of the book, then another and another. He hadn't said a word but she increasingly felt his alertness within her.

Too long later she glanced at the clock – it was way past her usual midnight bedtime.

'I need to get some sleep.' She didn't think she was actually going to get any, but her eyes were scratchy and sore from the viewing marathon.

'Leave it playing. I will listen while you sleep.'

Yeah, he was quite used to giving orders. Her panic resurged as she realised how little she knew of him.

'You don't need to sleep?'

'I have been sleeping for decades. I do not need more.'

'Okay,' she swallowed. 'I'll set it up so they play one after the other.'

'Good.'

Curiosity vied with fear. How come he knew all these languages? How come he read so well? Had he been privately educated? Was he even from Earth?

'What school did you go to, Tamás? What's your surname?' She'd Google him. Shame Facebook didn't go back that far.

'I did not go to school.'

She was surprised he'd answered – perhaps he sensed her need to understand just a little.

'How come you can read so fast?'

'The nuns taught me to read and write. Speed was something that came naturally after that.'

Because the guy was a genius?

'The nuns weren't at school?'

'They were at the orphanage.'

Ouch. Zelie paused for a second.

'Where was the orphanage?'

'Please put the next documentary on. I need to know.'

Didn't she need to know about him? But that had been another order. Seemed he wasn't interesting in talking further. Well, she wasn't interested in yet another documentary. She had the urge to not put it on just to spite him, except she had the feeling he'd make her headache return with unbearable intensity. Already she felt like knives were piercing her temples. She clicked another doco on and then turned her back on the glow from her monitor. While the audio would keep playing, the screen saver would roll across soon and she didn't want to see the photos tonight. She didn't want to see her mother's face and wish she could talk to her.

But she couldn't have talked to her about Tamás anyway. She couldn't talk to anyone about him. They'd slap her into the nearest psych unit in less than a minute.

She was terrified about tomorrow. She'd have to go to the Hearns' place and she dreaded seeing Kate with her bleeding ears and nose and stinking cloak of death. But now, as she burrowed into her bed and the darkness descended, she was terrified about something else too – the presence in her head from whom she couldn't escape.

'Can I ask you something?' she blurted the question.

No reply. Naturally. Why had she thought he'd answer? But she was damn well determined to ask anyway, even if she got nil response. 'Are you human?'

She waited. Still no answer. She tried to settle into some kind of relaxed position to let sleep come. Tried to forget.

'Mostly,' he said softly.

Her eyes flicked open. *Mostly*? What did *that* mean?

'You must sleep, Zelie.'

Oh, like that was going to happen now.

CHAPTER FIVE

ZELIE JERKED AWAKE, the images a blink away, just out of reach. But she couldn't snatch them back.

Horrors replayed in her subconscious night after night: her mother's room on that hideous day – strewn with flowers; the awful smell that had hit Zelie as she'd walked through the door and had lingered until they'd finally moved away; the futility of *trying*, of watching paramedics try despite the hopelessness. And every time she had the nightmare part of her couldn't help trying to grasp it anyway because it was *something* of her mother – the only thing she had left.

All the good things had gone. The brightness of her smile, the sound of her laughing and singing. The happy memories. Instead it was only the very last moments, the ugliest, that filled her head. She had to look at photos to see her mother's beauty because she couldn't remember it herself. Those wrong memories would never leave her.

Now she had another burden. She grasped the pendant, making sure it was still there. The metal was as cold as when she'd pulled it from the lake, the weight oppressive. The hint of warmth she'd thought she'd felt last night had gone.

She sat up, the dull pain thudding harder against her temples. Her computer speakers still emitted some BBC dude's commentary on the carnage of war – a deep monotone punctuated by dramatic pauses and horrible questions.

She staggered to her desk and tapped the mute button on another World War I documentary. How many had she selected last night? She clicked up another screen to check the headlines.

'Don't turn it off.'

So the autocrat was awake and sounding angrier than ever.

His English sounded smoother too – was that another example of his super-quick learning abilities? Was he going to have a BBC accent next?

'Haven't you heard enough?' She had and she'd slept through some of it at least. 'I don't know that this is helping you, Tamás.'

'It is. It's important I understand. Knowledge is everything, Zelie.'

Her mother used to say that: *Knowledge is power, education is everything.* But Zelie knew it wasn't. It didn't matter a damn. Look how educated her father was. But despite all his degrees he couldn't stop the worst happening. He couldn't bring her back. His precious research was meaningless.

Tamás sounded more ferocious now than when he'd first spoken to her yesterday. The constant analysis of destruction and despair was doing her head in, so who knew what it was doing to him – he'd had hours of nothing else.

'I have to get ready for school.' She turned away from the computer.

'You're going to school? What about Kate?'

Yeah, she didn't have the stomach for that yet. 'I can't miss class. My father will start running a million tests if I don't appear down there all healthy and ready to go.' If her dad started his over-medicalising act, she'd crack under the additional strain. 'I'll go to her house this afternoon. After school.' She went into the bathroom, desperate to wash away the sweat from the night terrors.

'What is the average life expectancy now?'

Zelie frowned, surprised by the left-field question. 'I don't know,' she said honestly. 'Seventy-five, eighty maybe if you're well fed and live in a decent place.'

'It used to be lower for humans.'

'Yeah.'

'So everyone I knew –'

Zelie squeezed too hard on the tube of toothpaste as he broke off. She hadn't thought of that. Did 'mostly human' creatures have the same life expectancy as 'all-human' creatures? Did mostly human creatures have family? He'd been in an orphanage so he must have lost his parents. But what about brothers or sisters? Or aunts or uncles?

No one born the same year as him would be alive now. Well,

maybe there was some random person in Tibet who was in *The Guinness Book of Records* as the world's oldest person, but everyone else would be dead. His parents. His siblings. His friends.

Zelie had lost her mother and that was bad enough. She couldn't imagine loss on that scale. 'Tamás, did you have family?'

No answer. Zelie felt the ache in her own heart deepen as the silence lengthened. Yeah, there was no improvement in his manners, but she could hardly blame him now. Instead she searched for answers, hoping he might not be so alone. Was it possible for him to have nieces or nephews or cousins or something? Some kind of descendants? Or was it possible that what had happened to him had happened to others of his kind?

'Is there a chance there might be others like you?'

'You mean bound?' he said roughly.

'Yes.'

'Not my family. They are dead.'

'How do you know?' She was half-afraid to ask, but she probably wouldn't get an answer anyway.

Yeah, none. She quickly brushed her teeth and then pressed a hot flannel to her face, trying to freshen up.

'I feel it.'

She almost didn't catch that lighter-than-air whisper.

Intuition was a scary thing. The feeling could be so unshakable, so certain. Zelie knew it could be accurate too. Hadn't she felt it? She'd raced into her mother's room as soon as that fear had struck, but it was already too late.

So she didn't question Tamás now, didn't try to say he might be wrong, didn't make it worse by trying to make it better. She didn't say sorry either. She felt for him, she was truly sorry for his loss. But she knew how useless it was to hear those platitudes. No one could understand. Grief was a solitary hell.

She stood in the shower, remembering to keep her eyes closed, and held the icy block of metal under the steaming water some more. Not that it did much good. She stayed on the far side of the room from the mirror and closed her eyes again as she dropped the towel and put her underwear on.

For the field trip they'd been allowed to wear whatever, but it was back to school uniform today. She pulled on the tights and then the long heavy kilt. She put a wool singlet on beneath the white shirt and looked in the mirror to ensure the chain couldn't be seen. Ancient magic necklaces were definitely not on the uniform list.

She didn't bother sitting for breakfast, just hurriedly chucked pre-packed snacks into Luke's lunchbox – this one day wouldn't matter – then put cereal and milk on the table for him. Usually she sat with him to ensure he ate but she couldn't face it today. She grabbed a piece of toast for herself and shrugged her coat on.

Luke wandered in, went straight to the table, tipped half the box of cereal into his bowl and started wolfing it down. He didn't look up and give her the coded look that meant he needed her help. He hadn't given it to her in weeks. She smiled. Maybe her little brother was going to be okay after all. She could only cross fingers that she would be too.

'I have to get some stuff done early today. You have a good day, okay?' she said to him. 'Don't be late.'

'I won't.'

She stepped outside into the silence. It was August. Back in Britain it would be hot and the holidays. Here in New Zealand it was the last, worst, month of winter and the middle of term. The snow must have fallen steadily through the night because a new, thick layer had covered the old. Beautifully pristine, no mud or tracks destroyed the perfect icing effect. The street lights had just gone off but the winter-weak, slow-rising sun was only just making headway against the dark.

Everything was monochrome, like all the colour had been leached from the world. A grader had been over the road earlier, carving a black line for the cars to travel over, but more snow was settling on it already. The leaf-bare branches of the trees showed black under the weight of white. Even the lake looked grey, its usual opaque cyan lost under the oppressive reflection of the clouds.

She scraped the tougher clumps of ice off her windscreen with her bank card and put her key in the lock, hoping it wouldn't be frozen. The loud click as she turned the key told her it wasn't. She tossed her backpack into the passenger seat, put the heater on high and carefully headed out along the icy roads.

'Cars are very fast now,' Tamás said.

'You think?'

Zelie couldn't help chuckling. She was such a slow driver – especially in these conditions. Yesterday she'd gone especially slow due to her headache. Now she had the urge to put her foot down and see if he screamed.

But she couldn't take the risk.

'You can see and hear what I do, right?' she asked. 'And taste.' She could hear his breathing and sense his presence like she could yesterday but her awareness of him was growing. Was the same happening for him?

'The taste is not as strong.'

She cleared her throat uncomfortably. 'And you can read my mind too? You hear my thoughts?'

He didn't answer for a while, which made her nervous. She really didn't like the lack of privacy thing. Not to have your thoughts as your own was twenty steps too far over the okay line.

'I cannot see what you are thinking, or know what you are feeling. I can access your senses to varying degrees – sight, taste, touch. But nothing more.'

She held her breath. Could she believe him? She had no real way to know if he was lying. She hunched deeper in her thick coat, lowering her chin into the collar as she pulled up outside the school. Usually she aimed to get here just as the bell rang – she had good social avoidance skills now – but she was far earlier this morning.

She felt as self-conscious as the day she'd worn a bra for the first time. Hard and cold on her chest, the pendant was foreign, slightly uncomfortable and never far from her thoughts. She felt like everyone would take one look and somehow know there was something different about her.

More paranoia.

But there already *was* something different about her. Several things in fact. Most obviously she wasn't from round here. Her voice betrayed her even when she said something as simple as hello. But she was different on the inside too. Experiences changed people. While the other kids were all talk about the school ball and what they were going to wear and how they were going to get there and which hairdresser they were booked with in the nearest town, she couldn't participate in that – as much as part of her wanted to. She had other issues taking up her brain space and an even bigger one now.

She watched other students carefully walking over the ice on the footpath into school. It was stupid, but suddenly getting inside without slipping over seemed monstrously important.

So much for bigger issues.

With each step came both relief that she hadn't slipped, and a rise in her anxiety. She hated the way people here looked at her – curious, judging. But when she got inside she saw she needn't have worried. There was a new kid to gawp at today and everyone was.

Kate Hearn was in the foyer with a backpack in her hand, obviously getting her bearings. Her jeans, jersey and beanie marked her out from the uniformed masses. She was still pale and knock-over-with-a-feather thin, but at least she didn't have blood dripping from her ears and nose.

Zelie was so surprised she let the door bang behind her. Kate turned her head and looked straight at her.

Zelie heard the intake of breath whistle in her ears. Then the feeling flooded her, filling every cell, nerve and muscle with its poison. Like a tsunami sparked from a hidden earthquake deep below the surface of the sea, it rose unexpectedly, unavoidably.

Rage. Pure, murderous rage.

And with it, the overwhelming urge to hurt Kate.

The only way to escape it was to run.

Zelie called on everything she had to move. She swivelled, forcing her feet to do the opposite of that horrendous foreign compulsion. She went down the corridor to her locker. She had to get away. *Her* intuition was working now, fighting the other instinct that was trying to dominate her. All she knew was that it was vitally important to get away from Kate.

'Look at her again.' Command central, that's what he thought he was.

'No.' Zelie rebelled.

She didn't trust him. Or Kate either. And she certainly didn't trust the feelings battling inside her. He'd said he couldn't read her thoughts and feelings, but these weren't *her* feelings.

'Zelie,' he snapped with staccato wrath. 'Look. At. Her.'

Zelie pulled her iPod from her bag, pushed in her earbuds with painful force and switched the music on live-concert loud to drown him out. Her heart banged, bruising her ribs, and her throat hurt as she tried to control her breathing. Her vision blurred. She rapidly blinked to right it, struggling to hold him back.

'Zelie!' His fury frothed over, shouting and cursing in his crazy language, his presence pounding against her will.

But she held fast, glaring into her locker, listening to the beat of the music, hoping her heart would slow.

The moment would pass. Soon it would pass. She could control this. She could control him. She had to. Because she'd felt what he wanted.

It took two tracks before her pulse slowed enough to stop her head spinning. Tamás had stopped swearing and gone back to heavy-breathing-stalker silence.

Finally she knew she couldn't stay frozen facing her locker any more. In a couple of minutes the bell would go and she'd have to be in class. He wanted her to follow Kate. She could feel that. But she could feel the other things he wanted too and they terrified her.

She fished her mobile from her pocket and took out her earbuds. That way she wouldn't look like a nutcase while she talked to him. 'Huff and puff all you want,' she said into the phone. 'I'm not going near her.'

Not if he was going to do what she thought.

'You do not understand how dangerous she is.'

'She's not.' *He* was the one who was dangerous. 'She can hardly walk unaided. What do you think she's going to do?'

CHAPTER SIX

ZELIE RUSHED INTO English and slumped into her usual seat. On the edge, towards the back, it was an unobtrusive, forget-you-were-there spot. She rummaged in her bag for her pens and book, still trying to distract herself from the anger within her. She wouldn't let him control her. She glared at the book, only now remembering she was supposed to have read a chapter last night. She'd keep her head down and hope she wasn't called on to answer any questions. Ordinarily she could get through a day of school without opening her mouth but it would just be her luck to have to contribute today.

Finally she risked a glance around, mainly to make sure Kate wasn't there. As she quickly took in who was present, she saw Otis looking at her. She stared right back at him.

He had a smile on. Not a big one, but definitely a smile. It was a shock – literally. A powerful current zinged through her body like she'd touched an electric fence. She flashed a return smile. Her spirits lifted. She'd far rather look at Otis Hayes than Kate Hearn. And looking at him made her awareness of Tamás subside.

Otis's smile broadened and Zelie's mind totally blanked under the spotlight. He had nice eyes, warm and friendly, cuddly-bear brown – and they smiled even more than his mouth.

'You spoke with him yesterday. He is not relevant.'

Tamás's rude dismissiveness made her stare all the longer at Otis and her smile widened. Looking at Otis flushed the poisonous intent of a few minutes ago from her system.

Otis winked. The ambient temperature of the room went up ten degrees in less than a second.

The sound of the door closing shattered the warm buzz. Zelie looked at the front of the class. The teacher stood tall and started on her spiel.

No Kate Hearn.

Thank God. Relief mixed with the lingering warmth from Otis's attention made Zelie's headache ease. Then she remembered again that she hadn't done her homework. She opened the book and wished she had Tamás's speed-reading abilities.

She didn't look up much during class other than the occasional sideways glance at Otis a couple of rows ahead. He didn't usually sit there; his spot was in the back row with his buddies. Now she could surreptitiously study him in the navy trousers and white shirt of the school uniform. He didn't fit well behind the student desk – too tall. If he didn't stretch out his feet his knees would hit the desk, and his shoulders were just about broader than the width of it. Yeah, he was built. And he was a great distraction.

'I need to see her.' Sounding cold and angry, Tamás interrupted her first happy thoughts in twenty-four hours.

She cleared her throat. Hoping he'd get the hint. She could hardly answer him in class.

'I need you to find her.'

Why? So he could use Zelie to take her out somehow? Zelie didn't think so. Zelie didn't do violence.

He muttered. She ignored him, ignored Otis now too, just stared at the book in front of her and counted the seconds until the lesson was over.

Fortunately Zelie didn't see Kate in geography, recess or bio. And the bonus was she'd managed to have to speak only once in all three classes – to confirm to Mr Webb that she was all better.

Kate had probably just been visiting the school, picking up some resource or something for her correspondence studies.

'This is a waste of time,' Tamás said shortly. 'Go to her house.'

'Later,' Zelie mumbled. Despite his curt tone, she knew he was more in control of himself. The knot in her stomach had eased. His tension had subsided – for now anyway. She went to the cafeteria for lunch. She wasn't hungry but if she didn't eat something her headache would worsen and she didn't want to go home early two days in a row. Her dad would give her a full physical and blood work. Joining the queue, she figured she'd make do with a muffin and then go to the library. She could check out some more histories of the twentieth century. That would keep Tamás happy for a couple more hours. She wanted to delay the trip to Kate's house – indefinitely if she could.

'Want to sit with us, Zelie?'

Zelie turned, so surprised she just stared and the girl had to repeat the question. Ella Robinson, flanked either side by Maddie Symon and Clare Jones. The coolest girls in the year had picked up their priority-packed, special diet lunches already, but they'd stopped to ask Zelie to sit with them? She looked over to where they usually sat with the prime view over the snow-covered sports field. And he was sprawled right in the middle of them, his brown bag already open.

Warmth radiated from her tummy out. Was this the Otis-effect? Had they noticed he'd talked to her? Or was it one step more – had he got them to ask her to join them? She knew she was blushing, could feel the heat in her cheeks and the back of her neck. If she said yes now she'd be on her way to breaking in. She could try to chat with them, try to find some common ground and start to settle. All she had to do was make the effort. All she had to do was say yes. Would she, should she, *could* she?

'Um.' She swallowed and looked away from their expectant, confident, friendly faces. Otis's lopsided smile danced across her vision. Her heart thudded faster.

And then she saw her – the stick figure all alone in the far corner.

It was like a bucket of ice-cold water had been tipped over her. The knot in her tummy pulled tight. Her heart stopped, then leapt uncontrollably. For a split second longer she wavered. But the feeling within her strengthened. Not scarily angry like it had been before, but insistent.

Zelie decided. She couldn't turn her back on the problem any longer. He'd pester her till she did it. At least here it was a public place and Tamás was under her control. She wasn't too sure how long that was going to be the case.

She turned back to Ella, wondering if she was about to commit social suicide. 'Actually, I promised to sit with someone else this time.' She regretted it, she really did. 'But thanks.'

Her stomach twisted, this time all her own emotion, not Tamás's. Had anyone ever said no to Ella Robinson? Zelie was sure this would be her one and only invite. Two days ago she wouldn't have cared. But now she'd been the recipient of that Otis smile. And now she *did* care.

She got the guts to look them in the eyes. Okay, it was social suicide. They weren't pleased. But they did that veneer of polite really well. Zelie grabbed her muffin and walked away from them.

As she walked closer to Kate she homed in on Otis – couldn't help it – for a second. He was tracking her with his eyes. A tiny frown scored his forehead but in the next nanosecond it was wiped clear as he laughed at something one of his mates said. He turned to reply – *away* from Zelie.

That's when the regret hit. She should have gone and sat with them. Should have beamed and taken up the offer. Kate and Tamás had strangled her first opportunity to be normal. And for the first time in forever, she'd actually wanted to be.

There were only a couple of tables between her and Kate now and the insistent feeling intensified. His power intensified.

'Tamás.' She whispered a warning, her pace slowing. She wasn't going to do this if he wouldn't behave. But he was Mr Silent all over again. She knew he was totally focused on Kate.

She got to where Kate sat alone with her back to the room. Zelie opened her mouth, but weirdly no sound came out. She shut it again, her jaws pressing so hard together her gums hurt. Then she tried again, prising her mouth apart. The words formed but still there was no sound. So here she was doing an impersonation of a constipated fish. It was like she was turning into a marionette – and he was the puppeteer. The horror kind.

Because he was livid. White-hot rage blurred her vision, she could only focus on Kate. On what he wanted her to *do* to Kate . . .

'Zelie?' Kate looked wary.

Zelie forced her head to move. She managed to jerk her chin down – it was almost a nod. And then she shoved her body into the seat opposite Kate's. Her muscles bunched. Her stomach clenched, like she was preparing for a blow – or to deal one. All over she tingled like she'd just done a five-minute warm-up in a gym class. Only she never did gym classes – not since her mum died. She'd quit the hockey team, pretty much quit everything.

Now she was hyperaware of the power rippling beneath her

surface. But she was determined to keep the surface smooth. She wouldn't let him break out.

'I can feel you,' she muttered through gritted teeth. Prowling around her mind, like he was searching for the smallest of gaps, a tiny tear through which he could force himself and his intentions. She closed her eyes and concentrated harder. He was getting stronger. She'd not felt him as intensely as this, not even when she'd first seen Kate this morning. Now she could feel what he wanted of her – she could *see* it.

'I will not let you control me.'

Deliberately she opened her eyes and gazed hard at Kate. Kate, who looked as freaked as Zelie felt. Kate, who stared right back at her, brows up high, eyes wide – revealing her uncertainty and fear.

Zelie didn't have the energy to reassure her. She had to deal with Tamás first. 'I can feel what you want me to do,' Zelie spoke harshly. 'But I will not let you make me.'

She was never hitting a person. Never hurting. Never causing someone to –

'Is everything all right, Zelie?' Kate swallowed.

'Do it,' Tamás growled.

'No,' Zelie snapped at him. 'Yes.' She looked at Kate. 'You're in trouble, you know that?'

Kate's eyes widened so much Zelie could see the yellowish whites all around the bright blue irises. 'Is he with you?'

Her question hit Zelie hard. 'You know?'

Blood leached from Kate's face, leaving it death-white. Zelie could see the veins at her temples, the thick one pulsing down her forehead. In her mind she saw Kate's blood splattering – thickening, pooling, cooling . . .

Not going to happen. She swallowed back her nausea at the horrendous image.

'How is he?' Kate whispered.

'Who?' Zelie tried to sound bland, but at the same moment Tamás let forth with one of his instructions.

'Don't answer her.'

Zelie waited.

Kate leaned over the table, her eyes still rounder than the sun, although not quite as yellow today. 'Is he all right?'

'Say nothing,' Tamás jumped in. 'Don't trust her.'

Zelie swallowed again. Don't trust *her*? Tamás was the one wanting to kill the girl. She didn't trust either of them. 'What do you know of him?'

'How are *you*?' Kate's colourless lips were dry and peeling.

'Fine,' Zelie lied. 'But I think I deserve some answers.'

Kate shook her head. 'I can't.'

Zelie lifted the chain, pulling the pendant from her skin.

'No!'

'No!'

They both shouted at once.

'You need to give me answers.' Zelie let the metal drop where it would blister her skin some more. 'I can't give you the chain, can I?'

Kate shook her head. 'You can't take it off.'

Yeah. She didn't need Kate to tell her that, she had the scrapes and bruises to remind her. But it also meant that Zelie held the power. For now. 'So what exactly is going to happen?'

'Have you had any strange effects since putting it on?' Kate asked.

Did suddenly having a boy in her head count as a strange effect?

'Other than Tamás,' Kate added belatedly.

Zelie jerked bolt upright at the sound of his name on Kate's lips. Sensation whooshed as he raged inside her, colouring her world crimson. Her muscles cramped as she fought to stay still.

'You'd better tell me everything you know,' she said quickly to Kate. 'And *you* better sit back and behave or I'll rip this damn thing off right now, even if I have to tear my head off to do it,' she said to Tamás.

The tension dropped, the relief instant, like he'd stepped back completely. But she knew he was still there – waiting. Zelie breathed in and out a couple of times to regroup.

Kate looked sideways at her. 'I'd heard about an old necklace –'

'Tell me the truth, Kate,' Zelie interrupted. 'You didn't just hear. You knew where it was and you knew what you were doing. Hell, you probably put it in there yourself, didn't you?'

'Don't judge me,' Kate said vehemently, not denying it. 'Don't judge me when you don't know what I've suffered.'

'She deserves to suffer,' Tamás growled.

Zelie closed her eyes and did another few deep breaths. 'One at a time, people. Tamás, let her speak.'

Kate leaned forwards again. 'He's talking to you?'

'All the time,' Zelie exaggerated, staring as the blue of Kate's eyes brightened and flickered.

'Witch,' Tamás spat. Zelie suspected that if he could he'd pull his finger across his throat in a murderous gesture like some Cold War villain.

'He says you're a witch,' Zelie said, deadpan.

'I am,' Kate answered, dead serious.

He muttered – soft and strange words but their meaning was unmistakable. A curse. A violent one. The hair on Zelie's arms rose, like an Antarctic wind was howling in the room. She swallowed.

Kate's eyes followed the movement of Zelie's throat down to the chain hanging beneath her blouse. 'I can't wear it. I'm not strong enough. I don't know that –'

'That what?' Zelie prompted.

'That you are either.'

Zelie looked at the goosebumps on her own arms. 'What do you think might happen to me?'

Kate's gaze slid to the lunchbox open in front of her. 'I don't know.'

'I told you to tell me the truth,' said Zelie.

'That is the truth,' Kate replied in a monotone. 'I can only guess.'

'Guess then.'

'Madness,' Kate whispered.

Zelie laughed. 'Well, I knew that already.' She shook her head. 'So why aren't you strong enough?'

'Look at me,' Kate bitterly looked up. 'The constant sickness is the price I pay for my great-great-great-grandmother's actions.'

'Your however-many-greats-grandma?' Now she was getting some info.

'Catriona,' Kate snapped. 'The one who did this to Tamás.'

Zelie's pulse quickened. *Catriona* – just as Tamás had said.

'What did she do exactly? And why?' Zelie leaned forwards.

'He has power she thought was needed later.'

'Later being now?' Zelie asked. 'Why? What's happening? The end of the world is nigh or something? Some clash between the underworld and the humans living above?' Zelie let all the sarcasm out. 'Am I right? Totally Hollywood, Kate. I've seen it in a million movies.'

She felt rather than heard Tamás grunt. Surprised, she almost grunted herself, because for a split second she felt amusement within, not anger.

'The time Catriona foresaw is not now,' Kate said gravely – clearly not one to appreciate sarcasm. Zelie looked closer at Kate and marvelled at the hint of colour blooming in her cheeks.

'I did not initiate his release because of the prophecy.'

The prophecy? Zelie rolled her eyes. Of course there was a prophecy. It went with Kate's sudden drop into medieval-sounding speak. 'So why did you start it then?'

'I did it for me.' Kate jerked her head up and glared at Zelie. 'I'm sick of being sick. I don't want to pay any more. My mother died young. As did her mother. And her mother before her. It'll happen to me too.'

'When did your mother die?'

'Two hours after I was born. And her mother died two hours after she was born. See the pattern? See why I have to break it? If I don't, I'll have a baby and then I'll die. I don't want that. I don't want to die.'

Have a baby? Where did the baby suddenly spring from?

'There is such a thing as contraception, Kate,' Zelie said bluntly. 'Or abstinence.'

'That's not how it works. If I don't free him I cannot stop fate. I cannot deny my duty.'

Zelie felt revolted. 'You're fated to have a baby and die young? This is in the prophecy too?'

'My family accepts it. They expect me to.'

Riiiiight. They clearly were a bunch of witches then. Zelie shook her head. 'No one wants a pregnant teen.'

'Until Tamás is free, that is the curse on the women in my family.'

'Who put the curse on you?'

A sad expression flitted across Kate's face and she shrugged. 'It's what happens when you meddle with greater forces. If you wield magic, there'll be a consequence. The pendulum will always swing back to strike a balance. When my ancestor bound Tamás, her life was shortened. That was her price. It's the price *all* her descendants will pay until he is free. None of us will live much beyond the age he was when he was bound. We know this, and at the same time we know we must continue our line because if we don't, he'll be lost forever. I can't let that happen either. My mother, my grandmother – they were stronger than me. Less selfish. They knew the time wasn't right, they accepted their sacrifice.' Kate leaned forwards, her expression hardening. 'But moments after the necklace touched your skin, I felt better. Already I am well enough to come to school. This is my first day, Zelie. The first day in my whole life that I'm healthy enough to come to school. The stronger he becomes, the stronger I become. And when he is free, I'll be free.'

Honestly, coming to school really wasn't all it was cracked up to be. Zelie wanted to joke that in less than a week Kate would wish she was home-schooling it again. But she didn't, because Kate was intensely serious.

'And that's why you did it?'

Kate nodded.

'Are you in trouble? With the family – or should I call them a coven?' Zelie asked.

Kate's gaze skittered away again. 'I'm forgiven,' she said slowly. 'The Witching are not all bad.'

'The "Witching"?'

'My kind.'

'What kind – you're more evolved than the rest of us or something? You've got fancy powers – you can cast spells, set fire to things with your mind, fly on broomsticks?'

Kate wasn't listening. Kate was lost, looking at nothing, staring off in the middle distance. 'If you saw how beautiful he is . . . what he can do . . .'

'How do you know what he can do?'

Kate's gaze lifted, the blue washing in wave-like swells over her irises. 'I have their memories. All their memories.'

'*All* the great-grandmothers'?'

'And my mother's.'

'Memories,' Zelie repeated. 'What, like you can talk to them?'

'No, they're not living in me the way Tamás is living within you. They're dead. But I have all their memories as well as my own. Like an elephant, I forget nothing of my own experience, or of theirs. From birth to death. Each life. So I know the torment – the pain of childbirth, then of bleeding out just after the most precious creation is born. And the pain of a kid who's lost her mother. I have these memories many times over. I felt it. I lost *my* mum. Do you understand now why I started this?'

Zelie didn't want to look at Kate. Didn't want to understand. But she kinda did. Losing her mum had been horrific – but to have the memories and feel the pain of several women who'd lost mothers, who'd died before being given the chance to love their children?

That'd suck.

'There's danger now, before the process completes. So I must be near you. It is my duty to help you.'

Her duty? Zelie's distrust sharpened. Was Kate really here to help her or was her job to keep an eye on her? Zelie sat back and ignored her muffin some more, trying to see any hint of honesty in Kate's carefully blank face.

'What's this process that needs completing?' she asked. 'When will it end? How?'

'Burn, blow, bury, bathe . . .' Kate murmured.

'You like alliteration.' Jeez, the girl was crazy.

'The *amulette* – forged in fire, blown so it expands to hold the spirit, buried to seal it, then bathed clean.'

'That's the spell?' Really? That was it?

Kate's sudden smile sparkled, but it wasn't friendly. More freaky. 'That's part of how he was bound.'

Zelie tensed, feeling Tamás's rage resurge.

'So I told you what you wanted to know. Now will you tell me what *he's* been saying?' Kate asked.

'Say nothing,' Tamás instructed.

Zelie gritted her teeth. Did he think she was a complete idiot?

'He hasn't been talking much. He's very moody.'

'I am not moody.'

'Most of what he does say is in a language I don't understand.' Zelie shrugged.

'A language you've never heard?' Kate leaned closer again.

'No,' Zelie smiled with satisfaction over how eager the girl looked. 'In French.'

The disappointment on Kate's face was comic.

Zelie had no idea what the other language Tamás spoke was but she wasn't sharing it with Kate.

'So let me get this straight.' Zelie shoved her muffin further away from her and glared at Kate. 'Tamás has some great power that Catriona, your great-great-whatever grandmother, decided was needed at a later time so she put some spell on him and now you've woken him up because you're sick of paying the price of that spell.'

'Yes.'

Zelie leaned her elbows on the table and rubbed her fingers hard over her forehead. 'Do you really expect me to believe this?'

'Do you really have a choice?'

It wasn't the first time Zelie had been asked that, and she knew the answer. But that didn't stop her asking for more proof. 'Do some magic for me then, Kate. Come on. I want a rabbit out of your hat.'

It was a soft wool hat that hid the thinness of her short, lank hair. Kate's hair was too wispy to grow long; Zelie could tell from the split ends that it broke. Just like the rest of her would if anyone put any pressure on her. And yet Kate was now talking with steel in her voice and a look in her eye that meant business.

'I'm not an illusionist, Zelie. I'm talking real magic.'

'Black or white?' Zelie wanted to joke just a little because her freaked-out feeling was flooding back.

Tamás wasn't the only one trapped. She was too.

'Nothing is black and white, Zelie,' Kate said quietly. 'Magic can be used or misused for a variety of reasons. It is anything but simple. And there is always a price.'

'So what price do I pay for being your pawn?'

Kate simply looked at her.

'Temporary insanity?' Zelie asked. Please let it only be temporary. Please let it be only as mild as that. Her anger bubbled as both Kate and Tamás stayed silent. She hadn't chosen this, she hadn't wanted this. 'Why me?'

'You were there.' Kate looked down, seeming to need to concentrate hard as she stirred her yoghurt.

'So you could have picked anyone?' Zelie felt oddly miffed. So supposedly there was all this magical stuff going on, but she was just in the wrong place at the wrong time?

'It had to be a female,' Kate conceded.

The vessel of life. Okay, she got that symbolism but really, it was a bit icky. And frankly, Zelie reckoned there was more to it. 'No, you called me. Is it cos I'm new in town?'

Kate lifted her head and stared at her for a long moment – her eyes wide, that flickering purplish blue swamping her pupils. Then she shook her head. 'You do not respond to me.'

'To what?' Zelie stared back at her – and it dawned. 'Your psycho-killer stare?' Zelie giggled. 'Is that all you've got? That's your magic?'

'Most people can be influenced.'

'Influenced? Like mind control?'

'Sort of.'

'Is that why you and your uncles go all silent and stare – you're trying to cast spells with your minds?' Zelie laughed some more. 'Sorry, but it doesn't work on me.'

'Exactly,' Kate said softly. 'Perhaps you have been protected.'

Protected? Oh, Zelie so didn't think so.

'My resistance is strong,' Zelie drawled. 'So I'm strong enough to be your vessel?' Ugh. 'Ever thought the reason your mind powers don't work is because you don't *have* any? That you're deluded?'

'I'm telling you the truth.'

What she thought was the truth, sure.

But though Zelie couldn't believe her, how else could she explain the presence of Tamás if it *wasn't* magic? She needed to know more. To test Kate. She tried out a scary stare of her own.

'You put the necklace in the water.'

'Yes.' Kate met her gaze and held it.

'You tricked me by asking me to get it out, forcing me to touch it.'

'Yes.'

Zelie leaned towards the thin girl and whispered. 'You can't be trusted.'

Kate looked down. Yeah – Zelie had known she wouldn't be able to maintain eye contact on that. Kate was a liar.

'You need to trust me,' Kate said softly.

'Never.' Zelie retrieved her muffin and broke off a bit, rubbing it into crumbs. 'What're you going to do with him once he's free?'

Silent, Kate continued to stir her spoon through the pink

yoghurt. She was as bad as Tamás with her selective hearing.

'What's his power?' Zelie asked.

Again she got no answer. Kate still didn't look at her. Not surprisingly Tamás remained silent at this point too.

Zelie tried another tack. 'How are you going to control him?'

Fear flickered in Kate's eyes and she dropped the spoon.

Zelie felt aggression flood her system, even her bones ached with tension as Tamás surged again – trying to take her over. She closed her eyes for a moment and breathed out.

Stay calm. Stay in control.

She pressed down on the fear that wanted to consume her. If he was this strong already, what would another day do?

'What's going to happen to *me* once he's free?' Her question croaked out.

Kate's focus was intent on Zelie now. 'If you survive the process, then nothing.'

If she survived. Great. 'So why shouldn't I let him do it? Why should I stop him from killing you now? That's what he wants to do.'

The faint yellow tinge in Kate's eyes deepened. 'She never meant harm to come to him. She thought she was protecting him.'

Zelie bit back the growl that rolled up in her chest – but not from her own soul.

'You need me to stop the real danger to him,' Kate said desperately.

'There's no danger,' Tamás said viciously. 'There is nothing that can stop it now. Once I am free, I am free. And I will have my revenge.'

Cranky boy was back. And sick girl was looking like she'd been on one too many rides at the fairground.

'There *is* danger, Zelie,' Kate pleaded. 'That's why I am here. I want to help you.'

'What's the danger?' Zelie asked. Why couldn't she get clear answers from them?

'She was trying to protect him,' Kate evaded. 'There are others who want to take advantage of him.'

'Other witches?'

'The Witching.'

Zelie rolled her eyes at Kate's pretentious name for her fellow nutters. From the vibes Zelie was getting, Tamás was totally capable of looking after himself. 'How long do you think it will take?'

'I don't know.'

Great. So she had a guy of seventeen – give or take a century – residing in her head for the foreseeable future.

'Be brave, Zelie. He's a force you cannot understand, and soon you won't be able to control him.'

What kind of threat was he? 'If I can't control him, what hope do you have?'

'I have some power of my own.'

'Oh please, your witch powers? You can't even heal yourself.' Zelie pushed her muffin away again. 'This is ridiculous.'

Kate reached across the table, grasped her arm. 'You need me to get you through this, Zelie.' Her hand was frozen and clammy. Zelie fought the urge to violently shake it off. Instead she slowly sat back, sliding her arm free. She felt like she'd been slimed by some cold underwater creature.

'I don't think so, Kate.'

Zelie was the one stuck with him. There was no way out. Not even metal cutters would work on this chain.

'You do,' Kate argued. 'And when you need me, I'll be there.'

That was weirdly emphatic. Why would Zelie need her? To help her fight Tamás?

Kate reckoned nothing was black and white. Was Tamás for good or bad? And what was his power?

'Watch out for strangers, Zelie.' Kate stood and walked away.

Great. Like she needed anything to feed her paranoia more.

Zelie's muscles ached with tension. That rage had been unlike anything she'd ever experienced. He'd wanted to kill Kate. He'd wanted to take her apart like some wild predator. But no matter what had happened in the past, Zelie didn't think a life should be taken. Certainly not by her.

She reached into her bag and got her phone. Pretended to punch numbers and put it to her ear. 'So what's this power of yours?' she asked Tamás.

She waited. Ten seconds later she wondered why she was bothering.

'Come on, I'm stuck with you now, I might as well learn the

whole story,' she drawled. 'You're telekinetic? Can make fires start, control other people's thoughts *à la* Kate?'

'More Hollywood, Zelie?'

'Yeah. It's all been covered, Tamás, so whatever it is you're not going to surprise me.'

'I don't have any special powers. Not anything that is unusual to my kind.'

'Your kind?' Jeez, he and Kate were so arrogantly hell-bent on being unique. 'So what is your "kind" exactly? Angel? Alien?'

'I already told you I am human.'

'Mostly,' Zelie reminded him. 'It's not normal to read as fast as you can. To remember things like you can.'

'I had good teachers.'

Like hell. He hadn't even gone to a proper school. 'You're not going to tell me, are you?'

'No.'

Why? He didn't trust her enough? Well, the feeling was mutual. 'Then I'll just have to find out for myself.'

CHAPTER SEVEN

SOMEHOW SHE SURVIVED the rest of the school day. Tamás might have stayed quiet but he was brooding and her whole body hurt because of it. She didn't see Kate again and did her best to avoid contact with everyone. Seeing how she usually did this anyway, it wasn't hard to achieve.

Of course, part of her wouldn't have minded seeing Otis – but she only caught one glimpse of him in the distance. Her refusal of the lunch invite had no doubt killed any fledgling attention there.

She drove home playing dance music loud enough for the vibrations to cause mini avalanches along the side of the road. Too wired to face another marathon in front of the computer just yet, she changed into trackies and trainers. She'd warm up and burn off the negative energy. Amazingly there were no complaints from Tamás.

'Go up that hill again so I can see over the lake,' he said as she got outside into the cold air.

She didn't acknowledge the demand, but didn't fight it either. She concentrated on the path ahead, watching for the ice, letting her mind relax by focusing only on not slipping. The problems could stew by themselves at the back of her brain for a while. But one of them wouldn't go away.

'You could hurt me, couldn't you?' she asked roughly, after she'd got into her stride.

'Why would I? I need you alive.'

'But you could hurt me anyway.' She puffed through the trees on the flat and past the ice rink and pool complex. 'Couldn't you?'

She stopped as she came out of the forest onto the open hillside, hands on her hips as she sucked in breaths big enough to satisfy her screaming lungs.

'I do not want to,' he said curtly.

For half a second she thought about flinging herself off the cliff and ending it all here and now. What if he was a demon? What if he was going to destroy the world? How could she help him if he was as destructive as she feared he was?

'Zelie, I will not hurt you or your family. Or anyone innocent. I promise,' he said, his words biting colder than the wind.

Who decided who was innocent? Who made him judge, jury and executioner? She turned to go back down the path. 'Is your promise worth much, Tamás?'

He didn't answer. Her mood – and his – soured.

Afterwards she poured an entire bottle of bubble bath under the hot tap so she had a mountain of bubbles to step into. Now she could shave her legs. If she wanted to swim in the hot pools this week she'd be in boy-leg swimmers because no way was she dealing with her bikini line as long as Tamás was around to watch.

Once dressed she raced to heat the casserole Megan had delivered last night. Hooray for no lumpy mince and raw onion. Luke would be home from playing at his friend's house soon. Zelie was grateful he'd found someone as mad on bugs as he was, but he'd be tired and grumpy so the sooner he ate dinner the better. Her father walked through from his lab and gave her an assessing look.

'I'm fine, Dad.' She pre-empted him with a forced smile as she tested the casserole's temperature. *So* good.

'Saw you go for a run earlier,' he said briefly.

'Yeah. Good to get fit.'

And that was it. Her father was straight back into distant mode. She heard the front door slam and went to meet Luke.

'Good day?' she asked.

He nodded.

'Will you set the table?' she prompted. 'We're having that casserole tonight.'

Real, home-made food.

Twenty minutes later the three of them sat at the table in silence. Zelie usually talked to Luke lots – asking him about his day. But she had too much else to think about.

'You made this, Zelie?' her father suddenly spoke, looking surprised.

'No. One of the local mums dropped it off.'

And it was incredibly delicious. Zelie hadn't tasted anything so flavoursome in weeks. It warmed her belly – would it help warm Tamás?

'She works at the observatory,' Luke piped up.

'Really?' Her father's eyes actually sparked with a hint of interest. 'An astronomer?'

'Yeah,' Luke confirmed.

But then her father fell silent again – lost in a world of science and theory and research.

After clearing up and getting Luke ready for bed, Zelie went up to her computer, ready to cue a million more dreaded documentaries. Tamás would listen to them while she slept. 'More on World War I, Zelie.'

She hesitated. Hadn't they covered that enough already?

'Are you sure?'

'Yes. And the 1918 influenza epidemic. Can you find more on that?' he asked.

The request tore at Zelie's heart. The last thing she wanted to hear about was that. She bit her lip, wondering if he had a sympathetic side she could appeal to. 'Tamás . . .'

'Just put it on, Zelie.'

No. No sympathy. He was all cold, angry business. She typed it into the search engine but refused to watch the documentaries. And he didn't ask her to, not saying a thing as she turned the screen off so only the audio played. Maybe he sensed she'd been pushed to the edge. She rolled into the darkness, pressing her face into her pillow. But the words sent images into her brain, twisted them with the memories she already had, the ones she tried to bury deepest.

It started out as it always did. She heard the argument – never saw it, but heard every shrill word. Her own defiance, her mother's soft pleas. Until her mother grew angry and shouted. And Zelie had shouted back. She'd screamed in a fit of petulant, teen rage.

She didn't remember all the words exchanged – only the defiance she'd felt as she'd stormed out of the house, reluctantly dragging Luke with her. Then the flash came – her mother's face, stiffened in a scream. The twisted agony and the terror within Zelie as she'd tried so hard to help. The futility as she'd looked around the room in desperation – her mother's sanctuary, a green space where so much grew. But it had been too late. She'd got home from the park way later than promised, walked in to find her mum already dead – her expression so contorted she was almost unrecognisable. That hideous mask settled in her mind as it always did, night after night. But tonight it transformed again – to the face of a youth. A terrified, screaming youth.

She didn't recognise his face – but she saw the same horror in his dull eyes.

Zelie tried to rouse herself out of the nightmare, tried to tell herself this wasn't real. This was only a *dream*. But her limbs were heavy, she couldn't move. It was like she was immersed in quicksand. And the faces kept coming at her – rigid, terrorised, desperate. New faces. So many of them. Yellow clouds of poisonous fog swept across her vision, hiding some faces, while others lunged out at her with mouths open and twisted. Noise echoed in her mind louder than a battery of drummers – but this noise was from human instruments. Voices – hundreds of voices lifted in screams, shouts of agony. Zelie squeezed her eyes tight but couldn't escape. These were scenes of war. The stench of death choked her – that putrid rot of infected flesh.

She woke with another vile headache.

'What's wrong?'

She groaned and opened her eyes to the blank wall, wished he'd gone. If he was going to ask about her health, he could at least sound genuine, not make it seem like an accusation.

'You wouldn't understand.'

She didn't want to discuss the dream that haunted her. And she certainly didn't want to delve into the extra scenes that had mashed into it last night. Were those horrors coming from his memory – from the war? Or was it just from all the docos she'd listened to? She really didn't want to know. Tears burned the backs of her eyes. She didn't ever want to sleep again.

'Will it be much longer?' she asked to change the topic. Please let it be over today.

'I don't know. I have to get warm enough to be able to move.'

'You can't move?'

'Not yet.'

'Where are you?'

'I don't know,' he snapped.

'But you can feel your body?' she persisted, desperate for assurance that progress was being made.

'I don't know.'

She backed off as he verbally slammed the door in her face. She didn't want to rouse his temper more, her head hurt enough already.

'You don't look well,' her father frowned as she went down to contemplate breakfast. 'Do you need to stay home today?'

She shook her head and instantly regretted it. Her brain thudded against her skull, each jolt leaving it feeling bruised and bloody. But staying home would only make it worse. Better to go through the motions of a normal day, not sit home with her father hovering with a thermometer. And she certainly didn't want to watch any more of those damn documentaries.

She left for school early again, driving with her window down so she could breathe fresh, cold air. She couldn't seem to get enough of it. She squinted as she saw something on the road ahead of her. She slowed, waiting for the feasting bird to take to the air. The mess was in the middle of the road; lethal positioning for the beautiful creature. She pulled over and opened up the boot, rummaged beneath the blanket and emergency first aid kit her father insisted on her carrying, to get what she needed.

'You okay, Zelie?'

She straightened so fast she bumped her head on the open door of the boot. 'Ow.' Like her aching brain needed that as well?

Because it hadn't been Tamás who'd asked the question. She turned around, rubbing her head with one hand as she heard a car door close. Otis was walking towards her, wearing a giant jacket over his uniform and a cautious smile. 'Sorry. You okay now?'

She could feel the warmth in her cheeks and it was all she could do to nod.

'What are you doing?' he asked, looking amused.

She looked out to the road to the carcass – a large, well squashed rabbit. 'I'm moving the roadkill. If they haven't been able to catch anything, sometimes falcons feed on carrion and get hit by cars themselves.' She shrugged, a bit sheepish. 'I like falcons.' She looked up to the one that was circling in the distance, like it knew they'd be gone soon and it could resume its desperate breakfast.

'They're beautiful, aren't they?' A soft, foreign whisper in her head.

She smiled. It was the first time she'd heard real warmth in Tamás's voice. The first time he'd showed much of any emotion other than anger.

'I watch them soaring,' he added.

She heard his wistfulness too. And then she felt it. The same kind of yearning she used to feel when driving along in a car and seeing horses running in a field – wishing she could run as fast and as free and with as much power. Did Tamás dream of flying?

'You always have a spade in the boot of your car?' Otis teased.

Zelie blinked, only then remembering Otis was even there.

'I do it too,' Otis was grinning at her. 'Can't bear to see any of them hurt.'

Tamás had gone so silent she couldn't even hear him breathe. Zelie was sorry. She wanted to hear more of him when he was like that. What else did he watch?

'They're beautiful creatures.' Otis took the shovel from her and walked out to the middle of the road. 'And this guy might as well have a final use in helping them.'

He scraped the shovel along the bitumen, lifted the rabbit remains up and went to the side of the road. He cleared some of the snow mound with his boot and put the carcass in the space. 'You have a little brother, right? Luke.' Otis dunked the end of the shovel in the snow bank a couple of times before walking back to her car and putting it in the boot for her.

'Yes.'

He slammed the boot shut and then turned to lean on it. 'What does he do after school? Do you have to go home to look after him?'

Zelie swallowed and shook her head. 'He goes to a carer, the mother of another kid at school. She looks after him till five and then drops him home.' She bent her head and focused on the positives her father had laid out for both of them. 'It's good for him to have a friend to play with after school. She makes him nice afternoon teas.'

'But what about you?'

A chill zipped all the way through Zelie. She looked up at Otis's serious expression. Did he think she was lazy? A mean sister for not being there for her brother? It wasn't her choice. She'd *wanted* to be there for him. If anything she was hurt that she'd been side-lined.

'I'm supposed to be concentrating on my studies.'

No way had she hidden the defensive tone.

'No,' Otis bent forwards so he could look in her eyes. 'I meant, who makes you afternoon tea?'

Oh. Zelie stared back at him, dimly registered his gentle smile, and ignored the garbled groan from Tamás. 'If I'm hungry I make myself some toast.'

'Come to my house and I'll make it for you.'

It was all Zelie could do to stop her mouth falling open. 'Um.'

'This afternoon. Come home with me and have afternoon tea.' Was Otis blushing? Or was that extra red in his upper cheeks just from the chill wind?

'Your family will be there?' She bit the inside of her cheek.

'Mum should be at the observatory and Dad never gets home till after six. It'll just be us.' Otis smiled and waited.

Zelie managed to blink – but that was all she managed for a few seconds.

'Unless you wanted to go to a café?' Otis suddenly said, like he thought she was anxious about going to his house. 'Mama Jo's does good toasties. And milkshakes. Or hot chocolate.' His brows lifted.

She didn't want to go to that café. Lots of the kids who travelled to and from school on the bus got off and went straight there. She didn't want to be stared at by them – and she would be if she went there with the Big O.

'You can't go.' Tamás broke in on her thoughts, right back to being angry. 'You shouldn't go to his house alone.'

'Um,' Zelie cleared her throat. Had it been so long she'd forgotten how to say yes? 'Thanks, Otis. Toast at your house would be great.'

'Alone?' Tamás sounded surprised. 'We do not have time to waste,' he added gruffly. 'You should not go.'

But as far as Zelie was concerned, moody spirit-boy could go back to being uncommunicative. His old-fashioned disapproval couldn't diminish the small bubble of happiness inside her now – if anything it made her smile all the more.

'Yeah?' Otis's white lopsided smile burst out. 'Great. I'll meet you by the gates and we can drive in convoy.'

'Sure,' Zelie nodded.

His eyes creased at the corners and the brown in the irises deepened. He had the loveliest smile. Zelie's brain started to go woolly with the happy vibes. Her headache eased.

'He's just a kid,' Tamás muttered.

So was she. She ignored Tamás.

'We'd better get going,' she said to Otis. 'We're going to be late.'

Otis nodded.

She got into her car and belted up. Then paused. She wanted Otis to pull out from behind and drive in front of her. Because it would be just her luck to graunch the gears or bunny-hop or something.

'Are you going to move?' Tamás asked.

'In a minute.' She was a good driver but so didn't want to stuff up in front of Otis. And life being what it was, she would. So she waited some more. But he had the polite thing going on and flicked his lights for her to go ahead. In her rear-view mirror she could see his wide smile behind his windscreen. Okay. She'd go first.

The fates were kind to her for once. She had no trouble starting or pulling out, and she sat on the speed limit for the remaining twenty-five-minute drive. The silence from Tamás was deafening.

Good, Zelie grinned, he could stay silent. The hottest guy in school had asked her on a quasi-date and the lost soul stuck inside her could just get over it.

She parked and Otis pulled into the space next to hers, walking with her into school. Zelie hugged her bag to her chest and tried not to care if anybody was noticing, tried not to concentrate too hard on not slipping. Then up ahead she caught sight of a rail-thin girl. Kate.

She was walking fast, like she had lots of energy. Zelie angled her head to keep an eye on her, knowing Tamás wanted to see her too. He was aggression-free for now, thankfully.

'You know her,' Otis said. More statement than question.

Zelie turned. Otis had caught her staring. 'A little. She sees Dad a bit.'

'Oh,' Otis nodded. 'Of course.'

'Do you know her?' Any info could be useful.

'No.' His boots crunched heavily on the ice. 'Everyone knows the family of course – they own Glencorrie Station. But they've always kept to themselves. Shame because Tim, one of her uncles, would be awesome in the ice-hockey team. I'd never actually seen Kate before yesterday. But she's looking better today, isn't she?'

'Yeah.' Zelie climbed the stairs.

Kate was looking a lot better. It was quite some miracle. And if her improvement correlated with Tamás's increasing strength, then his power was building up frighteningly quickly.

'It's nice you're friends with her,' Otis said. 'She must be lonely.'

Zelie didn't know what Kate was, but she sure wasn't a friend.

When Zelie walked into her French class later that morning she saw up close the changes in Kate.

'Are you okay, Zelie?' Kate came over as soon as Zelie walked in.

Zelie tensed, preparing for a fierce reaction from Tamás, but to her surprise he stayed quiet and still. The anger she felt was her own – that Kate had done this to *her*.

'I don't need you stalking me, Kate,' Zelie said coolly.

'I'm not.' Kate took the seat next to Zelie's. 'This is my class.'

'You take French?'

'I've been learning French at home for years. I can help you with yours if you like. Any phrases you want translated . . .' Kate sent her a meaningful look.

'No, that's okay.' Zelie stared at Kate. Her hair looked thicker, glossier. It was cute – gorgeous. A massive difference in just one day. Zelie glanced around the class. Yeah, she wasn't the only one staring. 'You're looking well.'

Kate smiled but her clear eyes were sharp, the blues rippling. 'You're not.'

Was she going to get all Kate's illnesses now? She hoped not. 'Just a headache.'

Kate leaned closer. 'He's getting to you, isn't he?'

He wasn't getting to her at all. He barely talked to her. He listened to his documentaries then retreated off into some dark cave. All right, so *that* was getting to her. The fact that he left her to carry all his baggage while he moped. She felt it like a physical burden. Hell, she even had his nightmares.

'If you want to talk . . .' Kate paused.

'Not in the least.' Zelie turned to face the front, building a barrier with her books.

It wasn't till the lesson was half over that it occurred to her that she'd just done to Kate exactly what Tamás had done to her – shut her out. Which was stupid when she needed more information from her. *Keep your friends close and your enemies closer*, wasn't that the adage? She'd never had enemies before. She should glean whatever info she could, however she could. Kate Hearn held more answers than she'd given up yesterday. Zelie wanted them all.

But Kate wasn't in the next class and Zelie, feeling self-conscious, hid in the library at lunchtime. She didn't want to see Otis – still couldn't quite believe his after-school invite and she didn't want to deal with him in a group situation. Not till she had her star-struck staring and blushing under control.

Last class was PE. A mandatory subject but fortunately it was only for a couple of sessions a week. She had managed an excuse for the first few weeks but this time she knew she was going to have to front up. Back in England she'd played hockey – like her mum had. She'd not touched a hockey stick since her mother's death.

Today was basketball in the gymnasium. She was stunned to see Kate in the change room, her bony limbs all angles in her trackies and long-sleeved tee.

'You're playing?' Zelie was so astounded she had to ask to be certain.

'Yeah.' Kate's face glowed.

Zelie was amazed that anyone could look that excited about participating in a school PE class. But she bit back the snarky comment and grovelled instead. 'I'm sorry I snapped at you earlier.'

'That's okay,' Kate muttered. 'I know you don't trust me. I don't blame you for that. But I do want to help you.'

Did she? Zelie suspected Kate was out for herself. After all, it was for a selfish reason that she'd started this whole thing.

She followed Kate into the gym. They lined up for ball skills and drills. Zelie deliberately partnered up with Kate. She felt Tamás's attention growing, felt him lurking like a predator, scoping out the right moment to attack. She wasn't going to let him.

Under the cover of the noise of thirty balls bouncing and echoing, Zelie asked Kate the first of her questions. 'How long has your family been living by the lake?'

Kate caught the ball and held it in her hands, looking at Zelie thoughtfully. Yeah, Zelie had hardly been subtle. But Kate tossed the ball lightly back and answered. 'My family originally came from Ireland. They moved to London. They were travellers, got money doing shoe repairs and leatherwork. Then came the war, and then the flu.'

Zelie's attention sharpened. The flu? Tamás had requested more info on that last night.

'The 1918 flu was terrible,' Kate elaborated. 'It didn't hit the children and old people like flu usually does, but the strong young people. The people who should have had the greatest immunity.'

'But maybe those people weren't that strong,' Zelie interrupted. 'They were fighting an awful war, surviving on rations, living in terrible conditions.'

'Maybe,' Kate acknowledged. 'But the same could be said for Tamás. He'd been in France. In the battlefields.'

He had? Zelie froze, as the blood iced in her veins. An image from her nightmare flashed in her mind. The mud. She could almost taste the stench. She gripped the ball. Tamás was stirring. Not in a good way.

'My family decided to leave Britain for the new world. They got on a boat for New Zealand. But the flu was on the ship. In Calais they picked up more passengers. Including Tamás. People were dying. Young people like him. He should have got it, but he didn't. The people around him didn't get it either. And those that had it recovered. There was something special about him.'

Zelie shook her head and threw the ball to Kate, trying to stay calm. But her pulse was skipping, uncomfortably missing beats as it sped up. She sensed Tamás's focus, his anger rising. 'Maybe it wasn't that bad a strain of the flu.'

Kate smiled. 'He saved the baby. That's when she knew.'

'Knew what?' Nervous apprehension attacked her insides. She could feel the malevolence now, the welling fury. Her breathing deepened. Her focus zeroed in on Kate. It was Tamás doing this – sharpening her senses. Like a hunter.

She swallowed, trying to keep calm. She jumped on the spot a couple of times to release energy, but still it built. A burning rage fuelled by a century of having to bide his time.

'What he was.' Kate lobbed the ball back. Kate, who was so happy to be playing a sport. Kate, who was smiling. Kate, who had no idea that Tamás *hated* this conversation. Hated her. 'We didn't think there were any left. Certainly none as pure as him. So rare. I know they can live for a lot longer than us, but I don't know where his parents had been hiding, because he was still young. And so strong.'

Zelie squinted to stop her vision clouding. Kate needed to stop talking. Even though Zelie longed for answers, she had to stop Kate. She had to stop Tamás. But Kate didn't stop.

'The proof was there when she saw him help the baby. Catriona saw it, all his power. She knew he needed to be kept safe.'

Something in Zelie burst, ripping. A roar, a scream, a flash of something so huge it blinded her to everything – stealing her consciousness, her control, her strength.

The ball shot from her hands like it was possessed, like it had been fired from a high-tech rocket launcher. Zelie gasped – terrified as she realised the target.

Kate flinched. The ball missed her head by a millimetre, bullet-slamming into the wall behind her with a monstrous bang.

Zelie froze, staring at the wall, half expecting to see a circular smash mark in the concrete. The noise reverberated around the gym.

Zelie looked at her hands, her trembling fingers. The rest of her began to shake. In her mind she saw what could have happened. What he'd wanted. Kate pinned to the wall in a brutal blow. Blood. *Vengeance.*

She realised the gym was deathly silent. She slowly turned. Everyone was staring at her. Kate moved to stand between her and the others, shielding her from their gaze.

Her face was white, but her blue eyes blazed – an almost purple edge to the blue fire. 'You can try, but you cannot hurt me,' she whispered, snarling. 'Because as you grow stronger, so do I. Remember that.'

And she was growing stronger: now proud colour filled her cheeks; her hair shone like she'd put glitter hairspray in it; she stood tall, her feet planted apart in the confident stance of a victor.

'Is everything okay?' The PE teacher strode over. 'What happened?'

'Nothing.' Kate swirled on the spot and smiled. 'We're fine.'

Zelie watched, amazed, as Kate effortlessly handled the teacher with a laugh and some more chat and unbelievably – her psycho-killer stare.

Silenced, Zelie focused on coping with the overwhelming reaction within her – the appalling realisation of how vicious she'd felt, how close she'd come to hurting someone so badly, how far out of her own control she'd been.

And now, she felt afraid – not only of Tamás, but of Kate too. What *wasn't* she telling Zelie? Because there was so much she wasn't saying.

The fright of what had almost happened made Zelie's legs give out. She staggered to the wall and leaned against it, turning her back to the other students, to Kate, who somehow now had the PE teacher talking about her trying out for the basketball team. It was insane. She focused inward, on the malevolent rage still swirling inside.

'Don't, Tamás,' she muttered.

'Don't listen to her,' he shouted. His voice broke on the last word – ragged, with pain?

'Why not?' Zelie said, almost in tears. 'She's telling me more than you ever have. Were you on that boat?'

No answer. Nothing. Of course. Tears prickled and stung. She was home to a monster. An absolute monster who wanted to kill.

'Yes.' A whisper. Lighter than a butterfly's wing.

She shuddered. Her eyes watered more. He'd finally answered and suddenly that terrible tension drained from her. 'Did you save the baby?' she muttered.

'Yes.'

She pressed her fists to her chest, pressing the pendant closer, overwhelmed by his admission. He'd done something *good*? She desperately needed him to tell her more. 'So that's your power?

You can save people's lives somehow?'

'Not exactly.'

'Well what, exactly?' She needed to know. She had to know there was something good in him, not just this murderous anger. 'None of those people got the flu when they were around you. The people who did have it got better. Kate gets better just from being near you. You're a healer, is that it?'

He didn't answer for a while and she wanted to thump the wall in frustration. He couldn't clam up on her now. It wasn't fair. She stood upright, ready to run screaming, but then he did answer.

'Some things I can heal,' he said quietly. 'Just because of the way I am and the things I can control. But I can't heal everything or everybody. It's not that simple. I'm not that special.' Bitterness roughly coated his last words.

Zelie drew in a jagged gasp of air like she hadn't breathed in years.

He'd finally told her something important about himself. And Zelie knew for sure she couldn't believe him.

CHAPTER EIGHT

'PEANUT BUTTER? JAM?' Otis sent her a sideways look. 'Marmite?'

Zelie pulled a face. She'd never get a taste for the New Zealand version of that thick black spread. 'Peanut butter please.'

'Smooth or crunchy?'

'Crunchy.' She leaned against the island bench in the middle of the large kitchen and watched him work on the other side of it. He'd pushed his sleeves up, had hot toast on the board in front of him and a second round already in the toaster.

Tamás was seemingly expressing his disapproval with silence.

Otis spread a piece of toast, put it on a plate and pushed it across the counter. 'Sit and eat.'

She hopped up onto one of the tall stools by the counter and glanced around the room again. It was all glass and light and gleaming steel appliances and was frighteningly tidy. She looked out the floor-to-ceiling windows that offered the most incredible views over the lake. A couple of telescopes were set up along the bi-folding doors that opened onto the deck. A big print of the night sky hung on the wall.

'You like it here in this country?' Otis finished slathering marmite on his toast and took a bite.

'It's very beautiful,' she said.

'It must be different,' he said out the side of his mouth.

'It's smaller, quieter.' A lot quieter. She'd gone from a city with a population of half a million to a town with a permanent resident population of less than four hundred.

'But there's a lot to do here. And there's a lot on at school.' He paused to swallow. 'Have you signed up to anything yet?'

'I just wanted to settle in for a bit first,' Zelie evaded, lifting her toast. 'I've only been at school two weeks.' And she'd been more interested in finding a part-time job than signing up to any clubs. Something to keep her busy so she could delay getting into the social game as long as possible.

But she'd never have thought someone like Otis would be interested in spending time with her.

He nodded. 'What happened at PE today?'

She put the toast back down, swallowing her discomfort instead and tried to pull on a smile. 'I lost control of the ball. Made an awful noise, didn't it?'

She waited a beat. Then he chuckled. Her smile eased.

'Sure did.' He put more bread in the toaster. 'You looked shook up.'

She hesitated again. 'Yeah.' Total understatement.

'You didn't want to move here, did you?'

Her breath was stolen by the direct question. She glanced up but he didn't look accusing. Rather, his eyes were that gentle brown again. She looked down. It wasn't that she hadn't wanted to move, truthfully she didn't want to be anywhere in particular. 'It wasn't my decision to come here.'

'You couldn't have stayed at your old school? Boarded or something?'

'I couldn't leave either Luke or Dad.'

'Is that because of your mum?'

Zelie pushed her uneaten toast round the plate. 'No secrets around here, are there?'

Otis picked up the knife and got to work spreading butter on another bit of browned bread. 'I'm sorry, I didn't mean to pry.'

'It's okay.' It was pretty obvious her mother wasn't around. No doubt everyone in town knew the new doctor was a widower. It was human nature to be curious.

'She died a year ago,' Zelie said quickly. 'It's taken us a bit of time.'

'Sure,' he fiddled with the lid of the peanut butter. 'You're close to your dad?'

Zelie nodded for form's sake, but it was a lie. He'd shut himself away. So her responsibility for Luke had trebled. 'I need to be here for Luke.'

She checked his maths homework with him. She gave him

goodnight cuddles. She talked about their mother – dredging up the few stories she could. Luke didn't have the same memory bank and Zelie plumbed her own to keep their mother real for him. After that awful fight Zelie owed it to her mum to do all she could for Luke. Not that he didn't annoy the hell out of her at times.

Guilt rubbed again.

'How'd she die?' Otis looked apologetic but it didn't stop him from asking. 'Sorry, is that too personal?'

'No. It's all right.' But it wasn't. She loathed thinking about it. She blanked the ugly scenes stirring in her head and tried to give the simple recitation she used to have down pat. But she hadn't been asked it for a while and the words were rusty.

'She got a virus. It started with a bad headache and flu symptoms but it progressed really quickly. She thought it was a migraine so she didn't call Dad home from work. By the time they got to her it was too late.'

It hadn't been quite that simple. Zelie and Luke had been home. Her mother had insisted Zelie take Luke to the park for an hour. Zelie never argued with her mum but that day they'd had a doozy. She hadn't wanted to go. She didn't want to be Luke's babysitter. She'd been a selfish brat and she'd snapped at her sick mum. Her mum had shouted at her in a way she'd never shouted before. Told her she wasn't to return to the house for at least an hour. To prove a petty point Zelie had taken Luke and stayed out two. As a result her mother's last living minutes had been spent alone and her last spoken words had been in anger. Zelie would never forgive herself for that.

'It must have been really hard,' Otis said. 'I remember when my aunt died, it was awful.'

Zelie nodded. She hated this kind of conversation, the pointless sharing of incomparable experiences. It might be the social norm, but she failed to see how it was supposed to help.

'I'm sorry I brought it up,' Otis said softly.

'It doesn't matter.' She forced a smile because he was genuine and she hadn't meant to make him feel uncomfortable. 'What about you? You're an only child?'

He nodded as he chewed on the toast. 'Used to getting my own way.' He grinned slyly, bringing some tease back.

Zelie felt her embarrassment rise, unsure quite what he meant by that. Had she imagined the innuendo? Was he almost flirting? The only thing she knew for sure was that he was amused and that his smile was so attractive.

The back door suddenly opened. A chilly blast howled into the room until it was shut out again as the slight woman leaned her whole body against the door to close it. Zelie automatically stood.

'Hi, Otis.' The woman's voice carried bell-like across the room. 'I didn't know you'd invited a friend over.'

'You've met Zelie, right?' Otis didn't look remotely embarrassed.

'Of course,' Megan smiled. 'Nice to see you again, Zelie.'

'You too,' Zelie trailed off, her tongue feeling swollen and useless. Her blush was violent now, judging by how hot her cheeks were. 'That casserole was so delicious, I should have brought the dish back by now –'

'Don't worry about it.' Megan moved forwards with a smile. 'Sit and enjoy your toast.' She shook her head at her son. 'You couldn't find anything nicer in the pantry?'

'Nothing nicer than toast on a cold afternoon.' Given that Otis was now on his third round, it wasn't just a line. 'You're not working tonight?'

'Snow coming. We won't see a thing through those clouds.' Megan flicked the kettle on and turned to flash her smile back on Zelie. 'But the forecast for Friday is good – if you're free, Zelie, bring Luke up and I'll show you guys around.'

'That would be awesome. He's really looking forward to it.'

'It's so great to finally have our own doctor in the village,' Megan added. 'Mostly we've had to go through to town two hours away. Is his patient list building?'

'Yes,' Zelie nodded. 'And he does a lot of research so he's kept busy.'

Megan nodded encouragingly. 'And Luke's getting on?'

'Yeah, he's settling in well.' Better than she was.

Megan gave her a long, considering look. Her eyes were different from Otis's, so blue they were almost black. And it was impossible to guess what she was thinking. Zelie shifted on her stool, uncomfortable with such an intense inspection. She glanced at Otis, half hoping for some respite, but he was too busy putting butter on yet more toast to notice.

'It takes a while, but you'll get there,' Megan said kindly. 'There's something about the lake that draws you in.'

'The lake *is* beautiful,' Zelie said quickly, wanting to make amends for not sounding enthused about the place.

'It's too cold to swim in though. Even in the height of summer I find the water freezing.' Megan's face lit up, making Zelie blink. And for a horrible second she was totally jealous of Otis. She'd give anything to see her mum again – to be nagged by her, teased by her, embarrassed by her.

Proud of her.

'We need to leave, Zelie!'

Zelie jumped, almost falling off the stool. Tamás had been quiet for so long she'd forgotten him. And now he'd just shouted at her?

'Is something wrong?' Megan's brows lifted.

Zelie tucked a loose lock of hair back behind her ear and shook her head. 'No. Sorry. I was thinking of something else.' The heat was running up under her skin again. Guilty. There was something wrong. Feelings churned inside her. Strong, dark and not her own.

'We need to leave,' Tamás repeated harshly.

Zelie clenched her teeth. Someone was being nice and interested. Not just someone but the most popular guy in school and he was lovely. Even his mother was nice. Admittedly the interest was a little overwhelming, but now she was past the initial questions it would be okay. She wanted to make an effort too – for the first time in ages. So Tamás could keep his attitude to himself. She toyed with her toast and tried to dredge up her corroded social skills.

'Zelie.' All impatience, Tamás pestered her again.

She ignored him.

The furious pressure inside grew. Her own anger rose too. Why was Tamás suddenly so annoyed? She sipped her water, but something went wrong. Tamás lashed out inside and Zelie choked, half spluttering water all over herself – making a worse mess than something Luke would do. Beyond embarrassed, she put the glass back on the bench. As she brushed the droplets from her blue school jumper she was aware of some unspoken communication going on between Otis and his mother. Great. When she finally knew she couldn't avoid it any more, she looked up at them.

Megan smiled and walked towards the door. 'I'll leave you guys to it.'

Zelie managed a nod and then stole a glance at Otis. He'd finished his toast fiesta and had the lopsided smile on again. But she couldn't smile back. The discomfort inside killed the fun. Tamás might do something else that she couldn't control. She checked her watch. 'I really should get back. Luke will be home soon and I better get dinner organised.'

His smile went even more lopsided. 'Sure. You're not going to eat your toast?'

She looked down at the plate. In answering all his questions she'd only managed to take one bite out of it. 'Too busy talking.'

'It's probably cold now anyway.' Otis made it easy for her. 'Come on, I'll walk you to your car.'

And that easiness just made her like him all the more, which in turn made her even more nervous. She negotiated the icy path with ridiculous care. Self-conscious about her slowness, she tried to escape him sooner. 'Go back inside. You'll freeze.'

He hadn't stopped to put his jacket on.

'I'm fine,' he said calmly.

Finally they got to her car. She fumbled with the keys. Stupidly nervous and uncertain. Why had he invited her? Was he just being nice to the new girl or was this something else again? And if so, what?

She wished he hadn't asked. Wished she hadn't said yes. Wished she hadn't made such an idiot of herself spilling half her water like that. Above all she wished she didn't have the moody one inside her making it even harder.

'I'm sorry she came home early,' Otis brushed some snow from the top of her car. 'I know you're shy.'

He did? She avoided answering by swinging her keys round on her finger, catching them in the palm of her hand again and again.

'It's the ball on Saturday night,' Otis said.

She nodded. She'd have had to be living on another planet not to have known that.

'Are you going?'

She caught the keys once more but didn't spin them again. Her throat thickened, making answering difficult. 'I wasn't planning to, no.' Starting school only a couple of weeks out from the big day, Zelie just hadn't wanted to go there at all. Everybody in their finery for the whole big deal, with the even bigger deal of after parties? Too many people to face.

'What if you went with me?' he said calmly. 'Would you go then?'

Zelie gaped. Eventually – three seconds too late – she pulled herself together, having given him a first-class view of her tonsils. 'You don't have a . . . someone to go with already?'

'I'd like you to be my date,' he leaned against her car, making it impossible for her to open her door.

She swallowed. He wanted her as his date? To the school ball? Her brain seemed to be processing nothing but white noise. She couldn't think, certainly couldn't speak. The Big O. The hottest guy in town had asked her to the biggest event in any school calendar?

He angled his head to catch her eyes. His teeth flashed whiter than the snow as he smiled. 'It's okay to talk you know. And it's okay to say yes.'

She nodded again and felt her cheeks go thermonuclear hot. 'Um, that would be great. Thank you.' She flipped her keys again, unable to cover her embarrassment and her breathless voice.

'Fantastic.' His face lit up even more. It almost hurt to look at him, he was like the brightest star in the sky. 'You want to let me know what colour your dress will be? It seems to be the thing to match or something.'

Oh. Dress? What on earth was she going to wear? She hadn't worn a dress since the day they'd buried her mother. She didn't own any now. She'd packed them all up and put them in a charity clothing bin before she had time to change her mind. She hadn't thought about them since – refused to regret it. She just wore jeans and T-shirts, the stupider the slogan the better. Somebody else's words. So people would think she was somebody else – if they thought of her at all. Because she didn't care what other people thought. Not usually anyway.

But now was different. Now was the ball. Now was Otis. And only four days to find some kind of dress. And just like that her brain flipped into one-track mode, unable to think of anything else. Maybe she wasn't so different from the other girls after all.

'I'll let you know, okay?' she half gasped, trying not to let the total panic be too obvious.

'I'm going to hold you to that,' he smiled. 'So I guess you'd better give me your number, huh?'

Oh, smooth. She smiled and pulled her brain together just enough to remember what her number was. He tapped it into his phone and straightened away from her car.

'See you tomorrow, Zelie.'

'Thanks,' she mumbled, opening the door.

This time, of course, the fates weren't so kind. She grated the gears, the car jerking randomly before she got truly underway. But she was a puddle of sweating mortification anyway, so what did it matter? She didn't dare glance in the mirror to see his reaction. Just concentrated on getting down the hill sort of safely.

But the further she got from Otis, the more she could feel Tamás's impatience and anger.

'What's the problem with you?' she asked him. 'Can't I have afternoon tea with a friend?' Or a possible friend – their status had yet to be confirmed but she was fairly sure they'd moved up from acquaintance. Hell, they might move to something more . . .

'You made me choke on my water.' She was mortified about that.

'Why didn't you tell me about your mother?'

She nearly choked again. '*What?*'

'Why didn't you tell me she'd died? Why keep it a secret?'

What did that have to do with anything in the last half hour? And why did he sound so angry about it? It wasn't like he cared. 'I didn't keep it a secret,' she snapped. 'You never asked.'

He'd hardly been Mr Interested. He hadn't asked a thing about her or her life, nothing personal. All he'd wanted from her was warmth and history facts.

There was a sharp silence as her irritation peaked.

'I'm sorry,' Tamás finally spoke. Stilted, soft. 'I have been selfish.'

Zelie braked as she came to the bottom of the hill, and spent too long checking it was safe to drive across the main road. She didn't answer him immediately, mainly because she couldn't believe he'd just apologised or that, for once, he'd sounded uncertain. 'It's understandable,' her voice cracked. 'You're in a pretty weird position.'

'So are you,' he said slowly. 'But you cope well. Better than I do.'

She felt her eyes smarting and sat lower in her seat so he couldn't see her in the rear-vision mirror.

'I am sorry for ruining your afternoon,' he added stiffly. 'I did not realise it was so important to you.'

Another apology? Strangely it made her feel worse. 'It wasn't that imp—' She sighed. Maybe it was. She'd wanted to be normal again for five minutes. But the fact was that even without Tamás she'd failed at that in the first five seconds. She couldn't seem to do the sit and chat thing easily like everyone else did. In some ways Otis's mother arriving home had been a relief as much as it had been a stress.

Now she was filled with a swirling mix of emotions and she couldn't tell which were hers and which were his any more. It was all a bubbling soup of anger, regret, anticipation, guilt, excitement and hurt.

'Why didn't you say anything about losing your mother when I realised everyone I knew had gone?' he asked, so quietly she almost missed it.

She turned down the music. The relentless dance-party beat didn't seem appropriate right now. 'Because I know how annoying it is when you're hurting and you're talking to someone about it and they immediately chip in with "Oh I know, when I lost my . . . whoever" and they start yapping to try to make you feel better.' She turned down her street. 'They don't know. No one can know what your grief feels like. No one can be in your head.'

'I'm in yours.'

'That's different,' she said with sarcastic slowness. 'And you don't know what I'm thinking, only what I see and hear and taste.' She pulled up outside the clinic but kept her hands on the steering wheel. 'You know what I mean. People offer platitudes. I know it's because there's nothing else they can do. But sometimes I wish they'd shut up. I think it's better just to listen.'

'Did anyone listen to you?'

She swallowed the sudden stab of pain. 'They wanted to help but they didn't really want to know. People in a happy place find the death and grief thing uncomfortable. Especially people our age. It's too raw, you feel too exposed.'

'Everyone goes through it, Zelie.'

'Eventually. And that doesn't really make it easier. It doesn't mean we all have the same experience of it.'

'I still wish you had told me.'

She couldn't tell if he was hurt or angry. 'Why?'

'Because I made you listen to that documentary about the flu,' he said harshly. 'It upset you.'

'No it didn't,' she lied.

'Yes it did,' he argued. 'Don't try to make me feel better. You slept badly. You had that headache when you woke.'

'That was . . .' she stopped. He had the kind of heartache not everyone went through.

'Because of the documentaries,' he said flatly. 'I'm sorry, Zelie. And I'm sorry there was no one you could talk to when you lost her.'

It wasn't just the documentaries. It was the dreams that had followed them. The dreams that tortured her more nights than she could bear and now were worse than ever. She blinked away the tears.

Tamás's gentleness was almost worse than when he was all uninterested and uncaring. 'It's okay. It was ages ago now.' She undid her seatbelt and reached for her backpack.

'It's like yesterday for you,' he challenged, softly.

CHAPTER NINE

'WE DON'T HAVE to do more research tonight if you don't want to.'

Zelie paused, bending over the dishwasher to put the last of the dinner dishes in. Was he kidding? No more history lessons?

'I've got a grip on a lot of it now,' he added. 'I have an overview.'

'No you haven't.' An imp of humour tickled her. 'Your education is totally lopsided. It's all been doom and gloom and serious. You need the arts and culture as well. And the laughs.'

'Hollywood?'

'That's right,' she grinned.

'Hollywood is the source of all evil in the modern world.'

'Oh my. See, you *have* been reading the wrong books.'

'It was a joke,' he said drily.

'Really?' she giggled. 'You need to practise some more.'

'Ha.'

'Ha ha ha. Keep them coming. You might actually belly laugh one day.' Her mood lifted. He was teasing her. The urge to tease him back became irresistible. 'You know there's a whole genre you don't know about.'

'What's that?'

'The musical.'

She banged the dishwasher shut and quickly rounded Luke up and made him go take a shower. Then she raced into her room and clicked onto YouTube. There were so many movies Tamás just *had* to see.

'Edited highlights please, Zelie.'

She smothered a chuckle at his wary request. 'Edited highlights'? He was a fast learner.

She played him a clip from a Fred Astaire movie. 'This is where it started. And then it went to this.' A mash-up of *Grease*, *Fame*, *Footloose*, *Dirty Dancing*. All the classics. 'And then this.' She updated him with some scenes from *Step Up*, cheesed it out with *High School Musical* and *Mamma Mia!* That's when he spat the dummy.

'Is this what your dance on Saturday is going to be like?' He sounded appalled.

Saturday? Pure excitement bubbled through her and she laughed, her spirits soaring freely for the first time in so long. 'It'll be better.' She turned the music up and danced round the room. 'Do you dance, Tamás?'

'No.'

'Not ever?' Curiosity bit hard too. What had the dating scene been like back then? 'Did you ever go to a ball?'

'No.' Flat, uncompromising, his humour had gone on holiday again.

'You didn't have many laughs did you?'

'Not in those last years. There was a war on, remember?'

She hadn't forgotten. But she wanted to. For just a few minutes she wanted to forget the sadness that hung in her and that burdened him too. She wanted five minutes of *fun*, for both of them.

'So dance now. Let's have a laugh.' She closed her eyes and spun around, letting the rhythm ripple through her body, moving her feet, swaying.

Her door opened and Luke peered round the edge, looking bright-eyed and sparkly clean from his shower. 'What are you doing?'

'Dancing.' She grinned, breathless. 'And what are you doing still awake so late?' She grabbed her brother's hand, pulling him into the middle of her room, then raced to her computer and changed the track. She whirled to face him when the opening chords twanged.

She saw the moment he recognised it. Saw his smile stretch wide. Her ten-year-old brother could be a groover when he wanted. She held his hands and they swung round and sang along – loudly.

'You can't sing, Zelie!' Luke shouted over the music.

'He is right,' Tamás added, but he sounded amused.

'Doesn't matter, because I can dance, baby.' She could hardly talk for laughing. 'Oh,' she gulped and straightened as the chorus hit. 'Here we go.'

ABBA's 'Dancing Queen'.

A three-minute dance party with Luke in his pyjamas. He giggled and she giggled and when it finally ended they flopped onto her bed, warm and happy. Her mum had done that. Spontaneously burst into song and done crazy dancing round the kitchen. Or put her favourite track up loud and let them bounce on the sofas. Always ABBA.

She looked at Luke. 'You okay?'

He nodded, his breathing as easy as hers – no asthma at all despite the full-on dance moves. Awesome.

She rolled towards him and blurted her secret. 'I'm going to a dance on Saturday. Don't know that they'll play that though. And I don't know what I'm going to wear.' She bit her lip but couldn't contain the smile.

'There's a box of Mum's dresses in the attic,' said Luke.

'There is?' Zelie sat bolt upright. How could she not know this?

Luke's eyes widened, the worry returning to them. 'I saw it up there when I was looking for jars the other day.'

It was like a large hand had grabbed her stomach and twisted it. Her mother's dresses. For a speck of a second she almost had a glimpse of a skirt swishing. Just as quickly it was gone. Damn.

'*He kept them?*'

Luke met her gaze, his big eyes full of shadows now. Silently he nodded.

'Oh.' She didn't say anything more, didn't mention aloud what they both knew she was going to do. If her father got angry, she didn't want Luke copping any of the fallout. But she was so going to see that box. As soon as possible.

'Found any tiger beetles recently?' She changed the subject, drawing them back to safety.

'Three.' Luke's smile chased away some of the shadows. He sat up, his eyes even brighter. 'But I found something far more cool.'

'More cool than a beetle?' she asked in mock wonder. 'What could be cooler than that?'

'Wait there.' He jumped off the bed and ran, banging her door and then his.

She sat up, half dreading whatever it was going to be. She wasn't sure she could manufacture glee over a slug. And now all she wanted was to sneak up to the attic. Her door opened wider as Luke kicked it open and then walked in backwards. It must be something exciting then.

'Ready?' His question and accompanying smile were all flourish but his hands held their burden carefully.

'*Papillon*,' Tamás breathed.

'A monarch!' Zelie exclaimed at the same time and looked in the glass tank her brother held. 'Oh Luke, it's beautiful.' And in the middle of winter? She'd never seen a butterfly in winter before. Not this kind of winter where snow and ice covered pretty much all there was of the world. She stared at the creature's fluttering orange wings with their black lines. 'I didn't think they were around in winter.'

'I know.' Luke beamed.

'Don't they only live for a day or something?'

'A month,' he nodded.

'So how is this one alive?' Brightly coloured, it looked like it had just come out of its chrysalis and was ready to take on the world.

'I looked it up,' Luke spoke super quickly in his excitement. 'It's the coolest thing, I think it's stopped growing.'

'What do you mean stopped growing?'

'It senses that the conditions aren't right to continue the life cycle, so it puts itself on pause.' Luke lifted the tank. 'The fancy name is "diapause". Lots of insects do it. Some when they're still slugs or when they're in pupal form, but some can do it when they're almost fully adult too.'

'Diapause?' Zelie had never heard of it before. Trust her bug-minded baby bro to know it all.

'They stop growing or maturing in unfavourable conditions.'

'Arrested development,' Tamás murmured.

'So what happens to it?' Both intrigued and worried, Zelie watched the butterfly flap its wings as it rested on a leaf.

'When it gets the right signals, it starts developing again,' Luke gazed at it.

'Like warmer weather or something?'

'Yeah.' Luke peered closer into the tank. 'This one must have got the signals wrong and woken up too soon. I can't wait to show it at school tomorrow.'

Zelie's concern multiplied. 'Where did you find it?'

'It was just by the back door. Can you believe that? So lucky.'

'Yeah.' Zelie nodded. But suddenly she wasn't sure it was luck at all. 'You'd better go to bed. Take care of it.'

'Absolutely.'

She walked across the room as he carried the heavy tank out and closed the door behind him.

'It's to do with you, isn't it?' Zelie muttered. 'Tamás?'

'What makes you think that?'

It was too coincidental. Butterflies hovering round the house in the middle of winter seemed about as unnatural as having a century-old teen boy's spirit inside you and an enchanted amulet stuck round your neck. An amulet with an insect wing engraved on it. 'It's what's happened to you. Something like diapause.'

'Clever, Zelie.'

'But how is that possible?' It was insects who did that sort of thing, not humans. 'Bears hibernate, is it like that?'

'No. It's more like diapause because my system has stopped maturing. At least I hope it has.'

'So your body should be as it was when you were seventeen?'

'Hopefully.'

Yeah, she understood that hope given it was almost a hundred years later. She shook her head; it was still impossible to believe. 'Kate said your kind live longer anyway. How long?'

'It depends. We used to live for a good thousand years –' he broke off as Zelie choked and then resumed once she could breathe again. 'But as we integrated that time shortened. Perhaps a few hundred years?'

'What do you mean integrated?' she asked, staggered.

'Mated with humans.'

Oh. Right. 'So it's not all because of some spell?'

'The spell worked because of what I am. I don't think it would work on an ordinary human.'

She swallowed. 'Are we going to have a ton of butterflies at the back door, Tamás? Because that's going to attract attention.'

'I do not think there will be any others.'

Were there no others like him either? She slumped back on the bed, her excitement about the ball snuffed. For a few minutes there as she'd danced she'd totally forgotten she had this crazy thing to live through. For all she knew she might not make it to the ball at all. Tamás might be whole again, and she might be dead.

'Are you going to go and find the box?' he asked.

There was that too. Her heart ached. She wanted to see the clothes. She *really* wanted to see them. They might help bring her mother back. But her father had hidden them away.

'I'm not sure I should.'

'Why not? Why else did he keep them?'

'I don't know. He doesn't like to talk about her or have any reminders. I think it hurts him too much.'

'What would she have wanted?' Tamás asked gently.

Her mum had been a dress person. Big swirling skirts and pretty sparkling fabrics and never, ever jeans. She'd made hundreds for Zelie too. Lots of frilly fairy ones when she was little. They'd flitted around the garden in them. Zelie tried to catch the sound of the laughter, her mother singing, but it was silent inside. But maybe if she saw the dresses again?

She walked out to the hallway and listened. Luke had put an audiobook on, some toilet humour boys' book. There was nothing but silence from her father's room. She was sure he was downstairs in the lab. Meaning she could sneak up into the attic now and look at the box.

She pulled down the stepladder before she thought better of it and quickly climbed. She flicked on the light when she got into the cramped space. Boxes were stacked along one side. Many book boxes, a few bigger ones. All meticulously labelled so it was easy to find the box Luke meant. It was at the furthest end of the attic and had only the one word on it.

Freya.

She stared, scared to open it. Although Luke must have already if he knew what was inside.

'Do you remember much about her?' Tamás asked.

'Not enough.' The only image locked in her mind was her mother's face in its final moments, thin and rigid with the pain etched on it. Death had made her beautiful mother ugly. It hadn't been an easy end.

She pushed her thumbnail through the tape, ran it down the seam and then opened up the cardboard flaps. Everything was still neatly packed. Luke must have only glanced at the contents, too afraid to touch for fear of what Dad would do.

Angered, Zelie lifted away the layers of tissue. The packing must have been professionally done. That thought angered her more. If she'd known, she'd have done it. She hated the idea of some stranger handling her mother's things.

On the top sat a small box. She opened it and lifted up a delicately beaded necklace. Zelie remembered that one. She concentrated on it, wanting to see it on her mother in her mind. But, as always, the image was just out of reach.

She put the smaller box to the side, the lump in her chest getting bigger and her breathing quickening. Then she started lifting the fabric. She knew that blouse. She pressed the cloth to her face and breathed in, hoping to catch that elusive scent – the beautiful one, not the terrifying stench of death that had hung in the house afterwards.

But that unique soft scent was gone and only a faint synthetic lavender and moth ball smell remained.

Zelie's hope crashed. There was nothing truly concrete of her mother here. Her initial excitement faded into nothing.

Powerlessness, the sense of hopelessness, swamped Zelie. Her knees pressed into the hard wooden floor and she bent her head.

'Keep looking,' Tamás quietly encouraged.

Why? What was the point? She shouldn't wear any of them anyway, shouldn't even go to the stupid dance.

'Keep looking.'

She sniffed and leaned over the box again, lifting them out one by one, the dresses that she knew, but that were nothing.

Her heart contracted when she saw it and she hesitated. Layers of pale green rested prettily. A delicate, floating sort of dress with hand-painted decoration on the lowest tier of silk – intertwined vines and flowers. Her mother had loved to grow things, had always had the loveliest of flowers growing year round and she'd loved to paint.

Zelie hadn't seen this dress in years but she instantly recognised it. It was the one her mother had worn when Zelie was in dress-up fairy mode so long ago, before Luke had even been born. Zelie had loved it so much as a toddler that her mother had made a miniature version of it for her. That was long lost now. So this dress must be almost twenty years old. Maybe more. She hadn't known her mother still had it because she hadn't worn it in recent years.

But here it was.

She held it up in front of her, her heart melting as memories flooded back – the laughter, the green of the grass, the heat of that summer's day when her mother had scooped her up and spun her around, singing. Zelie had been so thrilled to have a replica dress of her own. She closed her eyes, hearing her again, feeling warmth rising like a gentle tide deep inside.

She remembered. Oh, she finally remembered *something*.

She clutched the fabric closer. It was the only contender, it wouldn't matter if it was too fanciful for a formal. It wouldn't matter if it was slightly loose. It wasn't a fitted style anyway so she could get away with it.

But this was her dress. *Hers*.

She quickly put it to the side and put the other things back in the box. She didn't have time to try it on now, besides, she couldn't bear to. This time the liquid pooling in her eyes didn't sting, but soothed.

'Are you all right?' Tamás asked once they'd returned to her room and Zelie had hidden the dress at the bottom of her bag.

'Yeah.' She looked at the computer, not wanting to admit to him how close she was to crumpling into a heap and howling. 'Let's listen to some more history, Tamás.' She didn't want to have the space in her head for thought right now, she just wanted to curl up in the memory of that warmth. 'What about the Velvet Revolution?'

'The fall of communism in the former Czechoslovakia?'

Oh, he knew it all now, didn't he? 'There must be something we haven't covered.'

'Just put on some music, Zelie.'

She wiped a tear from her cheek. 'I thought you hated my music.'

She heard his smile as he answered.

'I can live with it for a while.'

CHAPTER TEN

'I'M GOING TO town after school to get some shoes,' she told her father over the breakfast table. Not that he heard – too buried in the pages of his periodical. Luke was beside himself with excitement about his butterfly and left to go down the road to school the minute he'd brushed his teeth, his glass-domed container carefully balanced in front of him.

Zelie put her bag and its precious contents in the back of her car. Driving to school, she tried to suck up the anxiety riddling her bones.

'You're nervous?' The laugh was in Tamás's voice again.

'How can you tell?' she asked grumpily. Yes, she was.

Despite the warm memory she'd found in the dress, the dreams in the night had been worse than ever. She didn't tell Tamás about the visions of war, the crowds, the face – the horror in some young man's eyes. She didn't mention Kate and her freakish recovery and even more freaky flickering eyes. It was all too weird. Too scary.

Too uncertain.

'You've forgotten the indicator,' he chuckled. 'It has been on for most of the ride.'

'Aren't you just a Formula One professional?' She flicked it off. But she didn't go faster, even though she could sense that Tamás wanted her to. He'd got used to cars very quickly – had the usual boy-lust for speed. Some things didn't change through the ages.

But she was too self-conscious to cope with arriving at school any sooner than the final bell. Would Otis have told anyone? Would he talk to her today? Had she dreamed the invitation to the ball thing?

But Otis wasn't in French at first period. Kate was, but Tamás stayed quiet. Zelie thought she could feel him more but maybe she was wrong, because the anger seemed to be tamed. At lunchtime she glanced in the cafeteria, but though his friends were there, Otis wasn't. She didn't see him all day. So all the nerves were wasted. Gloom grew in their place. It'd be just her luck that he'd come down with something and wouldn't be able to go to the ball at all.

As soon as the bell went at the end of the day she ran to her car and fired up. She didn't have long to get to the city before the shops shut. It would be the first time she'd travelled further from the town than school since Tamás had arrived and she didn't know if it was a good idea. She pulled the car out onto the road, heading further away from Tekapo.

'You're in the lake, aren't you?' She was sure he was. It just made sense.

'I think so,' he agreed. 'I can hear the water now. I can move a little bit.'

'So you can feel your body now?'

'Yes.'

That had to be positive, right? That had to be a step towards freedom from each other. 'So do you feel me less?'

'No. That's getting stronger too.'

Oh. Bang went that theory. 'Are you okay with going even further away from the lake for a while?'

'So far so good.'

Zelie chewed the inside of her cheek and lifted her foot from the accelerator. 'I don't know that we should.' She didn't want to do anything that could screw up Tamás's departure from her head.

'It will be fine.' He actually laughed. 'You need to get your shoes.'

'I might not even go.'

'He wouldn't have asked you if he didn't mean it.'

'Tamás, there's more than one movie where the loser girl is asked by the gorgeous guy to the prom as a joke, only to be publicly humiliated on the night.'

'You think he's gorgeous?' Tamás chuckled again.

'I'm probably dreaming the whole thing.' Zelie was too far gone in her humiliation to answer.

'It's not a movie, Zelie.'

'It feels like it.'

'Truth is stranger than fiction,' he teased. 'You should go and dance anyway, Zelie. You're a good dancer.'

'Stop being so nice,' she said, but she couldn't hold back her grin. 'It makes me think there's something really wrong with you.'

This time he laughed long and loud. His first real belly laugh. 'Am I that bad?'

'Mostly.' Now she couldn't stop smiling at the warmth in his voice. He had a lovely laugh. 'You're not exactly communicative.'

'What do you want me to communicate about?'

She bit her lip, pausing. Did she want to ruin this new lightness between them? She decided to go for the jugular. If he didn't want to tell her he wouldn't, so she might as well ask anyway. 'Tell me about your life. Your family. How come you were in an orphanage?'

He sighed, but didn't sound as pained as he had before.

'You're not asking a lot then.'

'We've got over an hour in the car,' she said, hoping he couldn't feel the way her heart was thudding. 'We might as well pass the time with something interesting.'

'You think it's interesting?'

'Of course it is. I'm a female and I'm dying of curiosity.'

'Well the last thing I want is for you to die,' he said ironically. 'So, skipping the century I've lost, I last saw my mother seven years ago.'

'She was alive?'

'Yes.'

His voice suddenly thinned. Zelie didn't know if it was because they were getting further from the lake or because he was unsure about talking about his family.

'What happened?' she asked quietly, holding her breath as she waited for the rejection she was sure was inevitable. She hoped it wouldn't happen, hoped they'd moved on and become sort of friends. But only the noise of the car growled in her ears. 'Tamás?'

A cold river of fear ran down her spine and she lifted her foot from the accelerator again. Was he still with her?

'We lived as travellers. What your old movies would call gypsies. We're not actually Romani but everyone thought we were and we let them think it. It was easier.'

She breathed out and picked up speed again. 'Why?'

'Because people kept away from us. Drawing attention was not something we wanted. We just wanted to live peacefully. And be safe.'

Safe from what? More questions flooded Zelie's mind, but she daren't interrupt him.

'In France travellers were not liked. Not in any of Europe either. But we were in a village in northern France. They accused her of stealing.'

Zelie swallowed.

'She didn't of course. But it was the . . . policy . . . to remove the children. They wanted to make them normal. Put them into school. Give them stability.'

'Is that what happened to you?' Zelie was aghast.

'For a so-called better life, they tore our family apart.'

'Forced integration.'

'You know about it?'

'It's happened in other places at other times. Recently even.' Her history class had spent a term on Australian history; similar policies had been used against the Aboriginal people. Divided families, a divided nation. And in some countries families were still being divided. 'Where did they take you?'

'They put us in an orphanage.'

But he hadn't been an orphan. He'd had a mother and they'd taken him from her with no real justification.

'Us?'

'My sister and I.'

'You have a sister?'

He didn't answer for a long time. '*Had* a sister.'

Shock reverberated through her. And from that rose the overwhelming desire to help. 'But we have to find out what happened to her.'

'There is nothing to know. She is dead.'

'But she might have –'

'Might have nothing.'

Zelie opted not to argue with him. Not yet. She didn't want to stop him telling her the rest. 'So what happened then?'

'We were lucky in that we were kept together and there was a very good nun who continued teaching us – reading more, writing. *Maman* had taught us much already. We worked on languages as well because there were some other foreign children in care. I did lots of work around the orphanage. The men had gone, they needed someone with some strength. If we wanted food we had to grow it. But the war was terrible. I had to do something to help. The village was not far from the front.'

'But weren't you underage?'

'I had no birth certificate. No proof that I wasn't older than I was.'

'So you went into the army?'

'No. I helped as best I could while still working at the orphanage. I ran supplies up the lines.'

'And your sister?'

'Cared for the younger children. But the line advanced and when I came back from a week with the cart, they'd all been forced to move.'

'From the orphanage? Where to?'

'I don't know. When I got back the place was empty and there was no one around who could tell me. I couldn't talk to her, or hear her. I never found her. I never found out.'

Zelie's whole body ached with the knowledge. 'And what about your mother?' she whispered. 'Did you find out what happened to her?'

'No.'

Zelie was shocked. 'What about your father?'

'He'd been gone a long time. It was just the three of us.'

She didn't know what to say. And in the end all she could do was fall back on the platitudes that had once been given to her – and had annoyed her. Yet it was all she had to offer. And she meant every word with all her heart.

'I'm sorry for what happened to you, Tamás. I'm sorry you don't have them anymore.'

She was sorry she couldn't give him more comfort. But she wasn't sorry she'd asked.

'It's like yesterday,' he said softly. 'But I know you understand that.'

Her eyes blurred.

'Don't cry, Zelie. We don't want to have an accident.'

She gave a watery chuckle. 'Thanks for telling me.'

Ten minutes later they came to the outskirts of Timaru, the city nearest Tekapo. Zelie slowed, falling in with the heavier traffic.

'These are traffic lights?'

'Yes,' she laughed.

A motorbike went past, old style with lots of power and gleaming chrome. She deliberately looked at it for a while. 'You like that?'

'Interesting. They're a lot more powerful now. *Everything* goes faster.'

Yeah, somehow she'd known riding in the open air at great speed would interest him – the guy who liked the thought of flying. She searched for a park along the main shopping street and felt her anxiety notch up over the stupid mission. 'This is hopeless. I've only got an hour and I don't know what I'm looking for.'

She went into the first shop and gazed at the shelves.

'I've never seen so many shoes in my life.' Tamás sounded stunned.

She chuckled, but too soon felt desperate. 'There's nothing here,' she muttered.

'Nothing?' he scoffed.

'Nothing *right*.'

'You're never going to find a pair to match the green of the dress,' Tamás said practically. 'Why don't you go with silver? That way they'll match the *amulette*.'

'Matching accessories?' Amazed, she wandered down the footpath to the next shop. 'Tamás, I'd never have thought you had it in you.' And she should have thought of it herself. It was the perfect solution.

She tried all three shoe shops on the main street but the only pair she liked were dangerously dainty with high heels and a huge price tag – and it was ten minutes till closing time.

Fifteen minutes later she was back in the car, a big shiny bag on the seat next to her and a serious case of post-purchase panic.

'You should have stopped me.' She shook her head. 'Shoepidity. I've never spent so much on shoes.'

He laughed. 'Women never change through the ages. My sister wanted shoes once and she cried about it for hours. So I'm glad you got them and you're not crying now.'

'I will be when I see that credit card bill. I'm hungry, are you?' She looked at a sign halfway down the road. 'Come on, there's something you've got to try.'

She went into the Thai restaurant. She'd get takeaway so she could talk to him – she was interested in his reaction to curry. Recklessly she got a few different options. Back in the car she drove down to the bay, parking where they could overlook the sea. In the distance the port was all lit up as the cranes and forklifts loaded and unloaded goods from the ships.

She inhaled the mix of aromas emanating from the bag from the restaurant. Yeah, she was hungry.

'What's this?' Tamás asked as Zelie unpacked the containers.

'Thai curry.' She lifted up the lid of the first one, dipped the spoon in and tasted it. Her brows shot to her hairline and her eyes watered. Wow, that one was too hot, she'd broken into a sweat already.

'That's goooood,' Tamás groaned.

'You've got to be kidding.' Zelie sucked in some air, trying to cool her burning throat.

'No. It's great,' he said. 'Have some more.'

'No way.' She put the lid back on it. When she got home she'd put it in the fridge. Her father could have the leftovers.

'Please,' Tamás begged.

Laughing, she ignored him, found her mild green curry and had some of that instead.

'That's good but not as good as the other one,' he said.

'The other one was nothing but whole chillies.'

'And so good. I've never had it before, Zelie,' he wheedled. 'Think about how much I've missed out on.'

'Oh all right.' Maybe it hadn't been so bad; she hadn't had Thai in a while. She cracked open the first container again, took another spoonful and stuck it in her mouth. Wincing, she swallowed it as fast as possible. 'It's too hot for me. It makes me sweat.' She reached for the bottle of lemonade and gulped half its contents.

'It's delicious. Stop watering it down. What else is there?'

'Another curry. Lots of rice.' She'd end up the size of a house if she ate like this all the time. But she ate more anyway. 'The sooner you get out of where ever it is you're trapped, the better. Then you can eat all the curry you want.'

'The taste is getting stronger.'

'I know,' Zelie said, switching to serious. '*You're* getting stronger.'

CHAPTER ELEVEN

ZELIE HIT THE road after eating all the curry she could handle, including another couple of spoonfuls of the super-hot one just to keep Tamás happy. The sun had long sunk below the horizon and any droplets of water were already icing over, making the roads treacherous. She drove slowly, carefully. It was funny how used to him she was now. How easy it was to talk to him. They argued about the music they'd listened to last night, with him eventually admitting there was some he actually liked.

She looked up at the house, surprised to see Luke's light still on.

'Luke's awake,' she said. Usually he was one of those early to bed, early to rise kids. Totally the opposite to her. A twist of anxiety soured her good feeling.

She called out hello to her father but then went straight up the stairs to check on her brother. His door was closed so she knocked. Even though there was no reply, she carefully opened it.

He was face down on the bed but turned his head as she stepped in. Her muscles failed when she saw his expression.

'What happened?' She dropped to sit on the bed beside him. He'd been crying, his eyes and nose all Rudolph red. His shoulders jerked as the tears started again, his face crumpling. She put her hands on him, panicking over the cause. She hadn't seen him looking like such a wreck since Mum had died. 'Luke, tell me, what's happened?'

'They killed it.'

'What?'

'The butterfly.'

'*What*?' Nausea roiled in her stomach. 'What happened to it?'

'They let it out. I told them not to but they did,' Luke wailed.

'But how did it die?' It had been okay out in the winter so far, what could have gone wrong?

'It flew to a tree, was on a branch. But the wind lifted. It got hit by a lump of snow falling from a branch above,' he sniffed. 'It just smashed to the ground.'

'Oh, Luke.' She pulled him into a hug.

'I know it's stupid. I know it is.' His words were muffled, his face hot. 'It was just a dumb butterfly.'

'It's not stupid. It matters. I know it matters.' Zelie put her cheek to his. 'They didn't mean to hurt it.'

'They should have listened to me. But they didn't. I could have looked after it.'

'Of course you could. I know you could.'

'It was special, Zelie.'

'I know.' She closed her eyes against her own tears. 'Want some hot chocolate?'

He shook his head, unable to answer through the sobs.

She pulled back the covers and encouraged him into bed. She stood and turned out the light but then went back to his bed to sit beside him and rub his back. Slowly the shuddering eased. Eventually he slept.

Her whole body ached as she quietly stood and left his room. Her brother hadn't needed that.

'Are you all right?' Tamás asked.

'Yeah,' she nodded as she brushed her teeth. 'Are you?'

'I think so.'

But she was worried. She curled under her duvet, put her hand to the pendant and felt how the cold had gone from it. It was warm now, and she knew that meant Tamás was on his way to being as strong as he needed to be.

How would the split happen? And what if it didn't work properly? What if she was stuck with him forever? What kind of life would that be? She heard him more clearly, she felt his reactions more strongly. She felt his will. And she suspected that one day soon his will might overpower hers, that he would be able to gain control of her body as he so briefly had on the basketball court. Only then it would be permanent.

Yet that thought didn't frighten her as much as it should. In fact, it was the separation that scared her more. At least like this she was sort of safe. It was a more than manageable existence. Every day became easier – and honestly? She actually liked him. She'd never have thought it but he had a sense of humour, he felt compassion. And while she didn't want anything bad to happen to her, she didn't want anything bad to happen to him either. What if the separation damaged them?

She tried to put it out of her head but couldn't. It was looming, coming closer and closer – the great unknown. Everything else went round and round in her head too. Everything he'd told her about his life and his family. She wanted to search for his sister for him. She wanted to find out if he had living relatives. But he didn't want her to and she wouldn't risk his anger by doing it anyway. Still, she hated not being able to help him. She sat up, frustrated with her inability to stop all the thoughts.

'Why are you still awake?' he asked.

'I can't sleep,' she sighed and went for the whole truth. 'I'm scared, Tamás.'

'Lie back down. I will tell you a bedtime story.'

'A fairy story or an autobiographical one?'

'Both.'

'Of course,' she giggled even as her heart twisted.

He started speaking. Slow, low in that strange exotic language.

'It doesn't count if I can't understand it,' she whispered.

'Just be quiet and listen,' he said firmly.

So she did. It was like being lulled by a soft music. The cadences rose and fell in long sentences, echoed in pauses. It was bewitching. She guessed it was Eastern European, maybe Russian or Hungarian? Who knew? It didn't matter anyway because it wasn't so much what he was saying but the sound of it that soothed her. She closed her eyes to listen better and suddenly saw it in her mind – the beautiful blue of the sky. And she was running beneath it on a vast stretch of bronze- and fawn-coloured plains – the tussock bending in a gentle breeze. She was the wild horse of her imagination, full of power and speed and strength. She looked to her side and saw it flying low alongside her, the gleaming-eyed falcon with its wings spread wide, effortlessly riding that breeze and keeping pace just ahead of her. The movement was so easy. She felt free. Weightless. Peaceful.

And suddenly she was flying too – above the earth, floating in the air.

Happy.

♦

She woke earlier than usual. Probably because she'd fallen asleep so early and stayed there so deeply and dreamlessly. She sat up, surprised – no dreams at all. No nightmare for the first time in over a year.

She heard muffled movements in the hallway and got out of bed to see what Luke was up to. He was coming back towards his bedroom, his face pale and puffy.

'I put the sheets in the machine already, Zelie.' He didn't look her in the eye.

'Oh, Luke. That's okay.' He hadn't had a bedwetting accident in ages. Zelie had hoped he was through it. He'd been mortified the first time it had happened a week or so after their mum had died. Her father hadn't known, was just blind to these things. And that's the way they wanted him to stay. They'd agreed it between them, that their dad had enough on his plate then and Zelie and Luke could handle it together.

She was awake so late into the nights in those early months after her mother's death that she'd snuck in and taken Luke to the toilet just in case. She'd got him a mattress protector as backup. It was nice that it hadn't been needed for so long.

She knew that showing her concern would only upset Luke more now so she tried to play it down. But she was as upset as he. The stress of yesterday had got to him and the grief was back burning fever-bright in his eyes.

'He'll be all right, Zelie,' Tamás said when she went back into her room.

'Yeah.' Because she'd be here for him. She'd make sure of it. They only had each other and he was everything to her. She owed him, and she owed it to her mother to take care of him. During the last couple of weeks she'd wondered if she could have stayed in the UK. Luke had seemed to be settling so well. And with her father insisting on him going to after-school care, Zelie hadn't felt very needed any more. But seeing him now confirmed how right it had been that she'd come. He was still vulnerable.

So was the other guy currently in her life. Not that he'd ever admit it. But she wanted to help him too.

'Tamás, I think we should find out what happened to the orphanage. We could find out what happened to your sister.' It was the one thing she could do for him.

'Zelie –'

'She might have married and had children, Tamás. You might have relatives. Have you thought of that?' She sat at her computer, jiggling the mouse to begin a search.

'Zelie –'

'We can email the local council or something. You can tell me what to write. You want to find out, don't you?'

'No.'

She didn't believe him. She was growing even more sensitive to his moods – their bond was strengthening. So she knew he was hurting and trying to hide it. 'You might –'

'I am not another brother for you to take care of, Zelie,' Tamás snapped.

She sat back from the screen, hurt by his rejection. 'Okay. Fine.' Did he have to be so savage?

She stomped to the bathroom, feeling both his anger and her own. She had an extra-long shower in the dark. Back in her room she wriggled into her underwear, holding the towel in place as she did, and then sat on the edge of the bed. She sighed as she fought the tangles in her hair with a comb. He could have relatives. She might be able to find them. Wouldn't that be fantastic? If his kind lived so long, he might not be alone after all. She couldn't understand his refusal to even consider it.

'Zelie, I can see everything you see, remember?' Tamás suddenly spoke furiously. 'Even in your peripheral vision. *Everything.*'

She blinked. She hadn't really been looking at anything, too busy working on her hair and mentally planning. She looked up, trying to see what it was he was seeing. Then she saw it. The mirror. Her towel had slipped. While she was focused on her hair, he was probably focused on her bra.

'I can *see* you, Zelie.' He sounded goaded.

Okay, definitely focused on her bra.

She stood, the towel falling to the floor, and for just a moment she looked at her reflection – her whole body. Then she turned, closed her eyes for good measure. Screwed them tight shut to stop the images suddenly crowding her head. But still they came. So stupid. She was decent in bra and undies, it was like a bikini at the beach.

Except it wasn't. It was much, much more intimate. She clamped on every muscle in her body to stop the reaction, the rising heat coursing through her.

It wasn't all embarrassment.

Just because she was a virgin, didn't meant she was an idiot. She knew what excitement felt like. She'd been kissed once back in England, she'd read *Cosmo*. And she wanted to stop the thoughts because she was sure he understood them and felt them too, spreading like wildfire.

Damn. She was blushing. She could feel her cheeks, every centimetre of her skin growing hotter and hotter. Heat burned from the inside too. Her tummy. Her bones melted so she locked her muscles around them, trying to stop them going to goo. Was she going to incinerate on the spot?

The amulet felt on fire – searing her skin. Worse than the ice burn of the first day. She bent forwards and caught it with her hand. 'Tamás!'

Covering her breasts with one arm, she peered at the mark on her chest. A small patch of red that still stung. She licked her finger and touched it gently to the spot.

'I'm sorry,' he said harshly. 'I didn't mean to hurt you.'

She immediately looked up, so he could no longer see the wound. 'It's okay. You didn't. What happened?'

'Um.' For the first time in ages he was back to not talking.

'Tamás?' she whispered. 'Are you okay?'

'Yeah.' Was that the hint of a laugh? 'I really am sorry.'

'I guess it's been a while since you –'

'Let's not talk about it. Please.'

She laughed. What else was there to do? And so did he. Faint, embarrassed chuckles that stopped almost as soon as they'd started. She quickly pulled on her uniform. Despite the embarrassment there was an easing or softening inside. Like a defence had been removed. She held the amulet again, protecting her sore skin while keeping him safe. It was still hotter than it had ever been, but not burning like it had only a minute ago.

And then she thought of something else. 'Tamás, you can see and hear and taste what I do, but can you feel as well? When I touch something?' She already knew the answer, but she half hoped he'd lie.

'Yes.'

Her breathing shallowed at his honesty. So when she was in the shower – when she shampooed her hair or ran the soap over her body, he could feel that – *her*?

Heat flared and rampaged again.

'I wish this was finished,' he said sharply.

She looked out the window to the hill and the trees and down to the lake, tried not to feel a stab of rejection at his words, tried to bluff through the chaos of her emotions. And the awareness that had her heart thundering. 'So do I.'

There was no snow falling today. Instead a cloudless, sunlit sky blazed above them, but the temperature was still freezing. She turned away from the brightness. 'I'd better get to school.'

It was French first period again. Zelie walked in two minutes before the bell and saw Kate already at her desk. Today she looked pale again, like the healthier colour of yesterday had washed off in the shower.

'Something's happened to her,' Tamás said.

'No kidding,' Zelie muttered.

'Find out what it is.'

She was already onto it. 'You don't look so well, Kate,' she said as she stopped by her desk. 'Are you okay?'

'Sort of.' Kate's eyes were red-rimmed. Not like Luke's tear-tired ones, more icky-infection swollen. 'How are you?'

'I'm fine.'

'And Tamás?' Kate sounded much more interested in him.

'He's fine too.' Zelie swallowed a rueful smile. He was definitely coming back to life.

'He is?' Kate looked confused. 'I wondered if . . .'

If what? 'We went to Timaru last night,' Zelie said, watching Kate's face closely. 'He had his first Thai curry.'

'You went that far away?'

'Yeah.' Was that why Kate was looking worse now – because Tamás had been so far from her?

Kate nodded, but didn't look any less anxious. 'It's a test today.'

'Oh shit.' Zelie had totally forgotten and she hadn't done any study because she'd spent the last week watching nothing but history programmes and musical movies. She took a couple of steps and slumped into her chair. What sort of teacher scheduled a test the day before the school ball?

Zelie glanced behind her as the teacher handed out the sheet of questions. No Otis again. And no smiles or anything from the others in his posse. So they didn't know he'd asked her to the ball? Ruthlessly she put it from her mind and picked up her pen, looking at the first question.

'*Le ticket coûte cinq euros.*' Tamás supplied the answer.

Her pen hovered above the paper as she bit back the giggle. She shook her head, unable to whisper in test conditions. *Don't, Tamás.* She hoped he'd get the vibe, she wasn't a cheat. But then she wrote the answer anyway.

He laughed the biggest, most infectious laugh she'd heard from him. Zelie felt like a lamp, glowing from the inside out. And like some ancient lamp, she even had a genie bottled inside her, dazzling her. She looked at the next question. Again, he gave her the answer.

'No,' she whispered very softly. But started to write it anyway – or kind of.

'No, you've spelt that wrong. You need an O before the U. The next one's "*tu veux*".'

She shook her head. She wasn't going to let him do this.

'As they say in the movies, you need to "loosen up",' he teased. 'How do you know it's the right answer anyway? I could be telling you to write something outrageous.'

She bit her lip to stop her jaw dropping. That wasn't just humour, that sounded almost flirtatious. She gripped her pen harder to stop the gooey thing happening to her body again but it was pointless, she was all warm tingle. Then she skipped to the next question and had to listen to him give her the answer in over-the-top, over-enunciated fashion.

She looked up, hoping no one could hear her giggle her way through the test. Kate was staring at her. Zelie's heat deepened and she looked back to the paper. Caught cheating by a terminally ill witch. Fantastic.

'Forget about her,' he said lightly.

Like he had? They both knew it was impossible. But at least he wasn't trying to kill Kate any more. Zelie read the next question but didn't start to answer.

'Why don't you write it? I know you know it.'

Did he? She hadn't said it, and he hadn't told her. So how did he know she knew it? The answer sprang to mind immediately but it was such a scary thought she blanked it. She had to be wrong. She wrote on the paper to distract her mind.

'That's the wrong answer,' he said. 'You know that's not right.'

Okay, so she knew. But she hadn't been studying. In the last year her grades had slipped from above average right on down to well below. It was going to be pretty weird if she suddenly got one hundred per cent on this test. He'd given her half the answers already so it was time to make some deliberate mistakes.

Later, as the bell for lunch rang, so did her mobile.

'Hey, Zelie, it's Otis.'

Hell, he sounded like he'd been smoking a hundred a day. 'Are you okay?'

'I'm fine. Well, almost. That's what I wanted to tell you. I've been laid out the last coupla days with a cold, but I'm better now. I'd have texted or something sooner, but mum banned all things electronic.' He sounded sheepish.

Zelie silently laughed; that was the kind of thing her dad would do. 'You just wanted to get out of the French test.'

'Yeah, you got me.' He chuckled. 'You're still on for tomorrow night?'

'Sure,' she hesitated. 'But are you sure you'll be up to it?'

'Why, what have you got planned for me?'

She flushed at that total flirt.

'I'm not missing my first date with you, Zelie,' he added softly.

She went even hotter. His first date? Did that mean he might want more? 'Well,' she cleared her throat. 'Okay then.'

'Mum wants to know if you'd still like to bring Luke to the observatory tonight.'

'Is she sure that's okay?'

'Absolutely.' He laughed a little. 'I'm gutted she gets to hang with you today instead of me.'

'Oh.' Zelie couldn't think how to answer. 'Look, I'm just in the library, I'd better go.'

'Sure thing, see you tomorrow. Bye.'

She could hear that grin again as he rang off.

She waited for some sarcastic comment to come from Tamás, but he was pointedly quiet. Which annoyed her more than if he'd said something to tease her.

She flicked through the newspaper. Not really reading it but figuring Tamás was.

She was glad she'd heard from Otis, but she wasn't as excited about the ball any more. There was something else that had captured her interest completely.

It was like the more she tried not to think about him, the more she did. Like when she'd tried to diet – as soon as she'd decided to restrict her chocolate intake, she was starving and it was all she could think about.

In the end she gave up trying to hold those thoughts back. If Tamás could read her thoughts – and she was sure now he could – then he knew anyway. Totally mortifying.

But he didn't comment. Didn't acknowledge it. He remained silent. Which was frustratingly chivalrous.

That evening, after an early dinner, Zelie drove Luke up to the observatory.

'No werewolves tonight,' she joked with him. 'The moon's at its smallest.'

'No such thing as werewolves,' Tamás piped up.

Oh really? Nothing would surprise her now.

'There's lots of stars though,' Luke said, sitting forwards to peer out the windscreen. 'Millions and millions.'

Megan was waiting for them as they parked. 'Come inside for a bit, before we go to the telescopes.'

She led them into the warm building, hot chocolates already on the table.

'Yum, thanks.' Luke lifted the nearest cup.

'You need to be warm, it's a clear sky but that wind is super-cold.' Megan went to a cupboard. 'You'll need to wrap up more warmly if you're going to look through the telescopes outside. Here.' She turned and held out a scarf to each of them.

Zelie put her hot chocolate down and went to wrap the scarf around her neck.

'That's a very pretty necklace, Zelie,' Megan said, her head tilted as she studied Zelie's collarbones.

'Oh,' Zelie clapped a hand over the chain. 'Yes. Thanks.'

'Is it a locket?'

'I don't really know.'

Megan's expression softened. 'Was it your mother's?'

Zelie shook her head, quickly wrapping the scarf round her neck to cover the chain. 'No, I found it . . . in an old junk shop. I just liked the look of it.'

'It's unusual.'

Zelie nodded.

'How big is the biggest telescope?' Luke asked from the other side of the room. 'Can we see another galaxy?'

'Yes we can.' Megan turned. 'I'll show you the Magellanic Clouds.'

'The what?' asked Luke.

Megan laughed and walked over to explain further.

Zelie grimaced wryly. Hooray for inquisitive little brothers.

But almost an hour later, she was over the billion questions. The kid had more whys in him than the sky had stars.

Zelie wasn't so interested in identifying the clusters and distant planets. It was enough to look through the lens and bring the universe that much closer. It was beautiful. But it was scary. There were so many things she had absolutely no clue about. Not in this world, let alone all the way out there.

'It is beautiful,' Tamás said quietly. 'There is so much knowledge in the stars.'

Were there aliens out there? Was that what he was – ET?

But he said nothing more.

Summoning all her tolerance, Zelie watched Luke drink in all the stats Megan fed him about the telescopes, the constellations, the behind-the-scenes work. The woman was unbelievably patient and polite. And seeing Luke's rapt expression, Zelie felt a rush of gratitude for her.

'I should let you guys get home,' Megan finally said with a smile. 'You have another late night tomorrow, Zelie.'

'Oh . . . yes.' She flushed. She so didn't want to talk about it with

Otis's mum. How embarrassing was that? Hell, maybe Megan had put her son up to asking her out – to be nice to the new girl or something? – and really Otis was dreading it . . .

'Thanks so much for taking the time to show us around.' Zelie nudged Luke.

'Yeah, thanks,' he added.

Driving back down the hill, Zelie's thoughts turned inwards. Tamás had barely spoken during that visit. He seemed to have retreated to the silence he'd kept at the start, even though she knew he was stronger, knew he was seeing, hearing and feeling everything as much as she was.

After putting Luke to bed, she grabbed courage with both hands and blurted her first question aloud. 'What do you look like?' She hated not being able to see him.

'Why?'

'So I can recognise you when you're free.' She sensed it was imminent; the amulet was holding body temperature, he was strong. And she really hoped that it went okay, that they survived. That they'd meet.

'You won't see me. I won't stay.'

Her heart dropped through both storeys of the house and smashed onto the icy ground below. She *wanted* to meet him. She wanted to know him.

She'd tried to lock away the secret part of her mind that wanted to wonder about him. But she couldn't control it now. Questions burned – what he looked like, what it was his powers were, what it would be like to come face to face with him . . . whether he was as intrigued by her as she was by him.

And now he was saying she wouldn't meet him? 'So what'll happen? You'll just disappear from me one day?'

'I think so. I hope so.'

What was she, nothing but the heater? The incubator? The storage container for his soul until his body was ready again? She was being used. But what made it worse was that she knew she was going to miss him.

So stupid to feel that, especially when all he did was make life difficult. She couldn't even look in the mirror any more.

'It is best that way.'

Was it?

'I don't know what my body will be like,' he said very quietly. 'I don't know how long I can live after this. I don't know what effects this may have on me in the long term. That is why it is better to leave.'

Tears prickled her eyes. She understood that he must be worried – hell, *she* was worried for him. But she just wanted to see him once, to know he'd got free okay. Didn't she at least deserve that? Living with someone twenty-four-seven led to such intimacy. It was impossible for it not to. And it also led to friendship, didn't it?

'I think we should watch a movie,' she declared with a defiant sniff. She was so not tired. She so didn't want another one of their shared nightmares. 'Something rebellious.'

Marlon Brando. James Dean. Peter Fonda.

She'd feed him the Hollywood rebel. Chrome and attitude and freedom.

But hours later as she dragged herself to bed, still her curiosity burned. 'So what *did* you look like?'

'Zelie,' he said crushingly, not even a slight smile in his tone.

'Why not say?'

'I looked like any other kid. I had arms, legs, a head,' he said irritably.

'Only one?'

He laughed then, but it became a groan. 'You're thinking about *mostly* human, aren't you?'

'Do you blame me?' she said. 'Come on, were you tall? Short?'

'I was short. Skinny. Really weak.'

She so didn't believe him. 'So you weren't that much use to the nuns then, were you? Digging in the garden for them. How on earth did you cart that stuff to the front line?'

'Zelie –'

'I'm not stupid, Tamás.'

'I know that,' he sighed. 'It's close, but I'm not there yet. But when I am, I'm leaving. I have to get out of here completely. I will live, no future, no care. I do not want anything else. You will not see me.'

'But how'll I know you're okay?' And how would he know she was okay? Or did he not *care*?

'Tamás?'

He didn't – answer or care. Her anger boiled over at his selfishness.

She grabbed the amulet in her hand, wishing she was mean enough to punish him, to let it hang in the air, not touching her skin for a few seconds. But she was too soft to do even that. All she managed was a pitiful challenge that sounded *too* pathetic.

'You won't even send me a postcard, will you?'

CHAPTER TWELVE

IN THE MORNING Luke looked like he'd hardly slept. Zelie knew the feeling. His eyes flashed the code, miserable and defiant. She hid her grump and went to strip his bed.

'I've got the morning shift up at the park,' she said to her father, who appeared once she'd sorted Luke's stuff. It would be good going to work today because it would keep her busy and not thinking about Tamás and worrying. 'Then I'm going to the school ball tonight.'

Her father actually looked up from his papers at that. 'You are?'

'Yes.' She stole Luke's toast and busily chewed to forestall any other questions as she walked out of the house.

Not that there were any.

The weather had turned. Low, heavy clouds threatened to dump rain or snow or buckets of both. She worked at the skate-hire desk: a steady stream of customers wanted skates, then skates of a different size, then help with their laces, then different sizes again. Music played loud over the rink and she hummed along, occupying her mind with lyrics and her hands with the demands of wind-bitten, excited tourists.

She wasn't talking to Tamás, or thinking about him. Too mad about his careless 'I'll be straight outta here' attitude.

Otis texted to tell her what time he'd pick her up. As soon as she replied she had a panic-attack moment. She'd been stupid to agree to go. How was she going to cope with an evening with him? With all of them? She barely knew him and now she had hours of close company to get through. She'd forgotten how to do small talk and easy social stuff. Just to prove the point, her almost-always-silent phone rang.

'How are you feeling?'

'Kate?' Zelie felt cold, despite the small heater blasting her feet under the counter. 'How did you get my number?'

'Just because you're immune to my psycho-stare, doesn't mean others are.'

Zelie's stomach churned. Kate sounded so damn smug. Who had she been messing with? Not Luke?

'What do you want?'

'You need to be careful. I'm stronger, Zelie. Much, much stronger.'

Yeah, well that wasn't a cause for celebration. 'Bully for you.' Zelie jabbed her phone off and shoved it in her pocket. Had that warning been about the upcoming split from Tamás, or a direct threat from Kate herself?

Another face appeared at the skate-hire queue and she had to go get on with it. But the butterflies fluttered faster and faster in her stomach like they were doing a mad dance to the death. She jogged home, feeling the temperature dropping quickly as she went down the hill. There was going to be snow for sure, the clouds had that lavender look in the grey.

She ran a deep bubble bath to warm up and relax. Nerves gave way to another kind of anticipation as she slipped free of her clothes, keeping her eyes on the patterned frieze near the ceiling.

There was no halting her thoughts of him.

Submerged in the water, she squeezed liquid soap onto her hand, lathering it into a silky-soft froth. She glided her fingers down her leg.

Her diaphragm spasmed – like a fist had clenched around it and twisted. She felt his tension rise in a sharp surge of what she guessed to be annoyance.

Too bad, she wasn't going to the ball with stubble on her legs.

She picked up the razor and concentrated. The only sound was the occasional drip of water as she ran her fingers down to soap, scrape then rinse her now-smooth skin. Steam hung in the room. She was vitally aware of her every movement.

From Tamás there was nothing but silence.

In her room, she sat in her robe and twisted her damp hair into several plaits so she'd get a curly effect later. Every other girl in class probably had an appointment with the hairdresser, but she was going with a cheap stage-school trick. She did have straightening irons but sleek wouldn't suit the dress, it had to be loosely curled and soft – that whole woodland nymph look would suit the flowers.

As she waited for her hair to dry she opened up the toiletries bag sitting on the back of her chest of drawers. She didn't wear much make-up but this was a special occasion, and she had a collection of free samples from magazines bought eons ago – back when she'd lived in Britain and been a normal teen with friends and a social calendar and a mum who'd laughed and encouraged her.

She massaged sweet-smelling moisturiser into her arms and hands, legs and feet. Then pulled her chair up to the mahogany mirror and carefully painted her toenails. She blew on them so they wouldn't smudge. She swore she heard a disgruntled sigh and couldn't help a small flash of satisfaction. She slipped on the pretty silver sandals and did up the straps.

Then she slid closer to the mirror and carefully applied make-up, determined to ignore the fact that she had a guy watching her every move, determined to stall her sick nerves. But if she was honest, which given the situation she refused to be, she'd admit she was taking her time deliberately to annoy him.

'You still with me, Tamás?' she asked as she slowly brushed mascara on her lashes.

Nothing. But she felt him – his rising irritation. The sensations were stronger now, tumbling through her, harder to control, unpredictable. She felt them as if they were her own. It was like getting a double whammy of hormones and impulses. One moment she wanted to giggle like a loon, the next weep over the agony of the world's failings.

She was definitely heading for a smash. Her heart raced as anger collided with anticipation. He wanted to seize control, she could feel how badly he wanted that. Yet he didn't. She didn't even have to fight him, she could feel his own self-control holding him rigid within her.

She undid the now-dry plaits and shook them out. She twisted a few locks up at the front, left some wisping down. Finally she reached for the dress. She'd hung it in the bathroom so the creases would fall out in the steam. She turned away from the mirror and dropped her robe. She almost pulled her arms out of her sockets in a way that a circus contortionist would envy, but finally she got the zip done up. Only then did she turn back and look in the mirror.

'What do you think?' she couldn't resist asking.

Then she waited. And waited.

Of course, why should she have expected a reply? He was back to the grumpy guy of the beginning.

'Tamás?' She gazed at her reflection, put her hands up by her eyes like blinkers so he couldn't focus on anything but her, and started counting.

She'd got to four hundred and three when he finally answered. 'You look nice.'

That was it? A lukewarm compliment in a heavier than usual accent? She turned her back on her reflection. Stupidly hurt.

'All right. You look beautiful. Is that what you wanted to hear?'

'What girl doesn't want to hear she looks beautiful when she's going to her school dance?' she said huskily.

'You don't need to hear it from me.'

Yes she did. His opinion mattered as much as anyone's. Maybe more than anyone's. Her heart thumped and she swallowed, trying to stop those thoughts.

She was nervous, that was all. That's why she had this crazy pulse going and this over-alert mind. She picked up the silver evening bag she'd found in the bottom of her mother's treasure box and tucked her mobile and lipstick into it. She glanced at the time and peered out the window just as Otis's car pulled up outside.

Now her nerves stretched unbearably. Not because of Otis or Tamás, but because of her father. She had no hope of getting out of the house without him seeing her. Slowly she went down the stairs, her shoes tapping out her entrance.

Luke, bless him, had already opened the front door, and Otis stepped through into the hallway at the same time that her dad walked out of the lounge.

Otis just stared at her. Luke turned and stared too – both round-eyed. But Zelie could only look at her father.

His face whitened. She was sure he winced. But he said nothing as he gazed down at her dress and back up again.

Her heart shrivelled. There wasn't condemnation in his eyes, but a controlled blankness that hurt more than if he'd yelled at her.

She wished that just for once he'd tell her how he felt, whether he minded her wearing the dress or whether he thought she looked nice in it. Why couldn't he care for her? She was his daughter, Luke his son.

But all he had room for was his grief.

She lifted her chin and went down the last two steps to meet Otis.

'Wow.' Otis, the super-cool, was actually blushing. 'You look amazing.' He held out a dainty ribboned white rosebud. 'I wasn't sure what colour you were wearing, so I went with simple.'

'Thank you.' Touched, she pinned it at the point where her shoulder strap met the material on the front of her dress. 'It's beautiful.'

'Not as beautiful as you.'

It was the same word Tamás had used, only this time delivered with sincerity. She looked up to meet his eyes, determined to forget about Tamás tonight.

Otis looked pretty wow himself in the tuxedo, his rugby-broad shoulders emphasised by a few sparkles where snowflakes had melted into droplets that now caught the light. His eyes were sparkling too.

Through the open doorway she saw snow falling lightly. Good thing the ball was at one of the hotels right here in Tekapo and not thirty minutes away in the school hall. For once it was the other students who had to drive a distance. The school had put buses on so they'd be fine to get home or they'd stay in the hotel, but Zelie would be able to get home no matter what the weather.

She lifted her jacket from the hook and put it round her shoulders.

Otis put his hand on her waist, warm and heavy. A chill zipped down Zelie's spine. Startled, she felt an urge to step away, but didn't want to be rude.

Yet something didn't feel quite right. Something more than nerves. She turned and glanced again at her father. He still hadn't said a thing. Still pale, he stared back, looking at her like she was a stranger. Which she figured she was.

Otis cleared his throat. 'I'm used to driving in these conditions, Dr Taylor. I'll take good care.'

Her father jerked his head. Maybe it was a nod, maybe it was some uncontrollable sign of the anger Zelie assumed he must be feeling. Defiantly Zelie lifted her chin. Why shouldn't she wear her mother's dress? Her mum would have wanted her to. Zelie longed for just a hint of approval.

There wasn't any.

Tamás too was silent. She cleared her throat, hoping to spur him into saying something – anything – she didn't care how joking or sarcastic. But there was nothing from him either.

Otis held the door for her. 'Don't be nervous,' he murmured in her ear.

She shivered as she walked outside. Was it that obvious?

'You'll get to know everyone better,' he said encouragingly as they went down the path, a concerned look in his eyes as if he'd felt the frosty atmosphere in her house. 'They're really all right once you get to know them.'

'I know.' But her nerves worsened.

She looked at her reflection in the car window as she bent to get in. She wished Tamás would say something. Anything to calm her somersaulting stomach. Hyper-aware of being alone with Otis, as his *date*, the insanity of the situation hit. What if he expected something from her? What if he made a move? She was never going to kiss Otis Hayes while Tamás was in her head. And with him in her head, she didn't want to kiss Otis anyway.

Far, far too late she realised she'd rather stay home and watch flicks with Tamás than go out and look at Otis and try to mingle with a hundred others.

She didn't want to go at all. She wanted to go back into her room and continue to hibernate.

'When the butterfly gets the right signals, it starts to come out of diapause,' Tamás suddenly said. 'It goes through a period of quiescence – a quiet time, waiting, reflecting, while its strength builds and it begins to grow. Then it flies.' A thread of iron underlaid the gentle way he was speaking.

Zelie didn't want to fly. She wasn't a butterfly. She was just a stupid messed-up fool.

'You'll have a good time,' he added. 'Just relax.'

That American talk-show kind of banality was the last thing she wanted to hear from Tamás. He wanted her to go out with Otis? He didn't want her to stay home and be alone with him?

'Are we meeting your friends there?' she asked Otis as he got into the driver's seat.

'Yeah. I thought you'd prefer that,' he smiled. 'You don't need to feel shy, they all like you.'

Well, they probably only liked her because Otis had singled her out. Until that had happened they'd been pretty uninterested. Mind you, she'd made zero effort too.

'I'm really glad you're coming,' Otis added. 'I wasn't sure you would. I wanted to ask you over a week ago but didn't think I had a chance.'

'Really? I didn't know.'

She'd thought she was invisible.

'I know,' Otis laughed. 'You're pretty much in your own world.'

Okay, so that was true, but it wasn't something she could explain.

It was only a few minutes' drive to the posh hotel on the main street of Tekapo that was the venue. There were a couple of buses already parked outside, meaning most of the others would have arrived already.

They entered the lobby. Mr Webb was there, supervising the coat collection and checking people weren't smuggling in contraband drinks. Otis took her jacket and joined the short queue.

'Nice to see you here tonight, Zelie,' Mr Webb nodded at her.

'Thanks,' she mumbled, feeling terrified.

She smiled as Otis stepped back, envying his casual ease as he greeted their teacher, before he pressed a guiding hand on her waist again.

She sucked up courage as they walked into the ballroom. She blinked, it looked amazing. It was a supernova theme and there were a ridiculous number of mirror balls and small mirrored decorations hanging everywhere, creating tiny rectangles of star-light all over the walls.

The girls in Otis's circle were key players in the ball committee so she knew to enthuse to them — and it was easy.

'It looks amazing. You've done a fantastic job.' Zelie smiled at Ella when she and Otis got to the prime table.

Ella's glance skittered over Zelie's dress, checking out her shoes. 'Is that a vintage dress?'

'Yes.' Designed and made by her mum a couple of decades ago.

'It's cool.' Ella smiled her approval.

'Thanks. I really like yours too.' Zelie danced some more in the flattery-will-gain-you-friends game. But the butterflies in her stomach flew more frantically. She *was* the only one who hadn't had her hair done by a professional hairdresser and that was why they were all staring at her. And what on earth was she going to talk about with them all night?

'Come on. Come and dance with me.' Otis took her embarrassingly clammy hand.

She nearly stumbled as she walked with him onto the floor, conscious of the entire senior school watching them. She wanted to hide. She hardly knew Otis and she had too much else going on to be able to deal with it. Coming here had been a massive mistake. Her breathing quickened, she couldn't seem to get enough oxygen to her lungs and the lights made her giddy.

'Relax, Zelie. Just have a good time. At least it's your sort of rubbish music.'

Tamás. She drew another ragged breath – but a deeper one. Just hearing his voice grounded her.

'You should be feeling sorry for me,' Tamás said fauxmournfully. 'It's my first ever ball and I have to dance with a man. And yes, I know that's fine in today's society, but personally I'd prefer a woman.'

Zelie chuckled, the tightness in her lungs easing.

'Just enjoy it.'

She was now that he was teasing her again. She pushed the strap of her pretty bag up her elbow so it hung out of the way as she moved into Otis's arms.

She stared up into Otis's brown eyes, smiling to herself. *Take that, Tamás . . .*

'Don't think I'm looking at him. I'm focusing on the girl in red behind his shoulder,' Tamás said calmly.

She choked on a giggle. And he wasn't that focused on the red dress; the amulet wasn't getting hotter at all. Not like it had that time he'd focused that way on *her.*

'What's so funny?' Otis tilted his head to one side to study her.

'Nothing.'

'You're doing it again.' Otis pulled her a bit closer.

'Doing what?' Zelie tried to keep her attention on him, but all her hearing was attuned to Tamás, waiting for his next words.

'Going off to Planet Zelie.' Otis's hand splayed heavily on her back. 'What goes on in your head?'

'If only he knew,' Tamás drawled, his accent thicker than usual.

Zelie bit her lip. *Be quiet, Tamás.* Even though she wanted to hear him so much.

But suddenly Tamás was in a challenging mood. 'I do not want to be quiet any more.'

With his words came a stirring inside, like a lick of electricity had hit her muscles, preparing them for action. Adrenalin surged, as if she was at the start line of a race.

'You get this look on your face,' Otis said in her ear. 'Like you're enjoying some secret joke. Like there's something the rest of us don't get. Totally Mona Lisa.' His fingers tightened on her skin. 'You're secretive, Zelie. And you don't want to participate. Why? Are you too good for us?'

'No.' She tilted her head back to look in his face, shocked he'd even think that.

'Then what is it?'

She wanted to pull away from him but felt bad for being so mentally absent and for making it so obvious. 'You were right before. I am shy. It's like I forgot how to do . . . all this.' She waved at the others surrounding them. 'It seems so easy for everyone else.'

Otis laughed, but it didn't lighten her worry load.

'It's not easy for anyone. It just takes practice.' The cheeky smile lifted one half of Otis's mouth. 'You should practise saying yes.'

'You think?'

'Uh huh. I challenge you to say yes three times tonight.'

'Oh that's – how do you say in the movies? A smooth line,' Tamás chimed in, ultra-sarcastic.

'It's going to depend on what the questions are, Otis,' Zelie said seriously. This was turning into a nightmare. Was he starting his Big O moves? With Tamás as commentator, and her a passive participant?

'You are not passive,' Tamás said. 'You cannot be. No matter how hard you try.'

Yeah, now she knew for sure he could read her thoughts. He could access *everything* inside her. Suddenly her pleasure at hearing him faded. Instead it infuriated her; *he* infuriated her.

'Uh oh,' Otis bent to look her in the face. 'I've lost you again. Your attention's gone.'

'I'm sorry,' she said, her anger growing. 'You're right, I was thinking of something else.'

Talking to Tamás wasn't fair on Otis. She should be having a ball with him – literally. And Tamás was right. She wasn't passive. Not any more. So she looked up at the tall, handsome boy who was here in front of her, who *wanted* to be with her. Otis. She was here with him, she'd tune into him, *not* Tamás. Not when he was so desperate to be freed from her, so reluctant to pay her even the slightest compliment. All her earlier anger returned as she thought of his lack of interest and his intention to leave without ever saying goodbye. That hurt. She smiled up at Otis, resolving to forget her internal intruder for the rest of the evening and not, definitely *not*, think anything personal. Especially not about *him*.

Otis smiled back with that open, warm look. 'It's okay. You're back with me now.' He pulled her closer in his arms, his gaze dropping to her mouth, then her neck. 'You always wear this. Does it have a picture of your mother inside?' The backs of his fingers grazed her neck as he touched the chain.

She felt a rush of cold air, like it wasn't a thin silver chain but a thick wool scarf that had been lifted from her. She panicked, quickly putting up her hand to push the pendant back into place.

She couldn't. The chain slid through Otis's fingers. He smiled, asking the simplest of questions that she didn't have time to listen to or answer. She had to stop it from leaving her skin.

But time went wacko. She tried to get her hand to the amulet, but it was moving so fast and her body was so slow. She heard a snap, but it was such a slight sound she didn't register what it was. It was slipping before she realised the truth. She looked down, bending forwards, but it slipped faster, further. Everything else blurred as her gaze followed the falling edge of silver. Further, further, further away from her hand. She couldn't move fast enough. She reached but she couldn't catch it. Suddenly she couldn't see it. Her other hand pressed wide against the material of her dress. The pale green floated on the edges of her vision as she frantically twisted and turned beneath the blinding prisms of light.

It was too late.

The pendant fell to the floor.

CHAPTER THIRTEEN

SHE DIDN'T HEAR the thud but she saw the metal hit the polished wooden floor and skitter across it.

'No!' Zelie barged between the couple dancing near her, searching in the darkness, frustrated by the mirror balls that revolved above her, offering only small patches of light that disappeared as soon as they landed.

'Tamás? Tamás!' In her head she called over and over.

Finally she saw it and crashed down on her knees between the legs of gyrating students.

'No,' she whispered, her throat as hoarse and sore as if she'd been screaming for hours.

Shaking, she snatched it up. It was neither hot nor cold. She rubbed it between her hands, trying to get it back to the almost-comfortable temperature it had been when it last hung around her neck.

'Oh man, sorry.' Otis crouched down beside her. The chain hung from his fingers – or part of it did.

'It just came apart in my hand.'

The music was a noise in her ears, and so was whatever Otis was saying. All the noise blanked out the thing she wanted to hear most. Holding the amulet in a clenched fist, her other hand wrapped around that, she strained to listen, to clear the fog that rolled in from every direction.

The burn mark on her chest had stopped hurting. There was nothing to hurt. Nothing to hear. Nothing to feel any more.

And that's when she knew – when she admitted the truth she'd been too scared and too embarrassed to face.

Tamás hadn't just been inside her head, but her heart too.

'Tamás?' Her lips moved but his name sounded only inside her – and echoed around those now-empty chambers.

He was gone.

Otis held the chain out to her but she ignored it. She stood, trying to break through the waves of panic so she could think. She had to think. He couldn't have gone. It had only been seconds.

But the chain had snapped. The pendant had lost touch with her skin and Tamás had been torn from her.

She uncurled her fingers. It hurt, but she had to see it. She stared at the amulet in the palm of her hand. A grey, lifeless lump of metal. Battered and tarnished. Damaged beyond repair. It might as well have been dust – like how life eventually crumbled to nothing.

'No!' she shrieked silently. 'No!'

'Zelie?'

She heard a voice at a distance. But it wasn't the voice she wanted.

'Zelie, I'm sorry.'

She gazed around the room, vaguely seeing the other students, the concern on Otis's face, Mr Webb suddenly walking towards her, looking even more worried.

None of that mattered.

She ran faster than she'd ever run in her life. Through the people, not seeing faces, only enough detail to dodge bodies on her way to the door. Outside was bitterly cold but she didn't care. She just needed to get beneath the black night sky. And once out there she had to get far enough away from the pain. So she ran and ran. Turning down the nearest street, heading into the darkness.

'Tamás?' She couldn't say his name any more for panting so hard. She stopped, took the deepest breath she could then screamed at the top of her lungs, 'Tamás!'

She circled around on the spot, straining her eyes in the gloom, hoping to see him, to see any kind of movement. But there was nothing but the steadily falling snow. The trees stood like giants, motionless black shadows that offered no help. There was nothing and no one who could help.

There was only the ringing silence.

Her breathing roughened, became louder as panic exploded through her. He hadn't been ready. Yes, he was stronger, but he hadn't been ready. She knew that. He'd *told* her that. That meant he must have died. She'd been supposed to protect him and he'd died. She'd failed. Again.

Immense pain flooded her. Like a vital organ had been ripped from her body without anaesthetic. She couldn't believe it. Couldn't understand it.

How had the chain broken so easily? It had been so strong. She'd tried to break it herself and couldn't. The magic must have been destroyed. But how? Why?

She held her hand against her breast, pushing the pendant harder into her palm. But no longer could she warm it. She didn't know how to bring him back.

There was only one person who might be able to help. She fumbled with the clasp on the small bag, finally pulling her mobile free. In the dark the screen glowed a cold blue. She selected the contact and touched it to connect. Waited, waited as it rang. It wasn't that late, surely she'd still be awake.

'Hello?'

'Kate?' Zelie whirled on the spot, shutting her eyes to listen better despite the blackness of night surrounding her.

'Zelie? What's wrong?'

The tears slipped beneath her lids and she could hardly talk.

'It's broken. The chain is broken. I can't hear him any more.'

'What?'

'He's gone.'

'Where are you?'

Kate's cold precision penetrated Zelie's emotional fog. She focused harder.

'Zelie?' Kate didn't sound panicked. Kate sounded calm. 'Where are you?' Too calm.

Zelie looked back up the darkened road to the distant lights of the hotel. She couldn't be seen from there, the weak town lights didn't reach far enough. It was deliberate so they didn't create light pollution for the observatory. This was the darkest night spot in the country. And while the stars often appeared in their millions overhead, tonight the clouds blocked all of them and the moon.

There was nothing but darkness.

Zelie's intuition spiked, a warning. Could she trust Kate?

No. Tamás never had. Tamás had said Kate was dangerous. And

Zelie trusted Tamás more than she trusted anyone. Maybe that was crazy, but he'd made her a promise and he'd kept it. He'd not hurt her. More than that, he'd actually cared for her. She *knew* he had.

She'd felt it.

So Zelie would keep her promise too. She'd stay away from Kate.

'Sorry . . .' Zelie waved the phone backwards and forwards in front of her mouth to create a distancing effect. 'You're breaking up. I can't hear y—'

She cut the connection and switched her phone off so it would go straight to voicemail. Now she knew. She should have thought of it before. It had all started with Kate at the lake. Later he'd heard the water, the freezing, deathly water. It was so obvious.

She had to get there now. Before Kate did.

She raced, kicking herself for dawdling so long and not having thought of it sooner. She ran and ran. Her lungs screamed as the exertion twisted sharp hot pain into them. The air burned despite the snow and cold and dark. She stumbled, her ankles twisting over the large rocks. Her stupid dainty dancing shoes were useless as she hit the stones, the heels too flimsy for her to maintain any speed, the soles too slippery. But she pushed herself on, driven by the need to get down to the water before Kate Hearn.

She could make it out ahead of her. Hear the soft lapping of the waves. A liquid pit, blacker than ink. She knew the dangers. Many boaties had drowned in the vast lake. Once a body went in, it was months before it was found – if ever. Too cold to fight for life, people sank like stones into the murky depths.

'Where are you? Where are you?' Maybe she muttered. Maybe she just thought it over and over. She didn't know, but her throat was tight and sore.

He had to be there. He had to be.

She scrabbled, slipped and put her hands forwards to break her twentieth stumble, scraping the skin up the side of her wrist. She forced herself back up and kept moving. Every breath took her forwards, a step closer, until finally she was right near the edge.

She nearly fell over the lump. She went down again, hands reaching out. Touching something – some*one*.

'Tamás?'

The black shape was a creature of some kind. She reached out to touch it again – the instinct to help overriding her terror. Even if it wasn't him, it was someone who sure as hell needed her this minute.

And this time, *this time*, she couldn't fail.

It had to be Tamás. Maybe it was hope or wishful thinking, but suddenly she was sure. She found his hand – her own fingers shook – but his were still and freezing. Gingerly she slid her hand up his arm. His skin was bare. She put both hands on him, brushing away the layer of snow, trying to feel for life, blinking to force her eyes to adjust so she could see more. Remnants of a shirt or something like it covered parts of his chest. His trousers were ripped below the knee on one leg. He was half curled on his side and shallow waves washed over his feet and legs. He'd hauled himself only far enough to clear his face from the water before collapsing.

Was he breathing? She touched the tips of her fingers to the inside of his wrist. Repelled by the slimy stuff that seemed to cover parts of him, she made herself hold on as she tried to feel his pulse. She bent her head close, blocking out the raging of the wind in her ears and the beat of her own blood.

There. It throbbed. Faint, but steady. Regular.

Compelled to check further, she lifted her other hand and spread it wide on his cold chest. Beneath her palm she could feel it, the sluggish thudding of his heart.

She willed the contact to have some kind of power. Wished that somehow the touch could transfer some of her life force to him. He had to stay alive.

His sudden tremor brought her back to reality.

What was she doing just sitting here? Hurry. She had to hurry. 'Just a few more minutes,' she muttered. A few more minutes.

She couldn't possibly move him on her own. She had to go for help. And fast.

Kate's family lived further round the lake. It was quite a drive but one she was sure they were breaking the speed limit on now.

She wiped the slimy gloop from his wrist onto her skirt. The stuff was weirdly thick and made her fingers tingle. With dry fingers she was able to undo the buckles on the straps of her sandals and kick them off. She'd be faster in bare feet. Then she twisted to undo her zip. She couldn't reach it. It had been hard enough to do it up. Now she had neither the time nor patience.

She ripped it, shaking with the effort it took to pull the seams apart enough to wriggle it down over her hips. She shook it out and spread the skirt wide to protect as much of his skin from the snow and wind as she could. It didn't make much of a blanket but it was better than the nothing he had now. As she lifted her hand away she felt something hard and moved to check, finding a strap looped over his shoulder. She followed it down, and half wedged beneath him was a canvas bag.

She didn't stop to open it, or to think. She lifted the strap off his shoulder and tugged it down his arm, rolling him just enough to get the bag free. She'd take it with her now. That at least she could keep safe for him.

She paused for a final half second, carefully touching his forehead.

'Hold on, Tamás,' she begged.

CHAPTER FOURTEEN

SHE TRIPPED BACK over the rocks. Feet slipping, the stitch searing. She pushed past it, dredging an impossible last scrap of energy to strike out, step after step. Barefoot, wearing only bra and knickers, all but blinded by snow and tears and the darkness of a moonless, starless night. She ran through the trees to her father's house, the pale snow on the path guiding her.

She had to hurry. Faster, faster, faster. She chanted in her head, pushing herself even though she knew she was slowing. But he was barely alive and his only chance lay with her. So she had to keep running.

The bag was heavy and banged hard against her thigh. She no longer felt her feet or her lungs, no longer heard her own mantra – only the bang, bang, bang of the bag.

Finally she got to the footpath, tried to push her leaden limbs on the smooth, snow-cleared, cold concrete. The lights of the clinic were on – dazzling safety. She got to the gate, wanted to scream for help but could barely breathe.

'Zelie? Are you okay?'

Zelie whirled. Otis was a few metres past the gate, looking like a ghost under the pale glow of the streetlight, his mouth open as he stared at her.

'What's happened?'

'I have to get my father.' Her mouth moved but whether there was sound she didn't know. She just had to get there. Only a few paces more to the door.

Otis ran towards her, his voice rising as his questions hurtled. 'Where's your dress? You're bleeding.' He swore. His hand reached out and grabbed her by the arm, stopping her desperate steps.

She tried to pull free but he tightened his fingers. 'Otis, I have to –'

The door opened and she turned towards the bright light and the tall silhouette in the middle of it. 'Dad. Dad!' He had to help her. 'Dad, please.'

'Zelie, what the hell is going on?' The gasp was unlike anything she'd heard from him. He stormed down the stairs.

'You have to come with me,' she puffed. 'You have to help me.'

Otis looked at her father, his hand dropping from her arm. 'Sir, I promise –'

'There isn't time to waste,' she interrupted as she lobbed her and Tamás's bags into the hallway behind her father. 'You have to come now. *Both* of you.' Zelie turned and ran back the way she'd come. No point getting the car, the only way to get to him was by foot.

'Zelie!'

They both shouted after her but she didn't stop. She couldn't stop, worried that if she did she wouldn't be able to start again. And she had to get back to him, to save him.

Otis was faster than her father. 'What's happened?' he shouted as he sprinted alongside her. He reached for her again but she put on an extra spurt. 'Zelie, I'm really sorry.'

'It doesn't matter. I need your help. We have to hurry.'

'Hurry where?'

'The lake,' she gasped, the numbness gone from her feet now, shooting pains making her hobble. 'He's by the lake.'

She couldn't talk any more. She just had to lead the way. She could hear the heavy feet and heavier breathing of her father behind them.

'Zelie, what's this all about?' he called out after her.

She didn't have time to explain, she just had to get back there before Kate and her family arrived. Before he got too cold.

It was eerily quiet now. The wind had dropped. The silent darkness terrified her. Her head hurt as she jolted up and down over the rocks, her face screwed up as every step hurt. Her heart clogged her throat. What if she couldn't find him again? What if she was too late?

But up ahead her dress was a shade paler in the blackness, like the patches of snow that settled on the tops of dark rocks. The white rose that Otis had given her decorated Tamás's shoulder now. She flung herself forwards over the last few feet, skidding over the stones to land on her skinned knees beside him.

He was there. Still alone. Untouched.

'Oh my God.' Otis crouched down beside her for the second time that night.

She should have thought to bring a torch. But just as she regretted not having one, a light appeared, pinpointing the dark lashes of eyes that were closed. She looked up, stunned.

'Maglite on the end of my key ring,' Otis explained shortly. 'Who's this?'

The circle of light was only coin-sized but it emphasised the paleness of Tamás's skin, its dampness and seeming lifelessness.

Already there was a dusting of snow over the dress that covered him. It was falling thicker as they stood. With no wind and no rain, the steady, heavy fall of snow came straight down, blanketing the world in the purest white.

Lethal.

Her father got to them and swore, something he never usually did in front of her.

'You have to help him, Dad. I think he's been in the lake.'

The rocks bruised her knees and the soles of her feet screamed. The distraction irritated her. Her damn feet didn't matter. Tamás mattered. She watched her father checking his vitals. She daren't ask the question.

'We need to get him to the clinic quickly,' he said shortly.

Still alive then. He was still alive.

The exhilaration gave her strained muscles a much-needed boost. They were in time. They could save him.

'I can't tell if there's a head trauma but we'll just have to carry him without a stretcher.' Her father stood. 'We have to get him warm if we're going to save him and we don't have time to wait for help.' He looked up at the sky. 'There'll be no reinforcements in this weather anyway. We'll just have to do our best. It's that or nothing.'

Revitalised, Zelie stood.

'Zelie, you hold his head steady while I get a grip under his shoulders. Otis, you take his legs.'

Zelie nodded.

'Put my jacket on.' Otis stripped it off as he prepared to help her father.

There was no time for a polite argument about it. She couldn't say no anyway, her teeth were chattering too much. It was warm and smelt of aftershave. She took his torch. 'Thanks.'

He went forwards to listen to her father's instructions.

'Good thing you're here,' Her father looked at Otis. 'You look strong.'

Otis nodded.

But trying to get a grip on a half-naked youth who was dripping wet in the middle of a snowstorm wasn't easy. Especially one with splodges of slime over him.

Her father grunted as he took the bulk of the weight, his feet slipping on the wet rocks. 'Hold the torch steady, Zelie, we need more light.'

Tamás was taller and broader than she'd expected – more man than boy. They started moving as soon as they had him. She slipped as she led the way, using the torch to light a small path as she talked, guiding them over the rocks. Both Otis and her father were puffing heavily, grunting as they carried the burden. They moved a bit faster as they hit the snow-covered grass but not by much because they were tiring as they trudged up the slope. But they were both determined, and sooner than Zelie had dared hope they got to the path.

Headlights lit up the trees down by the lake, the heavy wheels of a four-wheel drive crunching on the gravel car park. Snow chains rattled. The weather had hindered them too, but they were there now – the Hearns. Was one of them running to where Tamás had been lying only minutes before?

'Come on.' Zelie tried not to let the panic show in her voice. They needed to get him inside, away from the eyes of strangers – especially those dangerous ones. He had to be kept safe. He had to get well.

Zelie darted ahead as the clinic came into view, opening the door for them. She pushed the button on the heater, turning it up to full. Both Otis and her father were sweating but the body they were carrying was horribly blue.

Zelie guided his head as they laid him down on the narrow bed. Her father glowered as he whisked her mother's dress from where it half covered Tamás's body. But then he turned and reached for a towel, started rubbing over Tamás's chest with it.

'Get those clothes off him, Zelie. There are scissors on the trolley. Otis, there are heat blankets in the cupboard. Find them.'

Zelie got the scissors, her hands shaking as she tried to snip through the soggy fabric. It was impossible. In the end she just ripped it as she had her dress, tossing it from his body to the floor where the dress already lay crumpled.

'You'll have to help me, Zelie,' her father said. 'Keep this up for a moment.'

She took the towel he gave her, copying the circular motions her father had been making on Tamás's chest while he wrapped the blankets around their patient's lower half.

Then he reached for his phone. 'Damn this storm. I don't think the road will be open.'

With the snow falling heavier, the helicopter wouldn't be coming out either.

'We have to get him warm,' Zelie said. That had always been the problem. He'd had to warm up.

'Marion? I need you here asap, there's an emergency,' her father barked into the phone while pulling on gloves. 'Hypothermia.'

Zelie didn't dare stop and look at Tamás. Didn't want to be distracted, just had to focus on the job of rubbing, rubbing, rubbing. But when her father began putting in a needle for an IV line she stood back for a half moment and looked at the dark head on the pillow – at his pale face.

'Who is he?' her father finally had a chance to ask. 'What's his name?'

'Tamás. I think his name is Tamás.' Unless he was some tourist who'd drunk too much down by the lake and been robbed or something, but that was so unlikely. In her bones she was certain. Besides, his trousers weren't exactly the height of fashion and they'd been falling apart. Ancient.

It was him. With thick black hair and long dark lashes, cheekbones and jaw all masculine angles – and yet vulnerable, with a soft-looking mouth that was frighteningly colourless.

'Where's he from?' her father asked.

Zelie shook her head. 'I'm not sure.'

'We'll have to call the police.' Her father tapped the IV line.

'You need to get him well first,' said Zelie.

She glanced at Otis, who was standing in the back of the room, almost as pale as Tamás as he watched.

The front door opened. Marion, her father's nurse, flustered in. 'Who is it? What's happened?' She frowned as she looked at Tamás, immediately going to the sink to scrub her hands.

'You two out of here now.' Her father snapped back into professional mode. 'Go and get dry. Shower and get dressed, Zelie.'

She didn't want to leave but she recognised her father's expression – serious and concerned. 'Okay.' She'd get warm and come straight back.

Otis opened the door and she went through it. He followed her and she turned to face him in the hallway, but couldn't look him in the eye.

'Are you all right?' she asked, her mind still on that motionless body in her father's room.

'Fine.' He blew out a big breath. 'Why didn't you answer your phone?'

Phone? It took a moment for Zelie to shift gear. Of course, she'd switched it off after talking to Kate. And down at the lake she hadn't even thought of phoning her father for help. She'd just run. She'd had to act, couldn't have stood still and waited for help to come to her. Maybe that would have been better. But it was too late now. Besides, she'd got Tamás to the surgery before Kate and her family had arrived. Her nerves prickled. She needed to get back to Tamás.

'It wasn't working,' she said briefly. 'Otis, I'm really sorry for ruining your night.'

'Do you know that guy?'

'No. Sort of.' She shook her head, totally couldn't look at Otis now. 'It's hard to explain.'

'But you're worried about him.'

'Of course I am.' She couldn't hide that. She glanced up for his reaction then.

He was frowning. She could see a million more questions forming, but she couldn't cope with them right now. She had to get back and find out how Tamás was.

'Look, you better go home. You're soaked too.' She had to stop Otis from asking anything more. 'I'm really sorry. Your suit is . . .'

She looked down at the soggy jacket. Her hands hovered over the button at the front but the reality of her near nudity underneath made her hesitate.

'Keep it,' he said abruptly. 'I can get it later.' He took a step closer, his gaze suddenly intense.

Zelie ducked her head to avoid him, taking a small step backwards, pushing back the wet straggle of hair that had fallen across her face.

He flicked a glance at the clinic door behind her. 'You think he'll be all right?'

'I hope so.' She more than hoped. She was at the point of offering anything – even a devil's bargain – to know he was going to be okay.

'I really should get going.' Otis stepped back too.

Now she felt bad. Otis was a nice guy. Hell, he was *normal*, born in the same decade as her, definitely alive and largely uncomplicated. But it was too late. *She* hadn't been normal for quite some time, even before Tamás had taken up residence in her.

'I'm really sorry, Otis.'

'So am I.'

She followed him as he swiftly walked to the door.

'I'll text you to find out how he is in the morning.' He was all business now.

'Of course. I'll make sure my phone's on.' She pulled a coat from the rack. 'Please put this on, Otis. I don't want you getting sick too. You're only just over a cold as it is.'

'My car is only ten metres away,' he said shortly.

'Please put it on.'

At last he looked at her again, and slowly that lopsided smile appeared – a half-strength version of it anyway. 'Okay.' But he didn't try to get closer again.

It was there between them – *Tamás* was there, as he had been all night. Only now Otis knew it.

She stood at the door and watched him jogging through the snow, the pinprick of light from his torch dancing over the path ahead of him. Then she heard the engine of that four-wheel drive again. It had pulled into a park a hundred metres down the road, but the headlights were still on. She knew who it was. They'd followed her here. It was the obvious place she'd bring him. But it was too late, right?

She'd got him inside. Surely he was safe now he was with her father. What could they possibly do?

CHAPTER FIFTEEN

ZELIE SLAMMED THE door and bolted it. She grabbed the canvas bag that lay against the wall where she'd thrown it, along with her silver one beneath. Wincing with each step, she ran up the stairs and threw both bags under her bed. She'd look at the strange canvas satchel later. First she had to check on Tamás. She raced back down to the clinic door, thankful her harried father had left it slightly ajar as she shamelessly eavesdropped.

'He's not responding.' Marion sounded scared. 'Are you sure there's no way we can get a chopper in here?'

Zelie stepped closer to the door and peered through a gap in the curtain that was pulled across the glass window. Semi-retired, Marion worked part-time doing vaccinations and wart treatments. Being called on in the middle of the night to deal with a hypothermic stranger had her looking confused and frightened.

'The storm's too severe. The roads are closed,' her father said crisply. 'We'll have to try to get him through the night.'

Zelie nudged the door open more. She had to see Tamás. But it was her father she saw first. The lines on his face were etched deeper than usual. He was working hard, his eyebrows creased into one thick line.

Tamás was hooked up to machines. Not just the saline drip but a heart and oxygen monitor that recorded vital signs, bleeping them out for all to hear. Silver thermal blankets covered his body. Marion still worked with the rubbing.

Her father's frown grew as he read the digital thermometer. 'I can't get his body temperature up.'

'You want me to phone Timaru again?' Marion asked. 'There must be some way of getting through.'

'He's too unstable to move.' Her father looked grim. The beeps on the machine grew more erratic. Then the alarm.

Zelie didn't even know she was standing in the middle of the room until her father suddenly looked up from where he was frantically bending over Tamás, defibrillator pads in hand. 'You're freezing! You go shower now,' he shouted. 'Shower. Now, Zelie.'

'No.' She stood, bloodied feet planted on the floor.

Her father didn't bother speaking again, he was too busy.

Zelie winced, her own heart stopping as he shocked Tamás's body. There was no huge convulsion, hardly any response. He looked like a corpse already.

Zelie watched her father's face as he worked. She didn't breathe. Didn't blink. She just had to believe.

Her father used the machine again. The monitoring system sounded, fusing into one long blare.

She couldn't stand it.

Then it started, a series of beeps, still irregular, but beeps. Beep after beep after beep.

'Zelie!' Her father roared.

'I'll go,' she mouthed, her vocal cords frozen.

Horrified, she turned and ran. Couldn't bear to watch any more. Was he slipping away? Tears stung as she ran up the stairs. The phone started ringing but she ignored it. Knew she had to warm up fast so she could get back down there. If his life was ending she wanted to be with him. She didn't want him to be alone – or with no one he knew. He'd been alone for so long. Wrenching the taps on she jumped into the shower, bra, knickers and all. She stripped and rubbed her skin as her father had been rubbing Tamás's, in quick circles. Anything to get warm. She ignored her stinging scrapes. Blocking the sheer panic, forcing herself to move fast, she racked her brain to try to think how to help him. Surely she could help.

Nothing warms a cold body like the heat of another.

He'd told her at the very beginning on the bus. He'd needed her warmth. Now she badly wanted to give it to him. She'd hold him close and beg him to stay with her. But it wasn't like she could go and jump in the bed with him, even though her arms ached to embrace him. Back then it had been the pendant that had needed to get warm.

The amulet.

Zelie put on the first clothes she found, yanking on her jeans and pulling the woollen jumper over her head. She didn't even register the scratchy wool straight on her skin or her lack of underwear. She hastily stuck some plasters on the worst cuts on her feet, but only to stop herself from trailing more spots of blood around the house and freaking out her father.

The phone was still ringing incessantly. She snatched up her extension. 'Hello?'

'Is he with you? Is he alive?' This time Kate sounded desperate.

'I can't talk now.' Zelie slammed the phone back down, not caring that it missed the cradle and fell on the floor.

She snatched up her silver bag from the floor and in a moment of pure terror, encountered nothing but her mobile and the silk lining. But then her fingers curled around it. Triumph surged, immediately overtaken by more adrenalin. More drive. She had to get it to him. She ran to the stairs.

'Zelie?'

She turned. Luke stood at his door looking tousled and confused.

'It's okay. Just go back to sleep. Dad has a patient,' she whispered, trying to sound calm.

'How was the ball?'

'It was great.' She put her hands on his shoulders and turned him back towards his bed. 'Go back to sleep.' She gave him a push, trying to keep it, and her voice, gentle. 'I'll tell you about it in the morning.'

Downstairs it was scarily quiet. Utterly terrified, she peered into the room. While she could see Tamás, she couldn't see either Marion or her father. But now she could hear the machine beeping with reassuring regularity.

Her muscles sagged and she slumped against the wall as relief hit. But then she heard her father's voice. He was on the phone in the small office adjoining the surgery. She could hear him saying what he'd done for Tamás already, detailing meds and procedures. He must be consulting with someone at the hospital in the city. Asking advice.

Her fear resurged. Her father was a good doctor. If he was asking for help it meant Tamás was still in serious trouble. She pushed the door open and went in. As she walked across the room she saw Marion standing at the bench drawing up syringes full of something.

Zelie ran on tiptoes to the bed, casting a scared glance to the door where her father was. He'd have a fit if he found her here, but too bad. She had to do this now before he made her leave again.

She got to Tamás's side and looked down at his dark lashes, wishing he'd open his eyes and look at her. Given the colour of his hair she guessed his eyes would probably be brown. His skin was blue at the edges – his lips, his fingertips. A tremor shook him. So violent it made her shiver in response. Then he went totally still, like the movement had taken the last of his remaining energy. She could see the network of blue veins beneath his skin at his temples and eyelids. But for once the sight of sickness didn't freak her out. He needed something. And she had it.

She took his hand, turning it palm up. Its coldness increased her fear. But she forced it down, determined that she'd not fail him. Not like she'd failed her mother. She wasn't losing him. She placed the metal into his palm, curled his fingers around it and then pressed them close with both of her hands.

She listened hard. For a moment all she could hear was her own heart, as if her mind was shielding her from the truth and the regular thumping was just wishful thinking.

But then she really heard it. The beeping of the machine growing stronger, more regular. His vital signs were improving. Yes. She exhaled harshly and kept her eyes on her hands, his clasped within them. That was what he needed. The pendant. That last part of himself. It had made all the difference.

His chest rose and fell more easily in a gentle, regular rhythm. His muscles seemed to relax. No more vicious spasms shook him.

Magic? She truly believed in it now.

She pressed his fingers more tightly, helping him hold the amulet. She'd be here for as long as it took. She didn't want to leave him, not until she was sure.

She looked up as a shadow fell over his face. She hadn't known her father had even re-entered the room. 'Sorry, Dad.'

She was sorry for a lot of things – things she'd done and things her father hadn't done.

But he was watching the machines. 'He seems to be doing better.

He's warming up but he's not clear yet.' His frown deepened as he bent to look close at Tamás's face. 'It's taken so long for any treatment to have an effect. I thought I was going to lose him.'

Zelie swallowed and looked down at the black-haired guy. He was a complete stranger, yet so important to her. Her hands gripped him tighter.

She looked up and saw her father's gaze was on her hands too – at the way she held Tamás.

'What happened tonight, Zelie?' he asked. 'The last time I see you you're off to a ball with one boy, then you come home almost naked and there's another boy half dressed on the beach using your moth—' he broke off. 'Your dress as a blanket,' he ground the last words out.

She felt the flush. 'It's not like that . . .'

'No?' He pushed a couple of buttons on the monitor.

Zelie looked at the floor, but while Tamás's shredded clothes were still there, the dress had gone.

'What did you do with it?' Zelie's eyes filled as she saw the hard expression on her father's face.

'I destroyed it,' he said coldly. 'Put it on the fire.'

Zelie clenched her teeth, trying to stop the sob from breaking free.

'You'd ruined it already,' he added.

No, *he'd* done that. Hiding it and all her other stuff away. Never talking about her. Like she'd never existed. Her mother would have wanted her to wear the dress, she'd have wanted to see her. Zelie knew it.

'I'm staying in here.' She gripped Tamás's hand tighter.

'He had this strange stuff on him.' Her father ignored her defiance, picking up a small specimen jar from the trolley beside him. He held it out for her to see.

Zelie took a quick look. The slime stuff. She remembered how the tips of her fingers had tingled when she'd touched it. 'It looks like jelly.' Jelly that some toddler had sprinkled silver glitter in, because as she looked at it in the light, she could see that it kind of glowed.

'Not any jelly I've seen.' He looked sharply at her. 'Have you seen it before?'

She shook her head.

'Where was it?' Marion asked.

'Some on his fingers, some under his nose. Maybe there was more but it might have washed off in the lake.' Her father carefully put the container back on the bench. 'I'll check it out.'

Marion walked closer, her face relaxing as she looked over Tamás. 'The heat blankets didn't seem to be making a difference but they've kicked in now. If he keeps on like this over the next few hours, then I think he's going to be okay.'

'I agree.' Zelie's father moved to the foot of the bed. 'His turnaround is remarkable. But we'll keep watching him.'

Despite the fallout with her father, Zelie couldn't help her smile spreading. Marion was smiling too.

Relief swept through her, but tiredness was the chaser. She hooked her foot around the leg of the chair next to the bed and dragged it closer so she could sit without letting him go.

'You should get some sleep, Zelie,' Marion said.

Zelie didn't answer and her father didn't say anything either. In truth none of them would be resting well tonight.

The loud knocking made her jump. Someone was at the front door.

'I'll go.' Zelie's stomach churned, threatening to send its meagre contents up in protest. But she had to face them down. She let go of Tamás and walked as fast as she could on her shredded feet before the others could beat her to it. Before she could chicken out completely.

Her hand shook as she turned the porch light back on and opened the door.

'Hi, Zelie,' Kate said coolly. 'Can we come in?'

For a moment all Zelie could do was stare. She checked Kate's feet, but she wasn't wearing high heels, yet she looked taller. And her hair? Thick, glossy. Her eyes sparkled, that shocking blue. No yellow at all in the whites. She stood with the straight-backed confidence of someone who had strength and knew it. Like she was invincible. She'd had more than a makeover, it was like she'd been genetically enhanced or rebooted or robo-rebuilt Hollywood style. This much difference in only a few hours?

She looked capable of anything.

More scary than ever.

Her two uncles stood a step back on either side of her. Big, strong men who would have no trouble tossing a couple of sheep onto their shoulders and hefting them up steep mountainsides. They'd have no trouble with a body either.

They looked like assassins.

'We know he's here,' said Kate. 'We want to help.'

Zelie didn't believe that. She blocked the slight gap in the doorway, refusing to be freaked. Their psycho-stare didn't work on her, right?

'No,' she said loudly, so she'd sound authoritative. 'You can't come in.'

Anyway, nothing awful could happen with her father and Marion here. They were witnesses.

'Zelie?' Marion bustled up behind her. 'Who is it?'

Zelie glanced behind her and saw Marion take in the Hearns on the doorstep.

'Are you all right, Kate?' Marion reached above Zelie's arm and pulled the door open wider.

'I'm fine thanks, Marion.' Kate smiled.

'Well then I'm sorry, but we're very busy –' the older woman broke off.

Zelie frowned, surprised at her sudden stop. She glanced back at Marion. The woman was standing stock-still, her head slightly cocked like she was listening to something. Except no one was speaking.

Dread soured the spit in Zelie's mouth.

Slowly, feeling shit-scared, she looked back at robo-Kate and her overgrown, mute uncles.

The three of them were staring at Marion. Kate's blue eyes shone. With the uncles either side of her, the three sets of identical, unblinking blue eyes were so bright they were almost *blinding*.

'Stop,' Zelie called sharply but they ignored her.

Marion smiled and stepped aside. The two men and Kate filed past Zelie – a triumphant smile curling Kate's ruby lips.

'Zelie, why is the door open?' Her father shouted.

They were inside. She hadn't been able to stop them. Would they sway her father's mind as well? What were they going to do to Tamás – to all of them?

'Dr Taylor.' Perma-stubble uncle stepped forwards and actually spoke. 'I'm so sorry. We heard Tamás had been brought here.'

'You know him?' her father said sternly, only briefly glancing at the uncles as he walked out of the treatment room, closing the door behind him. 'What the hell was he doing down by the lake?'

For once Zelie was glad of her father's rudeness. But Kate didn't seem interested in trying the stare on the doctor – she was too busy gazing at the treatment room door. The small curtain had been pulled back, giving them a view of the patient bed. And its occupant.

'He's here,' Kate breathed.

The two uncles swapped looks. Zelie saw Perma-stubble pump a fist. The shorter one nodded. Yeah, they were interested.

'He's not in good shape,' her father said, still checking the chart in his hands. 'Suffering exposure, hypothermia. But he's making some improvement now.' He went to the receptionist's desk and pulled out a patient enrolment form. 'He needs to rest. He hasn't regained consciousness yet so we might as well fill this in while we wait. How do you know him?'

'He's an exchange student staying with us,' the uncle said.

Zelie's jaw nearly hit the floor. *Exchange student*?

'He's over from France for a few months. He only arrived last week.'

Her father nodded, totally buying it. 'I'll put your address down then. You'll contact his parents?'

'Of course,' Perma-stubble assured him.

'He didn't pick the best night to go swimming in the lake,' Zelie's father said drily.

'It was my fault,' Kate piped up in a clear voice. 'I dared him.'

'You *what*?' Zelie's father whipped round to glare at Kate.

'I know. It was stupid.' But Kate's flush wasn't from her illness or remorse. The fever in her eyes was excitement. And greed.

'Don't you realise how close to death he is? We nearly lost him only half an hour ago,' her father launched into lecture mode. 'What a crazy thing to do, Kate. You know what it's like to be susceptible to sickness.'

'We've spoken with Kate and she'll be punished,' the uncle said quickly. 'We'll ensure it doesn't happen again.'

Kate looked down as if contrite, but Zelie still caught the pent-up energy in her body. What was it they wanted from him?

'Do you think we can go in and see him now?' the other uncle asked.

Her father still had the stern look on. 'I'll go and check. As I said he's not conscious yet and more than anything he needs to rest. But a minute shouldn't hurt so long as you stay quiet. Just wait here, would you?'

He went into the room and whisked the curtain across the door.

The three Hearns turned and stared at her. Zelie's legs trembled but she locked her knees so she wouldn't sink to the floor. She wasn't going to let them know how much they freaked her out.

Perma-stubble's mouth opened and he took a breath, about to say something.

But the door opened and her father called. 'You can come in.'

They all turned back and moved forwards, rugby-scrum style. Yeah, Tamás was much more important to them than she was.

Terrified, Zelie hobbled in behind them, standing just to the side of the door as they formed a half-circle at the end of his bed. Could they hurt him while she and her father watched? She already knew they could do damage silently.

And they were scarily quiet now. Just looking down at him, their heads bowed like they were saying their evening prayers. No sound in the room other than the soft beeps from the monitor.

Perma-stubble shifted, turning to look at Zelie's father. 'Will he be well enough to come home with us tonight?'

Kate lifted her head too, as did the other uncle. The three of them directed the psycho-stare at her father.

Too petrified to do anything more, Zelie frantically shook her head from side to side like a side-show clown. *No, no and no.*

'No.'

A wave of relief made Zelie woozy. Thank heavens her dad had said it aloud with even more conviction than she felt – impossible as that was.

'He'll be here for a few days. Really he should go into town to the hospital –'

'That's not necessary is it, Doctor?' Perma-stubble said calmly. 'He's looking pretty good.'

He was too, his colour much more normal. He was still pale, but no longer blue-tinged. Instead his face was lightly flushed, his blood obviously circulating well. Zelie's comfort level lifted as she saw it. He was going to be all right. He had the amulet and it was working. So long as these guys kept their distance he'd be able to get well and get away.

She smothered her gasp when she saw his thick dark lashes quiver and then lift. He was waking up. She willed the others not to notice. Willed him to remain still until they had gone.

But clearly she didn't have the telepathic skills Kate did, because Tamás opened his eyes wide. And incredibly, his gaze bypassed the people nearest him and arrowed straight to Zelie. She bit her lip to stop from gasping again. For his eyes weren't brown at all, but the palest, palest blue. Like the colour of ice deep in the heart of a glacier, or of the sky at its most distant edge. Pale, clear, cold. And very, very focused.

'He's awake.' Kate had noticed too.

Heads practically snapped as everyone stared at him. The entire room went still – *time* went still – as Tamás unblinkingly looked back at Zelie.

'Tamás?' Kate's shorter uncle broke the charged silence. But the tableau held. They remained still, watching, almost as if afraid of what might happen.

No one knew, Zelie realised. No one knew what he might do. And everyone was just that bit afraid. Even – what was it Kate had called them? – even the Witching.

Everyone except her father and Marion, who had no clue. 'Are you okay, Tamás?' Her father stepped forwards and touched Tamás's hand.

Tamás didn't answer, but he did blink. Zelie saw the start of a frown, but slowly his lashes drooped before he opened them again with obvious effort. This time his focus wasn't as sharp. This time he slowly looked from one face to the next and then the next. Turning his head ever so slightly to see them all standing around him. Only Zelie stood back from the semicircle.

'You've given us such a fright.' Kate pushed forwards, training her gaze on him.

The uncles fell in behind with their own no-blink, pinprick-pupilled stares.

But Tamás looked at Kate for the scarcest of seconds. No hint of recognition in his eyes. Or interest. Then he looked past her, back to Zelie.

Relief flooded her again. Warmth bathed her – as did a wave of sheer protectiveness. She was blanketed in it – hoped he was too. Now fearless, she held his gaze.

It felt like a moment of forever.

But then, like he couldn't help it, his eyes closed again.

'He's very tired.' Zelie's father frowned and felt Tamás's pulse for himself, in spite of the machine's readings. 'All this can wait till the morning.'

'Of course.' Perma-stubble turned immediately and jerked his head at the other uncle, who turned and walked too. 'We're so sorry to bother you, Doctor. We'll be back first thing to check on him.'

'I'll call you with an update,' her father said firmly. 'He'll be here a couple of days at least, so there's no need to rush back.'

The uncles swapped another look but didn't argue.

Before she moved, Kate looked around. Her gaze swept the room, lingering on the pile of rags that Zelie had cut from Tamás's body. She even ducked her head and looked under the bed, but Zelie knew the rest of the floor was clear. Her father insisted on a scrupulously clean surgical-standard clinic. Whatever Kate was looking for wasn't there.

The men had all moved into the waiting room – she heard them saying goodbye – but Zelie stayed in place near the door. She wasn't leaving the room till Kate had. She tensed as Kate passed. Because Kate wasn't looking so happy now – she looked furious.

'Where did you find him?' she snapped. 'Where by the lake?'

Zelie just stared back at her, letting Kate find out how the silent treatment worked.

'Tell me,' Kate spat.

Fear shot back into Zelie's veins – because Kate's eyes weren't just blue now. Their irises were flickering the way flames did, ripples of indigo and navy shooting in all directions over her eyeballs. So not normal or natural. So not freaking human.

Zelie breathed out when Kate finally spun and marched to the front door. Faking calm, Zelie followed her – to flick the deadbolts behind her. But just as Kate was about to walk out, Zelie decided to send her on a pointless mission in the foul weather. Who knows, maybe she'd get sick again.

So softly, she answered Kate's question. 'On the rocks near the church.'

Kate moved quickly, breaking into a run, following the two men already striding out – not to their car, but to the dark waterfront ten minutes away.

'It's raining,' Zelie said softly, but Kate was too far away to hear now. 'The rain came down heavy.'

It would have washed those stones clean. And she had his bag hidden already. There was nothing for them to find.

CHAPTER SIXTEEN

'GO AND SLEEP, Zelie.' Her father opened the door, waiting for her to move. 'He's through the worst.'

She nodded, her throat aching with unasked questions. She'd sat with Tamás for another twenty minutes after Kate left, hoping he'd wake again, but he was in a deep sleep, his body relaxed. As a result, he was only continuing to improve. The amulet rested in the palm of his hand. Zelie got a plaster from the trolley and taped it in place, ignoring her father's stare.

He needed it.

She walked up the stairs and her feet and legs screamed their protest. She went into her bedroom and glanced at the mirror. It was weird to be in here and be truly alone. Empty. She half laughed, half sobbed. She missed him. She'd never thought that would happen.

She reached under her bed, pushing aside the various items of her 'floordrobe' and got hold of the bag. The mouldy canvas was tied with tough string. She went to her desk and found scissors. She hoped it wasn't as enchanted as the necklace, or she'd be in big trouble. But the string snapped between the blades. She peeled back the crusted-shut flap, one corner tearing as she applied pressure to force it. She didn't want to put her hand inside in case whatever was in there bit her – or worse – so she tipped the bag up.

A parcel slithered out, wrapped in a kind of waterproof fabric that had yet more string tied around it. Impatient, she snipped that off and unrolled the contents, hoping this wasn't going to be like pass-the-parcel. She groaned at the sight of more paper, but it turned out to be a folded sheet, not wrapped around anything.

Then something heavier slid out from underneath it and onto her bed. She stared. Four rectangular bars of thick, heavy yellow metal. Yeah, she'd seen a few movies and she knew what this had to be – gold.

Ingots.

Was this what Kate was after? Tamás was literally buried treasure? Where had it come from? How many people carried around bars of gold in the middle of World War I? She had no idea how much they'd be worth. She'd check on the net later. But first there was that much more intriguing piece of paper. Carefully she unfolded it, not wanting to rip it. A flowing, perfect script covered part of the page. The beginning of a letter.

She hesitated for a sliver of a second but the need to know was too strong, and her eyes had scanned it before she'd finished the moral debate.

It was written in French. For the first time Zelie regretted not paying as much attention in class as she should, because deciphering the cursive writing and translating at the same time was hard.

Gemelle,
Do not be afraid. I will find you. I cannot hear you, but I know you are there. I will leave this letter every day, everywhere. You will find it. And I will find you.

It wasn't signed off. It wasn't finished? She folded it up, feeling bad for invading his privacy. Like reading someone's diary, it was just wrong. But she'd only done it because she'd wanted to help him, right? Didn't that make it better? But she didn't feel better. Something twisted inside her, knowing that he'd written such a heartfelt letter. Every day? He obviously loved her – Gemelle.

She repacked his things in one of her old backpacks and stuffed it in her bottom drawer. She flopped back on her bed, not bothering to undress and get into her PJs. She turned out the light and stared up at the ceiling, listening to the relentless drumming rain.

Kate had been right. He was beautiful. More than she'd thought a boy could be. Not athletic gorgeous like Otis. While Tamás was big and looked strong, he didn't have the bulk Otis had. He was leaner, harder. He had intensely pale eyes and thick black lashes and the angles of his face were perfectly symmetrical – like he'd been carved from marble by a grand master. But he wasn't flawless. A thin red line that curved like a fishhook was scored deep across his shoulder. She longed to ask him how it had happened. She rolled to her side and drew her knees up, curling into a ball – unable to unwind from the tension of the night.

He was real. It wasn't a dream, wasn't a temporary madness. It was all true and he was here and he was going to be well and so was she, and he was *stunning*.

But she couldn't hear him. She ached to hear him speak to her once more. Now she knew just a few more of his secrets, she missed him all the more. And she wanted to help him all the more. Had he found Gemelle? She didn't think so, because he was still writing up to the day he'd been trapped by Kate's many-greats-grandma and locked away at the bottom of the lake.

The thought of Kate chilled her. They'd be back – first thing in the morning those scary people would be back. And who knows what they had planned.

She gave up on the idea of sleep altogether at exactly 4.23 a.m. She snuck down the stairs, wincing with each step, fearful that the creaky wooden boards would give her away. She peeped through the chink in the curtain covering the glass window. Marion was asleep in the armchair beside the table. Zelie figured her father had done the first shift while Marion slept in the spare room, and now he'd gone for some sleep himself. She pushed the door open and walked in.

The lamp on the desk in the corner was on, enabling her to see everything clearly. But all she looked at was him. No more shivering, no more sweats. The colour in his cheeks wasn't a feverish glow but enough to make him look content and comfortable. Peaceful. The rest of him had more colour too. Now the frozen pallor had gone she could see he had a faint bronzed tone, like his homeland knew something of the sun.

She couldn't resist moving closer to sit in the chair beside his bed again – touching his hand to feel for herself the blessedly normal warmth of him. The pendant was still taped in place. But after too short a moment she withdrew her hand. He was a stranger. In a funny way even more so now she knew that bit more about him – that there'd been someone he'd cared for so deeply and never mentioned.

He sighed. The muscles on his forehead quivered like he was about to frown. She froze. She hadn't meant to wake him.

But she had. He blinked a few times, trying to clear the bleariness from his vision as he looked at her. His eyes were still that palest blue but flecked with grey now too, like the floured rocks down by the lake.

She leaned closer. 'It is you, isn't it?'

He swallowed, closing his eyes as he did, like the action had hurt him.

'Tamás?'

His arm jerked. She looked at his hand, his fluttering fingers, and she glanced back at his face. His eyes were open again. Deliberately he looked at her hand, and then back at her.

She understood, or thought she did, and put her hand over his. She gasped as his fingers twisted to grip hers with far more strength than she expected.

Intensely he gazed at her. His eyes burned like the pale heart of a fire, the hottest point in an out-of-control blaze.

'Tamás.' She ventured a small smile, her heart beating half in fear, half in excitement.

His fingers tightened that bit more.

'You can't talk?'

A slight shake of his head.

She bit her lip and tried not to let her disappointment show. She'd wanted to hear him again so much. 'You need to sleep some more.'

The corners of his mouth turned up with the faintest of grins. The fear dropped like ballast and she shot up into the skies of happiness. She smiled back openly.

But he could hold his smile for only a moment, the intensity dimming until he closed his eyes, a frown pulling his brows together. He tried to blink a couple of times.

'You really do need to sleep,' she whispered.

His fingers tightened again and she gripped back just as firmly. But his weariness was evident as he struggled to keep his focus on her. She reached forwards and stroked his forehead with a tentative finger, like she did to Luke when he woke with a fright in the middle of the night. Tamás's eyes closed. And stayed closed.

For another hour she sat with her hand clasped tightly in his as he slept. The pendant pressed into both their palms. Tiredness sank into her too, pulling her down with its weight. But it was into a warm comfort. Finally she relaxed. Watching over him, knowing that, for now, he was safe.

Her back ached like she'd spent a week pointlessly lugging bricks from one pile to another. She stirred, realised she was leaning forwards on a chair, her head pressed on the side of a bed and her hands cold. She sat up sharply. Encountered that ice-cool blue gaze. It was focused this time, utterly alert and healthy. Tamás.

It all came flooding back. Quickly she tucked her hair back, gave her mouth a wipe with the back of her fingers. It'd be just her luck to have been drooling, or snoring.

'Are you okay?' she whispered.

A faint nod.

Zelie glanced around the room. Marion still slept like a kitten in the big armchair, but a creaking overhead meant either Luke or her father was awake. She and Tamás were as alone as they could be and it wasn't going to be for long.

'Do you want me to bring you some clothes? I could get some of Dad's,' she asked, sliding to the edge of the seat. 'Or I could get something from the shops when they open.' It would be tourist garb but it would be okay.

He shook his head, not smiling. In fact, he looked horribly serious, his mouth a firm line, not the soft curve it had been last night. She wished he'd smile. She'd like to see a proper smile just the once. 'I guess you'll take care of it, right?'

He nodded.

She sat back. He didn't want her help? He wasn't looking at her now either. 'I have your bag,' she said.

His face turned sharply towards her.

'It's safe,' she reassured him. 'I'll bring it down.'

He nodded, a quick jerk of his chin. But still no smile, still that remote expression. Cold tentacles of discomfort curled around her stomach. What was he thinking? Did he even remember that he'd gripped her hand so hard? Or did he think she was like some sad stalker chick, spending hours sitting here fawning over him while he was out to it?

It hadn't been like that. She'd been trying to protect him. 'Kate came,' she said roughly. 'She's coming back.' And he should be worried.

He didn't even blink.

'She's looking really strong. She looks scary.'

His expression remained impassive.

'I guess you'll take care of that too,' she said, suddenly fed up. He looked like he was capable. No doubt he'd wave his magic wand and defeat the enemy and fly off to his fabulous forever.

She stood, smoothing down her crumpled jeans. 'I'd better go check on Luke.'

The old excuse for running away. But her awkwardness was only growing because there was still no softening in his face. No concern. No warmth.

'I'll see you later,' she said, certain she would. He wasn't well enough for her father to let him leave yet. But then, Tamás had a bottomless well of determination in him. If he wanted to go, he would.

She walked towards the door, her misery deepening, but she was quite determined not to turn and look back at him.

'Zelie.'

She whirled around at that husky thread of voice. Oh it *was* him – her Tamás – with that deep, foreign accent that made a caress of her name. His gaze was fixed on her, the blue paler than any she'd seen.

He opened his mouth but it took a couple of goes before the words sounded. 'Thank you.'

'You can talk.' Her smile beamed, all over her body.

He winced as he answered. 'It hurts but it is improving.'

Their eyes met again and her smile faltered. They shared so much knowledge, yet he felt like such a stranger. Suddenly she was shy. Shy because of what she did know. What he knew too. Once again she wished that she knew what he was thinking. What he was feeling. Only a day ago she would have had some idea, his thoughts running parallel to hers, his feelings flowing through her veins. Now there was distance, silence. And uncertainty. 'I'd better go before she wakes up,' she said, pointing at Marion.

He nodded. She managed to get out of the room, up the stairs to her own bedroom. Then the tears came. A crazy mix of relief, loss and worry over what was to come, both for Tamás and for her. She crawled under her covers, her whole body one big ache as she pushed her face into her pillow to muffle the sobs. And then she slept.

The sun was just stealing in through her window when she woke with a start – was that a slammed door?

She sat bolt upright, heart accelerating.

She leaped off her bed and opened her door to listen – silence.

Silence wasn't necessarily good. She quickly snuck down the stairs, senses on full alert. It only took a second to peek through the surgery window – he was still there, still asleep. The clock showed it was only a little more than an hour since she'd left him. Her father stood checking the monitoring equipment. But Zelie knew all was okay.

She raced back up to her room, rubbing her arms as she remembered the moment the amulet had fallen. She'd just run out of the room – making such an idiot of herself. She knew it shouldn't matter. It didn't matter. All that mattered was that Tamás was okay. Even so, she was embarrassed. She still had to go to school tomorrow.

She hunted out her mobile and switched it on. It pinged twice in quick succession. The first was from Otis.

u ok? Tht guy ok? So sorry abt yr necklace

She'd reply, but first she had to think how. The other message was from Kate.

I need 2 c u NOW

Zelie looked out the window. There were no cars parked in the clinic car park, so Marion must have gone home. The rain had washed the snow from the road. The Hearns were on their way.

She hobbled to the bathroom and rubbed antiseptic cream on her sore feet, plastering the deepest cuts before pulling on thick-soled sports socks. She didn't want her dad to see her scratches or he'd give her some anti-germ injection or something hideous. Last night he'd been too preoccupied with Tamás to notice.

She quickly dressed in her usual jeans and tee and looked in the mirror. Then stripped off and put on another set. *Stupid*. He'd seen her whole wardrobe. He'd seen her brush her teeth. He'd probably seen everything at some point or other. So why was she so focused on what she was wearing now?

For the first time in days she could look in a mirror and not feel self-conscious that someone else was looking at her too. But instead of making the most of it and squeezing that zit up by her hairline, she turned her back on the glass and ran as best she could down the stairs.

He was awake. He looked up as she walked into the room, but looked away again just as quickly. No smile softened his face.

'How are you feeling?' she asked, conscious that her dad was in his office and that the door between them was open.

'Fine.'

So stilted. So uncomfortable.

'He's recovered amazingly well. I thought he'd be seeing the effects for days but he's really bounced back.' Her dad walked through. 'It's remarkable.'

'So he's going?' Zelie studied the rail along the side of the bed extra hard.

'No,' he said stiffly, as if they were strangers not father and daughter. 'I think we'll keep him here for another day yet.'

She darted a look at Tamás, saw the flash in his eyes and knew he was going sooner than that.

'I'm glad I got to meet you,' she said to Tamás, but she dropped her gaze as she spoke.

A terrible loneliness hit her when he didn't acknowledge her words. He was here, but any sense of friendship had ended. Maybe he'd been right: it would have been better if she hadn't ever met him. Not if he was going to act like this, like they'd shared nothing.

'I need my bag.' He didn't even look at her as he said it.

She glared at him and then whirled away.

Her father retreated too – closing his office door. Through the window she saw him bend over his microscope. Some complicated computer program was up on his screen. He hadn't noticed her limping. Hadn't asked if she was okay. He'd just hermetically sealed himself away.

She went back to Tamás with the backpack in hand. 'I put it in here because the bag fell apart when I opened it.' She refused to be embarrassed about going through it. 'Don't worry. I haven't taken anything.' She dumped it on the bed beside him.

Of course he didn't bother to answer. Anger erupted. She wasn't going to be treated like this.

'A thank you might be nice,' she said tartly.

He looked at her then with the first sign of emotion she'd seen in his expression since the previous night – his eyes gleamed challenge. But his earlier thank you didn't count. He'd been half asleep. Now, fully conscious and healthy, he just didn't want to know.

'Goodbye, Zelie.' Utterly final.

In other words, *don't come back*. He didn't want to see her. He just wanted to go.

What on earth had she fallen for? The mystery? The moods? No. It was his humour, his heartache, the secrets he kept and his protectiveness of her. He *had* cared. She knew he had. She stared at him a moment longer, willing him to respond, but he was back to unfathomable – *uninterested*.

She stormed out of the room, refusing to let him see how sore she was. But the minute she got out of sight she slowed to less than crawl speed. She pulled on gumboots and went outside, but the fresh air didn't cool her temper. In fact, the further she shuffled into the cold, grey afternoon, the hotter and angrier she became. She yelled at him in her head, really regretting the fact that he wasn't forced to listen to her any more.

She'd done everything she could for him. And he was so ungracious, so uncaring. It hurt.

Interpreting his silence now was easy, his intention obvious. She wouldn't ever see him again and that was exactly how he wanted it.

CHAPTER SEVENTEEN

SHE ONLY LASTED twenty minutes out in the snow before she realised she was starving – and that really she ought to stay at home in case the Hearns tried to get Tamás. Not that she thought she could stop them entering the house. But the least she could do was warn him when they arrived.

She shook off her boots and went inside via the treatment room, frowning when she saw the bed was empty. She ran to the kitchen. To her amazement her father was in the middle of cooking breakfast. He didn't look up from the pan, though he had to have heard her thumping down the hall. Was the food for Tamás? It was hardly going to be for her, not that she'd want to eat it no matter how hungry she was. She glanced in the sink and saw a dirty cereal bowl. Luke had got his own already. She didn't blame him.

She watched her dad silently plate up the food. But she had to broach the subject, no matter how awkward. 'Is Tamás in the shower?'

'He's gone. I couldn't stop him.' Her father put the plate on the table. Some partially frozen hash browns were piled in the middle while a couple of half-poached eggs slithered alongside.

Zelie's appetite dropped dead. 'Did he go with the Hearns?'

'Yes.'

'You saw him leave with them?' Open-mouthed, she stared at her father as he took a seat. In the twenty minutes she'd been gone they'd come and carted him away?

'They came to the door. Next thing, he was gone.' Her father calmly set about eating.

'Did you see him go with them?'

'I don't remember. I'm too tired to worry about it.' Her father forked in some hash brown and chewed. End of conversation.

Zelie gaped. Her dad was *never* too tired to worry about a patient. Was this Kate's scary-starey stuff at work?

And had Tamás voluntarily gone with the Hearns? She couldn't understand why he would. And if they'd trapped him all those years ago, they could do it again, right? He'd warned her not to go there, it wasn't safe for either of them.

Her father continued brutalising his breakfast and giving Zelie the silent treatment.

She fled to her room. Tried texting Kate.

Where r u? What hv u done with him?

No matter how many times she checked through the day, there was no reply. But maybe, just maybe, Tamás had escaped – if her father hadn't seen him leave with the Hearns.

Time ticked by, snail-slow. Clutching her phone close, Zelie sat at her window, watching for any kind of sign. But there was nothing but a normal cold blue sky out there. She glanced around her room and a flash of green caught her eye. Wow – her once-dead pot plant was now flourishing. Was that a sign? Was that from Tamás's magic?

Someone knocked on the front door. Zelie raced to the top of the stairs but, amazingly, her father answered it before she could even get there.

'I thought I'd bring this over on my way to work,' a perky voice said. 'I heard you had a late night last night.'

Megan? A lightly spiced aroma curled up the stairs – she'd brought another veggie casserole?

'Thank you,' Zelie's dad answered gruffly. 'We really appreciate it.'

'No problem.'

Zelie hesitated – she so didn't want to go down there and face Otis's mum. What had he told her about last night? She winced with embarrassment – they'd been kind to her and look how she'd treated him. But then she heard the door close.

Thank goodness.

For the first time since her mum had died, she couldn't face having dinner with her father. Not even for Luke. She told him she was just too tired.

But sleep was impossible in the silence, despite how little she'd had the night before. Her own thoughts weren't noisy enough now; she wanted Tamás to talk as well. But he'd left just as he'd said he would. She had to trust he was all right. He'd better bloody send her a postcard or she'd never forgive him – because the fear that the Hearns had him was growing stronger by the second.

But there wasn't a thing she could do about it.

In the end she put music on. But she was still wide awake in the small hours, wary of new dreams as well as the old. She opened her curtains and looked up at the sky. No doubt Megan would be working at the observatory – a zillion stars shone in the perfectly clear night.

She dreaded school – felt even more self-conscious now than when Tamás's soul had been within her. In a way he'd become a shield – her invisible friend. Now it was just her again and she'd made an idiot of herself in front of everyone, running out on the Big O.

Dread sat heavy in her stomach as she drove along the icy roads. The sun shone but without heat. With the precision born of plenty of practice she arrived exactly a minute ahead of the bell. As she locked the car another vehicle pulled into the park beside hers. She recognised the shiny red paintwork and her nerves shredded completely.

'How are you?' Otis asked as he got out of his car.

'Fine,' she lied, trying to smile.

'I . . . um . . . I'm really sorry about your necklace.'

'Oh . . . look, I overreacted about that. Really, it was silly,' she babbled. 'I shouldn't have run out like that. I'm so sorry if I embarrassed you.'

'You didn't. I was just worried you were upset.' He waited, falling into step with her slow pace. Zelie really just wanted to get inside and alone, but she couldn't walk any faster on her bruised feet.

'How is he?'

She'd known Otis would ask, so she didn't need to feel anxious about it. But still she did. 'He's fine. He's gone already.' She said it as lightly as she could, like it meant nothing to her.

'How do you know him?'

'Oh . . .' She shrugged dismissively, hoping he'd drop it.

He didn't. 'Through Kate?'

'Yes.' She was relieved she didn't have to lie more. She felt bad enough about Otis already.

'You want to catch up another day this week?' he asked with that smile. 'I've got training on Tuesday and Thursday but we could do Wednesday. Peanut butter toast on offer.'

'Um,' Zelie paused. He still wanted to hang out with her after she'd ditched him so badly the other night? Wow. That was so kinda noble of him, and she really, really should say yes. But she wanted to stay home. She wanted to sink into a pit. She missed Tamás. She was mad with Tamás. Even more than that, she was mad with herself for missing Tamás. But there was no point in moping and she couldn't hide away – not any more.

She saw a few of the girls looking at them. Yeah, Otis was doing her a favour, saving her from catty comments by pointedly walking with her, stopping her from being turned into a social pariah.

He was chivalrous and kind – more than could be said for Tamás. She was stupid not to spend more time with him. Besides, she owed him, didn't she? She made herself smile and answer. 'That'd be great. Thanks.'

His smile flared, but it didn't untie the knot deep inside her.

First lesson was science with Mr Webb, so Otis walked with her all the way to the classroom. Halfway through the door, Zelie stopped. Kate was sitting in the seat next to the one Zelie always took. What was *she* doing here?

A cold feeling swept through Zelie. Why was Kate looking so pale again?

'Zelie,' Mr Webb called.

Reluctantly, she walked over to his desk at the front of the room. He handed her a plastic bag.

'Here's the coat you left at the ball the other night,' he said in his too-loud teacher voice.

'Oh,' Zelie mumbled, knowing she'd gone raspberry-jam red. 'Thanks.'

'You got home okay?' Mr Webb wouldn't let it go.

'Yes, thanks.'

She kept her eyes lowered as she shuffled down the aisle to her seat – so not wanting to look at anyone.

'Are you all right?' Kate asked as soon as Zelie sat down.

'I'm fine.' Zelie concentrated on getting her book and pen from her bag, trying not to ask the burning question.

'Have you seen Tamás?' Kate asked.

'No.' Stunned that Kate had asked the exact question she wanted to ask herself, Zelie dropped her book. 'Have you?' She hated the breathlessness that afflicted her at just the thought of him.

'We don't know where he's gone.' Kate glanced around, her nerves on display.

Victory rocketed through Zelie's chest. So he'd got away. He was *free*. Yet Kate looked as terrified as a fox finally cornered by a pack of hounds on the hunt. What did she think was going to happen? That Tamás would appear from thin air and attack her?

'Are you afraid of him, Kate?'

'Yes. You should be too.'

No. Zelie wasn't afraid of him. She was afraid of not seeing him again.

'Are you with us, Kate? Zelie?' Mr Webb called out sarcastically.

'Sorry,' Zelie mumbled.

Kate sniffed. Zelie rummaged in her bag and pulled out a tissue, but by the time she had, Kate already had one and was wiping her nose. Zelie saw the red stain seeping through the white. Kate's fingernails were that awful blue again too.

Was that why she was looking so nervous? But if Tamás was free, Kate should be better. Yet here she was, getting worse again.

As class progressed Zelie could see that Kate's concentration was shot. Kate gripped her pen but her hand shook so much she couldn't draw a straight line.

'You should go home,' Zelie whispered.

'I'm getting worse.' Terrified, Kate stated the obvious. 'You don't know where he's gone?'

Zelie shook her head. If this was just an act to try to get her to tell, it was pretty good. The suffering in Kate's eyes looked genuine and made Zelie feel bad. But she didn't know where he was and even if she did . . .?

What the Hearns had done to Tamás was terrible. But Kate's illness was terrible too. It didn't seem right that she should have to pay for something her ancestor did generations ago. She'd suffered enough – burdened with all those memories. All that loss.

'When he was with you it worked,' Kate whispered. 'I was so much better.'

'I thought you said that when he was free, you'd be free.'

'That's what I thought would happen.'

'So either you were wrong or he's not free.'

Kate nodded, wincing as she swallowed.

Then they needed to find out. 'I really don't know where he's gone,' Zelie said.

'You can't contact him?' There was no denying the threads of hope in Kate's question.

'No. He's gone. I can't hear him.'

Kate's eyes dulled. 'That's it then.'

Zelie drew her lip between her teeth. 'Are you okay to get home?'

She nodded. 'I'll text my uncle after this.'

Finally the bell rang. The halls filled with bodies racing for lockers, eager to get food or phones. Zelie walked down the middle of the corridor alongside Kate, oddly removed from the others, right out to the main steps of the school.

'What do you think's going to happen?' Zelie asked.

'No idea.'

It was cold but not snowing or raining. The sky was as blue and clear as a summer's day, yet ice was everywhere. The sun wasn't warm enough to melt it. Zelie stood on the top step with Kate, watching as she texted her uncle.

In the distance a roaring grew louder. Zelie lifted her gaze to look down the road, waiting as it came closer. A motorbike turned into the street, heading towards the school. Her heart thudded at triple speed; she held her breath. Every cell jerked to attention, then screamed with tension. Was that who she thought it was?

No way. Surely he'd be miles away by now.

She glanced at Kate to see if she'd noticed, but she was just drawing in a shaky breath of chilly air and staring at her phone. The biker pulled over and took the park right at the front of the school – the one reserved for visitors. Legs astride the machine, his hands lifted to his helmet.

She knew her instinct was right. But she couldn't believe it. Only when the helmet was off did she breathe again.

Boom.

He'd taken that Hollywood bad-boy look way too seriously. But he'd made it oh-so-much-better in reality. Jeans, leather jacket and one hell of a sullen expression. Zelie's legs turned to jelly and she leaned against the stair railing. But she crossed her arms, determined not to look in the least impressed. Or worse, show her utter relief at seeing him again.

She glanced sideways to scope Kate's reaction. She was open-mouthed. A few others had come onto the steps for some air, and every one of them was staring at Tamás. The only person not watching him was Otis; his eyes were on her. She flashed him a small smile but, like everyone else, her attention was dragged back to Tamás.

It was some bike. But the bike had nothing on the guy walking away from it now. Some of the others went to inspect the machine, but Tamás cut through the crowd like a Samurai sword. He was taller than she'd realised; inches above Tom, even taller than Otis, who was standing at the foot of the stairs, just watching. Tamás didn't even look at him. As he climbed the stairs, unsmiling, he was looking at only one person.

Kate.

His eyes were that far-horizon blue, but cold, calculating, as he impaled the girl with a killer look. Only when he got to the top step did his attention flicker for a speck of a second to Zelie. There was no softening of his expression, no smile, not a hint of recognition. He simply looked right through her, then right past her as he went into the building.

Kate's raspy breathing was loud enough to be heard on the other side of the world. Her fingers frantically pressed buttons on her mobile. 'I'm staying.'

Zelie nodded but could say nothing, too crushed by that total blanking from Tamás. He hadn't come here for her. He wasn't interested in her. She'd known it already but it still hurt far more than she'd thought it could.

The bell went again and she drifted to her next class. What was he doing here? And what was it about Kate Hearn that was so damn special?

An hour later when she walked into history, he was there, on the far side of the room, his legs long in dark denim jeans as he leaned against the window frame. She walked over, determined not to let his remoteness intimidate her.

'You're coming to school now?' Her voice was pathetically thin.

'Obviously.' He kept gazing out the window.

'Why?'

'I have some things I need to do.'

'What things?'

'You don't need to know.' It was like he was dismissing a small child.

Zelie wasn't going to be sent packing so easily. 'Where are you staying?'

He paused, and she just knew he was going to be as rude as when he'd first taken up residence in her damn brain.

'How long are you staying?' she asked.

He looked at her then, his expression less mobile than a statue's. 'I don't know.'

'How did you get the motorbike, how come you can ride it?' Where had he got the licence from? How had the school accepted him with no question?

'Money can buy a lot,' he said cynically. 'You should get ready for class.'

In other words, *leave me alone.*

'You know she's contacted her uncles already.'

At that his lip curled. It wasn't a nice smile. 'Good.'

Other students trickled into the room. She could see the curious looks – interested ones from the girls. Tamás took a seat as far from her usual one as possible.

She tried again later in the day, caught up to him in the corridor just outside the café. 'How are you finding your first day?'

'Quite fascinating,' he answered, but he didn't stop, just kept walking away.

Indescribably hurt, Zelie watched him go. Maybe she should have had some pride. Maybe she should have just walked away. But she couldn't because she wanted their friendship back, as uneasy and weird as it had been. So she ran after him. 'Tamás.'

He didn't stop.

'Tamás.' She reached out and he veered sideways to escape her touch. But she got hold of his arm and finally he did stop. He looked at her, his mouth firm and forbidding.

'Why won't you talk to me?' She couldn't hide the wail in her voice. 'Why won't you even say hello?'

He swallowed but said nothing.

'I was there for you. I put up with you for days.'

He jammed his hands in his pockets and stared straight ahead. 'It is better if you don't become any more involved.'

Involved? Her fingers tightened. 'How much more involved can I be?'

'No, you *were* involved. You're not *now*.' He turned quickly, dislodging her hand. Suddenly he was too close and towering over her. 'Kate was right. There is danger. You don't need to be part of it any more.'

She tilted her head to hold his gaze. 'That's not fair.'

'Life isn't fair,' he said brutally. 'You should know that already.'

'Don't shut me out. I talked to you. You talked to me. We shared more than a body, Tamás.'

He stepped closer, his voice dropping to a menacing whisper. 'You didn't want to be caught up in this, remember?'

'But I'm in it now,' she argued. 'And I don't want to be cut loose. I can still help you.'

'No, you can't. There is nothing you can do. Stay out of it.' He turned away.

More orders?

'But my father took a swab of the stuff that coated your skin,' she said quickly, wanting him to know she could help – that she was still useful. 'He's going to analyse it.'

'He won't understand what it is. It doesn't matter.'

'It does matter. You don't know my father. He's obsessive –'

'So that's where you get it from.'

His smile held no warmth.

'Oh fine, Tamás,' she said witheringly. 'Just deal with it on your own. When all the damn scientists swarm into town you can sit there and explain it to them.'

'What do you mean?' He stepped after her.

'He's *analysing* it. Then he'll send whatever wacko conclusions he comes to off to his colleagues overseas. If it's something new, something they've never seen, they're all going to want to talk to you. They'll *hunt* you.' Because it *was* something new – something magic. She knew that the slimy stuff had been a vital part of the process that had kept him safe beneath the lake for so many decades.

His piercing blue gaze was trained on her. 'I won't be here for them to talk to. Forget it. Forget everything.'

Like she could do that?

But that's what *he* wanted to do. He wanted to forget about her. She stared, noting the way he'd turned away from her again. 'You don't want to know me.'

He'd just wanted her body. He'd used her. 'That's right,' he said, his accent clipped, his stance tense. 'I don't want to know. And I don't want you near me.'

She gaped, crushed by the blunt confirmation.

Then she rallied. One last spark of pride came to her rescue. She wasn't making a fool of herself a second longer. She tossed her head and turned away – blinking back the silly tears that she'd never show him.

Not worth it, he's not worth it.

She heard his sigh even though she was already five paces away. 'Zelie.'

It was only the third time he'd said her name since he'd washed up on shore.

She stopped but didn't turn.

'I do appreciate what you did for me.'

She jerked her head in a terse nod and carried on walking. He was talking past tense. If it was his call, they wouldn't be talking at all.

She walked into French ahead of him, focusing on her books, trying to hide how upset she was because Kate was watching. Kate, whose colour had returned in the short time since Zelie last saw her, whose cough had cleared, whose hair shone, and whose eyes had a scary glow.

Class sucked. The teacher was thrilled to have a native speaker in the class and all the girls were totally fascinated too. Zelie understood why, but that didn't make it any less hideous. If only he'd sent the damn postcard. If only he'd not come back. Then she might have been able to get over him, might have kept the memories but been spared the torment.

The French phrases from the letter he'd written floated in her mind like sticks down a gentle creek – slowly, some lodging on the sides and not moving on. She thought she had the translation right but she wished her mum was around to help. Her mum had been the one to insist she learn the language. Zelie had never asked why. Why *French*? How she wished she could ask her. She had so many questions to ask her.

But the ones she wanted to ask the most were also the most stupid – how do you get a boy to talk to you? To notice you? To want you? How do you right things when a friendship suddenly goes wrong? How do you communicate with someone like Tamás?

She banged her forehead into her hand, slumping as she tried to concentrate on class. She was such a fool.

A sound made her turn – Kate was laughing for some reason. Chuckling to herself as she bent over the paper she was supposed to be writing on. It wasn't a very sane chuckle.

Zelie shivered. If there was such a thing as intuition, she hadn't had it the day her mum had died. But now? Zelie's nerves screamed danger. Something was brewing. Something big. Something bad.

The bell finally rang. Tamás must have moved quickly because by the time she got outside, the motorbike was already roaring down the street. Yeah, she'd known he'd like to go fast. As near as he could get to flying.

Kate smiled at Zelie as she walked past to where her uncles stood waiting at the school gate, silent and staring as much as ever. Both men glared at Zelie for an uncomfortably long moment. Then, when Kate reached them, the three moved together, quickly getting into their ute and pulling away with a screech of wheels. The two sheepdogs chained on the back of it barked. No black cats for those witches.

Zelie stomped past the place where they'd stood to her car. She turned the key but the engine coughed, then died. She tried a couple more times but still the engine wouldn't spark. Cold sweat started to slide down her spine.

'Need a ride?' Otis had reached his car, still parked alongside hers.

But just as he asked, she turned the key again and it started.

'Thanks anyway,' she said loudly so he'd hear her through the window.

''Kay. I'll keep an eye out on the road for you.'

She nodded and slowly reversed out. To have trouble starting her car was strange – her dad had had it serviced recently, he was manic about it. It might be old but it was solid and reliable. Maybe it was the cold weather freezing the engine.

She listened to music loud as she drove back to Tekapo. Not ready to go home yet, she turned off the main road and cruised up the mountain to the lookout near the observatory. She left the engine idling and got out briefly to stand in the one spot where she could see two of the lakes in the region – Tekapo, with its weird cyan water, and Lake Alexandrina with the normal colour. She loved the contrast. But the wind was brutal.

She got back in the car, deciding to detour further and drive along Tekapo's waterfront. Passing the row of holiday cabins by the shore, she saw the motorbike parked on an angle outside one of them. So that's where he was staying. She turned her car around.

Because so far, so stalker. And that wasn't cool.

Slowly she headed back towards the tiny main strip of cafés and tourist shops. She saw shadows everywhere, heard threats in the silent snow.

Then a shadow appeared right in front of her. A black cloud – it took her a second to realise it was smoke.

She slammed on the brakes. That thick black plume was spewing out of the bonnet of *her* car. Stunned, she just sat still for a second. Now it was coming through the air conditioning unit, clouding up her small space. Frantically she killed the engine and yanked out the key, dropping it in her panic. She unfastened her seatbelt and pulled on the door handle.

It wouldn't open. Why wouldn't it open? She tried again. Jiggled it. Banged it. Kicked it.

She hadn't locked it, but it was jammed. She couldn't unwind the window either – it wouldn't budge. She'd have to turn the engine on again and she'd lost the key already. She reached across to the passenger door, but it wouldn't open either. She couldn't get out. And she was sitting on a full tank of fuel.

Her hands slipped on the steering wheel. Why she'd gripped it again, she didn't know. And then she knew what to do – she pounded her fist on the horn so it blared. And she didn't let up the pressure.

There was no point yelling – she didn't think she could anyway.

Terror had tightened her throat. She blinked as the smoke stung her eyes and made her cough.

Through half-closed lids she desperately peered through the windscreen, the windows – trying to see if someone was coming to help. The shops weren't too far away – surely someone would hear her?

And then she saw him. In the distance, across the snow-covered grass that led to the lake, Tamás stood watching.

Doing nothing.

He wasn't moving towards her, wasn't saying anything. He was just watching.

Zelie's fist loosened, her hand slipped from the horn. He'd once saved a baby, but he wouldn't lift a finger to help her?

That's when she heard the shouting. She turned her head – a crowd had gathered – mostly students. She saw Otis running towards her. Just behind him was Jo of Mama Jo's Café. She was carrying a kitchen extinguisher. She tried to get it to work, but failed. Otis grabbed it off her and tried.

Also failed.

The smoke was acrid, bitter, burning her lungs. She tried the door again, uselessly pounded on it. It still wouldn't open.

'Stand back,' she heard a strong male voice shout.

Mr Webb?

She could just see he had something in his hand.

'Shield your eyes!' he shouted at her.

She did. A split second later she heard the smash as he shattered the window beside her. She knelt on the driver's seat, sticking her head out to gulp untainted air.

'Come on.' Mr Webb gripped under her arms and hauled her out through the smashed window, half lifting, half dragging her to a safe distance. Zelie bent double, retching and gasping for air, wiping away the tears streaming from her eyes. A couple of Otis's friends had found a hose from who-knew-where and switched it on.

'You okay?' Mr Webb crouched down and looked up into her face. 'Zelie?'

'I'm fine. I'm just fine.' Just freaked. And embarrassed. And scared.

'You want me to take you home?' Otis ran up to them.

She shook her head. She didn't want anyone near her. She just wanted to be alone in her room and try to think for a moment. 'I'm fine,' she repeated. 'It's only a little walk.'

'Zelie?'

Megan?

Zelie glanced beyond Mr Webb and Otis and sure enough, Otis's mum was hurrying over from the row of shops, flanked by a couple of other women Zelie had seen around the town.

'I saw the smoke,' Megan said, stepping forwards from her friends. 'Are you all right, Zelie?'

Zelie nodded again.

'How did this happen?' Megan asked, turning to Mr Webb.

He still had a huge frown on. He shook his head. 'It'll need to be checked out –'

Ugh. Zelie couldn't handle hanging round here a second longer. 'I'm going to go home,' she whispered.

Both adults turned their heads, identical expressions of concern on their faces.

'Maybe you should come into the café for a bit,' Megan said.

'No. Thanks.'

Megan put her arm round Zelie's shoulders and gave her a gentle hug. 'All right, then. Otis will walk you home.'

Oh, it was mortifying, and all she wanted to do was be alone.

'Honestly, I'm fine. I'll be fine.'

Megan looked intently into her face – it was one of those shrewd looks that only mothers could deliver. Then she smiled. 'Sure. I understand. Have something hot and sweet to drink when you get there, though, you promise? You need something for the shock.'

Her instruction was so different to the cold, medical orders her father would bark. This was all smiles and warmth and made her heart ache.

She glanced back at her car. It was now drenched and no longer smoking. A couple of the volunteer fire guys had arrived and were ensuring it was safe. She knew they'd move it off the road.

It was okay for her to go.

'Thanks so much,' she muttered, not looking any of them in the eye.

She ran home. The phone was ringing as she got inside but

she ignored it and went straight to the shower to wash away that terrifying, charred smell.

Who could have done that? Because it wasn't an accident. She was sure of it. And there was only one person who came to mind.

Kate. That glow in her eyes when she'd walked out of school? Her uncles waiting in the car park? Had they done something to her car?

It had to be Kate.

That girl was going to pay.

CHAPTER EIGHTEEN

TRYING NOT TO watch him was like trying not to squeeze a zit. You know you shouldn't, that it'll only make it worse, but you just can't help it.

He made the most of the supposed language barrier. His accent sounded thicker, and he struggled to complete sentences when someone asked him a question. She knew it was a ploy to keep his distance. The girls were all intrigued – *Tamás the Mysterious*. On only his second day, the label was already affixed.

She wished she could ditch the awareness, but he was in every one of Kate's classes, so most of Zelie's as well. She felt skinned as he totally ignored her. Felt nothing but fury for him and Kate.

'Have lunch with us.' Otis caught up to her in the corridor, smiling in that easy, lopsided way.

'Thanks,' she smiled, grateful for the distraction.

'Scary shit yesterday,' said Otis as he walked with her to the café.

'Tell me about it. I'm driving Dad's car today.'

'You can always text me if you need a lift.'

'Thanks.'

Zelie wasn't hungry, but she grabbed a muffin and a can of lemonade and took the one vacant seat at Otis's table. The one right beside him.

She made herself smile at his friends. They were polite, but there was no hiding the over-bright curiosity in their eyes that made her too aware of her every movement.

She slowly sipped her lemonade, an avoidance activity. She still didn't know how to do the small talk with these people.

She glanced around the café. Kate sat in the corner, alone at a table. The way she stared at Zelie made her hair stand on end.

It was like she was willing things to happen to her – to those around her.

Zelie stared right back as if she could mentally warn Kate to back off. But she felt like she was watching a train crash in slow motion – knowing it was going to happen and there wasn't a thing she could do to stop it.

But nothing happened.

'Does she freak you out?'

Startled, Zelie turned back to the table.

'Kate Hearn,' Ella explained. 'She freaks me out. I know that's rude.' Ella shrugged with a small smile. 'But she's kinda creepy.'

If Ella only knew.

'She's a patient of Dad's,' Zelie said in a croaky voice.

Ella nodded. Zelie didn't know what else to say.

Still nothing happened. Not when she sat and played with her lunch because she'd lost her appetite. Not when the others chatted about things she had no clue about. Not even when Tamás appeared and bought a pie from the counter. Yeah, no ice cream for him, he liked his food hot.

Nothing happened. Nothing but Kate staring.

So Zelie waited.

After the never-ending torture of school she didn't want to be indoors, and didn't even bother going into her house. She threw her bag onto the porch and walked across the snow-lined path down to the lake. The water and the peace that she used to feel when near it called to her. She needed to salve wounds rubbed raw from a whole day of *nothing* from Tamás. She was afraid of being alone. But more afraid of being with her family in case something happened – something like the Hearns.

She tried to bury her recent memories of the waterfront. Of that frantic run, the battle to save him that wretched night. But she couldn't. She'd tried so hard, done as much as she could. Now he couldn't be bothered to say hello? Couldn't be bothered to help her when she was in trouble?

She strode faster towards the lake, ignoring her bruised feet and the twinge of isolation. She'd dunk her hands in the icy water and cool down. The swing at the children's playground ahead was empty, the elephant climbing frame was also bare. So was the sky – brilliant, cloudless blue. But cold.

She crunched over the icy patches and the baby pinecones, half squashed in the melting snow. The wind lifted, its noisy bitterness clogging her ears. She walked beneath the branches and began the descent to the water. From here she could see a long stretch of the lakefront. And then, as she turned her head to let the wind blow her hair from her face, she saw them. Right down where the freezing waves lapped the stones.

She stopped walking, thinking, breathing. Just stared.

Tamás had his back to Zelie, but his hands were on Kate's shoulders as she looked up at him. An intimate pose that fired a ball of burning acid into Zelie's stomach. She wanted to look away but she couldn't. There was something between him and Kate – something greater than what there had been between Tamás and her. They shared a huge, magical history.

Zelie knew Kate was the reason Tamás hadn't left. But seeing it as bluntly as this cut deep. Because she'd fallen for him. Before she'd even seen how unfairly beautiful he was, she'd fallen for his wounded self – his dry humour, his brilliant mind, even his arrogance was kind of appealing. So was his caring side, and the depth of feeling she knew he was capable of.

But he hadn't cared for her.

The wind shrieked louder in her ears. It carried his words over to her. Suddenly she could hear him clearly – speaking in that same language he'd told her the bedtime story in. But this wasn't soothing. This wasn't sweet.

Kate's face paled. She slowly shook her head. Her hands opened and clenched but grasped nothing but air. Her mouth went wide – like she wanted to cry out but couldn't. There was no sound from her at all.

Then Zelie understood.

Kate couldn't breathe. She was choking or suffocating or something. But how? From here all she could see was Tamás's hands on Kate's shoulders, not around her neck. He was only looking at her, merely speaking in that exotic language.

Kate's fists opened, curled again. As her head shook, her hair shone, almost sparkling in the sunlight. Zelie squinted. Kate's hair wasn't sparkling – it was *sparking* – tiny flashes of blue fire seemed to be shooting from the tips. And while her face might be pale, her fists were no longer empty. Small balls of fire, flickers of flame rested in each palm – and were growing with each release of her tight clench.

Kate's knees sagged, but Tamás held her up by her shoulders, still speaking. The words viciously whipped across the cold air. The fury on Kate's face burned into Zelie – her wide, frantic eyes and pale skin and the ugly strain in her face as she fought back.

Kate lifted a hand, shot the small flame at Tamás, igniting his shirt. Zelie gasped. But he turned his head slightly to the left, towards the flame, and seemed to squash it with a mere breath.

He could kill fire that quickly and he'd not helped her yesterday? And Kate could create fire from nothing?

Now Zelie was far beyond furious, she was incandescent.

She finally moved. Her rage-fogged brain cranked up just enough to push her forwards. But she couldn't call out. She couldn't get enough breath to make herself heard against this wind. All she could do was try to get there.

And sort them both out.

She ran – but not fast enough. Kate threw another flame, despite her lips going blue. Despite being barely able to stand. Tamás killed it again – but as he did so he seemed to release Kate from whatever hold it was that had stopped her from breathing, and she snatched a quick life-saving drag of oxygen.

Another flame, another crush of lungs. Another flame, another gust of wind. Another moment of rage.

And then Tamás threw his head back and swore. A huge, long shout that tore through the whistling wind. One word. English. Rude. He lifted his hands from Kate's shoulders, pushing her away as he stepped back. Kate fell but Tamás didn't stop. He stormed along the lake towards the forest, towards the hill rising above it, then broke into a run over the chunky rocks. He didn't see Zelie running towards Kate from behind.

Kate rose quickly to her knees – still working her fists – but oddly the flames were weakening.

Moments later Zelie got to her. 'Are you okay?'

Kate nodded, her breath coming in deep shudders. 'He couldn't do it,' she rasped, her words only just audible. But a hint of glee shone in her eyes. 'He couldn't do it.'

'Do what?' Zelie gazed down at her.

'Kill me.' Kate looked up, her blue irises rippling with those weird flames. 'He tried but he couldn't do it.'

Because she'd burned him? Because he couldn't?

Or because he *wouldn't*.

Zelie clenched *her* fist. She'd never believed he'd do it. Even though she'd felt his rage running through her own veins, she'd never believed he actually would. Not once she'd got to know him.

'He wanted to. He really wanted to. He hates me.' Kate stood, bending slightly to catch her breath.

Zelie kept her eyes on Kate's hands and took a step back. 'Are you really surprised about that?'

Kate shook her head. 'But he couldn't,' she panted, pressing her palm to her cheek. 'I've been through some scary things, Zelie, but that was the worst.'

'You held your own.' Zelie's fury surged again. 'You burned him.'

Kate shook her head. 'It didn't even touch him.'

'No? Not like it touched my bloody car.'

Kate frowned. 'What?'

'Don't try to deny it.'

Briefly Zelie twisted to look where Tamás had gone. The clouds looked low enough to touch now as fog settled over the lake and dampened her face. As the chill pierced through her skin all the way to bone, she felt it. The agony. The anger.

She froze. It was like those early days after she'd first put the amulet on, but it was unadulterated – *raw*. How she was feeling it, she didn't know. She had no chain linking him to her now and yet it was like he was back inside her head.

The wind lifted higher. She could smell the bitterness of smoke. Quickly she glanced back at Kate. 'You think you're going to burn me to a cinder?'

'What?'

Fear filled her as Kate straightened. Was she going to deny it? As if Zelie was that stupid. Though how the hell she thought she could get away from a wacked-out witch who threw fire, she didn't know. All she could do was run.

Adrenalin streamed into her muscles again and she sprinted, following the path Tamás had taken.

It was weird but she felt fitter than she ever had. Fitter than when she'd played hockey back in Britain before it all fell apart. It was like all the running she'd done in the last week had been some kind of fast-track boot camp. The cuts and scrapes on the soles of her feet seemed to have healed already because there was no pain any more. Her feet only felt *fast*. She breathed in regular shots of cold air, giving her muscles an additional energy kick. She raced up the hill, into the cover of the trees, dodging the iciest parts, the twigs that seemed determined to trip her up. It seemed she could now avoid them like the nimblest mountain fawn.

She was agile. Determined. And somehow sure she was doing the right thing. She listened to the wind, breathed harder, protecting the raw wound she still felt inside. *His* wound.

Finally she saw him, clear of the trees, up where the tussock was hidden by a covering of snow that made the hill as smooth as a freshly iced cake – but sterile and scary. His arms were outstretched, like he was reaching out to the cloud that hugged the lake.

'Tamás,' she called as she came near.

His arms dropped. So did his head.

'Leave.'

'Tamás.' Even if he didn't want her, she was his friend. She knew more about him than any other person alive, more than Kate did. Kate had truly thought he'd kill her, but Zelie had known he wouldn't. She was certain she was right about him.

And she was sure he was suffering right now. Because a part of her was suffering. From the nothing she'd felt in the shock of his departure, now an imprint was there. Honestly, she wanted it to stay. She wanted to understand him more. She liked having the link to him. But the wind was dropping, and with it the feelings were fading from within her. Back to silence.

His hands were on his hips but his fingers were curled into fists. His short-sleeved tee showed bunched biceps, the cotton across his back pulled taut as his stance went even more rigid. The bared bronze skin on his arms was smooth and free of goosebumps despite the cold.

'I wanted to make her pay,' he said quietly, like he was talking to himself. 'My family are dead and I wasn't there to be with them. I couldn't help them. I have missed out on everything because of her. I wanted her to die. I have wanted nothing more for days. But I couldn't do it. And it's your fault.'

'How?' she moved closer to the edge of the track to hear him better.

'It just is.'

She really didn't understand how. 'Tamás.' She put her hand out to touch him.

He whirled around before her fingers connected. 'I don't want to talk about it any more.'

She rolled her eyes. 'No, I guessed that.' She let the sarcasm drip to cover her high heart rate. 'You never want to talk at all, do you?'

'Zelie,' he roared with frustration. 'I couldn't look at you if I did it, I couldn't bear your judgment.'

Shocked, she stopped trying to move closer. 'But I wouldn't judge you, Tamás.' How could she? She understood his rage. They both knew what it was to suffer and lose, and the fury that went with that. She was glad he hadn't hurt Kate, but she understood why he'd wanted to. And she believed in his humanity – he'd saved that baby, hadn't he?

'And that's exactly it,' he said bitterly. 'You make it so damn easy it's impossible.'

She blinked. Not getting his logic at all.

'So are you going now?' Her heart stopped while it waited for his answer. He'd stayed for payback but couldn't follow through. Was there any other reason that would hold him here?

His hands fisted again, the aggression making the air ripple around him the way heat made the road shimmer on a record-smashing summer's day. 'Soon,' he said like he wished it was now. 'I can't leave yet.'

Her heart started again – faster than before – yet she could breathe that bit deeper. 'Why not?'

He looked everywhere but at her – around the hills, over the lake. 'They have knowledge, Zelie. I need that knowledge. I have to find out what they know about me and my kind. About what they've done. And then I have to deal with it.'

'Kate won't tell you?'

'Nothing more than what she's told me already. She's been blocked.'

Blocked? Zelie didn't want to know what that meant. And she didn't want to ask how he knew. But the image returned and stuck in her mind, Tamás towering over Kate as her body began to fail.

As he did whatever it was that could slowly kill her. He'd known exactly what to do — and how to fight Kate's own power. Even though Kate had been fighting back, it had looked like, ultimately, he'd have won.

'Can all witches throw fire like that?' she asked softly.

He shook his head. 'She's special.'

Zelie swallowed but still the curiosity spewed up, forcing her to ask the most awful question. Moments ago she'd been sure what his answer would be, now she wasn't. And she had to ask.

'Have you killed anyone before, Tamás?'

The change would have been imperceptible to anyone passing by. But she saw it, the way he absolutely froze. It was like she'd hit the button that paused time, but the only thing it had any effect on was him.

He didn't blink. Didn't breathe. Certainly didn't answer.

She bit her lip and thought about asking again. Wished that she'd never asked in the first place. Because finally he turned to look at her. His pale eyes reflected the grey clouds — devoid of ice-blue life. For a long moment he just looked at her. And even though he was motionless, she saw an unnatural calm rise inside him.

Then he answered. 'Yes.'

Zelie felt like he'd swung a knife and sliced her skin open.

She knew she shouldn't ask anything more. She knew she wasn't going to like the answers. But the curiosity was already killing her. Again. What had happened? Why had he? Who? When? And how? It could be more than one.

A hundred horrors flashed in her mind. Remnants of the nightmares that had plagued him now scurried through her head — the people, the faces. Yet still she couldn't quite believe it. Even though she knew he wasn't lying, that he really had killed, she couldn't believe he had been truly bad.

She was appalled with herself. Had she gone delusional because she wanted to like him so much? To believe in him? But the fact was she *did* believe in him. And she didn't believe he was capable of evil. He'd had more than one opportunity to take his revenge and he hadn't been able to. He could have used Zelie to kill Kate, could have smashed Kate's skull between basketball and wall that day. But he'd missed and Zelie was sure it'd been deliberate. In her gut she knew he was too powerful to make a mistake like that.

Maybe she should have felt frightened, but all she felt was sad. Someone's life lost, someone else's ruined. Suddenly she figured it out.

'Was it in the war?' Of course it would have been in the war. Even though it was still awful, it was a relief. A life was a life but there would have been a reason that Zelie could live with – defence. The defence of a people or a country or self or something. In battle the rules were different, weren't they?

He was watching her, his expression unfathomable. And when he spoke it was in that unemotional, factual, too-many-dry-history-lectures tone that she hated. 'It was in cold blood. He was defenceless.'

She blinked. Had to replay what he'd said in her head several times before she heard it, let alone understood it.

In cold blood?

Defenceless?

He'd killed. He was a killer. And right now he was as emotionless as someone capable of really bad things.

She still didn't understand it. Nothing inside her moved except her heart, which thudded against her ribs sickeningly fast. Tamás was a murderer?

No. She shook her head slowly. *No.* 'I don't believe you.' But inside was a kernel of doubt.

He grabbed her shoulders. 'I killed him. Don't you get it? I killed him.' He shook her, shouting each word.

Stunned, she stared up at him, shocked at his bluntness, revolted by the ugly, metallic truth in his expression. It seemed wrong. So wrong that he could have or would have. She'd thought she knew him. But she hadn't. Because she believed him now. It was there in his dirty-ice eyes.

Her own instinct had betrayed her. It was unreliable. She couldn't trust in anything they'd shared now. In anything she'd believed of him. She didn't know whose side she was on any more, or what the *thing* was looming ahead of them.

Until now she'd thought she could trust him. Now she knew she couldn't.

Now she was scared.

Finally she wrenched her gaze from his, only then realising that his hands were still clamped on her shoulders, his fingers digging into her bones. Wasn't this exactly how he'd stood over Kate only minutes earlier?

Zelie's heart thumped. Fear froze her to the spot.

'Stay away from me,' he said roughly, shoving her away. 'Stay away. I'm not safe.'

CHAPTER NINETEEN

ZELIE DIDN'T SEE the lake, the mountains, the trees. She kept her eyes on the grey rocks, the greyer footpath, the dirty mounds of snow on the edge of the rough gravel and the black tar of the road. She sprinted down the hill and into the village, past the clinic, past the shops. She didn't want to stop. All she could hear was the sound of her own breathing, hard and hurried. But the thoughts swirled, merging, growing bigger until they screamed at her.

He'd stayed to kill Kate. That was why he hadn't left right away. He'd wanted revenge. But he hadn't been able to do it.

Now he was even more angry. And for the first time that anger was directed at Zelie. He blamed her for his inability to destroy Kate.

So let him be angry. Because wanting to destroy Kate was wrong. And she was glad he'd learned it was wrong. He may have killed before but he couldn't now – at least not today.

Emptiness echoed in her head. The space he'd taken up rang hollow. She wished the rest of her would swallow up that gap but it was like her mind had been widened – stretched to accommodate his – and it wouldn't shrink back. That part of her waited for his return. And it hurt.

She could only hope that time would fix it.

Her legs ached but she forced through the nagging warning, because the pain in her skull was worse. He was a cold-blooded killer.

But still her stupidly soft heart sought to justify, to understand. For she'd killed too, hadn't she? Through negligence. In her own way, wasn't she as guilty? She'd been too absorbed in her own selfishness to see what was going on. She should have got help sooner. Her mother might still be alive today if she had. And her brother would have had a whole family. They wouldn't be left living like three strangers in the one house; weird flatmates whose paths crossed only at meal times, and half the time not even then.

So how could she judge?

Nothing, but nothing, was black and white. Right?

Devastated, she stopped, looking down at the school uniform hanging wet and heavy on her. It looked so everyday. She turned and started to walk home. She had to remember her responsibilities – and Luke.

It felt ridiculous to be preparing dinner in the light of what she'd witnessed only half an hour ago. But it had to be done. She looked at her brother sitting quietly at the kitchen table, lost in his bug world a million miles away. She was kidding herself. What good did she do for him really? They hardly ever talked, not about anything important.

The least she could do was help him to have some fun – to forget all the heartache that lingered so heavily in their lives. If everything was going to turn to custard – which it most definitely was – then shouldn't they have a laugh now?

'Let's go skating,' she said.

'Really?' Luke looked so surprised Zelie felt even more guilty.

'Yeah.' She'd obviously been a total grouch recently. 'Go grab your skates.'

She went upstairs and got hers. They'd eat later – the lasagne would keep warm in the oven. Her father was lost in his lab. She'd hardly seen him since Sunday. Since he'd saved Tamás. Since he'd destroyed what had been left of her mother's dress.

Since they'd stopped speaking altogether.

Zelie longed to escape, and Luke looked like he did too. As they walked she asked Luke about his day at school. Light conversation that would distract and bring normality back.

'We'll only be twenty minutes,' Zelie promised Glen, the playpark manager, knowing they were pushing it given closing time was in five. But one of the perks about working at the winter park was being able to skate and swim for free.

'Okay,' Glen grinned. 'I'm doing the tills and the pools. I'll be back after that to do the ice.'

'Thanks.'

Just enough time to exhaust herself so not even the memories could move in her head. She wanted to forget all of it; flaming Kate and especially Tamás.

Luke was already pulling his skates on. They couldn't talk any more because the music blared so loudly from the speakers. But it didn't matter. His smile said it all as he slid out onto the ice. A thin layer of water skimmed out like the wake from a ship at the end of his blades, pooling at the edges of the rink. Overnight the machines would run and thicken it up again. The frost would add to it, but right now, after a day with many skaters on the rink, there were grooves in the ice and marks under the puddles at the edges. If either of them went down they'd get really wet.

Luke stretched out and glided down the centre of the rink, skating from one end to the other like the little pro he was. She understood his attraction to skating. He could go fast with little effort. His lungs wouldn't let him sprint. It wasn't that he was unfit, in fact he kept fit to fight the asthma, but running hard wasn't something he could manage. So this was like the nearest he'd ever get to flying. And like Zelie, he loved it. They'd skated with Mum – holding hands, making a train, with her going backwards in front of them. Skating was a way of chasing those happy memories.

Zelie got onto the ice herself, feeling her thighs protest. Despite all the running it felt good to stretch out and feel the cold beat over her face. It felt free.

She coasted to the lake end of the rink and looked at the view. The village lights were like tiny fireflies below, barely impacting on the darkness that had descended. The lake had disappeared, only the snow-capped mountains around it could be seen in the pale starlight. Somewhere down there was Tamás.

The darkness suddenly deepened as Glen shut down the big bright lights. But through the windows, the internal lights from the complex sent a small glow onto the ice.

She turned, noticing the silence beneath the beat of the music. No sound of Luke's skates. She scanned the empty rink. It took too long to locate him. Her anxiety rocketed.

He was down, his lower back against the railing as he hunched over his knees. Even from this distance she could see his shoulders heaving. She sped over, the water sloshing with each slice of her blades.

'Can you breathe?' she called as she got within range.

She thumped against the railing and put her hand on his back, feeling how hard he was fighting to get air in. With every shudder he got less oxygen, and grew more terrified.

'Where's your inhaler?' she asked.

'Don't have . . . it. Been better . . . really . . . good,' he panted. 'Thought it . . . was better.'

'Damn it, Luke.' Panic sharpened her tone. Asthma didn't miraculously get better, it was a life-long ailment that could be managed fine if he had his damn medicine with him.

But he didn't and she was freaked. She couldn't let this happen. She should have checked he had it. He was her responsibility. He glanced up at her, his expression tensing further as he saw hers.

She wasn't helping. She bent closer, rubbed his back more gently. 'It's okay. It's going to be okay.'

She didn't believe it. Luke didn't either. Because his breathing was worse already, his face taut. Even in the dim light she could see his lips turning blue.

Her father was too far away. So was the volunteer fire crew. She had to get him oxygen. But she couldn't leave him. She couldn't leave him alone. She could never do that again. But she wasn't doing any good just standing here watching him. Glen wouldn't be able to hear her shouting over the music.

'Luke,' she bent down, trying not to show the tearing agony at having to leave him. 'I have to get Glen. We'll get oxygen for you.' Even better, Ventolin – maybe they had some in the first aid kit.

'Please,' she muttered beneath her breath as she turned to skate back across the rink. 'Please, please, please.' Let them have something. Let him be okay for the minute she had to be gone.

'What's happened?' a strong voice called out.

Not Glen.

'Tamás?' Zelie spun round, stunned to see him running down between the viewing seats. 'Where did you come from?' Had he been in the trees beyond the back of the rink?

He jumped over the railing and looked at Luke. 'You're having trouble breathing?'

Luke's chest rose and fell in violent bursts, the struggle even more evident in his face, the jerky movements of his arms, the hideous gasping as he grew tired.

'I'm going to help you.' Tamás crouched down beside him.

Zelie hovered, unsure whether to go get Glen now. But Tamás put his hands on her brother's shoulders and Luke suddenly looked slight and vulnerable. Zelie's heart pounded. The last time she'd seen Tamás do that, Kate had been choking and Tamás *hadn't* been helping. He'd been the cause of it. She remembered the feeling that had flooded her that first day when he'd seen Kate. His hate, his almost uncontrollable violence.

As much as she didn't want to believe it, Tamás killed people.

'Tamás?' Her voice sounded three octaves too high.

'Just relax, Luke.' Tamás ignored her again and answered Luke's frightened look instead. 'Don't be afraid. Think about winning Alien Eaters.'

His favourite game. Tamás only knew that because of his time with Zelie. But Luke was too scared to question anything.

Zelie was so terrified she couldn't move, couldn't speak, could hardly watch.

The air around Tamás seemed to shimmer. Not with aggression this time but something else. No longer was there a pale cloud of frozen breath coming from his mouth, but something brighter that soon surrounded him completely. She squinted into the aura of light, unable to believe the glow to his skin. It had gone opalescent – flickering with pale, creamy light. His eyes shone, their colour deepening to the turquoise blue of the lake.

Luke stilled. Transfixed, he looked up at Tamás and the eerie glow he cast – that now half surrounded Luke as well.

Zelie said nothing, couldn't move for fear. But in the timeless moments she could see her little brother relaxing, his breathing deepening, settling, *normalising*.

The shimmering ceased, evaporated in a blink. Frowning, Zelie couldn't be sure she'd seen it at all. She *thought* she had, but now it seemed too fantastic. Unreal. All she was sure of was that Luke was okay. That Luke was smiling. That he was breathing easily and blinking a couple of times like he'd been looking into a bright light.

It was only then that she realised she hadn't been breathing either. She inhaled deeply, puffed out the tension and let relief flow in as she bent and gave her brother a hug. His arms clutched around her neck, surprisingly strong for a weedy kid. She grinned at him and then stood up to thank Tamás. To ask him what on earth he'd done.

But now he was the one helplessly leaning against the railing. His eyes were screwed shut like he was suffering intense pain. Immediately she moved closer, putting herself between him and Luke so her little brother couldn't see how dreadful he looked.

'What's wrong?' She was back to deathly afraid in less than a heartbeat. He'd turned whiter than the ice they stood on.

'I just need a moment. It takes a moment.' His voice was so thin she hardly heard him.

'For what?'

His face screwed up again in a grimace. 'To get my strength back.'

'Can I do anything?' Instinctively she put her hand on his as he clenched the top of the railing.

He shook his head.

She felt the muscles in his hand moving beneath hers as he gripped the railing harder and then harder again. She felt the warm life-force beating beneath his skin, stronger, faster.

'Take him home, Zelie,' Tamás whispered. 'He'll be fine.'

'What about you?' She wasn't leaving him, not like this.

'I'll be fine too. Just go.'

'No.'

He sighed but didn't try to argue more. She waited an endless moment as he rested against the barrier. His fingers suddenly twisted, tightened – clinging to hers. But afterwards she wondered if it had happened at all or if it was just wishful thinking on her part, because in the flash before the next second he'd withdrawn his hand and stepped away.

'Better now?' She tried to hide her disappointment at the loss of contact.

He shrugged, the colour back to normal in his cheeks. 'It's like being light-headed for a moment.'

It looked a lot worse than that.

'Zelie?' Luke stood uncertainly.

'He'll be all right,' Tamás said quietly.

'It's my fault.' She wrapped her arms around her brother and hugged him close again. 'I should have checked he had his inhaler.'

'It's not your fault, Zelie.' Tamás smiled for the first time in days.

A small, sad smile. 'Not all the bad things are your fault.'

She looked down. The water came halfway up the soles of his trainers. She frowned – surely he should have mud on them if he'd come running through the forest.

'I'll walk down with you.' He moved forwards.

'Thanks.'

They left the rink. She helped Luke get his skates off and quickly stuffed her feet into her trainers.

'Everything okay?' Glen called out from the office as they walked through the doors.

'Fine,' Zelie waved. She slung both sets of skates over her shoulder and walked between Tamás and Luke down the path. She had her torch and let its light flicker ahead so they could see their way down. But their faces were in shadow, their thoughts shadowed too. Luke said nothing, just tucked his hand in hers. Yeah, that meant he was feeling weird.

Tamás said nothing either and Zelie was too afraid of saying the wrong thing. Her tension rose as they walked past the motor camp. But he didn't turn in; he stayed walking on the path with her, past the village shops and right up to her father's house.

She stopped outside. 'I'll be inside in a second, Luke. You get the plates ready.'

Her brother sent Tamás an uncertain smile and went inside.

'I don't think he'll say anything.' Zelie turned to face Tamás.

'He's forgotten most of the detail already.'

'Really?' Because of something Tamás had done? Just now? Was he about to do that to her?

Tamás looked into her eyes, like he was trying to read her thoughts.

'What did you do?' she had to ask. But his expression just grew more intense and he said nothing. 'Tamás?' She stepped closer to him, whispered. But she knew he could hear what she barely breathed. 'I don't believe you when you say you're dangerous. I'm safe with you, Tamás.'

He shook his head.

She spoke more vehemently. 'You just saved my brother. I know you won't hurt me.' He didn't answer so she filled in the blank herself. 'You're a healer.'

A smile tweaked his mouth and her annoyance multiplied. He

had just saved Luke's life – somehow. And yet he'd taken life too. So now she was totally confused, and cross with him for not being honest with her. 'Are you some kind of god?'

He laughed then. 'No.'

'Can you tell me, please?' she asked simply. 'Because I'm tired of not knowing.'

She strained her eyes to see deeper into his. But it was pointless; in the shadows she saw nothing. And she truly was tired. 'I deserve to know, Tamás.'

He reached out and touched her hair. 'Yes you do.' He caught a strand between finger and thumb and stroked down its length, tugging gently at the bottom. 'I'm so sorry, Zelie.'

For what? Still not talking to her? Still not telling her a thing? As they stood in the darkness he seemed to come to a decision.

'Tonight.' His hand dropped and he stepped back. 'I'll come to your room tonight.'

'What about Kate – she tried to hurt you. And me. And –'

'She won't bother you tonight.'

How did he know?

'Trust me. I'll tell you everything you want to know. Tonight.'

'Okay.' She had little choice but to trust him. 'Should I leave the back door unlocked?' she asked wryly.

He shook his head as he turned away. 'I'll come in your window.'

She stared after him. Her bedroom was on the second floor and there was no balcony outside her window. Was flying on his list of abilities?

She wouldn't be surprised if it was.

She walked into the house only a few minutes after Luke, but there were other voices in the kitchen.

'I was just showing Megan that swab. One scientist to another.' Her father smiled at Luke and ignored the fact that he hadn't talked to Zelie in two days.

'It might be something to do with the rock flour from the glacier.' Megan was holding the container to the light, checking out the sparkles.

'So it's not from outer space?' Zelie tried to joke.

'Where have you and Luke been?' her father asked. 'It's past dinnertime.'

His paternal concern annoyed her. 'Skating.' She let the skates thud by the back door to emphasise the obvious.

Her father's expression tightened, but he immediately turned back into mad-scientist mode, carefully taking the container of slime from Megan and packing it into a box.

Zelie realised what the box was – a courier pack. 'Where are you sending it?'

'Up to the university. They have better equipment there to run tests.'

'What kind of tests?'

'Every kind.' Her father couldn't contain his excitement, despite his lingering displeasure with her. 'It's the most amazing stuff. So rich in nutrients. I've never seen anything like it. I can't wait to see what they think it is. I had a look at it using the science lab at your school but again, the instruments weren't precise enough.'

He'd been to school? Had he shown Mr Webb the slime too?

'What do you think it is?' Zelie asked.

'I think it's something world-changing.'

Zelie glanced at Megan to see how she was taking this side of her father, but she was smiling benignly at Luke.

'Something happened to that boy in the lake. He should have died. Five minutes in the water on a night like that should have seen him drown. But he lived.' Her father taped the box closed. 'Science has an answer for everything. We just have to work it out.' He looked out the window. 'There's something special in that lake.'

It wasn't the lake that was special. But her father didn't know that and she intended it to stay that way. If he found out Tamás was riddled with exceptional abilities he'd pack *Tamás* into the lab. And Tamás had been in a prison long enough. No matter the scientific possibilities, she wasn't going to let that happen to him. He deserved privacy and freedom.

'I need to catch the courier. This is precious, there's only a small sample left. Excuse me,' he said to Megan. No smile now, just back to business.

'Of course.' Megan stood. 'I need to get up to the observatory. The forecast is clear so it'll be a good night.' She smiled.

Zelie nodded, totally distracted. She had to warn Tamás.

She served up the lasagne while her father saw Megan to the front door. She heard the courier driver call out hello as he came to collect the day's medical samples. Tonight he'd drive them to Timaru – together with that one special package.

Despite the asthma attack, Luke ate well. Had he really forgotten it? Zelie barely ate at all. She pushed her food around until enough time had passed for her to legitimately leave the table and escape upstairs. She needed to talk to Tamás *now*. Minutes were being wasted. Somehow they had to stop the sample getting to the university.

She closed her bedroom door, saw the movement out of the corner of her eye. 'Tamás?' she whispered frantically.

'What's wrong?' he asked, climbing through her window and quickly pulling it to behind him.

She paused, briefly distracted by his mad climbing abilities. 'It's Dad –'

'What's happened to him?' Tamás strode to her door like he was about to turn into super rescue man again.

She blinked at his speed. 'Nothing. But he's got that stuff that was on you – that slime. He's sending it away to the university to be analysed.'

'Oh.' Tamás turned, instantly relaxing.

Zelie walked right up to him. 'We have to stop it from getting there.'

He looked at her.

'No one can know, Tamás. It'll be the end of your life.' She wanted to shake the consequences into him. 'They'll find out it's magic. It kept you safe, didn't it? All those years on the bottom of the lake. It's like the holy grail – cryogenics or something that can stop someone from aging. The possibility of eternal life, or a greatly lengthened one at least. There are people who would kill for that.' She had to get him to understand. 'And if they figure out that's what happened to you, your life will be over. You'll be more of a prisoner than you've been these last decades. It'll be worse because they'll do tests on you all the time, stick needles in. Everything.'

'You've seen this in a movie, right?'

'I'm *serious*.'

Arms folded across his chest, he shrugged his shoulders. 'So what do you want to do?'

'Get the samples. Destroy them. Unless . . .' She bit her lip.

'Unless you tell Dad too. Tell him everything. You could ask him to keep your secret, Tamás.'

Only she couldn't be sure her father would.

Tamás shook his head. 'The less he knows the safer it is for all of us.' He tilted his chin, the colour of his eyes deepening again. 'There are more people involved than just you and me.'

So she was back in it now, was she? She wished she had the time to savour the sweet feeling that admission had given her.

Part of her was relieved that he wasn't willing to trust her father. She didn't want either her father or Luke in harm's way, and she sensed that Tamás was smack in the middle of serious danger. 'Then you have to go and get it. He's already given the parcel to the courier.'

'What about his lab? Would he still have a sample there?'

She bit her lip. 'Maybe one. He said there was very little left.'

Tamás walked towards her desk, turning to lean a hip against it. 'Can you get it?'

She clasped her fingers together and pulled on them to ease the terrible tension. 'If his world-changing slime vanishes, it could crucify his career. Back in Britain he got sidelined because of his mad flu obsession, so to have this end up as a figment of his imagination?' She shook her head. 'He's a great doctor but he's just . . .'

'Just what?' Tamás kept his back to her.

'Irrational when it comes to his virus fears. It's why we moved. After what happened to Mum he was so paranoid about us getting the flu. He wanted to come to a place where we could easily be isolated. And he's off on this massive research project to try to find a cure-all vaccine or something. Controversial research. Some of the other scientists think it's crazy. If he's spouted off to someone at the university about some amazing discovery, then he's going to look even more of a freak when it doesn't show up.'

Tamás paused. 'Do you not want to do it?'

'Of course I don't. And I do.' She flicked her fingers, spreading them wide in front of her. She wanted to protect both Tamás and her father. 'I don't know what to do.'

Tamás said nothing.

'Okay, I do know what to do.' She lifted her head and lowered her hands to her sides. 'I'll do the lab. You do the courier parcel.'

She chewed the inside of her cheek. 'How are you going to get it?'

'It'll be in the courier van, right?' He turned to face her again.

'He's taken it already, it'll be on its way to town.'

'Then I'll take care of that.' He walked to the window.

She watched. She didn't want to know how he planned to do it, but she couldn't help checking one little detail. 'No one will get hurt, right?'

His smile flashed. 'Don't worry, Zelie.' He pushed the window open wider. 'I'd better go deal with it now.' He paused, his hand on the pane. 'Trust me. We'll talk.'

He put his foot up on the ledge, and with a smooth movement leaped right out the window. Zelie gasped and rushed across the room. Brushing aside the leaves of her confused, once winter-dead, suddenly mad-growing plant, she leaned out the window, straining to see how he could safely land from such a height.

But he'd already disappeared.

CHAPTER TWENTY

THE WIND HOWLED like starved wolves – wild and hungry. It rattled the windows and doors, trying to break in and destroy whatever was in its way. In the height of the roaring, Zelie slowly snuck down the stairs to her father's lab, wincing at every creaky step, waiting for the big gusts to provide audio camouflage.

Just as she got halfway down the stairs a door up on the landing behind her opened.

Luke.

'Can't you sleep?' Zelie whispered, freezing. *Please don't let Dad wake.*

Luke rubbed his eyes.

'Come on, take a quick trip to the loo and I'll rub your back.'

She sat nervously, rubbing his back for what felt like hours until she was sure he'd fallen back into a deep sleep. Then she tried to get down to the lab again.

She held her breath and moved in absolute slow motion. This time she made it.

Wrapping her clammy fingers in a cloth she took the sample from the industrial fridge. It was so easy to find with her father's meticulous labelling. She held it under the tap, rinsing the gloop out and swooshing it down the drain. She left a small bit of water in the bottom. Perhaps her father would think it had dissolved or something. She raced up the stairs and dived guiltily into bed.

She couldn't sleep at all after that – too much energy trapped inside her, too many thoughts. Had Tamás got the other sample and, if so, *how*? Was he okay? Was the courier guy okay? And what was her father's reaction going to be when he found out both samples had disappeared? If he found out she was responsible –

and she worried that was inevitable – she knew he'd never forgive her. What little was left of their relationship would be destroyed.

She got up early, got busy. Tried to pretend life was normal by putting the cereal on the table and packing Luke's lunch. Totally unable to look at her father when he came down later. But that was the norm now anyway.

As soon as she was ready she threw her bag into her dad's car and scraped the ice from the windscreen. So much for Megan saying there would be a clear sky last night. Rain had bucketed down in a violent wind before a frost had struck. Signs of the storm's brutality were everywhere – drifts of dirty snow, tree branches scattered across the roads and fields.

She switched on the radio as she let the car crawl towards school, hoping to spin the thirty-minute drive into forty-five. But she couldn't linger at home a minute longer. She didn't want to be there when her father discovered what had happened to the sample. But she'd done the right thing, hadn't she?

She slowed the car even more as she listened to the local news report. A van had been blown off the road in the high winds as it went through the mountain pass. The driver had sustained mild injuries but had already been discharged from hospital.

A courier van.

Zelie gripped the steering wheel tighter and pushed on the accelerator. She was heading into the pass now herself. Fifteen minutes of exposed road through the barren basin of the high country. Had the van been towed already? What of its parcels? And what of Tamás? Had he made the wind blow like that? It was impossible. Yet she was certain it had been him.

She couldn't get there fast enough now, annoyed by the slippery blackness and the low-lying clouds that made everything difficult to see. But halfway along the straight road she braked sharply. Something partially blocked her side of the road ahead. It wasn't the yellow courier van. This was smaller. A snow-covered branch perhaps? She pulled over and popped her car boot so she could get her spade. She'd have to shift whatever it was. Then she walked a few metres closer to see it clearly.

From the near side she could see only snow, but when she walked around the object she saw something bright peeking out from beneath the white powder. A bit of fluoro material – like a

high-vis safety vest. She swallowed, not liking the sick feeling that
had risen below her ribs. She squatted down and gingerly brushed
off the snow, which slid away with just that small movement.

She fell backwards as she saw the face. Immediately she shut her
eyes but the image remained. It was frozen in an expression of pain
and terror. She pressed her fists hard to her eyes as the other image
rose, her mother's face wearing an identical expression. She saw
once again the loneliness and awful agony her mum had suffered
in death.

She made herself lower her hands and look at those empty,
frightening eyes again. She didn't recognise him, although she
knew he'd have looked vastly different when alive. Her mother
had looked nothing like herself in death.

She made herself move, her throat tight and aching as she got
onto her knees beside him. She needed help. He needed help. But
this time, just like that time before, she knew it was too late.

'No.' Her thoughts tumbled. 'No, no, no.'

She couldn't sit back. She had to go nearer to see if there was
something she could do. But once more she was alone and unable
to do anything useful.

'Tamás,' she managed to whisper. She wished he was with her
now. He'd tell her what to do. He'd help somehow. 'Please, Tamás.'

She put a hand on the man's shoulder, brushing more snow away,
and as she glanced beyond him she saw part of a wheel poking
from the snow bank at the side of the road. He'd been cycling in
this weather? So had he been hit by a car? Or was it hypothermia?

'What's happened?'

Startled, she looked up. He was in black – black jersey, black jeans,
black beanie, his skin only saved from pallor by that underlying hint
of bronze. She gazed at him, her brain rendered useless. He'd tan
overnight in summer, whereas she'd go red'n'crispy if she didn't
slop SPF 280 on every inch of skin. Random, irrelevant, ridiculous
thoughts flew through her mind.

'Zelie?' He bent down beside her.

Relief hit. He was there already. Like she'd wished for him and
he'd appeared.

'How do you keep doing that?' she whispered.

'What?'

'Appearing out of thin air.'

The slightest smile softened his tense expression. Then he looked again at the man lying in front of her and that hint of amusement vanished. 'Who is he?'

'I don't know.' Her composure crumpled. 'A tourist?' Her relief was sucked out as panic rose instead. Dread filled her with icy doubts. What was Tamás doing here? How had he got here so quickly? Had he been waiting here? Did he have something to do with whatever had happened to this man?

She shuddered as she tried to breathe, tried to collect her scattered, scary thoughts enough to challenge him.

'It's not anything to do with the accident the courier van had last night?'

He met her stare calmly. 'This one has nothing to do with me.' He crouched down, sweeping the snow from the man's chin and neck.

Zelie watched the gentleness of his actions and felt her shoulders ease. His words reassured her. She didn't think Tamás had ever lied to her – except for when he'd reckoned he wasn't special. But that was humility. When it came to the most important things, he might not have given her answers sometimes, but when he did it was the truth.

She looked again at the body. There was no blood, no sign of injury. Maybe he'd got caught in the storm and the expression on his face was from bracing against the cold.

'Isn't there something we can do?' Zelie badly wanted to help him. She couldn't be a useless witness again. She had to do something, anything, for this man. She turned to Tamás.

'I can't help him, Zelie.'

'Why not?' she asked. 'You survived hypothermia. You were nearly dead and you lived. And you helped Luke. Why can't you help him?'

'Zelie,' Tamás said gently. 'He's already dead. I can't bring him back.'

'But you help people breathe. Can't you make him breathe again?' Pleading, she stared at the glacier-blue eyes of the boy she was sure could do something. He was magical, wasn't he? Couldn't he manage a miracle? 'Maybe it's not been that long?' Tears hurt her eyes. She begged. 'Couldn't you try?'

Tamás looked worried. 'Zelie . . .'

'Please . . .' The word was half lost in a sob.

He shook his head slightly. Zelie's tears ran down her cheeks. He wasn't going to.

But then Tamás went right down on his knees, put his hands on the man's shoulders and leaned close to his face. Zelie shivered, almost too afraid to watch, yet she couldn't look away. The aura wasn't as obvious in the daylight but she could still see the opalescent sheen of his skin – the milky wash that gave him a kind of silvery-white glow as he did whatever it was that he did.

She knelt closer, watching Tamás, then scanning the still body in front of them to see if there was any change. The glow grew like a bubble, stretching to encompass the man's head and shoulders. The pearly sheen touched his skin but it didn't light him up at all.

She turned back to Tamás. His frown had deepened, his gaze even more intense on the man's face. Zelie watched beads of sweat form on Tamás's forehead. His chest rose and fell rapidly as he expended whatever power he had to create the strange magic. Zelie watched, transfixed by the beauty of him in the pale light. But his frown twisted in pain. His breathing grew louder and more ragged. His fists were clenched. All his muscles bunched. And all of a sudden the glow flashed blindingly bright for a split second. Then disappeared.

Zelie blinked to get rid of the black spots flickering in front of her eyes.

'I can't help him.' Tamás was hunched over, his breathing harsh, his hands on his thighs. 'It's not natural.'

'What?'

'He's been hurt.' Tamás sounded as shocked as he was breathless. 'If someone's been shot or something . . . I can't help . . . I can ease the suffering with anaesthetic . . . but I can't stop the wrong. He's been wronged, Zelie . . . Not a natural death. And it's too late.'

'Are you saying someone's *killed* him?' Horror added to the agony already twisting her innards. 'I thought he was hypothermic or something.'

Tamás bent closer to the ground, his ribs jerking, his head shaking. 'Poison.'

'How can you tell?' she asked, but then she tapped her fingers on her forehead. 'Don't answer that.' She wouldn't understand it anyway and he needed to recover.

Tamás was as out of breath as an overweight, unfit asthmatic trying to do the Death Valley ultramarathon. She gazed at the poor dead man. More questions, more fear. 'Why would someone do that?' Why would someone poison some random person in the middle of absolutely nowhere? It didn't make sense.

'They'll put it down to cardiac arrest, that's the result of the poison. But I can sense it in him.' Tamás straightened painfully and groaned, his face screwed up in agony, his breathing still not coming any easier.

'Are you okay?' She was getting scared for him now. He wasn't recovering.

He jerked his head and bent over again like he was trying to get the blood back to his brain.

'Tamás?' She reached out to touch him.

'Scraping up the roadkill again, Zelie?'

Zelie spun on her knees so fast she slipped and put out a hand, grazing it on the icy bitumen. Otis. She hadn't even heard his vehicle come up behind them, she'd been too focused on Tamás and trying to help the man.

'Otis.' She rubbed her hand on her jersey and stood. 'Something terrible has happened.' Her legs wobbled but she walked towards him. She wanted to distract him from how weak Tamás was. She sensed Tamás would hate him to see it.

Otis walked closer. 'Oh my God, who's that?'

'We don't know. We just found him.'

Otis looked quickly from her to Tamás, his mouth tightening. He looked back to the body. 'Is he dead?'

Zelie nodded.

Colour drained from Otis's cheeks. 'Zelie –'

She looked past him as another car came up fast. The brakes squealed and the passenger door opened before it had even stopped. Zelie's senses sprang to attention.

Kate. And she wasn't alone.

Zelie glanced back at Tamás. He was still on his knees. She took a couple of steps to shield him from the Hearns. It was taking much too long for him to recover. And she didn't like the way Kate was walking towards them with her uncles bringing up the rear, as if closing in on their prey. The three of them looked not at the body, but right through Zelie to Tamás.

'Have you called the police?' Otis asked, still staring at the body.

'My phone's out,' Zelie said to cover her inaction. They hadn't got to that yet. 'Can you?'

'Yeah.' He stuffed his hand into his pocket.

Zelie kept her eyes on Kate. She was quick to check out the situation and was the only one not to blanch at the sight of death. How ironic that Kate now looked healthier than all of them.

'Let me see, Zelie.' Kate walked closer.

Zelie held her ground. She knew Kate didn't mean the body.

'Let me see him,' Kate repeated. 'I might be able to help.'

'There's no helping him,' Otis said, unaware they were talking about Tamás.

Zelie relaxed as she heard yet another vehicle approach. It was as 'rush hour' as it got on this road. This time it was the school bus, rattling loudly as the driver pushed it to its maximum speed – still well below the legal limit. Its brakes screeched even louder than Kate's had, preventing any attempt at conversation for a few seconds.

Zelie had never been so relieved to see the old rust-bucket. The kids on board were all staring. Even better, she saw that Mr Webb had pulled in behind the bus. *Witnesses*. Nothing could happen now. It was okay to move. Kate looked up at the noses pressed against the windows of the bus, turned and nodded to one of her uncles, the shorter of the two.

'I'll phone the police,' he said as he stepped back towards the car.

'They'll be here soon,' Otis called to him. 'A patrol car's already heading into the pass – it was on speeding-student duty.' He walked closer to Tamás. 'You guys'll have to answer questions.'

'Can't we cover him or something?' Zelie asked, agitated. 'It doesn't seem right that everyone sees him like this.'

'I'll get the bus to move on,' Mr Webb said as he walked up beside them. 'You okay, Zelie?'

She nodded, turning as she saw her teacher frown at Tamás.

Yeah, he still looked awful, his breathing ragged. Zelie resumed her position between him and the others. Kate's uncles quietly talked to the bus driver and Mr Webb. It was only a minute before the driver walked back to the bus, muttering something to the gawping students pressing against the windows.

Otis moved closer to Zelie and watched the bus slowly pull past and park at a safe distance. 'How'd you get here?' he frowned at Tamás.

'I was giving him a ride to school,' Zelie said quickly.

Kate stared at Tamás, all wide eyes and open curiosity. Her glance flickered to the body briefly then back to Tamás. Chills slithered down Zelie's spine. Did Kate understand how vulnerable Tamás was at this moment? Did she know something of what had just happened? Because she didn't seem shocked to see a body. She didn't seem afraid. She just had that avid interest in Tamás.

Zelie felt sick. There was a murderer around. And maybe that murderer was a lot nearer than she wanted to think.

She bent and quietly instructed Tamás, 'Get in the car.'

He sent her an outraged look but could hardly argue. It took all he had to stand, but she didn't offend his dignity by offering her arm. His fists were clenched and she could feel the waves of emotion rolling off him. She opened the passenger door and waited for him to sit in the seat. He more fell than sat, his teeth gritted. He hated this and she couldn't blame him. He'd totally lost his so-cool-and-in-control aura. If she weren't so worried about him, or appalled that a man had been killed, she might have smiled.

'We'll get out of here as soon as we can,' she said softly.

He didn't answer. Her worry lifted another notch when she saw the twist of pain on his face. What had it cost him, trying to breathe life back into that body? She didn't know what his powers were, or the price he paid for using them. But she was desperate to get him away from Kate while he was so weakened.

'Are you all right, Zelie?' Mr Webb walked over to her.

'I'm okay,' Zelie answered. 'It was just a shock.'

'I've some coffee in a thermos if you'd like some. What about Tamás?'

Zelie glanced into the car and saw the slight shake of Tamás's head. 'It's okay. Thanks anyway, Mr Webb.'

He turned that narrow gaze on her for another moment – and then Tamás – before going back and quietening the kids on the bus who weren't handling the scene too well.

Fortunately it was only another few minutes until the police car pulled up, lights flashing. The cops swung into action immediately, setting up cones and taking photos while they waited for the ambulance and additional backup that was already en route from Timaru.

The interview didn't take as long as she'd feared. The officers took one look at them both and clued in pretty quick to their shock. They interviewed Tamás where he sat in the passenger seat, still whiter than a sheet and visibly trembling, while Zelie leaned against the car.

Once the police had asked their questions and got their details they told Zelie and Tamás to take the day off school and go home. Zelie couldn't wait to get Tamás out of there, but she had to wait until the bus and other cars had moved on as they were blocking hers.

'Zelie.'

She ignored Kate's call. She wasn't interested in anything Kate had to say, not till she was sure Tamás was okay. And she wasn't leaving him alone for a moment while those uncles were around. So she just shook her head and turned away.

Kate's uncle started up the ute. Slowly the three of them drove past, the bus following them. Tamás lifted his head and watched. Zelie saw the look pass between him and Kate – the flash of Kate's brows and the glint in her eyes, the way Tamás clamped his jaw to stop his teeth chattering as he stonily stared back.

Then only Otis remained. 'Are you sure you're okay to drive home?' he asked as he walked up to Zelie.

'I'll be fine.' She smiled at him, relieved that the Hearns had gone. 'Thanks.'

'You still want to meet up later? After I'm done at school?' Otis held her gaze and matched her smile, ignoring Tamás in her front seat.

'Um,' Zelie hesitated.

Otis's smile broadened to that all-winning one. 'What about a walk by the lake? It'll be good to clear your head. There's something I need to give you anyway.'

He made it impossible to refuse. She couldn't be rude to him. She genuinely liked him. Just not the same way she did Tamás.

'Sure,' she said. 'This afternoon. But I'm going to take Tamás to see Dad now.'

'Yeah,' Otis flicked a derisive look to her car. 'Not handling it well, is he?'

Zelie bridled, but said nothing. Tamás had more courage and strength than anyone she knew. 'He'll be fine.'

But she wasn't sure he would. Out of the corner of her eye, she saw the way Tamás's fingers trembled, the sheen of sweat on his skin, the frown deepening further still. He looked tortured.

She got into the car and drove as fast as she dared on the treacherous road. She shouldn't have made him try to help. He was suffering now.

'I'm sorry, Tamás.'

A tremor shook him from top to toe and she pressed her foot harder on the accelerator, scaring herself with her speed. 'Is there anything I can do?'

He sat silent, his eyes still screwed shut, anger emanating from him. Her heart raced and her head spun with unanswered questions. Was this some kind of sickness brought on by his efforts? Or was this the impact of all those years under the water? Had he somehow absorbed some of the poison that had killed that man? She gritted her teeth, closing her mind to the chaos, making herself focus on the one thing she could control – driving home. Her father would help Tamás. Then she could ask the questions she wanted to ask. She needed him to tell her all the things he hadn't had time to tell her last night.

She drove into one of the patient car parks and watched Tamás stagger his way inside. He looked too angry for her to risk offering help. Despite his weakness she could feel his aggression, and she just knew he'd bite her head off if she did.

Her father wasn't there. She guessed he must be doing house calls. For once she hoped to see him sooner rather than later, only he was on foot for his visits as she had taken his car. She strode to the kitchen and put the jug on to boil – pointlessly, because she didn't want coffee or tea and Tamás probably didn't either. Helplessly, she looked over to where he leaned against the doorframe, his eyes still closed.

'Sit down.' She tried to be firm.

'No!'

Zelie jumped. Oh man, he was angry.

'No!' He shouted it again. But Tamás wasn't looking at her. He seemed to be talking to himself.

She stepped closer to the door. Some colour had returned to

his cheeks but he still didn't look healthy. His fists clenched and he groaned between his teeth.

'Tamás?' She walked right up to him and went on tiptoes, angling her head so she could see right into his face. 'Look at –'

Before she could finish, his eyes snapped open and he stared hard right at her. His blue eyes were tinged with bruised purple. And that's when she realised. It wasn't physical weakness doing this to him, it was all emotion.

'I killed him.'

'*What?*'

'He was a boy. Maybe my age.'

Not that man on the road. Zelie's lungs started working again, but only at half strength. Tamás was looking at her, but not seeing her. He was lost in his own agonising memories. His voice came rough and unsteady as the words streamed out.

'He was in a trench. He'd been shot, his stomach blown open. There was no one else around. Not alive, anyway. I was scurrying through to get a supply message. I tried.' He shuddered. 'I tried, I tried. I *tried*. And he was begging me to stop the pain.' Tamás lifted his head, distress creasing his face into a mess of twisted lines. 'I tried everything I knew, but nothing helped. I couldn't do anything. I can't help someone who's been hurt like that. It wasn't anything airborne like a flu or virus – I'd dealt with lots of those – or cleaning a cut. But this?' His voice rose in a strangled plea. 'He was in agony.'

Now she understood. 'You ended it for him.'

His eyes were huge as he stared at her. Blue, purple and grey clashing – begging for understanding. For forgiveness. For absolution.

She ached for him to cry. But his eyes were hollow – empty of their tears and ability to soothe, unable to let the pain flow out through stinging salt water. Their visible dryness hurt her own eyes, so she cried for him. Thick, hot, silent tears that dripped to the floor.

'I'll never know if it was the right thing. I try not to, but I think about it all the time. I always worry that I could have done something more. I should have been able to.' He bowed his head, hiding his gaze from hers. 'I took the pain away,' he insisted. 'I thinned the oxygen out slowly so he just went to sleep. Thinned it out more until eventually he died.' His voice dropped to the slightest of whispers. 'There was no struggle, no horror, he just slept. Because I couldn't stand his screams, Zelie. I still hear them.'

'Tamás —'

'I'd do it again,' he said strongly, stubbornly. 'I'd do it again.' He looked directly at her, anguish burning in his eyes. 'But it killed a part of me too. It killed the good in me.'

CHAPTER TWENTY-ONE

'TAMÁS.' SHE REACHED around him and tried to pull him into her embrace. She felt the resistance in his muscles, so she softened and leaned closer – moulding against his hard planes. It was comfort he needed, and comfort she ached to give. There was nothing she could say to make it better. This was all she could think to do.

For a moment longer he stood even more rigidly. And then she felt his sigh as he lifted his hands to her waist. He didn't grip her hard, didn't push her away, just carefully rested his hands on her hips. 'He wouldn't have lived,' he pleaded. 'There was no way . . .'

'It's okay.' She put her fingers to his lips, he didn't need to explain it more.

'It's not.' His head jerked back from her touch. 'I killed him.'

'You eased his pain as he died.' She put her hand over his heart. 'He was dying anyway, Tamás. You made it better for him.' Didn't doctors do that with cancer patients? Wasn't there a difficult line between giving enough anaesthetic to relieve pain and hastening the death that was coming anyway?

'I should have been able to help him.'

'You did.' She spread her fingers wider, wanting to hold the hurt in his heart for him. 'You made the end better for him.' She'd give anything to have been able to do that for her mother. She hadn't even been able to offer her the comfort of a handhold or a whisper of love. Her mother had died a painful death all alone after a horrible, petty argument that Zelie had instigated.

Tamás closed his eyes. 'That's when I decided to get out of there. Go somewhere far enough away for me to forget everything. But the influenza was on the boat and I couldn't let that baby die.' His fingers tightened on her waist. 'I wanted to make up for him.'

'Tamás –'

'I can't be with my kind any more. I'm not what I am supposed to be. I can't do what I'm supposed to do.'

'What are you supposed to do?'

'Protect.' His eyes snapped open, revealing the stormy blue-grey. 'Keep the balance.'

'Balance of what?' She spread her fingers wider on his soft wool jersey, right over his heart. She badly wanted to understand.

His eyes went even more intense, locking on hers, shadows and secrets snapping in the deepening blue. 'What are the four elements?'

Mesmerised, she barely had to think to answer. 'Fire, water, earth –'

'And air.'

'Air,' she echoed slowly. *Air* – the wind, the weather, the stuff she breathed.

'And what if those four elements had Guardians, gatekeepers to keep them under control.'

'Magical creatures?'

'Sort of.'

'You're a Guardian of the air.'

'I am air,' he whispered. 'Or I was.'

Zelie's skin tingled.

'We've been in legends of old forever. Humans have always suspected. The Witching kind have always known. And there have been many names – the forest people of the earth, the mermaids or Ondines of the water, the phoenix of fire.'

'And of air?'

He hesitated. 'Sometimes they're called sylphs.'

'What?' Zelie couldn't help a small smile slipping out. 'You're a sylph?' The only sylphs she'd ever heard of were in ballet. Her mother had taken her one time. Women dressed in long white tutus – wispy creatures with fine bones and delicate features. Harmless. Zelie had found them a bit boring. 'You don't look very sylph-like.' He looked young, strong and tough.

A wry look crossed his face. 'I know.'

'This is impossible to believe.'

'Like magic is? Or that the consciousness of one could be trapped in the body of another?' His laugh was edged with bitterness. 'You can't understand, but you do believe.'

She nodded slowly. 'The four elements.'

'We maintain them. Try to stop them hurting people, and stop people from hurting them.'

'Balance.' She understood. 'So what happened?'

'We were discovered of course, as the Witching grew stronger, with the development of science and knowledge. And so, as the humans emerged from the Dark Ages, we were forced to integrate, to protect ourselves.'

'To integrate with the Witching.' Kate had said as much. 'So you're human as well.'

'Partly. On my mother's side.'

'Can you fly?'

'In a way. My human form is heavy, but for a while I can float on the breeze. Guide the wind to take me where I need to.'

'That's how you got to me so quickly?' That's how he could jump out of a second-storey window and just disappear, literally, into thin air.

He nodded. 'I can hear you. Every word you speak I can catch on the lightest of breezes. Even your faintest whispers.'

She felt hotter; wondered if he could feel her pulse tripping. 'Only me?' she breathed. 'What I say?'

'Anyone I choose to,' he shrugged.

And he chose to listen to her? Was it weird that she was both pissed and pleased at that? She tried to focus on what his revelation meant. 'You caused the storm last night, the one that blew the van off the road.'

He nodded. 'And I got the parcel out. The driver is fine.'

'I know.' She couldn't hide her feelings now. 'You're amazing.'

'No,' he said, gently shaking his head. 'I'm a liability. Being here puts you in danger.'

'How?'

'For a while we coexisted okay. We kept our powers hidden, thought we were safe. Truth became fairy tale. Old stories were embroidered so that no one believed in them any more.'

Zelie remembered the look of pure fascination on Kate's face when she'd first seen Tamás. 'Except the Witching.'

'Some of them have Guardian elements,' he nodded. 'It's like any gene – such as red hair – it gets passed on to some, but not all. The lines are weakened. Powers are diluted. They've always kept searching for more Guardians. Some were destroyed, but some hid. We hid well. People are driven by greed, Zelie. People with power always want more.'

'The Witching wanted to get stronger. They wanted to control you.' Around her, she felt the muscles in his arms tense.

'Of course. To control the air, the water, the movements of the earth. What happens with water can make people rich or poor. Nations can starve or become wealthy with the treasure they can dig from the earth. Control the powers that can control the elements, and you have ultimate power. Wars could be won in an instant.'

'But are you powerful enough to control all the air?'

'No,' he shook his head. 'Certainly not now. You can see the effect even the smallest effort has on me. It's the price of the diapause I think. My strength isn't all back. I don't know if it ever will be. I can't figure out how to feed it again.'

'Are there others?'

'I don't know. That was what I wanted to find out from the history searches – signs of others, that Guardians had been at work. But there seems to be only chaos now. Earthquakes, hurricanes, fires and floods. We couldn't stop those from happening at all, but there was more balance before – and we were able to stop ourselves from taking advantage. I needed to find out whether the Hearns had got other Guardians. But I don't think they have.' He frowned. 'I don't know why they bound me for so long. Why she freed me now.'

So now she knew. Now it made sense. He was a higher being. Literally. A being of the air. 'You're like an angel.'

'No,' he grimaced. 'I'm far from that. I'm just supposed to keep the balance. But being human has also given me the weaknesses of humanity. Greed. Selfishness. Hate.'

'Is that why you've stayed?' Zelie asked. 'Because you wanted revenge on the Hearns – on Kate?'

'I needed to find out why, what they wanted. Whether they have more Guardians.' His lashes drooped, hiding most of the stormy blue, but she knew he still stared at her. 'But that's not the only thing that made me stay.'

She couldn't move, couldn't breathe. Couldn't dare think.

Suddenly he pushed her away and took a step back into the hall. 'I don't know what you're thinking any more. I can't feel it.' He glared, folding his arms across his chest. 'I can't stand it.'

'Join the club,' she snapped, hurt that he'd pushed her away when they were finally communicating. 'I've never been able to figure you out.' Boldly, she marched the two paces back to him and talked right into his face. 'How do you think I feel? We go from being practically one to absolutely nothing. You wouldn't even talk to me.'

'I thought –' He bit back the words and took another step back. Unfortunately for him that brought him against the wall. And Zelie stepped after him again.

He sighed, leaning right back, his attention suddenly focused on the carpet. 'I was worried about what could happen to you. And you were going to the ball with Otis. I know how you felt about him.'

'You didn't.' Zelie flushed. He was so wrong about that.

'I did. I could feel your thoughts, your desires,' he mumbled, his accent thickening. 'I could see everything, Zelie.'

'Really? Then you must know the rest, too.' She pushed through the embarrassment. 'Yes, I thought he was attractive – and he's a nice guy. But you know I didn't feel right with him. Not on the night. And you know how badly I wanted to see you.' She couldn't look him in the eyes any more, so she looked at his jersey. 'And you weren't going to let that happen. You pushed me away.'

'I watched you dressing for him.' Goaded, he grasped her shoulders, shocking her into facing up to him again. 'Spending so long on your hair. On your make-up.'

'That wasn't for him.' For a supposedly higher being, he was a complete idiot. Totally exasperated, she blurted it all. 'The truth is I took so damn long over it to get a reaction from *you*. You were so quiet. I wanted you to notice me.'

His fingers tightened almost to the point of pain. 'How could I not notice you? I was part of you.'

'I didn't want you to notice me because of that. I wanted more.' She'd wanted him to like her, to feel the same attraction she felt to him. 'I wanted –'

Ugh. She broke off. Did she really want to wade even deeper into the mud of humiliation?

'What?'

'Never mind.' She dismissed it, annoyed with his obtuseness. How obvious did she have to be?

He smiled. A slow, heart-stopping, totally unfair smile. The kind of smile that transformed his beautiful but sombre self into a bright star – full of life and laughter and . . .

'Don't be mean, Tamás,' she pleaded softly. She couldn't believe her eyes. It wasn't fair that he knew she had feelings for him when he'd been so unfriendly since he'd got out of the lake.

'I'm not being mean,' he answered gently, but his hands firmly slid down her arms to grip her elbows. 'Zelie, how can you possibly doubt what I feel for you?' He lifted away from the wall, coming so close she thought she was about to die from the sensations rippling through her – from the anticipation.

'How can you doubt *me*?' She didn't know why they were whispering. It was like the words were too precious, too secret, too important just to be tossed out. Instead they were spoken with quiet care. And with fear.

She looked into his storm-tossed eyes and felt herself hurtling towards a cliff over which she couldn't see. But it didn't matter. She was going over anyway – happy to. She was right where she wanted to be most. With the person she wanted more than she wanted her next breath. And she wanted –

'Zelie?'

They froze, their gaze locked for a sweet, secret, guilty moment. Then Tamás dropped his hands as if he'd suddenly got third-degree burns from her.

'Sorry.' Her father closed the front door behind him with a bang. He definitely didn't sound sorry. His brows took an age to sink to their usual spot. They'd been almost higher than his hairline when he'd first spoken.

Zelie took a step away from Tamás at the exact moment he took one from her.

'I heard what happened. Are you okay?'

'I'm fine.'

'You, Tamás?' Her father sent him a sharp glance. 'I heard you were in a bad way.'

'I'm better now. Thank you.' Tamás directed his answer low to the floor. 'I'd better go.' He glanced at her father for a nanosecond and then away again even quicker. 'Goodbye.'

Zelie's heart sank lower with every step Tamás took past her father and out the front door. She could hardly run after him with her dad watching. But she wanted to – even more when she remembered the samples they'd destroyed.

'I didn't mean to scare him off.' Her father brushed past her into the kitchen. Zelie braced herself, forcing her feet to follow him. She switched the kettle on to boil again, desperately trying to think of a change of topic. But all she could think about was the sample. She was terrified of how he'd react when he found out. Restless, she got cups from the shelf to make some hot chocolate. Her father liked it too, and doing something nice for him might ease her guilt over the samples a smidgeon.

Silently he put his bag on the floor and pulled out a chair. She'd been right about him doing house calls. But he didn't sit. Instead he stared grimly at the centre of the dining table. She knew that look – he was a million miles away.

He suddenly spoke. 'There's something I want you to have.' Brusquely he left the room, and came back in barely a minute. Then tossed a box on the table.

Zelie stared at it. Utterly shocked.

'Zelie –'

'Dad, can we not have this conversation?' she interrupted, holding up a hand but unable to look at him. She turned away and spooned the hot chocolate powder into the mugs with jerky movements. Her father had put a box of condoms on the kitchen table – *condoms*?

'It's important, Zelie. I don't want you getting into trouble –'

'That's not going to happen.' She opened the fridge to find the milk, hoping the cold air would have a calming effect on her burning skin. Oh, could this please not be happening.

'Well, you can hardly go and buy condoms down at the corner shop in a town this size, and there's no other doctor you can go to here.'

She slammed the fridge door shut. Oh right, so it was about his image? He didn't want her buying them from the shop and the world finding out she was sexually active – except she wasn't.

'You're my only daughter. I'll never be ready for it. But I'm even less ready to be a grandfather and Luke's too young to be an uncle. And nor do I want your fertility destroyed by some STI.'

Zelie gaped and spun to face him. 'Dad, I haven't even kissed . . .' She trailed off, not wanting to say his name. Suddenly she wondered if he was listening in to this conversation, and hoped like hell he wasn't. It was bad enough to have to live through it, let alone think there might be a witness to this humiliation.

'Well it looked . . . um.' Her father was clearly uncomfortable as he searched for a word. 'Intense.'

Zelie turned back to the bench. Unbelievable. Her father was commenting on how things looked with Tamás. Intense pretty much covered it – for her anyway. If only her father hadn't walked in at just that moment, because Tamás had been going to kiss her. He'd wanted to kiss her. *She'd* wanted it more than anything.

And her father had seen that.

Awkward? The whole situation was appalling. Especially now he'd made the leap from a simple kiss to a full-on sexual relationship.

Her anger flared. All her father cared about was her reproductive health. What about her *emotional* health? Why didn't he even ask if Tamás was her boyfriend, or if she was happy or anything? And why wasn't he like a normal dad who'd be polishing up his shotgun at the thought of some boy getting it on with his daughter?

What did he think of her? Did he even care? Or was it just about keeping her as physically safe as possible? Zelie wanted to have a decent first time with someone who she cared about and who cared about her. She wanted it to be special. Did her father not even want to try to ensure she felt that way? Did he not care so long as her heart was beating and her body infection-free? Furious, she poured her mug of hot chocolate down the sink. Turned the tap on *loudly* to wash it away, wishing she could wash her father's actions away.

'Take them, Zelie.' He'd come up behind her, put the box on the bench right next to her. 'Just don't take this as permission.' He choked. 'But you're almost all grown up. And I want you to be safe.' He cleared his throat. 'And, uh, if you ever want to talk . . .'

Zelie glanced at him as his voice trailed away. He looked like he wanted to run away from there as much as she did, but he was almost smiling – something he never did much of these days. Even if it was a bit of a rueful smile. Her heart contracted as she saw the concern that was lurking there in the back of his eyes.

'I wish your mum was alive.'

The faintest whisper. His first mention of her in months.

'So do I,' she whispered back. Afraid to move in case this moment would be shattered.

'I'm sorry, Zelie.'

Her heart broke. For the first time in months he was actually *trying*. And it was in the only way he could – the emotionless, impartial, doctorish way. Now she felt worse than ever that she'd betrayed him.

'It's okay.' She was sorry too. She hid her face by putting the mug in the dishwasher. She had adult responsibilities and adult burdens. She'd had them since the day she'd discovered her mother dead. But the burden of guilt was heaviest of all. And now it doubled.

'I better get going. I have another house call.'

'Of course.'

She dragged herself upststairs, clicked on one of her favourite You Tube channels. A good hour passed as she tried to take her mind off everything.

But she couldn't relax. Too guilty. Too scared. Too confused.

She shut down the computer, glanced at the plant that had sprouted yet more leaves overnight. There was too much weird going on. Too much out of control.

She had to get out. She didn't want to be in the house when her father found the destroyed sample. Part of her longed to confess everything, but she'd promised Tamás she wouldn't. Anyway, there was no way her father would ever believe her.

She wondered where Tamás had gone. But she didn't call to him. How was it possible to go from the agony of uncertainty to almost ecstasy and on to rotten guilt in just minutes?

It was too early for her to meet Otis but she'd head out anyway. She'd kill another hour at Mama Jo's Café. She might feel safer with other people around. She might be able to forget for a while. It only took two minutes to walk there and order another hot chocolate that she didn't drink. She sat at the computer they had for tourists to use and randomly surfed the net.

But in the end her fingers typed his name – because he was all she could think of. A baby names database was first on the list, giving origins and meanings. She clicked on it just to see. Tamás meant twin. Zelie stared at the screen as the meaning hit her like a ton of bricks. She typed in Gemelle. A Latin variant of Gemini, it also meant twin.

She froze. How could she not have realised? It was so obvious. Poor Tamás. She Googled both names together. Aside from the baby names database there was only one other hit – a French website. Zelie's heart raced through twenty beats as she waited for the page to load. *L'Étoile Abbey* had one of those home-built kind of websites, mainly text, no logo or pretty pictures.

She squinted as she tried to translate it, guessing at the hardest words. It was a brief history. The monastery was still there, but it seemed the orphanage had closed in the 1930s. But as she scrolled down she saw the lists – children's names, listed under the years they'd been at the orphanage, provided now for family history purposes. Names, birthdays, some with question marks. She scrolled down further and her suspicion was confirmed.

Tamás didn't just have a sister. He had a twin.

Zelie closed her eyes. It was so obvious; she'd been so stupid. Of course he'd written to her. He couldn't hear her, he was afraid she'd gone.

Had Gemelle been a sylph too? Had she survived the war? Had she gone on to have a family? Zelie was determined to find out. He'd said he couldn't be with his people, but maybe he could.

'Zelie.'

She flinched, her skin chilling like she'd been dipped in the lake. She quickly clicked away the page and turned. 'You're following me.'

Kate didn't deny it.

'I know what he is.' Zelie went straight into attack mode. 'He's getting stronger. He's leaving soon. So leave me alone, Kate, you won't win.'

But Kate already knew Tamás was stronger because she was looking stronger herself. Clear skin, gleaming eyes that now sharpened with frustration. 'You don't understand, Zelie. That man this morning –'

'Died. I know. But it wasn't anything to do with Tamás.'

'I'm not so sure about that.' Kate rubbed her finger back and forth over her lower lip. Her nails were no longer blue and broken, but long and strong.

'You don't know him.'

'Neither do you.'

But she *did*. She knew it now – more than he'd told her himself. She stood from the stool so she could look in Kate's eyes on the same level.

'How did you know I was going to be at the lake that day? How did you find me? My getting the necklace wasn't an accident. You chose me deliberately. You planned it. Why?'

'It had to be an equal to him.'

'But I'm not his equal. I'm as normal as anyone.'

Kate looked down.

'What?' Zelie asked. 'How can you know anything about me?'

A sad smile half curved Kate's lips. 'When you know what you're looking for, it's easy to see.'

'And what do you see? What were you looking for?'

'Strength.'

Zelie shook her head. 'I'm not strong.'

'Yes you are,' Kate said. 'You resisted me – even when I was with my uncles. Someone had protected you. It was a strong spell for a reason.'

'Spell?'

'And you have compassion,' Kate continued, ignoring her interruption. 'You helped me. You didn't want to but you did.'

'Only because there was no one else around.'

'I know.' Kate smiled. 'But you still did. When backed into a corner, Zelie, you'll do the right thing.'

Right thing for whom? And who was the judge? Had she done the right thing for her father? Destroying the sample so that his discovery would never be made public? Was that the right thing? Zelie stood, suddenly impatient to get down to the lake. 'It's finished now, Kate. He's free, you're free. It's over. Leave it.'

'I'm worried for you,' Kate said quickly. 'Things are happening.'

But Zelie had heard enough. 'I'm sick of your vagueness. *What* exactly is happening?'

'I'm not sure. But I feel it. It's bad.'

'Take an antacid. I don't want to hear about it any more.' She strode out of the café and along the path towards the lake, texting Otis to let him know she'd be down by the water. She looked through the trees towards the motor camp. Hopefully Tamás was inside his cabin. She badly needed to see him again, just to be sure what she thought she'd seen in his eyes earlier really had been there. She'd find him after seeing Otis.

She paused and looked back at the row of shops she'd just left. She could see the thin figure watching from the café window. She turned back and jumped down to the stones – found some small flat ones to try to skim into the lake. She owed Otis some kind of explanation, but she didn't know what to say. Kate was wrong – Zelie wasn't strong, she was a coward.

'Maybe it'll rain,' she whispered – *wished*. But the only ripples on the water were from the splashes of the stones she threw. Soon enough she heard the scrunching of heavy feet over stones. She waited for him, smiled because he *was* a nice guy. And it wasn't his fault he'd been overshadowed by someone otherworldly. 'How was school?'

'The usual.' Otis bent and selected a few skimming stones too. 'Everyone was talking about that man this morning.'

'It was awful, wasn't it?' Zelie shivered. She watched as the stone he threw bounced four times before sinking.

'Yeah – are you okay?'

She nodded. He didn't mention Tamás and she was too chicken to bring him up.

Otis pulled something out of his pocket. A small box. 'I have something for you.'

She looked at it, her discomfort increasing. 'Otis –'

'I wanted to replace the one I broke. It's for you to put your pendant on.'

'You didn't have to do that.' She felt her colour rising as she looked at the chain. It didn't seem right to be accepting jewellery from him when she was so totally in love with someone else.

'Is the pendant back at your house?'

She shook her head. It was with Tamás. 'I was just borrowing it. That's why I was so worried when it broke.'

He looked up from lifting the silver necklace out of the box. 'So you'll give this to the proper owner too?'

'Yes.' She felt a weird kind of relief that she could think of it like that.

He looked down at the pretty links. 'Can I put it on you anyway? Just to see how it looks?'

She hesitated. She couldn't really refuse, not when he'd gone to the trouble and expense of choosing a new one for her. And she felt guilty for running out on him that night, and for caring so much more about Tamás. So she stood still and lifted her ponytail out of the way.

But as the cold silver touched her skin, something felt really, really wrong.

CHAPTER TWENTY-TWO

SHE TURNED TO face him and smiled, forcing away the scary vibe. This was just Otis. This was just a chain. 'Look all right?'

'Yeah,' he grinned.

She didn't know what to say next, but to her intense relief she felt the first drops of rain on her face. So wishes did come true. She lifted a hand to point it out. 'We should get back.'

He nodded and threw the last of his stones into the lake.

'Thanks.' She cleared her throat. It felt scratchy. It figured. After all the sleeplessness of the last week she was bound to get a cold.

'You'll be back at school tomorrow?'

She nodded, put her fingers to her neck. The necklace felt strange. 'Otis, would you mind taking this off for me? I'll put it in the box and keep it for the pendant.' It felt uncomfortable, and with a horrible sense of déjà vu she realised couldn't find the clasp.

She stood still, waiting for him to undo it. His fingers brushed the back of her neck. She wished it was Tamás.

'Um . . .' Otis sounded unsure.

'What's wrong?' Her throat tightened.

'I can't manage it.'

She turned to face him. The bad vibe intensified. 'You can't take it off?'

She put both hands to her neck as he shook his head. She saw the puzzlement in his face, but lost focus on him as she struggled to feel her way round the links.

It was funny, but the chain wasn't hanging as low as when he'd first put it on her. It was right on her collarbones now, and even in the few seconds it took to run her fingers around it, it seemed to tighten again. 'Otis, is something wrong with this?'

He stood staring at her neck like he couldn't believe his eyes. But he wasn't doing anything. She needed someone to do something – because it was tightening more.

Panic flooded her.

'Tamás!' Pure instinct made her scream for him. The wind lifted for a moment, a blast of cool air that she barely registered. But then he was there, running over the rocks towards her.

He shoved Otis out of the way. 'What's wrong?'

'I can't get this off.'

Otis staggered over the stones as he righted himself. 'That's so weird. How can that be possible?'

'*What* be possible?' Zelie asked.

'One link of the chain is being swallowed by another. Then another. The necklace is shrinking.'

Tamás paled.

'Tamás?' Kate called from halfway across the white field, panting as she ran. 'What is it?'

Zelie stared at Tamás as he studied the necklace. She saw him mutter beneath his breath. Then she glanced at Kate, who'd tripped down the last of the stones, who was now also intent on the chain, her eyes widening as she watched it.

'What's happening?' Zelie's voice had gone croaky. 'Can you stop it?'

'I . . .' Tamás didn't finish. He looked into her eyes, his own blazing. 'I'm not going to let this happen.'

Let what happen? 'Why won't it come off? Why is it getting shorter?'

'It's cursed.' Kate circled around her slowly. 'That explains the man this morning.'

'What?' Tamás whirled and grabbed Kate's arm, shaking her fiercely. 'Was this you?'

'Of course not,' Kate shouted back at him, trying to wrench her arm free. 'I've told you before, Tamás, that's not how we operate.'

'Break it.' He pulled her towards Zelie.

Kate met Zelie's eyes for a moment, and hers were pity filled. 'I don't know that I can.'

'You're descended from the most powerful witch who ever walked the earth,' Tamás lashed out, jerking her closer to Zelie. 'Break the bloody spell!'

Kate quailed. 'I'll try.' She started to mutter in that mad-sounding language.

Tamás was back in front of Zelie, watching as with increasing speed the necklace shortened.

'Try harder,' he said loudly to Kate, putting his fingers beneath the chain.

Zelie winced. It only made it worse.

He saw her reaction and whipped his fingers out. Turned to tower over Kate. 'Break the damn spell.'

She nodded, didn't stop the chanting.

'Do it, Kate, or –'

'I'm trying!' she shouted at him. 'Let me concentrate.'

Fear overwhelmed Zelie. She reached out with her hands. 'Tamás?'

In an instant he was back with her, his hands on her shoulders. 'I'll keep you breathing, understand? Trust me. I can keep you breathing.'

Kate pinched a couple of links of the chain. Zelie whimpered.

'Hold tight,' Tamás urged her.

She put her hands on his chest, feeling the force of his heartbeat. Trying to be reassured. She wanted to believe him. But she knew he couldn't save her. She felt light-headed. She wasn't sure if it was because of the necklace or because she was so scared.

Kate's voice had risen higher and higher, an eerie, inhuman cawing sound. Her eyes glowed – blue fire rippled over her irises, her pupils disappeared. The side of Zelie's neck heated – the side Kate stood on was *burning*.

She cried out.

'She's trying to melt the chain,' Tamás said, his voice hoarse. 'I'm increasing the oxygen. I'll make it pure.'

The necklace was unbearably tight now. Her vision wobbled. Red-tinged darkness swooped in front of her, like a curtain that was whisked across her eyes and back again.

'I will keep you breathing.'

He would try. She could see his aura lighting up, his skin shining like he was made of opal. But he couldn't succeed.

It was a trap. In the brilliant clarity of the moment before death, Zelie saw it all. It was a trap to weaken him enough to control him.

'You bitch,' she cried hoarsely at Kate. She'd actually started to believe her when she'd said she meant him no harm. But it was a lie.

Zelie shook her head at Tamás. But she could see him concentrating harder, the glow around him brightening.

The chain was cutting into her neck. Funny how the pain stopped after a moment as the giddy feeling made her sway.

His arms were right around her now. She'd wanted that for so long. She'd wanted him to hold her and for her to hold him. She'd wanted to feel his warmth. Wanted to feel his length against hers. She'd wanted to love him so much.

His eyes were brilliant blue. Like the sky when the sun was at its zenith and there were no clouds in any direction. Just the blazing sun and the blinding blue.

Her eyes were bursting with the pressure as the chain tightened yet further around her. It didn't matter if he could keep the air flowing into her, the metal would slice through her skin, she'd bleed to death. In the end it would sever her spinal cord.

And the end result would be his weakness. Tamás so vulnerable they could manipulate him however they chose.

'Break the bloody spell,' he called to Kate. His fingers were at her neck, scrabbling for a hold on the poisoned chain. But it was slippery and sly and he couldn't get a grip.

'I'm so sorry. If I hadn't interfered with the necklace none of this ever would have happened.' Kate was crying.

Zelie hated her deceit all the more.

'Now's not the time to develop a conscience,' Tamás yelled. 'Just fix it.'

Otis had pulled out a pocket knife and ran forwards. 'Let me try.'

'No,' Kate cried. 'It'll kill her.'

Zelie looked from Kate to Otis. As her vision fragmented she saw at last the similarity. One pale and thin, one tanned and strong. But their eyes – the bone structure around the eyes was the same. And the chin. The same family, the same skills.

Witching. Ones who'd use any means to secure the power and control they wanted.

She looked again at Tamás, seeing him once more before the stinging tears and the burning red blinded her.

A trap. It had all been such an elaborate trap.

And whatever he tried, it no longer mattered. He couldn't save her. He couldn't stop this murder. She shook her head in his direction.

'Go,' she screamed. 'Go!'

The anger in his voice blasted her. 'Never.'

Kate had resumed muttering beneath her breath. Whispers of words in yet another eerie-sounding language that no one normal would ever use. And suddenly Kate was shrieking them. Wailing them up into a wind that roared. With her eyes squeezed shut in agony, Zelie's hearing sharpened and so did her sense of smell. And she could smell it strongly now, the metallic stench of blood and that underlying, indescribable note of death.

Bile burned its way up her throat; she'd choke on it. Couldn't get any air in now as hot sick filled her mouth.

The screaming became so high and loud her eardrums banged, about to burst. She couldn't take it any more. She couldn't hold on any more.

But she wanted to. She wanted to more than anything. Luke needed her. Her father needed her. Tamás needed her. And she needed all of them.

She snapped – screaming her rage and fury, longing and love. Tamás caught her in his arms as the ground seemed to shake beneath her.

But then Kate collapsed, staggering to her knees on the stones.

In the sudden, total silence the chain skittered onto the rocks at Tamás's feet. With blurry vision Zelie saw Kate snatch it up, saw the flash of a red-splattered white hand. But Kate was running. As fast and as far away as anyone could.

Zelie drew a breath – a long, life-saving, painful breath.

Tamás looked over at Otis, who was bracing himself against one of the big boulders, his face as white as Kate's had been. 'Go! Go now!' he roared.

Zelie held tight to Tamás, anchoring him, not wanting his violence to be unleashed. She needed him with her now, more than he needed to vent his anger.

Otis backed away, staring at Zelie with a shocked, pleading expression, his head shaking. 'Sorry. I'm so sorry.'

Zelie didn't answer, she just gripped Tamás's shirt hard, holding him. Because she'd felt him flinch, knew he wanted to follow – to hurt Otis.

Otis turned suddenly, running away back towards the town.

Zelie twisted her fingers tighter in Tamás's top. 'Let him go. Please let him go.'

Tamás's face screwed up in an agony of anger and pain. 'Still you want him?' he turned his head and yelled at her. 'He just tried to kill you!'

'No.' She was so confused. She'd thought she'd seen a connection between Kate and Otis. But now she could think kind of clearly, she recalled the absolute horror that had been written all over Otis's face. He'd been as shocked as she. He'd never seen anything like that. Zelie was sure of it.

'You're so blind, Zelie.' Tamás lowered her to her feet and struck out, uselessly punching through air.

'I'm not the one who's blind!' she shouted. Her voice was hoarse, her neck bleeding and bruised, but it was nothing on her heart. Now was not the time for his unfounded jealousy. 'He's not the one I want and you know it.'

Tamás turned, his expression still bitter, still furious.

'Damn it, Tamás.' Her tears tumbled. 'I don't want you to hurt him. Or *anyone*. And do you know why?' she sobbed. 'Because the only person you hurt if you do that is yourself.' She punched his chest. 'It goes against your nature, Tamás. You were born to protect, not to destroy.' It would be better for *her* to avenge the attack, not him. It would cost him too much.

'Oh, Zelie.' His arms came round her again and he pulled her to him. 'Don't cry. It's over. You're safe now.'

'That's not why I'm crying,' she crumpled completely into him. 'I want you to hold me again. And don't let me go.'

'Zelie.' He ducked his head down to look at her. His face was pale too. The effort to keep her breathing had cost him and he'd yet to recover. But the trap she'd feared hadn't materialised, at least not yet. And right now she didn't care. She was too hurt, too angry to hide anything any more. She just needed him.

He said nothing more, but lifted her chin with a firm hand. And slowly, so gently, pressed his lips to hers. Her head fell back as she melted into the kiss. He groaned deep in his throat. She stretched onto tiptoes to get even closer. It was like his pale light was tumbling through her veins – healing, strengthening, revitalising. And so warm, so deliciously warm. She needed more of it. *More*.

But he pulled away, too quickly, his face twisted into a bitter frown. 'I'm taking too much from you.'

'No,' she gasped as the zing of energy jolted her heart. '*I'm* taking too much from *you*.'

The dreaded frown descended further but then suddenly lifted. A bright flash as some kind of recognition gleamed in his eyes. The smile broke him wide open. But she got way too short a glimpse of its incredible beauty, because he hauled her to him and kissed her again.

He kissed her and kissed her. Gentle and firm and fast and slow and over and over and still it wasn't enough. It would never be enough.

She wasn't floating, she was right there, grounded with him, close to him and feeling his strength pouring into her. Her heart thundered against his. He was so warm, so vital. She ran her fingers through his hair, holding him close as she arched up to meet him, her body pressed to his, the heat quickening more.

'I should have done this sooner,' he muttered.

He sure should have. His smile made her eyes water all the more.

'Zelie,' he whispered and kissed her again and again.

She couldn't answer. Her throat more tight with tears now than when the poisoned necklace had been strangling her.

'Thank you so much,' he murmured against her.

'I didn't do anything.'

'You did. It wasn't the *amulette* that made me whole, Zelie. It was you. It was your strength, your warmth. You don't know what you are.'

She shook her head. 'I'm nothing special, Tamás.'

'That's where you're wrong. So wrong. I've been so blind.' He kissed down her jaw, down to her bruised neck. His lips butterfly-light on the thin line of broken skin on her neck.

Even through her closed eyes she could see the glow. 'You can't make it better,' she teased. But she didn't want him to stop – it felt so warm and light and complete.

'Pure air will accelerate its healing. I don't want it to get infected. It was an evil magic.'

She opened her eyes and saw she was enveloped in his shining beauty. She leaned into it, leaned against him. It wasn't blood but bliss that coursed through her body. She didn't think she could ever feel happier than this. Living ecstasy, embraced in security and hope and love.

He wanted her. He cared for her. He was here for her. And she forgot about everything else. She lifted her chin and let him kiss her again. Kissed him back with undisguised joy.

'Zelie. Forgive me. I should have known sooner.'

'Known what?'

He didn't answer. His hand lifted and he toyed with her hair, loosening it from the ponytail. His smile was tender, almost wondrous as he looked so closely at her, the look in his eyes soft and beautiful. It was an expression she hadn't dared dream he'd ever reveal to her, not so open and caring. It almost hurt. 'Tamás.'

He kissed her again. One of those deep kisses that had her tumbling even further in love with him. 'Forgive me now,' he murmured.

'Forgive what?'

He held her face up to his. Kissed her nose, her cheeks, her mouth. Light, sweet kisses. Drugging kisses. Everything was so right and she was warm and sleepy. Too sleepy. 'Tamás?' she stirred in his arms. 'What are you doing?'

But she couldn't keep her eyes open any more.

For a wonderful moment she was lifted in his arms. Then she felt softness beneath her. The sofa? Her bed? Another light brushing kiss. And the last thing she heard was his soft whisper in her ear. 'You need to rest.'

ZELIE WOKE WITH a start, like something in her subconscious had kicked her awake. She stared at the ceiling – her bedroom ceiling. She was on her bed. How had she got back here? She winced as she turned to look out the window, her neck was so sore.

'Tamás?'

Silence.

Fear rocketed into her. He'd put her to sleep. Put something in her air to make her drowsy. She looked at her watch. It had only been twenty minutes. But anything could happen in twenty minutes. As she now knew, anything could happen in far less time. In the flash of a second, life could change irrevocably. Life could end.

She had to find him.

She knew what he'd gone to do. It wasn't Kate this time. Kate had saved her. Zelie had been wrong about her. And so wrong about Otis.

Otis, who'd given her the necklace. Otis, who'd looked so horrified when he'd seen what was happening. Otis, who'd barely lifted a finger to help.

Disbelief? Was that what it had been? Or was it guilt? Tamás had been right. It had to be Otis.

She pulled out her mobile and stabbed the buttons. It felt like eons till he answered. She ran down the stairs and out the door as she talked. 'Who gave you the necklace, Otis? Where did you get it from?'

'My mother gave it to me,' he sounded breathless. 'She said you'd like it.'

Megan? Zelie stumbled. But Megan was like super-mum with her yummy casseroles and cool career.

'She got it for me. She thought it was important I replace the one I broke. She wanted me to give it to you.'

Zelie heard the panicked edge to his words.

'I swear I didn't know that it was . . . whatever it was. I didn't, Zelie.'

Zelie ran faster. 'Have you spoken with her?'

'She was angry that Kate was there. We were supposed to have been alone.'

Zelie couldn't believe her ears. 'Was Megan *there*?'

'She was watching from the house.'

With one of those freaking telescopes?

'Otis –'

'I'm sorry,' he panted. Was he running too? 'I honestly had no idea . . .'

Really? He hadn't known? Hadn't set her up?

Tamás didn't know that. Zelie knew he wouldn't believe Otis. He was too angry. Zelie understood that, but it that didn't mean he should do whatever it was he was thinking of. Vengeance never satisfied, it only destroyed.

She had to get to Tamás. 'Where is your mum?'

'Not at home, I'm here now. Dad's away for work and Mum's not answering her phone.'

'Where would she have gone?'

'I'm guessing the observatory. I'm going there. I'm worried.'

He wasn't the only one. 'Have you seen Tamás?'

'No.'

Zelie raced along the path that ran parallel to the lake. She looked up to the hill where most of the houses were, and saw Otis running down towards her. He caught up to her where the sealed path became a dirt track. She said nothing to him. Didn't want to *know* him. She was so angry. He'd set them up. Him asking her to the ball had probably all been part of the plan.

He was a total jerk.

She looked up the hill. There were no tour parties tonight. Supposedly there was just a lone scientist studying the skies. But Megan wasn't that at all. Why had she tried to kill Zelie this afternoon?

Zelie was certain she'd seen a connection between Kate and Otis. That there was a family resemblance. But she couldn't figure it out. The person they all wanted was Tamás. Hurting her would weaken Tamás if he tried to save her. Kate knew that – but so did Otis. He must have guessed when he saw Tamás with that body this morning. But Kate had been the one to save Zelie. Tamás had tried too – and weirdly he'd displayed no ill effects after helping her. Not the extreme vulnerability he'd had earlier today. If anything he'd seemed stronger afterwards.

So Megan hadn't made a move. Not then. Had she known Tamás would come to find her? Had she set a trap at the observatory? The spider enticing the prey to her parlour?

Otis matched Zelie stride for stride. Only once did she look at him. He was watching her, like he was waiting for the moment she made contact.

'I swear, Zelie. I didn't know.'

'Didn't know what? How crazy your mum is?' Zelie couldn't trust a word he said.

'Truly. I didn't.'

Zelie glanced at him and suddenly halted her mad run. His face was so pale. His customary cool-and-casual demeanour had vanished.

She glanced away, suddenly more afraid. 'I have to stop Tamás.' She moved. She had to make Tamás run rather than fight. Because if Megan's own son had no idea of her true power, then that meant she was powerful indeed.

But as they scrambled through the trees the wind picked up – whistling from a breeze to a gale in a heartbeat. When they came out from the shelter of the trees, it hit them like they'd run smack into a concrete wall. Zelie could hardly take a step. She leaned forwards as far as she could, trying to drive into the wind that was so determined to push them back. Her hair whipped around her face like swishes of wet rope. Otis slipped, crashing onto his stomach on the icy path. He started crawling commando style. Seeing him actually make progress, she threw herself down and copied him. It was cold and hard but at least she was able to move forwards, inch by painful inch.

The hill was so exposed to the elements. One of the town's claims to fame was that the fastest wind speed in the country had been recorded there. But Tamás was making it worse tonight.

The tips of her fingers were numb from the cold, her palms were burned by it. As the wind almost suffocated her, she understood. He was trying to prevent them from going up there.

'Stop it, Tamás,' she shouted up into the sky. 'You're only wasting your energy.' She was furious with him. 'I can help you!' she screamed.

There was one great gust, a howling sound that ripped her soul and twisted through the trees below – pure fury. Then the wind dropped completely. For a second she couldn't move at all, struck by the fear that it meant his power had been broken. Then she scrambled to her feet and started running again, powering up the track as if the ground suddenly had springs and was helping her push forwards faster. Step by step, Otis fell slightly further behind.

But it took too long. Every breath hurt, her neck stung. Finally she saw it; the research building, the café and then the telescopes. There were several of them in the complex, each one safe in its white dome. They looked like a fairy ring of metal mushrooms circling round the summit of the hill. But to the south was a path that led to a rocky outcrop. The perfect place to get a view of the surrounding countryside. And it was there that Tamás stood, facing Megan, with Kate standing between them. He was a tall, dark shadow, barely visible in the rapidly fading light.

Zelie stopped at the dome nearest them to catch her breath. To try to size the situation up. But she couldn't concentrate on figuring it out. Could only *see*.

Kate stood, feet apart, like she was about to do battle. It was ridiculous; she was still twig-thin and Zelie could see her trembling even from a distance – where were her flames?

'What is it you want?' Kate asked.

'You know what I want,' Megan said confidently.

'You can't ever control me,' Tamás said. But Zelie wasn't so sure.

'No?' Megan laughed. 'You know I can.'

'I won't let you.' Kate was putting up a good show. Zelie mentally cheered her on.

'What would you do with him, Kate? Let him waste more time? You didn't like it under the lake, did you, Tamás? I wouldn't do that to you.'

'You killed that man. You needed to for the spell on the necklace,' Kate spoke up.

'That's right.' Megan smiled.

Zelie clapped her hand over her mouth to stop her cry from sounding. Megan had murdered that poor man – how?

'Magic makes magic. Poison makes poison.' Megan was still talking. 'You want to create something big, there must be a big sacrifice.'

'That's not a kind of magic I'll ever practise.' Kate stood firm, but to Zelie she looked too damn frail.

'Are you sure about that?' Megan smirked at Kate. 'You could be quite powerful if you wanted. You have the fire. A very pretty phoenix. We could enhance your power. You have her blood too.'

'And I've had her suffering. All their suffering.'

'All the more reason to embrace all of your power – the dark and the light. Think how strong you could be. You could live forever if you wanted. You could take on the Matriarch with me. Together we could control what she's collected. It could all be ours –'

'No.'

'It's just that you're tired, Kate,' Megan said in scary caring-mum fashion. 'Destroying the necklace took it out of you. Tamás is tired too. If you turn to me, you'll never be tired again. Never be sick again.'

It had been a set-up. She'd played them all.

'I'd rather die.' Zelie saw Kate's fingers fluttering like they had this afternoon when she'd been working her magic. But there was nothing now. No fire.

Megan was right. Kate was wiped out.

'Okay,' Megan shrugged as she walked towards Kate with that too-yummy-mummy hip sway. 'You can't stop me.'

A punch. That's all it took. Nothing supernatural at all. But Kate's neck snapped back. Her body fell. And as she hit the ground her head crunched on the half-buried rocks. Zelie shut her eyes, but she could still see the way Kate's head had bounced up and down twice, like a damn basketball.

'Mum!' Otis shouted, shocked.

At the same time Zelie burst cover, running towards the outcrop where Kate lay like a rag doll.

Megan brushed her hands together, like she'd got some imaginary speck of dust on them. 'So you made it.' She glanced dismissively at her son and then at Zelie. 'And her too.'

Zelie couldn't stop staring at Kate. Her eyes were open but she wasn't seeing anything. There was blood on her forehead. Zelie didn't know if she was dead or not. Didn't know if she should go to her. Everything in her own head was scrambling as panic set in.

'You shouldn't have brought her, Otis,' Megan berated her son. 'She knows too much already.'

'Too much of what?' Otis stared at his mother like she was a total stranger.

Megan huffed a vicious grunt. 'Of course, you're too useless to understand anything.'

Zelie gaped at Megan, stunned at the cruelty in her voice.

'Mum, what are you doing?' Otis knelt by Kate and put his hand on her wrist.

'Winning, Otis. Winning it all.'

'Do you think so, Megan?' Tamás asked.

At the sound of his voice, some reason returned to Zelie. She looked at him, knowing she needed to pull herself together if she was going to be of any use. He looked pale but not as ill as Zelie had feared he would. But this was bad, this was really, really bad.

He walked towards them. She shook her head at him. He should be running. He should be doing whatever it was he did to disappear into the air and be sent away with the wind. But he didn't, he just kept walking right towards her.

'I have the amulet, Tamás. I've already activated it.' Megan held out her fist and slowly unfurled her fingers. The battered lump of matte metal sat in it – it glowed red, like it had been sitting in an inferno. 'How silly of you to leave it in your cabin where it could be found. But you had to help her, didn't you? You couldn't let her die.'

Zelie stopped breathing. Megan had the amulet? Oh no. He couldn't be ensnared again. But Tamás didn't falter, just kept walking right into her trap.

'Light up for me, Tamás,' Megan taunted. 'Be a little firefly. Shall I hurt your girl again? Would that make you do it?'

'It's useless, Megan,' he said. 'Don't you know what she is? Don't you *recognise* her?'

Zelie stared at Tamás. What the hell was he talking about?

Megan's gaze darted to Zelie. 'She's nothing. She's just a vessel. Okay, so she's strong. She should never have survived your occupation.'

'She's more than strong.' Tamás moved closer to Zelie. 'Take another look.' He reached Zelie's side. 'Look into her eyes.'

Zelie dragged her gaze from Tamás to Megan. And for the first time she saw the malevolence there. Her desire for power was a hunger that could never be filled. She'd never have enough. Zelie saw the threat to Tamás. Suddenly it was like she could see right into Megan's head to the thoughts churning inside. The mess of evil and endlessly gnawing greed.

'Nooooo,' Megan said slowly. She inspected Zelie inch by inch – from top to toe and back to her eyes. Searching deeply into them in a way that made those TV hypnotists look like rank amateurs. 'It's not possible.'

Zelie felt as if her insides were being rummaged through by that manic stare.

'Yes.' Tamás reached out and took Zelie's hand. She experienced the zing that she always felt – like a current of electricity – and the instant sense of security that came with it. Only it never lasted. And this time it was gone before she could blink.

Trust me.

She heard him in her head again. Or was she dreaming? Anyway, he didn't need to tell her that, she trusted him entirely. She tore her gaze from Megan's, looked at Tamás and tried to tell him that with her eyes.

I can beat her, Zelie. Stay strong.

'But they were all destroyed or taken.' Megan looked enraptured. 'There aren't any left outside – none truly strong.'

Tamás said nothing.

'The Matriarch said they were gone,' Megan continued, her voice hushed. 'Those that wouldn't fall in with her vision were deliberately wiped out.'

'Not all of them.'

Megan walked towards Zelie, apparently captivated. 'The Matriarch doesn't know about her?' Her smile widened. 'How perfect.'

Zelie took a pace back. Her hand slipped from Tamás's. She didn't like this. She didn't understand this. Because now it seemed Megan was more interested in *her* than in Tamás. What was going on?

'The girl doesn't know either, does she?' Megan laughed. 'And if she doesn't know, she can't control it. Can't use it.' She followed

Zelie. 'But I'll teach you. My pretty little girl. The girl I should have had.'

The woman was completely unhinged. Zelie felt the queasiness returning. She looked at Tamás. But Megan spoke again.

'Come on, Zelie. Come with me. Come home.'

Unable to resist, Zelie looked at her again. There was something compelling about Megan's voice.

'We'll take Tamás with us too. You like him, don't you? We'll all go home together.'

Dimly Zelie figured out what it was – Megan sounded like her mother. *Exactly* like her mother. How was that possible? Zelie looked at Megan again, only now her hair was darker, like Zelie's own. She looked like – 'Mum?'

Zelie's mother held out her hand and smiled. That most beautiful smile that Zelie had longed to see again.

'Touch her, Megan, and I'll kill you,' Tamás said so quietly Zelie thought she might have dreamed it. She blinked.

In that instant Megan was back to Megan, looking and sounding like the crazy witch she was. The nausea rose in Zelie. She wanted to be sick but she couldn't; she didn't want to go near the woman but she couldn't stop herself. Her feet dragged but inexorably moved her forwards. It was like she was a zombie with no will of her own. She couldn't turn to look at Tamás. She couldn't see him or hear him or feel him.

'You can't kill me, Tamás.' Megan laughed, her face lighting up with genuine amusement. 'You can't hurt anything. You're not capable of it.'

But he was. Zelie knew it. In the right circumstances, if he had to protect, to defend or show courage in the face of something horrific, then he was capable of anything. Megan had no idea of his true strength. The human part of him meant he knew how to hate. But he could also love. And he'd learned to be merciful.

Megan had her hands on Zelie now, hands with a horrible biting strength in the fingers. Being drugged by Tamás had been much nicer. This tasted bitter and scary. Helplessly, she walked with the woman, a step, another step.

'You'll like it, Zelie.' Her mother's voice again.

She'd wanted to hear her again so much. So very much.

'We'll have lots of fun together.'

Her mind was going woolly now, like everything was at a distance. She wondered idly why Tamás wasn't following them. Wasn't he coming too? She made herself look. It took a lot to turn her head but, oh, there he was.

She frowned, it took effort. He was walking the other way, higher up the rocky outcrop. The wrong way.

'Tamás?' Her voice was distant too.

'He'll come too, Zelie, you'll see. He likes you too much not to. Such a weakness.'

But Zelie stopped walking. She wasn't going without Tamás. That much she could hold on to in the fog of her mind. The woman holding her arm had to stop. She was frowning as she turned to her.

'Come on, Zelie –' Megan broke off.

Tamás was lit up like there was a spotlight beneath him.

'You want what I have, Megan? You want to control this?' Tamás leaped higher up the rocks. Lifted his head and arms high to the sky.

Zelie stared at him.

He wasn't just opalescent this time, his whole body flashed iridescent. A myriad of tiny rainbows shot out from his skin, lighting up the night sky with diamond facets of bright colour. His power hummed. It was so beautiful it was blinding.

Megan laughed. A high-pitched, delighted cackle – there was no other word for it. She released Zelie's arm so quickly that Zelie fell to her knees.

She looked up to see Megan leaping up towards him, running fast, holding the amulet outstretched to suck up his power. And as she neared Tamás, the metal glowed a vibrant orange. And all those rainbows and sparks shooting from Tamás seemed to lean towards it – as if they were going to be sucked inside the metal.

What was he doing? Why was he giving her what she wanted? Megan was going to trap him back in the amulet.

No.

She could never let him be imprisoned again.

Zelie moved. Not feeling her body any more, not aware of instructing it. All she saw was the turquoise sweater that Megan was wearing – she focused on bringing it nearer and nearer to her. Fast, faster. Close, closer. She reached out her hand to stop Megan from getting to him, but she still wasn't close enough.

And Tamás was just hovering there. Why didn't he fly away?

'Stay back, Zelie,' Tamás shouted at her.

She wouldn't. She couldn't. But she couldn't *get* there. Rage, terror, determination gripped her.

'NO!'

Tamás turned his attention from Megan to Zelie and, for a split second, their eyes met.

'No!' Zelie shouted again.

The rumbling caught her by surprise. She jumped, planting her feet wide as the earth shifted beneath them. Instinctively she stretched out her hands, like she was surfing the slippery, chaotic wave of snow that had been shoved up by a push from deep below.

Megan didn't seem bothered by the tremor. She still reached out, her hard face illuminated by Tamás's radiance. Her expression was pure greed.

Pure fury surged through Zelie, rippling out of every cell in her body. And the ground shuddered again. A loud boom sounded, rocks crashed, punctuating the shriek of the howling wind. As the ground tossed, Zelie somehow stood tall. Somehow was able to stand fast through the tumult.

Megan's outstretched arm jerked as she was unbalanced – her once sure foothold tossed up by the angry earth. Her grip on the amulet loosened. The snow-slick rocks skidded around her, as she teetered on the edge she'd been drawn to.

And Megan slipped.

'No!' Otis screamed.

Tamás and Zelie were silent. And so was Megan. In the moment of eternity that it took for her to smash onto the rocks twenty feet below, there was no sound at all.

CHAPTER TWENTY-FOUR

'YOU'RE COUSINS.' ZELIE looked at Kate. 'You and Otis.'

She'd been right about the resemblance she'd spotted. But neither Kate nor Otis had known it. It was only now that Kate had worked out the link – now she'd figured out Megan's alias.

'Yes.' Despite her black eye, Kate peered closer at the old book spread wide on her knees. 'Megan's father was Catriona's older brother. You know, my lotsa-greats grandma who trapped Tamás under the lake.' The one who'd wanted to hold him until the time was right. The one who had thought she was doing something good.

'Not possible.' Zelie leaned closer, trying to read over Kate's shoulder. 'That would make Megan like, ancient.'

Kate looked at her pityingly. 'She killed one guy to create the power in that chain. You think she wouldn't kill for longer life too? My uncles think there's worse happening. That's why we needed to speak with Tamás. He might know if there are more like him. He can help us find them.'

More Guardians? But that's what Tamás had wanted to find out from *them*. 'So you weren't after his gold?'

'Don't you get it yet, Zelie? Tamás *is* the treasure.' Kate turned back to the indecipherable scrawls in the battered book.

Zelie tried to read it again, but there was no understanding the mess that was supposed to be writing.

She glanced around the room. The Hearn homestead wasn't anywhere near as huge as she'd expected it to be. It was more of a cottage, cosy, and the walls were lined with crammed bookcases and framed pictures. In the centre of the dining-room-come-library-come-lounge was a massive free-standing fire that currently blazed. Zelie had never seen another like it – on a bonfire night maybe, but not in the middle of a house. The heat should have been overwhelming, but the room was merely comfortable. It definitely wasn't a normal kind of fire.

'The family broke apart when they landed in New Zealand,' siad Kate. 'They were supposed to be searching out the best place to settle. Catriona and a brother went with Tamás, while Megan's father went with another brother and their baby sister.' Kate looked worried. 'That was the baby on the boat.'

Zelie's jaw dropped. 'The baby Tamás saved?'

Kate nodded. '*She's* the Matriarch.'

'The Matriarch?'

Kate's face paled. 'Most of the Witching now belong to the one coven, they follow one leader. Her. She doesn't practise good magic, Zelie. Catriona hid Tamás and then hid from the rest of her family, because she sensed something wasn't right. So we've been alone ever since.'

Zelie curled her legs beneath her on the sofa, fear making her draw herself into a smaller ball. 'So that baby is still alive?'

And she was bad? Tamás's sense of betrayal was going to be immense. He'd saved that child, only for her and her family to turn on him? She didn't want him hurt by that knowledge. 'Don't tell Tamás.'

'I think he already knows.' Kate looked sorry. 'I never even suspected Megan was Witching. She must have had strong power to remain undetected. Or maybe I was just lazy.'

'It's not your fault.' Zelie shook her head. 'You were so sick. How come she didn't spot you?'

'My uncles are amazing blockers.'

'Blockers?'

'It's what male Witching can do. They're strong. They can amplify another Witching's magic – beam it. Or they can block it. They can block knowledge, thoughts, feelings.'

'That's how they protected you? Is that why you couldn't tell Tamás whatever it was he wanted to know?' That day down by the lake when Zelie had thought Tamás was going to kill Kate. 'So the women have the power but the men can augment it.'

'Exactly. I had to hide my plan to activate the *amulette* from my uncles. I had to get away from them long enough to be able to give it to you. So it is all my fault.'

'No.'

'Yes. Wasn't it me who gave you the necklace in the first place?'

'And I'll never regret that you did.' Zelie had found something so precious. But now wasn't the time to think of that happiness. She had to understand the history more. 'So is Otis a witch too?'

Kate shook her head. 'I don't think so. Most often it's only the women who have the transference skills – the magic. The men beam or block, and some have mind powers. But for both male and female, the skills aren't necessarily inherited – so some daughters don't get it. Nor do some sons.'

Was that why Megan had spoken so cruelly to him up on the mountain? Why she'd gone on about Zelie being the daughter she'd never had? Because Otis had disappointed her by not having any of the Witching power?

Now Kate stared down at the writing on the pages. Zelie couldn't read any of it – didn't recognise the squiggles as any kind of alphabet. She watched Kate growing paler. The bruises on her head were purple and black and obviously painful. 'Are you okay?'

'Tamás is near,' she nodded carefully. 'I'm okay.'

Zelie frowned and looked over the other side of the fire where Tamás stood talking in low tones to Kate's uncles. All three turned and looked sombrely at her and Kate. But Zelie refused to be afraid. Tamás looked stronger than ever. After that huge release of light, he hadn't needed any time to recover. She suspected he was finally free from the diapause. He was whole. So shouldn't Kate be whole too?

'I was wrong,' Kate whispered, her features crumpling. 'I'm still dependent on him.'

Zelie turned back to her. 'You're saying you have to be near him to stay well?'

'If I'm not I'll die.' Tears slid from Kate's wide eyes. 'I'm sorry, Zelie.'

Yeah, it hurt. It shouldn't, but it did. Zelie didn't like Kate having that kind of claim on him. 'So something is still out of balance?'

'We're going to have to find out what.' Kate drew in a shaky breath. 'I think we're going to have to try to find the Matriarch.'

Cold fear swept through Zelie. 'I'm sorry I didn't trust you.' She made herself look directly at Kate, made herself show her contrition. 'You saved my life.'

Kate's shoulders lifted slightly. 'You'd already saved mine.'

'No.' Zelie hadn't. 'He stopped before I arrived.'

'But it was because of you that he did,' Kate said. 'He was in such a terrible place, but you brought him back. You gave him love.'

Zelie didn't deny it, and she appreciated that Kate could see what was between them. But love hurt. She knew that was why she'd retreated – socially, emotionally. She'd been so hurt when she'd lost her mother, she couldn't bear the idea of it happening again. So she'd understood something in Tamás. She'd sympathised. But in doing that she'd opened up to him, as he had to her. And both had hurtled to the place neither had wanted to be; in love and vulnerable.

And yet it was the most natural, magical thing in the world.

Tamás walked over. 'I'll see you home, Zelie.'

She stood, so glad he'd come for her. She ached to be alone with him.

The book thudded as Kate closed it. 'Take this with you, Zelie, you need to read it.'

'Like that's going to be possible.'

Kate chuckled. 'Tamás will explain.'

Too tired to argue, Zelie simply waited while Kate wrapped it in a soft cloth and put it into an old bag for her. When she was done, Tamás held out his hand for it.

Kate paused. A look passed between her and Tamás – one of those 'shared secrets' kind of looks that Zelie loathed – then Kate gave the bag to him.

They walked out to the Hearns' four-wheel drive. Tamás opened the passenger door for her and she climbed in. A minute later he was driving them along the narrow gravel road back towards town.

It was very early in the morning, the dawn light only slightly piercing the darkness. But Zelie knew that for Otis the nightmare was just beginning. Tamás had literally airbrushed the scene, leaving no trace that he, Zelie, Kate and Otis had been near the observatory. It would be put down to a terrible accident: the astronomer had walked out on the hill and had slipped in the snow – gone over the edge of the rocks to her death below.

Otis had been inconsolable. Confused, incoherent, uncontrollably shaking. In the end Tamás had somehow drugged him so he was calm enough to get home. Then Tamás had put him to bed and helped him sleep.

'Do you think he'll say anything?'

'He knows she tried to kill you. That she killed that man. He'll never say a word.'

Zelie nodded. And as if anyone would believe Otis about the Witching.

She felt awful about leaving Megan's body out in the open at the bottom of the cliff, but Kate and Tamás had insisted. Megan was gone, there was nothing they could do for her. The priority had been to protect Otis and themselves.

'What'll happen to him?' Zelie asked. 'He'll be so angry.'

Tamás sighed. 'I don't think he knew anything about her. You were right about that. Just talk to him. It'll be hard but he'll get through. You'll be a good friend for him.'

She doubted it. 'He'll hate me.' Anyway, couldn't Tamás be his friend too?

Tamás smiled. 'It's impossible to hate you.'

Yeah, but in part because of her, Otis's mother was dead. That wasn't something you just got over.

'It was an accident, Zelie,' Tamás said quietly.

Was it? Hadn't she and Tamás both been trying to stop her – fighting for their lives however they could? She'd been running, prepared to do *anything* to help Tamás. Pay whatever price necessary. And he'd been prepared to do the same for her.

But fate had helped them out, right? That tremor had caused Megan to slip over the edge . . .

Zelie squeezed her eyes tight shut. She didn't want to remember it.

Tamás put a heavy, reassuring hand on her thigh.

'He'll learn more about his background,' he said calmly. 'Kate's uncles will talk to him and explain.'

As he slowly drove on they were silent for a few minutes, mulling over thoughts too fragile to be spoken aloud. About a kilometre out from Tekapo, Tamás pulled over. 'Let's walk from here so we don't wake anyone.'

She nodded.

The lake was eerily calm; in the half-light the world looked monochromatic again, all black and white and shades of grey.

'Your mother didn't die of flu complications,' Tamás suddenly said.

Zelie nearly stumbled, had to take a quick step to right herself. 'Yes she did. I was there, Tamás.'

'I was there too. When you dreamed it – again and again. I watched what happened in your dreams. I saw what you saw when you got back to your house and found her.'

Appalled, Zelie pulled away from him. She hated that nightmare. She hated the image that rose before her now.

He looked apologetic but he reached for her hand, tugging it so she stopped walking. He moved in front to face her. 'I was blinded by my anger. And then by my attraction to you, Zelie. Well, by my *not* wanting to be attracted to you. So I should have seen it so much sooner. I didn't even pick it up in the dreams, wasn't paying close enough attention. I was too busy trying not to care for you. I didn't want to feel, Zelie. It hurts so much when you lose someone . . .' he trailed off.

She knew. And she knew how much he'd lost. 'But I've replayed your dream,' he said. 'I know you saw my nightmare. I saw yours too.'

She shivered. He'd replayed her nightmare in his head *voluntarily*?

'I saw it all, Zelie. The things you missed because you didn't know what you were looking for.' He breathed deeply. 'She was a Guardian.'

Zelie frowned. Like Tamás was? 'You're saying Mum was another *mostly* human person?'

'Yes. But she was more than that. She was Witching too – almost all Guardians now have Witching blood. Remember how I told you that when we first went into hiding that some of the Guardians integrated with Witching? But that combination proved too powerful and too threatening to some, and too enticing for others. While I was in the lake, the Matriarch has been hunting all Witching with strong Guardian elements left. Ed Hearn says she's bound them and has been leaching them of their power to feed her own. But your mother resisted. She sensed they were coming that day. She put protection on you and on Luke and sent you out. You've never noticed that you and Luke were missing from the photo frames?'

Zelie shook her head, stunned. 'You saw that detail in my dreams?'

'And more,' he answered. 'Her drawings gave it away – all those beautiful, intricate pictures of trees and flowers revealed her connection to the natural world. She knew what they wanted, and she refused to give them herself – or you. Protecting you weakened her, and in that fight they wiped her out.' He shook his head. 'They wouldn't have meant to. The Matriarch would have been furious.'

'You're saying the Matriarch killed her?' Zelie stared at him and saw he meant every word.

'The Matriarch's minions.' He nodded. 'She'd have sent them to get your mother – and any offspring. I believe the Matriarch has been drawing on Witching power and any and all Guardians she can find.'

Her mother had been murdered? Zelie was horrified. And anger ignited. A need for justice. But just as powerful was a smashing wave of hopelessness. How could she ever do anything?

'Your mother was strong, Zelie. It took them a long time to find her, and even when they did, she kept you secret.'

Why had she kept her secret? Adrenalin spiralled with uncertainty, fuelling Zelie with an excitement that was frightening.

'That's why she sent you out when they came,' Tamás continued. 'She died protecting you.'

'Protecting me from what?' she breathed, sure she didn't want to know.

He stepped closer. 'From them doing the same to you.'

'Why would they want to do that?' She had a suspicion, half a one, but she couldn't follow the thought through. She couldn't possibly believe it.

'Because you're Guardian too,' Tamás said it for her. 'And you're Witching.'

'I'm not.' Zelie took a step back, shaking her head.

'You're her only daughter. And you definitely have her skills.'

It was impossible. She had no powers, there was nothing in her memory, nothing weird that had ever happened until she'd come here. 'I think you've got me confused with someone else.'

'Zelie,' he half laughed. 'I'm healed inside, because of you. You restored my power. Every time we touch – when I was in the clinic, at the ice rink, but even more so when we kissed . . .'

Was that why he'd kissed her? Because she was like his personal rechargeable battery?

He laughed again then. 'You're so much more than that, Zelie. There's the balance of our two elements – we feed each other's power. But there's also passion. And that's something different.' He gazed hard at her. Yes, she felt the passion, the wildness that made her want to touch and cling, take and *love*.

He seemed to have access to her thoughts again and she saw the darkening of his eyes. But she didn't want to taste that passion again yet. She had to clear up his complete confusion first. Because he was so totally wrong on this one. 'Why didn't she tell me?'

'I think she would have, but you were too young and then she ran out of time. If you didn't control your thoughts, they'd find you, so she kept it secret.'

'So they might find me now?'

'No, you have the strength now, Zelie. You have incredible strength.'

'No. I don't have any special powers,' she said glumly. 'It's not like I can fly.'

'I think your mother contained your gifts when you were young, to protect you. And that final magic she worked to protect the three of you was fierce. That's why the Hearns couldn't use mind control on your father. Or you. And nor could Megan. That's what drew her interest in you at first. But it wasn't until you came into your own, till you accessed your power, that the remnants of your mother's protection fell and she could clearly see what you are. How powerful.'

'But Kate knew.'

He nodded. 'And she protected you too. She didn't tell her uncles. Didn't tell me. I know neither of us believed her, but she was trying to help you.'

Because she'd wanted to be free? And for Tamás to be free. Poor Kate. Because it hadn't quite worked out that way.

'What about Luke?' Zelie asked.

'He's still a little young to be sure; most Guardians grow into their domain in their early teens. But the signs are there.'

So Luke was special too?

It was a seductive fantasy that she couldn't believe. Because it was also scary. And Tamás looked so serious, so honest. She couldn't hold back the question any longer. 'So what am I Guardian of?'

'Your element is earth.'

Oh. Total let-down. He got to be air and fly and she got to be mud-woman. She still didn't really believe him. 'And what do they call me? A gnome? A leprechaun?'

He ignored her weak sarcasm. 'If you want a mythological term, I'd call you an Amazon.'

Zelie stared for a second and then laughed. A loud laugh that didn't sound funny and hurt her throat. 'An *Amazon*?'

'A female warrior – powerful, beautiful, strong.'

'I'm none of those things.'

'You're all those and more. You're brave, Zelie, and you have courage. The courage to help me when you were afraid, to care for Luke, to stand up to your father. You're filled with courage. Your mother wanted you to come here. She put the idea into your father's head.'

Zelie gulped. 'Did she know you were here?'

'I'm not sure,' Tamás shrugged. 'Perhaps she sensed the Hearns. That Kate could help you. Kate has Guardian in her too.'

Now that wasn't so much of a surprise. 'Fire.'

Tamás nodded. 'A phoenix. And she and Megan share blood. Megan also had phoenix powers.'

'She's not going to be reborn?' Zelie quailed at the thought.

'No. But she started some fires before she died.'

Zelie's car.

And Zelie'd thought that Kate had done it. But Kate and her silent, scary uncles really were on their side. Poor Kate had only wanted Zelie's strength to free Tamás, so she could be free herself, but that hadn't worked.

And now it seemed there were other, bigger problems.

Zelie looked at Tamás, the pieces slowly coming together to create a head-hurting, half-completed puzzle. 'You're a super-special Guardian aren't you?'

'I'm only quarter human.'

'I thought you said "mostly".'

'I exaggerated.'

'So your ability is stronger.'

'Yes.'

'But there are others with Guardian power. You know Kate has some – she's not strong but she has it. There will be others like her still out there, not yet captured by the Matriarch.'

'Megan obviously thought so. I think that's why she was here, to study the skies. She was watching for sylph; looking for others.' He glanced up to the clouds. 'When I influence the air there's a flash of light.'

She nodded, she'd sure seen that. 'Like lightning.' Except it seemed to last longer.

'Or like a meteorite shower. That's what she was watching for. There'll be other Witching like Megan stationed at observatories around the world.'

Zelie suddenly gripped his wrist. 'I'm sure there are more Guardians, Tamás. I found out about Gemelle.'

He froze. 'I didn't tell you her name.'

'I know about her, she was your twin. She might have lived, Tamás. She might have had childr—'

'How did you find out, Zelie?' Sharply he pulled his arm away.

'I saw the letter in your bag. And then I searched the net. Like I said I could.'

'I told you not to!'

She flinched.

He put his hands over his eyes and groaned harsh and loud. Zelie panicked. Okay. So she'd made a mistake. Totally touched a raw nerve. 'I'm sorry, I thought –'

'You'll have alerted them,' he waved a hand in the air. 'They'll be watching there too. They'll follow through on any query about that part of France back then. They knew about me but they can't have known where I'd been hidden.' He walked faster towards the village, shoving the bag under his arm. 'Now they'll know.'

'I didn't use my computer. I used the one at the café.' She ran after him.

'It's still the town.'

Oh – they'd search the IP address. She was such a dunce. 'I'm sorry, Tamás.' Had she put him in danger? Herself?

'It's okay.' He visibly tried to calm down. 'Megan had probably told someone anyway, but I'd hoped to keep your identity out of it for now. But you can still hide here.' He kicked at a stone in his path. 'Zelie, this is serious. I have to go right away.'

'What?' she stopped. 'You mean you're going to leave *now*?'

He stopped too, but didn't turn to face her. 'Now.'

She'd always known. He'd always said he'd leave, but that hadn't stopped her hoping he wouldn't. 'Why?'

'I can distract them away from you. I can keep you safe. I have to go now to do that.'

'Can't I keep myself safe, if I have all these mysterious powers? Can't I fight them all off?'

'Not yet.'

She hadn't meant it seriously. 'So what will I be able to do? Can I fly or whatever it is you do?'

He managed a tiny smile. 'No. You're earth, sweetheart.'

What, so she'd be able to magically dig holes or something? How totally unglam.

'Remember with the necklace? When it almost claimed you – you screamed and the earth shuddered.'

She gaped. 'Was that for real?'

He spoke softly. 'You caused an earthquake.'

'You're kidding.'

He shook his head. Zelie's smile faded. There was something else he wasn't saying. Something guaranteed to make her feel even more rotten.

'That quake last night,' she began, suddenly horrified. 'When Megan fell –'

She broke off as hot tears stung her eyes. He wrapped his arms around her tightly as if knowing her legs had turned to water.

Had Zelie killed her? Had Zelie caused the shaking that had seen Megan slip?

Nausea rose. 'No . . .'

'It's okay,' he murmured against her hair.

She shook her head, pressing her face closer against him. It wasn't. 'I'm scared.' She'd had no control over that power. No awareness even. Didn't that make her some kind of monster?

Tamás suddenly framed her face with his hands, firmly holding her still. 'Zelie.' He commanded her attention.

Eyes watering, gasping for breath, she struggled to concentrate.

'You'll learn to harness it.'

'It's too late.'

She'd already hurt someone.

'She slipped. It was an accident.' He inhaled a deep, shuddering breath. 'She was trying to kill me.'

Zelie would have done anything to protect him. And it seemed she had.

'Your skill will develop quickly. The book –'

'I can't understand the damn squiggles,' she hissed.

'You look at the pictures first,' he said simply. 'Like a kid looking at the colour plates in a fairy-tale book, you look at the pictures first.'

'Colour plates?' she repeated. 'You're showing your time-warp status again.'

He breathed a little laugh. 'Look right into the pictures, then you'll understand the words.'

It was that simple?

'The Hearns will beam for you, they'll accelerate your understanding. Trust them.'

Perma-stubble and his sidekick were going to actually be useful? Slowly Zelie nodded, her panic subsiding. She could look at pictures. She could ask the uncles everything. But while she was doing that, what was Tamás going to be doing?

She tensed, bracing herself. 'You have to take Kate with you, don't you?'

His eyes were dark with apology. 'What would you have me do, Zelie?'

Okay, so maybe she hadn't kept her tone jealousy-free. 'You can't leave her,' she admitted. 'You're not a killer, Tamás. You can't leave her to die. It's not in your nature.'

'I don't want to take her.'

'I don't want you to go.'

'I'll come back. But I have to go, Zelie. There are things I have to do.'

'The Matriarch.' Zelie nodded dully. 'Do you know where she is?'

'I have an idea.'

'You'll stay safe yourself, won't you? And you'll come back?'

'I promise.' He drew her close again.

She wanted to believe him. She knew that he meant it. But she was afraid something would stop him. Something really bad.

'You know how male Witching can block the powers of a

female?' he said. 'I've learned other things can block powers too – grief can block. Your powers were hidden and blocked partly by your grief for your mother. When you started to re-engage, your powers came to you.' He drew in a shuddering breath. 'So perhaps it's possible that my grief has blocked my ability to hear Gemelle – or other Guardians. It's possible that she was bound by the Matriarch. I have to go find out, Zelie.'

'Of course you do.' She nodded and her tears spilled onto the ground. 'But why can't I come too?' She hated having to ask him. Wished she was stronger and could just take it on the chin. But the question slid out, almost a whine. 'Wouldn't I be safe with you? Like Kate is?'

'I can't guarantee her safety. And I can't put you in more danger. I have to know you're safe, and you *can* be here – with the Hearns – so long as you don't go leaving trails on the internet.' He dropped the bag with a thud and put his hands on her shoulders. 'And you're needed here.'

Luke. Even her father. And didn't she owe him given she destroyed that sample and killed his chance to discover something that would turbo-boost his career?

'I thought you needed me,' she said desperately. 'I thought you needed what I gave you.'

'You've given me everything, Zelie. I'll always have it.'

She looked up at him. Yes. He was complete. Strong and vital, full of life and light – that opalescent sheen was present now. *Luminescent.*

'You have to stay,' he said roughly - like he was telling himself as much as her. 'Your father needs you. So does Luke.'

'But *I* need *you*.' Would her latent strength wane without him? Like the way Kate got sick?

'It's within you, Zelie. You'll find out,' he understood her fears immediately. 'It won't leave, it'll only grow if you let it. And yes, it's better when elements are together – we're stronger. But even alone, you'll grow. Study the book, Zelie, you'll understand.'

She glanced at the bag and suppressed a shiver. 'I don't know what's going to happen.'

'You know this.' He drew her into his arms. 'You know *us*.'

But the 'us' was separating. And after what, less than a day of togetherness? It was so unfair. So horribly unfair. She stood on tiptoes, turned her face into his neck, feeling his warmth, smelling the scents of forest, air and snow on him.

'You'll go to school,' he instructed in her ear. 'Luke will go to school. You'll stay hidden, the Hearns will help, you'll be fine. And I'll come back, Zelie. I will come back.'

'I'm scared.'

'You're a warrior, Zelie. You're a fighter.'

'If that's what I am, why did you try to stop me coming after you tonight?' She was still mad about that.

'Because I didn't want you to be hurt.' He pushed her away so he could look into her face. 'You've been hurt enough, Zelie.'

Zelie's insides melted at the raw emotion in his voice.

'I'm sorry I was mean to you when I got out of the lake.' He whispered it so quietly it was a wonder she heard him.

'You ignored me.' Her mumble wasn't much louder than his had been.

'I tried to but I couldn't.' His muscles bunched with tension again. 'That day in the gym when I made you throw the ball at Kate, I felt what you thought of me. You thought I was a monster. And that was awful. It changed everything – what you thought of me mattered. But I never thought you'd like me the way you liked Otis.'

She spread her palm on his chest, right where his heart beat strongly. 'I've never liked Otis the way I like you. I don't know him the way I do you. I've never shared anything with him the way I have with you. He's good-looking, but I fell for your soul before I even saw how beautiful you are. You must have known that the night of the ball.'

His colour had risen now. 'By then I wanted you to be safe. And when I came out of the lake, I wanted to make Kate pay, but I couldn't because of you. I had to push you away because I didn't want you hurt, and being near me would put you in danger.'

'You didn't try to help me when my car caught fire.'

'I was watching. Listening. Would have helped in a heartbeat if you'd really needed me. But I saw the others coming – Otis. I knew he'd help, he likes you almost as much as I do. And at that time I didn't want to mess you around any more. But in the end I couldn't stay away from you.'

'And thank God you couldn't, because you saved Luke.' Her

fingers curled and she clutched his shirt. 'I can't even manage him, Tamás, how can I be Guardian of anything?'

He cupped her face. 'You do manage him, you care for him and he still needs you. He's special. You're special. And your mother knew that. Zelie, that day you did exactly what she needed you to do. I know you resisted her, but you did the right thing – what she wanted you to do. And you'll be what she needs you to be.'

She knew then. There was nothing she could have done to help her mother. And the horrible feeling about their last words – that stupid argument – eased. Her mother had sent her away to be safe. The guilt lessened, but the sadness only increased. She gazed into Tamás's blue eyes. She was going to miss him so badly. 'I don't want you to go.'

He didn't try to argue with her any more. He kissed her, letting his strength, his belief in her flow through the tightness of his embrace. She clutched him, the elation in their closeness surpassing the bitterness of the parting to come. A few more moments. Just a few more moments of heaven.

She drew back, smiled at him. 'I want to know you – know everything. Like your scar . . .'

He smiled ruefully. 'You saw that?'

Her cheeks heated. 'You were naked the night you came out of the lake.'

'Guess that's "payback", as you say, for those times I saw you . . .'

'Those *times*?'

He kissed her. Sweet, hot, until she clung to him.

'I want you to be with me. Just once.' She ached everywhere, most especially her heart. She didn't want him to leave without them having been together. What if they never had the chance again? She wanted it to be him.

He grabbed her hands, pulled them to his chest as he shook his head. 'I know you. I know you as no other man can ever know you.'

'But I want you to –'

'No,' he said harshly, his eyes tortured. 'For one thing, there isn't the time to do it the way I want to. I have to go, Zelie. I have to go *now*.'

Zelie trembled but his grip firmed, only he held her slightly away rather than drawing her closer. 'Our time will come.'

'I thought you didn't believe in any kind of future,' she said angrily. Hurt by his rejection. 'I thought you were just going to get on and live your own life. Not care about anyone else.'

'But I do care, Zelie. You made me believe again.' He looked near to tears himself. 'I can only leave now because I believe in my future. Our future. Because I believe in you.' But there was a shadow in his eyes, a remnant of that desolate emptiness.

'It is only because of you that I can do this,' he said suddenly, anger lifting his voice also. 'You have to believe in me too, Zelie.'

'I do.' Her voice broke. 'I've always believed in you.'

He let her go, reached into his pocket. 'I want you to have this. Keep it safe for me.' He put the amulet in her hand.

Hot tears tracked down her face, splashing onto their linked hands. 'I don't want it. It's just a lump of metal. It isn't *you*.'

'Keeping this safe keeps me safe. I trust only you, Zelie.'

His arms came back around her and she collapsed against his strong, tense heat. She felt a quiver run through him as they pressed close. He lifted her chin, seeing past her sniffing and the tears that still trickled down her cheeks. And then he kissed her. She sobbed into his mouth, could hardly kiss him for the way her lips trembled. But then the magic blossomed. She softened as he kissed her both sweetly and with the kind of passion that made her blood thunder. And this time she was flying – soaring – as the iridescent glow surrounded them, the sparkling light that was the visible proof of the bliss between them. Resentment burned equally hot because she couldn't have him the way she wanted.

'You have a part of me, Zelie. You know you do.'

She closed her eyes.

But somehow, impossibly, he was in her head again.

My heart. You'll always have my heart.

Another kiss. More desperate, more heated. Their mouths clinging. Her fingers tightened on him. She wasn't going to let him go.

Her heart tore, a slow rip right the way through, and she couldn't stop it. Couldn't stop the hurt that was compounding with every last second they had together.

She couldn't do it. Just couldn't do it. He was wrong. She wasn't strong. She couldn't bear to let him leave. She slid her fingers through his hair, desperate to be in the heart of the rainbow again.

He was so magic, so special. And she loved him in a way she'd never known it was possible to love anyone. Every cell ached to hold him, to protect him, to love him. And for him to do that for her.

He wrenched away. The cold air swept in as they separated. She could feel it on her face, on her chest, her stomach. She refused to open her eyes. Not for long minutes. Until the sounds of his movement had long since ceased and all that could be heard was the gentle stirring of the breeze in the trees.

She blinked. On the dusty rocks beside the lake she was alone. She couldn't even see him in the distance.

She looked at the village. Dad and Luke would soon wake; she needed to get home before they discovered she wasn't there. Luke had to get to school. Her father would go into the clinic – he'd be furious about the missing sample. They needed a bridge to link them – somehow she had to be that bridge.

Tamás's words turned round in her head, over and over. A mantra. The only thing that she could hold on to in the difficult minutes, hours, days and months she had ahead of her.

Our time will come.

But first there was now.